THE SAFE GAP

LISA STUKEL

THE SAFE GAP by Lisa Stukel
Copyright©2023 by Lisa Stukel

All rights reserved.
No part of this publication may be reproduced, stored in a retrieval system or transmitted in any form or by any means, including electronic or mechanical. Photocopying, recording or otherwise reproducing any portion of this work without the prior written permission of the author is prohibited except for brief quotations used in a review.

Print ISBN: 9798218258344
eBook ISBN: 9798218306441
LCCN: 2023916532

Cover and Interior designed by Ellie Searl, Publishista®

TwinStar Press
Chicago, IL

Dedication and Acknowledgments

To Tom, my North Star, my everything who inspires me to persevere. You are my one and only light, always.

My Dante and Ezra . . . we hold plastic stars in our hands every day that guide our path. An abundance of gratitude to both of you for encouraging my dream of writing this book while sitting at our dining room table in Oak Park.

To Mom and Dad for giving me the gift of life, taking pen to paper, and storytelling.

To my friends and family who took delight in pushing me to finish this all the way to the end.

To all those who sit in front of a fire. May it bring you back to being one with nature while enjoying life's storytelling and moments.

Chapter One

Tammy

> *"The soul that sees beauty may sometimes walk alone."*
> *- Johann Wolfgang von Goethe*

Darkness dominates until splattered colors of gray filter into the ominous hue of my psyche. The splattering of gray creates translucent images in my field of vision as I lay listening to the quiet voices around me. The atmosphere is languorous while I hover over the cold room seeping into the dream-like landscape of a painting hanging on the wall. The scintillating colors catch my eye and illuminate methodically towards a faint aroma of a fire burning. I pursue this familiar aroma with my entire being. I elevate myself into the painting looking out on the cold, odorless space I am trapped in. I proceed delicately in this colorful painting because I could fall out of it if I move too fast. I am one with the trees who occupy this space. In the background of the odorless space, I hear a steady vibrating movement: people talking, faint beeps, extemporaneous noises clouding my better judgment. I hear voices next to me but can't reach out and touch them, unresponsive to my close environment. I walk deeper into the painting, moving further away from the noise behind me in the crowded room.

I am inside looking out.

It is quiet.

I turn back around to see the hands of the clock on the wall seemingly standing still, but my mind gravitates forward to follow a peaceful stillness that hangs in the balance. I hear my heartbeat pumping blood through my broken body at a slow melodic movement. I find myself lucid, dancing around the edge of a precipice until the noises fade again, like the silence that appeared before a vital storm.

While waiting idly viewing a mysterious opening, I gravitate towards the mesquite smell crackling over burning wood. I find myself at the end of the driveway walking up to the home I grew up in. Large sprawling oak trees line the deep front lawn majestically. The driveway steers in an upside down "u" shape that leads to the front door. It looks just as I left it many moons ago.

The house my dad helped build was set way back off the road. It was painted white with green shutters on every window. A verdant space with a few sprawling acres in the backyard was a heavenly oasis as a kid. The house being set back off the street was far enough away to feel secluded, while the hum of the cars blended in with the cicadas buzzing from the street. Way down in front, cars continued to pass through the western suburbs on their way to Chicago. Even though the house was set back in the woods with a long driveway, it was still close enough to a strip mall with cookie cutter neighborhoods. Will the people flying by in the cars find a perfect mate like the cicadas that were buzzing in the trees? Do they have to make loud shrieking noises to attract the opposite sex, luring them into a frenzy of ecstasy until it ends abruptly?

I feel confused about being here but elated at the same time. I walk innately up the front steps to the porch. The second step creaks the same as it did years ago, filling my ears with a sweet familiar sound of safety. I hear my mom's melodic laughter with my sister. They are telling stories as the pots cling and dishes are being set on the table. My chest is expanding with delight, and I can't wait to join them. But when I turn the knob to enter, the house fades and I am left standing on an empty lot. I wince with a sigh of deep despondency being so close to my family but still so far out of reach.

I am inside looking out. They are outside looking in.

I can still hear voices. They roam further away from me now, just light chatter in the distance over a moonlit fire.

The only things I see are giant oak trees and the remnants of the driveway that used to lead to the house. There are weeds sticking out of the cement, all overgrown and green. I see one particular oak tree I used to stare at every day out of my bedroom window on the second floor. It is beyond therapeutic to see this majestic beauty again. I wonder what this tree has seen since I left years ago. I stand under it with tears stretching out to engulf it in a big, loving hug. All of a sudden my head doesn't hurt. I don't want to leave the tree's presence again. The beeps and chatter fade away over the open space.

What has this tree seen since I left? I imagine the warmth on the leaves from the hot summer sun, the storms it had to endure, the gale winds that ripped at its bark, and the snow left on its branches under a cold blue, yet frigid winter sky. Twigs and branches would fall, relieving the weight of its stature. But the tree remains. The leaves would return back and forth with the season, cyclical, not breaking the familiar chain of events for years. Each season would bring a rebirth of change, but our roots were still deep in the earth, grounded into the hard clay.

My feet touch the ground in a moonwalk way as I try to locate the remnants of a firepit in the backyard behind the house. I helped my dad dig this pit one humid summer night when I was five years old. My Dad always had a way to make me feel included. He told me never to think I couldn't do something because I was a girl. I wish I had him around for longer because I know everything would have turned out much differently in my life, but we don't hold full control over what paths we take. I want to see him again. I hope he is here starting the fire for us to sit before it, one with nature.

No sounds emerge but the soft sound of my feet sinking into the grass. I stop to watch a bee pollinating a wildflower. Had I lived thirty-six years of my life and never stopped to watch this miracle? Being here watching nature makes me wish I had a book to read in this peace.

I am an avid reader. I think about when I was growing up and really getting my hands into any book I could. I would often be found under these trees reading. Reading was a way for me to escape the pain of not having a friend, and that pain was deep as the fire pit. I wanted good friends, or at least one I could connect with, but that never seemed to happen. It didn't help that I didn't live in a neighborhood, but I knew nothing different. I did have some shallow acquaintances who popped into my life at times, but nothing lasting surfaced. I honestly just preferred to be independent after a while. I chose to find my friends in books that I devoured night after night. Besides my parents, it just seemed no one in my life quite understood me. It sounds pathetic, but books were my only friend; something to take refuge in. I remember a favorite high school teacher recommending I read *The Color Purple*. I remember how the title meant that not seeing the beauty around the world aggravated God. I loved this concept after reading the book and wanted to live like this.

I continue to watch this bee pollinate the flower. Maybe I've been aggravating God for years. Did I truly live life this way? I feel so at peace though, not afraid, and where I am now feels nothing like a punishment or Christian guilt. I feel similar to how I feel eating comfort food. But I find myself wondering: Why I am here at my birth home standing by my favorite oak tree in front of an empty lot along a bumpy driveway uprooted from trees?

Then suddenly I'm covered with a blanket of despair from the obvious abandonment of a once lively place. The lights dim in the cold, odorless room, and then the painting goes dark. I picture my old house at night, lights casting shadows in the dark forest, warmth on the inside while my family eats dinner and shares stories of life.

It's quiet again. I embrace the stillness.

The path on the driveway leads to an empty space larger than the hole I have in my stomach right now. My head pounds like it never has before. I feel a need to lie down again and climb out of the painting to restart, but I can't. I know I must stay now that I have entered. A light wind causes me to shiver while I wait to catch my breath. A small patch of grass is illuminated from a sliver of light creeping through the trees where the fire pit once stood. Forgetting the darkness, I am lured back to the mesquite smell of crackling wood burning again. But no sign of Dad anywhere . . .

Chapter 2

Ashley

> *"Happiness will never come to those who fail to appreciate what they already have."*
> *- Gauthama the Lord Buddha*

I used to love the fall when the wildflowers gleamed bright yellow under an abated, golden sun. The bees arrived in growing numbers annoying everyone at picnics holding on to the last remnants of sugar drifting in the wind. When the cold air swooped in overnight changing everything in its path, the bees would hibernate, clustering together in the hive for the arduous task of surviving winter's frigid wrath. The sun hung lower, the daylight diminished each day by steadfast minutes, the colors of the trees changed, and the days of summer fell off the edge of the Earth.

Instead of feeling rejuvenated with a change of season, all I think about is the brown barren trees and the ugly color of brown that will be here for months on end with gray skies. How fucking depressing.

I have my window open a slight crack and can hear the low hum of the crickets. They used to lull me to sleep on a warm summer night, now their putrid attempt at creating noise is a sign of their demise and ultimately silence. My head rests on the cloud of regrets on my pillow.

I can hear the kids making noise in the kitchen, bowls hitting the quartz countertop and silverware clanking. Only two kids and it sounds like a noisy diner at a truck stop. My head pounds harder on this soft cloud with each clank in the kitchen. I can't hear the crickets anymore. How defeated they must feel to sing and dance under the moonlight so felicitously, then quickly discarded from such bliss. The thought of winter on its path of vengeance makes me brace for impact. I am a queen bee creating a high temperature for all the others to cling to breathing in their last bit of warmth to last for a while. I don't want to get out of this warm beehive but there are knocks on my door. Each knock collides with the fortress of my hive. Ava's whiny voice appears muffled through this wall of darkness. Her tone drowns out the last cricket's breath.

"Aren't you driving us to school today Mom?"

Silence.

"Mom?"

How many times will she say this?

"Mom!" Her voice gets louder. I can hear it a little more pronounced now. My brain still lays in a murky swamp, resting. I can't find my voice.

"Mom!" Ava says louder than the first time. Then the knocks again relentlessly, each pitch chipping time off my life. She opens the door and the harsh bright light flows in with her existence. She shakes me to the core.

"We have to go Mom. Can you get up so we are not late already? It's like you are dead, Mom. Like how can you sleep so late?"

She can't talk normally. She is an out of tune chime destroying the peaceful air on a harvest moon evening. She is standing over me swirling with noise and likes. She can't complete a sentence without adding likes.

"Yes, I'm getting up. Who else is going to drive you? I overslept, give me a break, will ya?" I am being pulled from the hive and dethroned. I sit up, my feet hanging from the bed into no existence. Without looking at her because my head is too dizzy to make eye contact, I find my voice, "What time are the games for both of you after school? I can't pick you up today because I have a tennis tournament that may go on the whole day. I also can't be at two places at one time and your dad is out of town, again. I can call Naomi and see if she can help."

"Whatevs Mom, but we need to get to school, so can you like, get dressed?"

I am annoyed at all the fucking activities my kids are in. Couple bottles of wine last night filled me with invisible thoughts. Ava leaves clomping down the stairs waking up the world in her fury. I hear her bitching at Noah that she had to come up and get me. She hates waking people up. I don't hear a word from Noah. Maybe he was sleeping too and she had to get him up as well. But now I have no choice but to get up. Naomi would never make it here that fast to help me, and of course Chris is conveniently not home. He is out sailing on a summer wind somewhere else, still pulsing with an insect's instinctual need for mating. After the shit storm settles here late this evening he will be home with his here-I-come-to-save-the-day bullshit. But he'll be too late. And on top of all that he'll want a piece of ass not skipping a beat since he's been gone.

"Fuck," I say angrily to myself with a dull sulfate headache. I can hear them both now calling my name. I yell down from the head of my doorway, "Just everyone be quiet already. I'm getting ready and will be down in a couple of minutes."

I grab my phone and text Naomi. Hopefully she can get the kids and bring them to their fall ball games after school.

"Ok," came Noah's monotone voice as he was gathering his things from the mudroom. I guess he was up this whole time. He is unbothered, unlike Ava.

Ava's whiney voice retorts back, her voice ricocheting off the walls at the bottom of the stairs. "Can't you like drive me and stay at the game Mom?" she says in an annoying tone that sounds awfully familiar to how she sounded during her terrible twos. Not much has changed.

I can only hope she doesn't talk to her friends like this because I can't imagine anyone wanting to be around her. I can only handle a few minutes of her before I'm ready to blow. It sucks, but true.

"I told you I have a match and not sure what time I'll be done. I'm texting Naomi to see if she can get you from school, bring you home to change and then back to the field. Why did you both have to sign up for fall ball anyways? Didn't you have enough balling this summer?"

I grab the shit I need and stuff it in a bag. I can just change at the club and get my Starbucks on the way over. When I get to the top of the stairs on the landing I look down. I see Ava and her neediness with her hands on her hips. She is a porcelain doll that should be pushed off a nightstand. She looks at me, then rolls her eyes, and sits down on the bench. I stare right back at her without a noise. She pulls up her socks while buckling her black Mary Jane patent shoes slowly stalling for time. What a little bitch she has become already at her young age.

"Fine Mom, whatever. It will be nice to see Naomi," Ava says back. I heard her mumble, "At least she cares."

I wince a little because I don't like feeling disdain for my daughter but I can't figure out another way to reach her. I leave the conversation there though because if I say anything else, it digs Ava in deeper and I have to listen to her bitching. I know when to stop. I sit down on my bed taking my time like Ava just trying to get my motivation for the day. I need a few minutes to wake up, so I start thinking about the relationship, or the lack thereof that I have with my kids.

If I were going to watch my kids do something substantial, I would be able to bear it somewhat and make it a point to get to the games after my match. I'm simply not interested. My kids are okay athletes, but their games are boring and they are just going through the motions of doing something because Chris feels our kids needed to be stars. Then he can go around and brag about them like trophy pieces, but ironically, he is never around to push them. He is the once-a-week father, and to his dismay, our kids aren't even medal worthy in a medal-for-everyone society. Somehow their inadequacies are my fault because he tells me this when he does show up for games.

My kids see their friends running the race to nowhere, so they feel they have to do this too. At times they both seem happy, but I know they would rather watch their YouTube videos of endless shit and waste time because that is just easier than working your ass off to get better than everyone else. Many, many times, I bite my tongue because I want to unleash, crack the whip and become the Tiger Mother I had growing up, but I walk the line carefully here with my kids. I clearly remember nothing but misery and feel the pain still to this day. My mother wanted nothing more for me than to be an extension of where she left off as a professional dancer.

"Mom please? Are you almost ready?" Ava won't let me be.

"We are not going to be late, I'm almost ready." I yell down the stairs. I secretly like making her squirm a little. This is good for her. I just need a few minutes to myself while I start thinking again. Without a job to get to I've got a lot of time on my hands. I often drift into the past trying to fix the present.

Growing up, I was a Barbie Doll clad in all new clothes, make-up and hair to match. Everyone wanted to be around me as far back as I can remember stemming back to kindergarten. I was put together like a mannequin for the shop window, all polished and clean but hollow on the inside. I had the kids all fooled, and even the teachers because my outside appearance was picture perfect, but no one bothered to look at the vacancy in my eyes. After a while I looked down a lot to avoid a gaze from an observant person for fear of my weakness being exposed. So, I wanted my kids to own the freedom to be who they wanted themselves to be, not what I wanted, and if it meant they weren't the stars of the show, so be it.

But when I look at Ava, she seems hollow in a different way. I don't know how to repair this now that she's entered her tweens. My lackadaisical approach is the source of many volatile arguments for Chris and me. I start to wonder why I had these kids in the first place. Chris is never around to help, which is why I hired Naomi, my German nanny. Yet even with help, most days I can't keep my kids' schedule straight. I often wonder just what the hell I used to do with all my time before I became a mom. All I am now is an Uber driver and it is interfering with my time.

Noah barely looks up and says "Hey," as we walk out of the house. I take this as a good sign because it tells me he is breathing. He rarely gets involved in our superficial conversations anymore. He is a few years away from getting his license. I know once he gets that plastic card of freedom, he will be driving far from the wreckage of our home.

When we get into the car it is filled with baseball dirt, an open Gatorade bottle with no liquid, and a stench of wilted egos. The car rolls off and I go into a daydreaming mode again. The lull of the car always brings me to a different place. No one is talking, so it's easy to wander off in thoughts.

I remember living in LA like it was yesterday. When I graduated from UCLA, I knew I had no intention to come home to Chicago. My parents got me an apartment with my roommate and we started interviewing right away after graduation. I loved California. My parents sent me an allowance until my Dad got me a job in pharmaceutical sales, so I was able to start earning my own money in addition to what they were sending me. I didn't even want to work, but it landed in my lap, so I accepted it because I hadn't found Mr. Right yet. I continued running around drinking and dancing with my friends similar to my high school/college days on the weekends. That was the easy life, palm trees, eighty degrees, and sunshine all the time. Why I decided to abandon that life is beyond me. What a big fucking mistake.

It did feel good to have my independence and make my own money, but there was always a voice in my head that told me if a man was there to help me along the path, I wasn't going to turn it down. Somehow my mother's energy seeped into every particle of my bones because she never did anything but use my father's money to become nothing but a lost busy body. My dad picks up my mom's many moving pieces even to this day.

The difference is Chris doesn't want to pick my pieces up anymore.

So after a short time of working, I had no interest in working for the long haul. I was getting drawn into the idea that it would be delightful to be like Barbie, living in a dream house while Ken came to pick me up in his Corvette. I really wanted my life to serendipitously fall into place, kind of like when you're shuffling the deck of cards. Sometimes I would lose my grip and the cards would fly all over the place. At some point, I needed to pick them up, put them all the same way and reshuffle to restart the game, or better yet, find someone else that was able to pick them up for me. Life was kind of like a nice little gift neatly packaged for me from my Dad, and then Chris picked up my cards when they scattered on the ground in a heap of disillusionment.

There is not much to talk about in the car and Ava decides to turn on the radio. This jolts me out of my daydreaming and reminds me that I'm driving. These pop songs make my headache even worse. We pass a public school on the way to the private school where my kids go. When I pull up to the intersection it is buzzing with kids, Moms, Dads, and Nannies. There is a crossing guard corralling all the kids and adults. She is not very tall, but she wears a bright yellow vest the size of a tent to cover her insanely large body. Her tummy has multiple rolls that lean precariously over her tan pants. Her feet pronate inward due to the weight from above. She blocks the sun but wears sunglasses to hide the fat that litters her face. She is chewing gum so hard that I can feel it through the car windows. This is the same crossing guard I have seen for a while on our daily route. She walks heavily in front of my car with pronating heavy clamps. I feel sorry for her but am more repulsed than sympathetic. The whole world which is racing from here to there stops. We all stare at her, watching her every slow, glutinous move. This morning's scene starts like a tornado moving down its path only to stop, halt for a moment, hover in silence while we all pause in annoyance that we have to stop for a few seconds from this barge of a woman. As soon as her foot hits the last white line, I accelerate over the space she is in hoping not to enter a sinkhole after she weighs down that street. We all go back to running away from the tornado and its path glad to be on the move again.

"What's wrong?" Noah says, tapping me back into reality.

"Oh nothing, I just spaced out for a moment."

"You do that a lot," says Noah, my intuitive son.

"I see that lady every day back and forth from school," I say. "I wonder if this is her actual job. Who would want to do this every day? I wonder if she is one of the teachers at that school," I say to the kids.

"I don't know," says Ava with no emotion, not even taking her face off her phone screen with all kinds of lights flashing back and forth. She is not interested at all.

"She always looks happy and she talks to all the kids," says Noah. "Don't you see how she is smiling all the time?" He is always my co-pilot in the front seat. He has his phone, but at least he looks up from it a few times in the morning.

"She's not happy, Noah, trust me," I say. "She chomps on that gum like a cow. How can someone be that fat and happy at the same time?".

"I don't get it either. How did she get so big? That's like, so gross," Ava says all of the sudden, finding interest.

"I don't know," I mumble. "She must eat a lot of McDonald's HAPPY Meals," and we all start laughing. I actually make my kids laugh even though they don't look up from their phones. That doesn't happen too often so I feel good about myself. This woman is at least three hundred plus pounds. She moves like a large hippo grazing in the field, and out of breath walking back and forth, yet very confident while doing so. Every day I see her duplicate everything she did the day before. I think of her a lot. Each day I drive by I find myself making up scenarios about her life and where she comes from, who she was with. I wonder if she is a mom, too. Did her Mom torture her like mine? Is this why she was so fat?

All of a sudden the school is upon me. I pull into the lot with monotone gray minivans flying in on two wheels. "Ok, see you later Ava. Hope you have a good game today. I texted Naomi and I'm waiting for her to text back to see if she could come watch you and bring you home later. But I'll text either way with what's happening, so watch your phone."

"Ok," Ava says and slams the door without saying goodbye. She never looks up from her phone.

Noah is finishing a text and looking down. He has one foot out the door, looks up and says, "Mark just texted and said his mom can drop me off at home and then take me to my game, so all good."

I think I should be a mom for once, so I dig down deep for cliched slogans. "Ok Noah, listen to your coaches, be a team player, and own up to your own mistakes, yes?"

He actually takes his gaze off his phone and I see his green eyes. He has a better presence than his father that I really enjoy watching.

"Cool Mom, thanks."

I can talk to Noah like this because he gets it, not like Ava who loves to hear herself complain. He nods with an adorable dimple and slow smile and walks into school. I can see the kids walking towards him as soon as his feet hit the pavement. He even walks like his father.

Off to the tennis courts not too far away but my daydreams return on the drive. A horn beeps behind me at the light reminding me I'm in a moving vehicle surrounded by others. I could give a fuck about the drivers behind me. Beep all you want. Then I get lured back in a daydream.

My pharmaceutical job was just a job. For me, it was simple. My motto was 'do what you need to do to get to the top,' and I had this banner hanging in my room at school all four years of college. My Dad had said this phrase many times over the years being a corporate lawyer, and that's why he was successful. My brother never really fell for this mantra since he stayed in Colorado after college majoring in environmental studies. He loved his simple life in nature and did the exact opposite of what my dad wanted him to do, and he's as happy as a clam. My Dad doesn't speak to my brother much. I am his favorite because I hang on to his every word. At one point though, I was really good at pitching a sale, so I started making a large amount of money rather quickly. When I was working, I was a hamster on a wheel just like the rest of the animals in this rat race. And this life as a mom feels oddly similar without the rewards of making my own money. I can remember rolling by the same landscape of the world I was in, day after day, just like now making up scenarios about people I didn't know. One day on my way out of a doctor's office, I stared at this building I would pass regularly. The palm trees lined the building so delicately. But there was one palm tree that was caged behind a fence. I kept staring at it every day because it was speaking directly to me like an epiphany. How can something so beautiful be trapped? I felt caged. Now as a mom with no job and everything I need, I'm still that palm tree caged behind the fence.

I eventually quit my job and ended up getting married to my x-boyfriend Chris from college and not long after I was pregnant with my first child. Chris really didn't want me to work once I had our son Noah because he was making more than enough money. I let myself go, just like a kite that took forever to get up into the right wind. The kite hovered in the sky for a while feeling the power of the air fiercely moving back and forth, only to feel the tugging of the string slowly losing steam, then down to the ground to lay limp and never achieve that height again. I once welcomed a new change that would alter the redundancy in my life, until a new life created another unsettled redundancy.

And for my parents, especially my mom, she was not too thrilled at being a long-distance grandparent. After my son was born, I could tell she wanted to put her hooks into my baby, and this would especially hold true when I had my daughter, Ava. She wanted to have another go at her granddaughter becoming a professional dancer since she failed with me, but I won't give her the chance to even attempt this dream. My older brother also made it clear that he was not having kids and loved being on his own with his wife. I lived my life in California. It was a win-win situation for both of us escaping the claws of our parents. We all saw each other occasionally and at holidays and special events. We were okay with the arrangement of seeing our parents for short periods of time, then being able to fly back to our own lives, but my mom was never satisfied with this. Although, and as always, my mother is a woman who gets what she wants. She ended up getting her wish for being a nearby grandparent, because when Noah was fifteen months old, Chris got a transfer to Chicago. Even close by, I did my best to keep my mother at arm's length because I didn't want her to infect my son and my daughter, like those super viruses you just can't kick. She had done enough damage to me. I was not going to let her take over my own children.

When it came time to move back to Illinois from California, I remember feeling a shock that I was heading back to my hometown of gray skies, torrential snow build-ups, zero temperature winters, and humid summers, but part of me was happy that I would at least be closer to my dad. We found a sprawling suburban city-like town close to Chicago. We wanted a spacious house that was up to our living standards and what we wanted for our kids. I had no choice on moving because I wasn't the one bringing in the dough when I was up to my ears in diapers. I settled into being a suburban mom for a little while at least, but not one of those moms that starts to wear Mom jeans, forgets to shave her legs, and gets fat.

I had to uphold my image.

I didn't want my own mom helping, so I asked Chris for a Nanny to help me. Naomi is a Godsend, most of the time, because she does everything for the kids, including all the housework, laundry, and even cooking meals. It gave me the freedom to walk out in the middle of terrible-two tantrums and leave when I got sick of hearing Elmo on Sesame Street for the twentieth time. Because I needed to keep up with the façade of being the best Mom, I joined a little class at the library, but all the moms just put a bad taste in my mouth. They were like little robots in their oversize moo-moos, and hemp diaper bags just cooing and falling all over their babies. I couldn't take it anymore, so Naomi just took over for me. And even with a new way of living, I just felt lost sometimes and would gaze off into the distance, like deer wanting to graze in the abundance of an open field. This feeling still comes and goes, and especially while driving. I eventually started to drink these feelings away slowly, day by day to make that gnawing feeling of boredom go away. Sometimes it works, sometimes it doesn't

I pull up to the tennis club and have no recollection of the ride over here after dropping off Noah because that seemed like a long daydream. I am on autopilot often when I'm driving with the past right next to me in the passenger seat. Naomi finally texts back and says she can pick up the kids from school and bring them to their games. I tell her Noah is all good, but Ava will need a ride. Thank God someone else will do this for me.

But of course I am late as always. I couldn't get my shit together with all this baggage because these kids weighed more than my car. My tennis bag slings over my shoulder and I feel lighter as I make my way into the club. I don't see any of my friends. I am sure they have already started, but I need to change and go to the bathroom because I ran out in a hurry.

On my way to the locker room Naomi is calling me now. "Hey Ash," she says, all happy like a cheerleader with way too much energy. "You didn't tell me which field Ava needs to go to. I just wanted to make sure I'm going to the right places."

I am just getting ready to answer her but she cuts me off. She likes to interrupt me any chance she can get. She feels the need to assert the authority she thinks she has.

"Spring Lake for Ava?" she says in a split second of peppiness.

"Yes, you got it." I say trying to get her off the phone. I don't know why she called if she knew where she was going. But this is the shit she pulls. She always needs verification of her own decisions to make her feel important. But she's not. She is just my nanny. Honestly, she's like taking care of a child too.

"Don't worry about Noah," I remind her. "He has a ride there and back, so all good."

"Ok cool, Ash. See you later." I think she stayed on to wait for a thanks but I have to get ready so I just click the red end button and move on. Too bad I can't hit a red button for all the people I can't stand in my life. I change super quickly and run out on the courts. I see Lola looking awfully familiar to the way Ava was looking at me with her hand on her hip this morning at the bottom of my stairs.

"You're late," snarks Lola. And Char looks agitated. Anna is hitting the ball against the board aimlessly and with anger.

"I know, try having kids without a full-time nanny." They keep swinging while I pull out my water bottle and racket ready to swing away from my motherhood.

I catch myself drifting off again while tidying up my shit and tying my shoes. I think about the crossing guard again. Did she get fat because of her mom? She wouldn't be able to get one foot across this court. I can blame my mom for so much of my shitty sides because her personality could change on a dime when I was growing up. One day she would tell me I was great, and the next day she would tell me that I would make someone miserable. So, I guess I just never knew where I stood with her and these ambiguous messages messed with my mind fiercely. To this day, I feel like a vending machine where I put my money in. I watched the mechanical wire spin and listened to the noise anxiously while waiting, but the candy never fell down in the bottom of the machine.

It got stuck.

It always gets stuck. I curse and shake the machine.

The ball lands directly in front of me and I miss it completely.

"What the fuck Ashley?" Lola says defensively. "Are you here with us or what? First you're late and now you're acting like a zombie for God's sake," she says, shaking her head. "Have you already been drinking?"

"Fuck off already Lola. I've had a rough morning."

Now I am playing tennis with these bitches I don't even like. Char and Anna are standing there with blank stares. The ball goes into motion without a word from anyone. It is hitting the pavement forcefully in my agitation, yet flatly and without purpose. They are surprised at my strength. The sun is in my eyes and I honestly do not have one goal as to where my life is heading now, but I'm hitting the ball fucking hard.

With a swing of the racket I think, "What kind of mother am I?"

With a swing of the racket, "What kind of wife am I?"

Another swing of the racket.

CHAPTER 3

Tammy

> *"The guilt of eating another piece of cake, claws at my stomach walls in distress. I curse myself at every calorie intake. I can feel my body expand as I obsess."*
> *- Anonymous*

I sit down where the firepit once stood on the bare patch of grass. The ground is cold and a little damp, but it feels good to sit and relax and think about my family. My sister Dawn is a few years older than me and we could not be more different. We had our fair share of fights, but for the most part we got along when we were little. She really was my only friend until she became a teenager and that's when she decided she really didn't want anything to do with me anymore.

My mom would say, "Don't worry Tammy. Your sister will always be your friend. It's just right now, she wants to be with the older girls."

"Why can't I hang with them too," I would say.

"They are older than you and have different interests. Just let her be and she will come around, I promise," Mom said.

"She is nice to me at home and then when her friends come over, she doesn't like me anymore."

"Tammy, you need to stop worrying about it. It will all work out, you'll see," my mom would say.

"Don't worry about it," was one of her favorite phrases, but this advice didn't help me because I did worry. I spent many nights lying in bed crying knowing I had lost the only friend I had, despite Mom telling me the opposite. As the days went on, the distance widened like a new highway being built from a two-lane road. And when Dawn left for college, I thought my whole world had ended because she got on that highway and never looked back. My mom was wrong that Dawn would grow out of a phase and be my best friend because she rarely came home when she went to school, so our friendship never rekindled itself. Therefore, I no longer pushed something that wasn't going to be because I knew she left me behind for good. I never caught up to meet her where she was at in life, and after Dad died, she felt being away from the sorrow was the best thing for her. Out of sight, out of mind, I guess.

After college, she stayed in Michigan, got married, had kids, and started her own life. And over time, the distance separated our hearts more than the miles between us. I could count on one hand how many times I talked to her in the last six months. I would see Dawn on occasion when she would visit, or we would visit her, but she was a minimal part of my adult life with my son and my husband. I know some of the detachment was because of distance, but this was just an easy excuse to use because if she lived a mile away our relationship may have been the same. When we were together, she felt like a stranger to me. I had to ask her questions to get to know her all over again and our relationship seemed forced. I pretended often that this arrangement was okay, but losing my sister's friendship was similar to clinging to your old stuffed animal that was worn out only to find it was ripped in pieces and unrepairable.

I can almost hear the fire crackle while sitting here on this bare patch of grass. I think about when my sister and I were little girls. I look up and the silence gives way to laughter from innocence. We played nicely with the kids that lived close by and those are memories I will always hold dearly. Because we lived on a large acre of land near a busy street, we were forced to be with each other because the closest neighbor on both sides required a supervised walk. As we got older, our parents trusted us that we could take the backyard trails to our neighbors' houses so we were able to branch out with other kids that lived nearby. We also didn't have that suburban block living like many kids had in the suburbs or city where they could go next door and ring a doorbell. Our walk to other kids that lived nearby was composed of secret trails behind our houses that took on the adventurous side of our childhood. It was like we were part of a Peter Pan tale and on that first day when our parents let us go on the trail to see our friends unattended; it seemed like a new world had opened up, free of the albatross around our necks to go where we wanted to go. We knew the forest and those trails like the back of our hands and took great pride in our territory.

There was a time when I had friends at school, from our softball teams or dance classes. And those friends from these places loved to come to our house because they felt like they were in a secret garden when we would go out on the trails. On the other hand, when visiting their houses, I always felt so constricted. There were cookie cutter houses and immature trees that tried to make a presence on the street, but it all felt so foreign and fake to me. I felt like I was in a prison of station wagons and grilled cheese sandwiches on their cut-out patios, so I didn't want to go over there very much. It was more often that kids came to see us and that's the way it was for most of my childhood.

I stand up to stretch a moment and my eye is drawn to where the remnants of the old swing set once stood. There are a few pieces of tattered wood still standing ominously in the fresh air I was breathing. Dad was a carpenter and built the swing set for us right here in the backyard, complete with a full sandbox, so we often spent most of our days playing here at this spot.

Mom was a stay-at-home mom, and I never was quite sure what she did all day long. I know now that she had the best job of all and also the most tiring. She did have a day job in her whole other life that she had before us, but she rarely talked about it, almost as if it happened in an alternate universe. She would come play games with us, read to us all the time, and taught us to be self-sufficient girls. She had the patience of a saint, as they say. I could count on one hand how many times I have been mad at her in my life. Our relationship was much closer than that of her and Dawn because I was the one that was there for her the most.

I turn around and stare at the blank space and picture the soft light glowing above the kitchen window. Most of my fondest memories were spent in that kitchen with Mom and Dawn. Our kitchen was one of the largest rooms in the house and I would say the most lived in. The kitchen was as yellow as the sun with curtains of white complete with a lovely bay window above the sink. The bay window had a large shelf that held plenty of green plants along with a splendid view of the large backyard. The best feature was an island that Dad built for Mom because he knew how much she loved to cook, and he knew good cooks needed space. A phone hung on the kitchen wall with a long cord that stretched as my mom paced back and forth chatting between the kitchen and the dining room while making dinner sometimes. If she didn't want us to hear her conversations, she would walk around the other side of the wall like she was in a private office. I used to laugh and tell her that the cord had to be twenty feet long from walking back and forth. Dad would say he would have to replace floors sooner than usual due to the path she created back and forth while solving the world's problems.

After school, my sister and I would run up the long driveway, drop our backpacks at the door, and run into the kitchen for a snack.

We couldn't wait to start cooking with Mom. One of my most favorite things to do together with Mom and my sister was when we baked cookies. I am convinced we became the sharpest readers in class because the kitchen was where Mom would read recipes to us and we would help her make dinners with step-by-step directions. But with baking cookies, I loved making the batter the best. I would often get in trouble from my mom because I would steal batter from the bowl and just throw globs of it down my throat.

One time we were making batter for sugar cookies. There was flour everywhere, blenders going and good smells like a warm blanket on a cold night. My Mom went to answer the phone and then walked around into her private office in the dining room.

"Dawn," I said. "Where did Mom go?"

"She's on the phone with Grandma," said Dawn.

"Watch this," I said. I proceeded to grab a huge pile of dough and ate it as fast as I could. Dawn was chuckling at my antics, and the more she chuckled, the more I ate. Dawn started to eat some too, but not as much as I did, and then all of a sudden, her tone changed.

"Tammy, you fat pig. Why do you have to eat like that? It's gross."

"I'm not fat. Why are you saying that? You like the batter too," I said back. I felt like I could easily eat the whole bowl of batter.

I was short in stature, but boy could I put away the food. Many people in my family would comment on my appetite as well when we were at a holiday party or at a picnic.

"Man, where do you put all that food Tammy?" my aunt would ask.

"You are so short Tammy. Where does that food go?" my uncle would tease.

I would not know how to answer these harsh questions, but in my mind, it was something I was proud of because someone noticed something about me. I could eat well, how about that? It was like I had put another trophy on the mantle for being the best eater in the family.

"Tammy, really, you look fat to me lately. I only had a little bit of the batter because it's called control." She walked over and picked up the empty bowl and looked at me with skeptical eyes. "How did you eat that whole bowl of batter?" Dawn walked closer to me and lifted up my shirt. I pushed her away because I thought she was going to tickle me.

Instead, she pushed my hands away and said, "I can pinch-an-inch Tammy. You are getting fat like the Pillsbury Doughboy!" She started laughing and making pig noises circling me with pig snorts.

"Stop saying that to me Dawn! You were eating the batter too." I went up to her and pulled up her shirt forcefully and tried to pinch-an-inch like she did to me. But I was surprised to find that I couldn't do this. Her stomach was a washboard, hard and smooth.

"You can't pinch an inch dummy because I don't eat like you, fatso. Keep eating the batter like that and you'll be the fattest girl in your class, and then I won't want anyone to know you're my sister!" she said meanly.

This was the ultimate blow to my heart. How could she not want anyone to know I was her sister? I was just trying to have fun.

"You are so mean to me, Dawn. I am telling Mom on you!" I started crying.

My sister and I kept arguing, and I was crying loudly enough for Mom to hear this quarrel in her private office so she hung up the phone with my grandma. When my mom came back to the kitchen she was horrified. "Where on Earth did all the batter go?" she said with a high-pitched tone in her voice. I could tell she was really angry. "I walk away for ten minutes and I come back to all of the ingredients missing?"

My sister and I looked at each other and my overeating turned to a feeling of guilt. We could tell this was not something she was just going to blow off, like she did most of the time.

"Well, I am waiting for an explanation," she said as she stood there with her arms crossed.

"Sorry Mom," Dawn said. She was used to being the older sister so she always stepped in first. "Tammy started eating some of the batter and I did too. But then she was shoving it down her throat and then I decided to tell her that she was getting fat. You know, how we talked about it before? You said we needed to keep an eye on how she was eating. I didn't want her to eat the whole thing, but she did even though I told her not to."

"I'm sorry too," I chimed in pathetically. I tried to pull the puppy dog's youngest kid look, but it didn't go over very well. But then I quickly realized my mom and sister had been talking about my weight without me knowing.

"What do you mean that she has to watch over me and what I eat? Is this about the baby fat you were telling me about Mom? The batter was good, that's all."

"Yes, we have been watching over you because you have been eating a lot Tammy, and we want to make sure you don't go overboard. But that is not the point right now!" she said, looking at both of us "Do you realize I have to pay for all of these extra ingredients? Do you also know that your father works his ass off to feed us, and then you think it is funny to shove food down your throats and basically take everything we do here for you for granted?"

We just stood in silence. My Mom rarely swore, and when she did you knew that she had been pushed to her limit. I never even thought about the things she brought to our attention. I was also sure my sister didn't think of them either based on the look she had on her face.

My mom was not done.

Listening to my mom's rants was similar to watching politicians run for office. They would say something powerful and the people would all stop for a moment and clap, cheer. The speaker would stand and wait and then move on for the next reaction. My Mom stood and stared in between her shrilling sentences. She had all the poise and wisdom of a presidential candidate; in fact, I'm quite sure she could have run for office and won. She had that kind of presence when she was firm.

She threw down the oven mitts and walked over to the stove and turned it off. She was ready to speak again. She sighed, took a deep breath and said, "Furthermore, and besides the whole money point I was trying to make," she looked right at us, but through us, "Do you know what gluttony is?"

"What?" said Dawn.

"You heard me," she said. "Gluttony." This time she said it slowly. "I want the two of you to repeat that word to me three times.

My sister and I looked at each other with dazed looks, but we weren't going to cross this candidate. We did what she said.

"Gluttony, gluttony, gluttony," we echoed together.

"Ok," Mom said. Now that you are familiar with how to say it, let me tell you what it means." My Mom loved words. She studied them and she used them very carefully like a research doctor looking to find the cure for cancer.

"It means that you are greedy with your hunger, that you eat too much and you are abusing food." She stopped and started again; man, she was the best speaker. We stood there with not one thing to say. We were stunned.

"So, how do you feel about yourselves now? Do you feel gluttonous?"

I did not want to admit she was right, but she was right. I feel bad about it now many years later. Even though I felt bad, my sister was not going to take the blame for something she didn't do.

Dawn piped in, "I get it Mom, but I didn't eat the batter. It was Tammy who ate it, not me."

"I have a stomachache and feel like I could puke," I said through my tears.

"Well, serves you right if you do," Mom smirked.

What bothered me the most, and I couldn't say it, was that I did not have a stomachache at all. I made that up just to get out of the situation. In fact, I still felt hungry for more, but I wouldn't dare say anything.

"That's it, Dawn? Why are you standing there not saying a damn thing? Do you have anything to say? You're supposed to be the older sister and set an example for Tammy."

"I told her to stop," Dawn said. "She just kept going and I couldn't stop her. I'm sorry."

"Well, your apology doesn't mean anything to me right now. I could get more emotion out of a wet mop. You both ruined the evening, but I hope you learned something from all of this."

Without saying anything, Mom took off her apron, turned off the stove, and said, "Clean everything up, take a shower, and go to bed. We can talk more in the morning."

My sister and I cleaned up in complete silence and at one point Dawn left to go to the bathroom and didn't come back. My people pleasing, naïve ways, and guilty eating had just been born right there in our kitchen, quite unknowingly to me at such a young age, but was with me subconsciously.

I see the kitchen light go out and I stare down at the firepit. Darkness emerges in the backyard like the light going off in the refrigerator cutting off my food supply. I feel hungry again.

Chapter 4

Ashley

> *"The reason why daughters love their dads most is because they know there is at least one man out there who will never hurt them."*
> *- Unknown*

It feels good to swing a racket and forget about my problems if only for a little bit. It has been a long day of playing, so a drink of wine always feels good to unwind even before heading back to my chaos, even with the dull headache still lingering from the night before. I stall there for a bit to avoid going to the games. But when the conversation gets old and the wine is gone, it is time to go home. I get up without a word. I take a shower at the club to polish my appearance and leave without saying goodbye.

When I start my car and turn on my set list, "Fly Me to the Moon" is playing. I turn it up as loud as I can and think of my carefree days as a child and think of my Dad. I turn left out of the club and hear honking over the music. Holy shit. I hadn't seen that guy coming, so I accelerate fast to make up for my blunder. My mind reverts back again.

I always felt like a princess who walked into a palace when I would come home. In my house there was a grand foyer and light from the sparkling chandelier, complete with a baby grand piano just east of the foyer in the living room. There were always perfect lines drawn in this room from the vacuum that resembled lines on a musical score. If a footprint was left in this room after the piano was played, the cleaning lady was instructed to vacuum again immediately to recreate the lines. My mother settled for nothing less than her house being damn well close to perfect at all times and she always had help around to cater to her every need.

At the end of the long corridor, the walls opened up to a large and sprawling kitchen straight out of *Better Homes and Gardens*. In fact, this kitchen was displayed in that magazine, and Mom was interviewed and pictured in the article. She lifted not one finger to decorate it. She didn't earn one dime to design this kitchen, yet she took all the credit for the splendor of this room like she was the architect. My dad let her hold all this glory even though he was the one with the design idea and the money that made it happen.

To complete the ambiance of the room, there was a sound system where music would bounce off the walls to the sound of sizzling smells for dinner. I used to love watching our chef cook and sometimes my mom would join in occasionally if it fit her mood. I loved to sit on the island chair and color while music was playing softly in the background.

One of my favorite and earliest memories was dancing with my dad in the kitchen. He would often come home late, mostly after we were already done eating, but he found time for me when eating his lonesome leftovers.

"Ashley, my darling. I want you to hear this song that made me think of you."

"Yes Daddy, what is it? I missed you." I would give him the biggest hugs.

He would turn the music up and motion for me to come by him.

"Step on my feet sweetie."

The music would start, my feet would move to the beat of the music, and I would laugh and giggle with delight.

"Count with me: one, two, three, four," he would say while snapping his fingers.

"One, two, three, four," I would say, holding his hands. I was able to feel his warmth, take in the smell of his cologne, and feel his suit and tie caressing my face. He always reminded me of a movie star like Cary Grant, always poised and put together.

"Twirl me again, Daddy. Twirl me again," I would repeat.

"You're such a good dancer Ashley," my dad would say as he twirled me around until I was dizzy with laughter.

Even though I can't remember family dinners in the kitchen, the dancing was what I remembered forever because our routine happened almost nightly for the longest time. I was secretly happy to have my dinners with dad once everyone left him to fend for himself when he had come home from a long day of work or a business trip. I knew he appreciated my presence because I was the only person he hugged when he walked over the threshold each day.

Dad would play all different songs from all different genres, but one night he said, "I have a new song for you tonight my little Ashley. "Stand on my toes and move with me. Listen very carefully to the words because this is our song. It will always be our song."

"What is it Daddy? Is it a good song?"

"Probably one of the best dance songs you will hear in your lifetime. It's by Frank Sinatra."

"Who's Frank Sinatra?" I inquired.

"He sings 'Fly Me to the Moon,'" Dad said.

"Fly me to the moon? Is it really about going to the moon, Daddy?"

"Not really, but it's about a man who loves his special lady and he's so happy that he's over the moon. It's just a saying. When I dance with you, I feel I am over the moon sweetie pie. That's why this is our song, ok?"

"Ok, Daddy. I love it too."

Then the drums tapped lightly as if the drummer was in the room, and the piano started, and then the words: *Fly me to the moon. Let me play among the stars. Let me see what spring is like on Jupiter and Mars. In other words, hold my hand; in other words, baby kiss me.*

"Play it again Daddy; play it again," I would say when Frank Sinatra's velvety voice stopped. I just couldn't get enough. That song was in my heart, and with my feet on Dad's, I felt a spring in my step that no matter what happened in my life, I had my dad.

Yep, that is the song that is always in my heart. I was a Daddy's girl dancing in that kitchen on our elaborate stage of marble floors.I hit repeat a few times and listen to it again and again on my way back home.

When it ends, the demon-like silence seeps in like my mother. On the other hand, she was a different story. She seemed to be always scowling at me at a young age and even worse when I became a teenager. As early as I can remember, I sensed her jealousy of my dad's love for me. Because my mother was a professional dancer, she always felt the need to insert her expertise at all the wrong moments.

Frank Sinatra's loving voice would pipe through the kitchen, but my mother would dampen the mood. "You know you led Ashley with the wrong foot," she would say while we were in the middle of the dance. My dad would glance at her and I ignored her, but she would continue to insert her opinion.

"You shouldn't twirl her like that dear; she might get sick."

"I think I know what I am doing. Thanks, we got it," said Dad.

"Why don't you pick a different song? She is probably tired of this song because you play the same one all the time. There are so many more options," she said with her know-it-all advice.

"But I like this song, Mommy," I would say.

"Ashley and I love this song, so why does it bother you so much?"

And that shut her up. My mother would walk away like a queen giving up her crown.

Finally, Dad just stopped listening to her and we eventually got wise and would not dance together until she was gone. It was just easier that way because she could never just let us be without her judgment.

Funny enough, she never really had issues with my brother Brett who was a few years older than me. In her eyes, he could do no wrong, and all she did was defend him in any situation just to piss off my dad. I was convinced of this. But eventually Brett grew tired of my mom's smothering ways, and he figured out really quickly his best option would be to stay away as often as he could. Plus, my father and Brett had a relationship similar to a cat and a mouse. There was always one running from the other until eventually the chase would end at a standstill. So, to dance with me was something Dad longed to do because we hit it off right from the start. He taught me how to dance with love. He taught me how to let go and be free, to love and be me. I danced with him to that song for years with my feet on top of his all the way until I left for college. I can go back in time and feel that song, taste the smells of dinner brewing in the kitchen, hear Frank Sinatra's soothing voice, and feel the warmth.

I danced to "Fly Me To The Moon" at my wedding on a gorgeous July summer evening with white lights, clinking glasses, and surrounded by lilies under candlelight. This time we had both feet on the ground while we glided over the dance floor.

"I love you to the moon, Ashley," he whispered in my ear while his voice shook with tears. "I will always love you to the moon." He paused and a tear came down his cheek. "Why did you have to grow up so fast?"

The music was enrapturing while I twirled dizzy in delight. I could hear the applause from our guests. Among my twirling rhythm, I caught a glance of my mom standing on the edge of the circle crying. I think she was crying not because of the sentiment, but more so that she got my father back for herself or to trap him for only her to keep. Her tears melted away like whitecaps gliding over the water to fizzle out, foam, and then to glide right back in.

Big shouts echoed as Dad gave me a dramatic dip while he picked me up and circled me around the dance floor as the white matte satin cascaded in rhythm with the bass. We were heading to the moon at the moment and I wasn't sure I wanted to come back. I will never forget that moment.Thank goodness for my dad, I thought after hearing our song.

On my darkest days I play this song and think of dancing on air. I honestly couldn't recall a time when I felt happier than on those nights dancing with my dad. My dad told me he loved me to the moon every night of my childhood, over the phone, in letters and birthday cards, and on the day I got married. I truly believed no one else could love me like my father.

As our hands parted that night after that dance and he took my hand and put it in Chris's, I couldn't help but feel myself floating away from the moon. I loved Chris intently, explicitly; yet, I just felt this unsettling feeling come over me.

The baseball field where Noah is on is on the way home. I had a few moments to spare so thought I'd see if I could catch the end of the game. I glide towards the stoplight and text Noah's friend's mom to let her know I'm picking Noah up. When I get there I see Noah's team all walking off the field with their heads down. I just missed the game. Noah is walking alone, not with the other group. The coach calls them all into a huddle. I feel it may be better to wait in the car. It looked like Noah needed a pep talk. I remember the pep talks well. Sometimes they worked, but many times they failed to help me. I didn't want to fuck this up. I find anger welling up in me because it would be nice if Chris were here to help pick up these pieces and be a father. This was all too much for me. I start humming "Fly Me to the Moon." My mind is still in the clouds as I wander: "Will anyone ever love me like my dad?"

CHAPTER 5

Tammy

> *"Keep your face always towards the sunshine and shadows will fall behind you."*
> *- Walt Whitman*

I sit back down in the darkness on the bare patch of grass and wish there is a fire blazing to light up the yard like when I was a child. This black sky evening with only a sliver of a moon leads me to feel the throbbing pain in my head and think about my crazy corner in life.

Being a crossing guard took a steady commitment of consistency, a relationship of trust from unknown drivers, and completing odd hours of work during the day. The intersection of Maple and Chestnut Street where I would stand each day was a busy, bustling area in the morning and in the afternoon rush hour. Even though this intersection was chaotic most of the time, I loved being part of the madness. What made this crossing area a little more difficult to manage was that the intersection provided many different variables, all colliding in one spot.

First, this intersection was a four way stop and not a light. This meant more drivers would often roll through quickly, or all wait for each other in annoyance, or almost collide because they both thought they had the right-of-way. I saw many road rage altercations in this intersection of people simply not taking their turn politely. It was like a scene in the elementary school of cutting in line and who could get ahead of who first to save a few seconds on the commute. I dubbed my space here at one time: "The Crazy Corners."

Second, there was a bridge that went over one of Chicago's busiest interstates, and at the bottom of the bridge at Chestnut Street was me waiting to cross people. The cars would come over the bridge very fast and I would have to second guess whether or not the drivers were going to notice the stop sign at the bottom.

Third, many commuters would take this road to avoid sitting in the inevitable stand-still of cars down under the bridge. Under the highway of the bridge was a transit line taking people into the city all from the surrounding towns, so many of the commuters would cross my intersection to get to the top of the bridge.

Fourth, there were two schools: one private and one public. And if this wasn't enough of a crowded beehive, there was a huge candy factory on the corner of Maple and Chestnut Street, so scores of workers would cross from the adjacent parking lot across the street. Because of the many people crossing at a four way stop, I had to be at the intersection at least an hour before school started and afterward, due to all the different schedules of the variety of commuters. Throw in the weather to this mix and you had a recipe for disaster for anyone of a weak mind. Being in the Chicagoland area the weather was rarely ideal, so I would plan for all the elements. Honestly, I could walk out on a gorgeous sunny, eighty-degree morning, and then it could be sixty and raining a few hours later at the kindergarten 11:40 dismissal, then maybe hot again, or heck even snowing by the 3:15 end of the day rush.

When most people come by and chat, the discussion inevitably turns into a discussion about weather.

"Oh my gosh, these winds are ridiculous!"

"It is nice and hot out, but this humidity is terrible!"

"Yes, you are right, but at least we are alive," I would chime back.

I love this one; "It was literally just raining cats and dogs ten minutes ago."

So, first off, the word literally is so overused, and it drives me crazy every time I hear it used as an exaggeration. If it was literally raining cats and dogs I would have been pounded into the ground by heaps of animals. Anyone who has lived in this area knows that the weather can turn on a dime, so why are we so surprised when the weather shifts rapidly? Can't anyone walk on by and say, "What a beautiful day?" Do we need the weather complaints for us just to be grateful we are here? I guess it is small talk, as so many people need to fill the air with words and their loquacious ways…just can't walk on by and smile, I guess.

This is what I did here at this corner though. I waved, I talked to the kids, to the adults; sometimes I would just smile, and yes sometimes I would partake in the dangling artificial conversations about the weather, too. I think it's just human nature. I watched the patterns of the rats in cages, and I saw mostly the same people every day. I knew when that red car was going to come flying over the bridge and make a right-hand turn to get on the highway before everyone else. I knew the minivan brigade of moms flying on two wheels to get to the gym for the spin-class. I marveled at the California rolls at the stop sign with streams of little children trying to get to school. Were we all in that big of a hurry not to stop for one second, pause and move on?

My head throbs a little now and I see now how none of these little things in life really matter.

I saw the man who walked his dog everyday no matter what the weather was, along with runners that did the same thing: running, rain or shine, cold or hot, or anything in between. The cars cascaded up and down the bridge like horses on a carousel. I was always there, the Lone Ranger, the lady who walked folks across the street, like the ticket holder at the merry-go-round. When I walked out into the intersection, all noise and obstacles would come to a stand-still, the safe gap: this is the time when we become still at this short moment in our lives and can hear the shoes of the pedestrians crossing while the hum of the cars come to a silent hush, tires rolling back to a halt.

I feel this gap now, no longer a pain throbbing in my head.

As soon as I walked back to the curb, the wheels were set into motion, back and forth, fast to still, until I made my way to the end of my time and set off to go home.

I arrive home now on this bare patch of grass in the dark.

Back on that corner, I visualized where everyone was going and how they would do without my presence there. Maybe they were going to work, or the guy who runs, maybe he ran every day because he wanted to get away from his nagging wife and that was his only time to get away. When I watched the kids, I wondered what kind of home they came from, did they have brothers and sisters, and I wondered what their favorite thing was at school. I talked to the kids daily and knew all of them by name. Some of them were shy and wouldn't talk at first, but after a few weeks I would get to know the behaviors of everyone and who to warm up to and who were my favorites that I would see each day.

"Hi Miss Tammy. How are you? I won my soccer game this weekend."

"Oh, that's good. I am sure you practiced," I would say back.

"It's my mom's birthday today," said a little girl.

"Oh, tell her I said happy birthday. And you be a good girl, ok?" I would say smiling. These were my favorite times of the day.

The kids I crossed were in elementary school, so most of them actually looked you in the eye and talked to you. The middle schoolers were a different story. They had a plan and I was not part of that at all because I was not snap-chatting or insta-gramming. I was not sure they knew how to have a genuine conversation face to face. The little kids didn't have phones or iPads that they carried around so they were forced to have face to face talks and it was always quite refreshing. However, I knew all too well that the refreshing feeling would lose its luster, like chewing fresh gum only for it to lose its flavor shortly upon opening it. But the adults I could say with conviction were the worst on their phones. I would worry someone would get hit by a car because of walking with their heads down sucked into a phone as if they were in another world, oblivious to simply walking down the street being aware of their surroundings.

"Good morning," I would say to anyone who walked by whether they were on the phone or not.

"Morning," a man would say, not even looking at me because his head was down texting.

"Good morning," I smiled.

The middle school girls passed me by chuckling. I heard them talking about my weight, so I knew for sure they were laughing at me. I was used to this.

"Good morning," I would say to the middle school boys. Some would say hi, and some would not even acknowledge my presence. I saw some boys pretending to waddle from being overweight and then laughing. I am quite sure some of these boys would make fun of my weight probably because their moms made their weight a big deal so as to not look like me. I put up with the ignorance, the silence, the bad manners, and the general polite etiquette back and forth with people every day.

I myself left my phone in my back pocket in case my son Alex needed me, but for the many years I had been on that corner, he never called once. I had very strict rules from the school that I was not to be on a phone.

My job was more than walking people across streets. I established relationships. I made most people smile. Some knew about me and I knew most of them. I provided a safe gap for a small piece of pleasure in their day even if only for less than thirty seconds.

Most outsiders who looked at me probably thought something completely different about me. See, it was not every day that folks would see someone who was three-hundred-and-eighty pounds walking people across the street. Yep, that was me in all my glory. Just like I would watch them every day, study their patterns, make judgements or speculate about their life, I often wondered what they thought of me.

I look up at the sliver of a moon. Does it really matter now? I stood on that corner smelling the aroma of candy-making from the huge factory that stood across the street. This factory made me think of the Oompa Loompas from *Charlie and The Chocolate Factory*: "No one comes in and no one ever comes out."

I stopped once a week at the small street side shop of the factory where you could buy candy by the pound. I loaded up on licorice, lemonheads, burnt peanuts, and my favorite, peach rings. I wished that I was not a regular here. It was just that the candy smelled so good while standing on that corner luring me in like an alcoholic who needed a drink. The cashier knew me by my first name.

I look out into the darkness again on a still night. I wonder if anyone would miss me and my heavy feet at that corner? Strange enough though, I didn't feel my weight anymore sitting here in my glorious backyard.

I felt light.

I felt safe.

I was home.

Chapter 6

Ashley

> *"Take what you need, do what you should, you will get what you want."*
> *-Gottfried Liebniz*

I wave from the car to get Noah's attention. He sees me and his face stays monotone. The door opens heavily and Noah sinks in with dust like Pig Pen behind him.

With no second to spare he says, "How long have you been here?" I don't know what to say. I think about lying and telling him I saw the last inning. But I know I can't because he may ask me about a play or something. I don't want to get him more upset.

"Well, I just got here. I was thinking I'd be able to catch the last part of the game." I can tell he is skeptical about my whereabouts and why I'm just arriving.

"Good thing you didn't get here early, Mom. It ended early because I made all the errors and cost us the entire game." His voice is youthful, with hints of tears, yet on the cusp of becoming a young man. I find this stage of boyhood to be so awkward. A piece of my heart sinks when he says this. I really feel for him.

"Hey, you can't blame the whole loss on one person. I don't know a lot about baseball, but I do know it's a team effort. It's not like tennis where it's you, solo out there in front of everyone. Stop doing that to yourself Noah. You'll make the loss worse. You gotta lose sometimes."

"Stop comparing this to tennis Mom. Baseball has nothing to do with tennis. That's not helping me right now!" His voice starts to sound deeper as he yells at me. He has that same look on his face that Chris does when we argue. This is when I get quiet for a while then slowly burn into an outburst I can't take back. I held my tongue here.

"You didn't see me miss routine ground balls, overthrow to first base and strike out three times. I suck!" He pounds his fists on the dashboard. It makes me jump because Noah rarely gets riled up. I don't know what to say so I just sit there. It must have been really bad like he said. I don't want to make excuses for him.

"I wish Dad was home to help me! You can't help!" This is when he puts his face in his hands and starts crying. I am not expecting this at all. Before I know what to say, my phone is ringing. It is Ava. I take a deep breath and answer the phone.

"Hey Mom, we lost. We are at home now. Like where are you at?" She sounds very stressed as if the world is ending. The world is always ending in her mind.

I don't want to tell her I am with Noah because I know she will freak out but I can't hide this one.

"I just picked Noah up from his game now. We are on our way home." I sit waiting for the wrath of Ava. And then it comes as expected a millisecond later.

"You can go to Noah's game but not mine? You must love him better than me!" She starts to cry. I can hear her whimpering over the phone. My heart doesn't sink like it did for Noah.

"Ava. Ava. Ava!" I hear more whimpering and then Naomi gets on the phone.

"Ash, sorry. It was a rough game for Ava. She was pitching today and made a lot of mistakes. She got quite emotional. I wish the coach would've pulled her off because the last pitch she hit a batter pretty hard. I think it was because of her anger. The girl had to go to the emergency room. Ava hit her right in the wrist. The girl couldn't move it so they were taking her to get x-rayed. I was just getting ready to call you."

"What the fuck?" I yell.

"What is it Mom? Is Ava okay?" Noah takes his hands off his face, diverted from his own agony.

"Do I now need to get a hold of this girl's parents? What the fuck was she doing? Does she not know how to pitch? All this money on lessons and this is what I get? A kid who can't throw a fucking ball across the plate!"

There was whimpering in the background. I can hear Ava sobbing. Again, she sounds eerily annoying to how she did when she was two. I almost wish she was the one that got hit.

"You know Chris said he was going to work with her on the pitching, Noah too. But where the fuck is he? Who the fuck knows. Listen, I gotta get going here with Noah. We'll be home soon. You can leave if you want, Naomi. Maybe she needs to be left alone to figure her shit out. I'll deal with her when I get home. Right now Noah's got some issues too." I wait for her speech of how everything will be okay.

"I can't leave Ava now, Ash. She's a trainwreck. I'll feel horrible if I leave her here by herself. I'll just wait with her until you get home. My mom always says that this too shall pass."

I can feel her phony positivity circulating over the airwaves. "Alright, suit yourself," and I hit the red button.

"What happened?" Noah says.

"Ava made a lot of errors like you and hit a batter. They have to get the girl's wrist x-rayed to make sure it's not broken," I sigh.

"Well, I guess her situation is worse," says Noah. "At least I didn't hit anyone." We both chuckle a little bit, then right back to gloom and doom. I keep thinking this is just a game. But I know what it feels like to lose and that shit was no fun when I was going through it. Now here I am with two kids who are trainwrecks. I have no clue how to make it right but to move it back to Chris. I don't feel like dealing with it.

"Well when your Dad gets home I think you both should go out in the backyard with him and practice. We are paying all these coaches and private lessons for what?"

Apparently that isn't the right thing to say because Noah puts his hands in his face again and shakes his head. "That's not it Mom!" Through his muffled tears he says, "When's he coming home anyways?"

"His flight comes in tonight at eight Noah. You can talk to him then."

Noah doesn't say a word. He picks his head up and pulls his baseball hat down over his forehead. He leans down in the seat and shifts his body over to face the window. The quiet side comes back. "I don't want to talk about it anymore," he says gloomily.

"Okay. I understand." I let him be for lack of words myself.

I start the car and pull out of there. I hum *Fly Me to the Moon* in my head because I don't dare put the song on the radio. I think about my dad. What would he do in this situation? I think about calling him for a hot minute but don't want to drag him into my mess. My dad was always put together and always knew what to say because he is a corporate lawyer. I learned more about him the older I got and heard he is quite shrewd. I go back to daydreaming.

Early on, I never really knew exactly what my dad did when he left the house, but I knew he was busy because he was rarely home. He often left the house early, came home at odd hours, and traveled a lot. I would hear him sometimes on the phone yelling at people and making all kinds of demands and wonder if this was the same man who would braid my hair and dance in the kitchen with me when my mom would go on her Caribbean trips with her girlfriends. Sometimes

I would ask him why he was yelling at someone on the phone and he would answer with, "It's nothing personal honey, it's just business." This response would satisfy my curiosity because I didn't really care to be honest. He was there when I needed him and always at the important events in my life. I didn't care what he did when he was gone. He was my dad and loved me no matter what. Furthermore, he took us all on fancy vacations, we lived in a lovely house, my mom didn't have to work, and my brother and I were never told we couldn't have something. We had the best clothes, cars at age sixteen, went to private schools, and debt free college experiences to great schools.

When I first went into college, I thought about being a teacher for a brief moment because there were many girls in my sorority that were thinking about this path. It seemed like the easier route, summers off, and your day ends at three. But the starting salary was enough to make me laugh out loud. My dad was also not convinced I would be able to do anything productive with a teaching career. He certainly didn't want to spend all of his money for me to go to UCLA and walk out as a teacher barely able to keep food on the table on a pathetic salary. He was relentless about changing my thoughts on teaching and went through many schemes to get me to fold. I was the only person in his life that he never wanted to disappoint, so he let me have what I wanted without any questions, but there was no budging on this one.

My dad made his living on being persuasive. I think I may have been the only case he lost in his whole career because he tried to talk me into law, but my heart wasn't in that either. Like a true lawyer, he tried one angle after the next until he found something. He told me that he had never seen any child sell as much lemonade as I did from my childhood years. I would chuckle and say, "That was all you and Mom. Mom made the lemonade and you started me off with a twenty-dollar bill, so I was already ahead. You probably paid your friends to come over!"

"No sweets, that was all you. People see that hair, blue eyes and charming smile, and the enchantment begins!" He gave me that know-it-all look with a dimpled grin. He paused, took a breath, and said, "I'm not telling you what to do, but I think you should go into business. You would be famous at creating your own business or selling for someone. Think about it."

He was right, but I never really wanted a job. But to suffice my Dad I switched my major to business and never looked back.

Upon graduating, I knew my dad would have loved for me to relocate back home to the Chicago suburbs, plus he knew scores of people in the city and he'd land me a job in a minute. Yet, on the other hand, he also knew there was no way I could come back home and live with my mother because our relationship was almost nonexistent when I left for college. The space and miles from my mother did me wonders, although it hadn't been easy on my dad. It seemed as though my parents had started living separate lives even though they were in the same home. I didn't ask him many questions, but I saw the exhaustion on his face when I would visit.

Living with her was similar to a runner who just finished a marathon while running with a sprained knee. I don't even know how she had any friends. But she did, and she spent all of her time playing tennis, drinking wine after the matches, dizzy and drunk to arrive home, pass out, go shopping, and then do the whole thing over the next day. I was privy to this behavior when I would come home from breaks, and I wanted out, similar to a prisoner wanting to escape from Alcatraz.

I could see why my dad just lived his own life, not wanting to deal with that shit, but part of me was starting to wonder if I was turning into the same woman.

For my college graduation, I got my Dad's BMW because he used me as an excuse for needing a to buy himself a new toy, preferably a fast car where he could hit the gas and go from zero to sixty to get the fuck away from my mother. Once my dad got me the job as a pharmaceutical rep, I was offered a company car, but decided to forgo that and drive around in the beamer. I felt it looked better for my image because I was working in mostly very wealthy areas in LA. I got a condo in West LA and made my way through the territories of Bel Air, Pacific Palisades, Brentwood, Porter Ranch, and as far as Santa Monica and Malibu.

My body was in the very best shape I had been in in my entire life, even surpassing my dancing years. Living in LA required a whole new subset of standards for myself and fitness. I entered UCLA in great shape after dancing all those years, but the dancing I did in college was nowhere near the regimen I had for many years prior. It was strange to go from working out every day to barely walking around the block most of my freshman year. I realized pretty quickly that there were many other women around me who looked just as good as I did and I had to keep up. I did keep up somewhat, but in between the late-night binge eating and drinking, it started to creep up on me, and I honestly felt like this was one of the reasons Chris called it quits before we graduated. It was kind of like the elephant in the room.

We had other issues too, and I knew he would never admit it, but I do think part of it was he was afraid of what my figure would turn into down the road if I stopped working out. I have heard men say this out loud in conversations: "I hope she doesn't get fat, or I am outta here." Or, "The day her ass gets big is the day I am gone." Guys would drone on and on about fat women, but it was okay for men to walk around looking like they were nine months pregnant, I guess. But still, I didn't want to be a fat mom or fat lady in my whole life. I also didn't want to be with a fat man, or friends with a fat woman.

Being fat was a deadly fate hard to escape the judgment of society. I wanted no part of that so I went to extremes to make sure it didn't happen. Believe me, in no way was I fat. But by LA standards, I was pushing in that direction. It was a whole other level when you lived in a climate of having to be crop-top ready under the sprawling sun.

Once I was on my own, my roommate and I joined a posh gym and a fancy dance studio where I got wind of an audition for a dance squad in a semi-professional basketball league. It sounded intriguing, and while I hadn't danced in a while, it was worth the shot because I was really feeling toned and up for the challenge. I ended up making the squad, making friends, and having the time of life, especially that my mom was nowhere near to control my every move.

In between my sales job during the day, I found myself at countless basketball games in the evenings, promotional functions on the weekends and practice before and after work almost five to six days a week, as well as finding time to hit the clubs, party, and fool around with some really hot guys. To live in LA was a whole different experience. It felt like summer every day, and that energy was enough to make me feel happy constantly, but even with all this action, I still had this lost feeling. My job started becoming a chore. I never really liked it but I liked the money.

In the midst of all this chaos, I ended up running into Chris at a club in LA. I was having a great night just dancing with my friends on a rooftop, sweating after five g-and-ts and had to go to the bathroom. As I was coming out, Chris was going into the men's bathroom and we ran into each other. I had heard from him occasionally via email but had not physically seen him in almost three years.

"Ash, Holy shit it's you!" he said with utter shock.

I had to do a double take myself because I was in shock too. Five drinks caused my flirtatious nature, so I hopped up onto his hips, wrapped my legs around him, pulled my arms up around his neck and clung there for an eternity. I didn't want to let go of this instantly exquisite hug. I lingered there for a moment taking in his smell, his lure, like a hypnotist who just cast a spell on me. I was ensconced with his rock-hard body. I could tell he hadn't missed a beat. He was still strong, biceps bulging and looked even more muscular since I saw him last. Now was the time to turn on the charm, and I turned it on as fast as an insect getting zapped in a bug trap.

I had made up my mind to make him my Mr. Right.

I leaned in and whispered softly and sultry like, "I missed you, Chris. Why did you leave me?" I kissed his neck ever so gently with my tongue.

He paused for a moment, cocked his head back and said, "I'm here now, am I not? Just like when I first met you. It's time to save the day again, yes?" he said slyly, grinning. He put me down, stepped back and said, "Wow, you look smoking hot! Washboard stomach and all Ashley, I'm impressed. What are you doing to look this way?"

"Well, in order to live in LA you gotta work your ass off, don't you?" I said.

"Yep, that's true, that's true," he said.

I filled him in on everything, but not before he led me down to the bar for more drinks and storytelling for three years of lost time.

I woke up the next morning in his bed feeling like I had finally been rescued. All the guys I was with and good times were just that, good times. I felt at home with him. He was the one who knew me the most. I took it as a good sign that out of all the places and girls in LA, he found me. He was doing great himself and feeling just like I was: happy, but somewhat lost at the same time. He needed me and I needed him.

I continued on the dance squad for the basketball team for a bit until I couldn't do it anymore. It was good while it lasted and honestly it made my mom feel happy. It was kind of nice because she couldn't be involved because she was too far away, although she did come in for a few events, and a few times I would travel and she got to see me dance in Chicago. But the yearly auditions were tough and each season was a new tryout where a new crop of girls would come in. The competition was stiff and I was just getting tired, unsure of myself with these younger girls with a new set of subskills. It was time, I could feel it. When I didn't make the fourth season, I knew it was okay because it really didn't bother me much. I had my time and it was time for someone else to enjoy the show. So, I ended up moving in with Chris and working my job, enjoying my evenings and running and workout regimens with Chris, fancy parties for his work friends, long weekends exploring California landmarks, in addition to traveling all over the world together as well.

My job was a job, but my dad was right. I was really good at convincing and selling, 'sealing the deal' so to say. I ended up enjoying it more once I was assigned to selling Ritalin to pediatricians. I had not heard about this drug until I started at my company because I knew nothing about kids. It wasn't until I had to start selling this drug that I became interested in what was happening with kids in classrooms. I would hear my teacher friends talk often about how kids couldn't sit still, especially the boys. I started hearing about ADD and ADHD and found out this could be quite lucrative if I played my cards right. This was a trend created by a drug infested culture, but also by many teachers, and Ritalin was used to get kids to sit still and do their homework and concentrate because they weren't capable of doing this themselves. It didn't take long for the parents to jump on the bandwagon either, because it was easier to give your child a pill than to be a parent.

I never really thought twice about the idea of essentially being a drug dealer for children, even at ages as low as five. I wanted to make the most money I could for myself and for the company. That was the ultimate goal. And selling Ritalin in the nineties was like striking oil beneath the surface. I couldn't sell it fast enough. I was a surfer riding ever so stoically under the huge weight of a wave. By the time Ritalin had reached its peak, many started bringing up concerning issues, like long term effects, or the overall effectiveness and shortness that the pill lasted but a new drug had taken its place and that was Adderall. I just simply shifted gears and started this pitch of how Adderall was longer lasting, and with fewer side effects, and boom, I was financially safe as a kitten. As long as there were kids in schools driving their parents and teachers crazy, I would have a job. So many times I would hear, "That kid needs to be medicated." But all I heard was "Kaching. Kaching. Kaching."

The money was flowing like the Mississippi River, and you can't stop the 'Ole' Miss. If the doctors said these pills were okay for kids, it must have been and not my fault. I was just giving everyone what they wanted.

The parents were happy.

The teachers were happy.

The kids were sedated and supposedly learning.

I couldn't see anything wrong with this.

Noah nudges me and asks if I am paying attention to the road. I snap out of my trance. He still is looking out the window with his body turned, half dead.

"Did you pick up my medication today Mom? I'm out."

"Oh, shit Noah. I'll bet Ava is out too. We'll need to stop at Walgreens before we head home. That will help both of you out with these feelings." Noah nods grudgingly. He continues to stare out the window.

"Uh, can you just send Naomi to get it so we can go right home? I'm tired from the game and need to go to bed." He continues to stare out the window, not looking at me.

"Nope," I say. "Medication is my specialty, not Naomi's."

CHAPTER 7

Tammy

> *"Let parents bequeath to their children not riches, but the spirit of reverence."*
> *- Plato*

I can almost hear the crackling fire and see my dad throwing small twigs in the pit to keep it going. I try to figure out how my dad was able to start the fire and keep it going. Off in the distance I can see my sister Dawn demonstrating a cartwheel that she learned how to do in gymnastics class. The air is crisp, that smell of burning wood always reminds me of the fall. My mom is in the kitchen getting marshmallows and chocolate. I can hear the cabinets banging as she is trying to find those fancy skewers she got one Christmas to make the s'mores.

When I was about eight or nine years old, Dad showed my sister and me how to start a fire. I could remember thinking in my head how hard could this be? You light a match, throw it in, and a fire starts. I sure was wrong about that, like many things I thought were easy until I tried them on my own. My Dad stacked small twigs like a pyramid and told us the fire had to have air. If the fire was smothered, no oxygen would get through and the fire would die out. Therefore, the logs and sticks would have to be stacked carefully, not just all thrown in a bundle. We are all such a delicate balance here in this life, one stick stacked on another, needing air and room to breathe. We kept trying with many failed attempts, but my dad remained patient before we finally got the fire going.

These are the times I remember and cherish as I look out into the bare space where the fire pit was. I start to dig back in my memory about my mom and dad together.

Most of my memories are of my parents separately because my mom did most of the taking care of my sister and me at home and with school, shopping, and everything we needed basically. My dad worked long hours as a carpenter and I would see him at dinner and then on weekends. He always seemed worn out to me. As far as him with my mom, I can't recall seeing any affection between them. It's not that they didn't love each other; they just weren't the couple that sat on the same side of the booth. They also didn't see a reason to sit right on top of each other in the two-seater pick-up truck leaving a wide gap open on the passenger side. When we went on vacation, they weren't the mom and dad holding hands strolling aimlessly, letting the world know they were in love; they simply didn't need to. I've always questioned those public displays of people—the couple making out in front of everyone, the hand holders, or the put-my-hand-in your back-pocket kind of couple.

I feel a small breeze of warmth, and to my absolute delight, a fire starts simply before me, rising into a slow rolling blaze of light on the bare patch of grass. It makes me think of sitting around the fire listening to the story about when my parents first met. It is a story I heard many times but never got tired of hearing. In fact, I felt like each time the story was told, I was replaying a movie in my head of a world where my parents were living life and I was there watching from the outside in. To fantasize about this was like watching your favorite episode of a tv show. It just never gets old.

In high school, my Dad told us that he was sure the first time he saw Mom he knew he would never be able to go up to her and say something, because he instantly fell in love with her, butterflies in the stomach, weak in the knees, and hot under-the-collar kind of love. He was so shy and just didn't have it in him to go up to her, but he knew he had to somehow find a way to talk to her because he was convinced that she was his only true love. My mom is one of those ladies that doesn't wear a stitch of make-up and looks beautiful. Her eyebrows are naturally curved, with deep brown-orange eyes set over high cheekbones. When she did decide to put some makeup on when going out, she honestly looked like a movie star, but her head was not so far up in the clouds, making her even more alluring because of her authenticity. My dad observed her moves, watched what classes she went to, which way she would go home, and who she was hanging out with after school.

She was not in any of his classes, but one time he had come face-to-face with her in the high school cafeteria quite surprisingly. She had bumped into him as he was behind her and she turned around to grab a fork she forgot and didn't realize he was standing right there. This was the perfect opportunity for Dad to say something, anything. He told us that at that moment, all breath left his body and it was as if someone had removed his tongue out of his mouth to forbid any kind of talking. He blew it. He told his friends this story when he sat down to eat and they just roared, egged him on, and threatened to throw food in her direction to get her attention. He pleaded with them not to do so, and miraculously they listened. Dad said the only thing he could think of was to ask his best friend Roger to go up to her and ask her if she would consider going on a date with my dad.

Well, Roger did just that, and Mom said, "If he wants to ask me out, then he'll have to do so himself. Just tell him to come talk to me."

When Roger came back with that news, Dad knew she was a woman who wasn't going to put up with any bullshit, so he had to do just that: shit because the bull was getting tired.

He somehow mustered up all the strength he had the next day when he saw her in the cafeteria. He told us she moved across the floor like she was a dancer on stage under a spotlight. She was an elegant goddess who cast spells on all the young boys worthy enough to be in her presence. This was my mom he was talking about so affectionately, so admiringly, and it made me love her even more.

She said, "Yes, of course I will go out for pizza with you." And that was it.

I'm convinced that love at first sight is real and that it doesn't happen all of the time, so when it does, grasp on tightly, or that time is nothing but empty space in an avenue of broken dreams.

The fire crackles softly. My head is at peace so I take it all in while I can.

Chapter 8

Ashley

> *"What the daughter does, the mother did."*
> *- Anonymous*

WHEN we get home Naomi is there trying to solve the broken pieces of our world. Little does she know that words cannot repair this carnage, only medication can. Ava is laying on the couch watching tv and doesn't even look up when we come in.

"I got food," says Naomi. "Ava ate and there's your favorite meal from Delia's on the table. My mom always says a little food makes the heart feel good."

"Well, I guess. Listen, you can head out now because I'm sure the kids will do their homework and head to bed. Chris will be rolling in tonight so I'll have him talk to the kids." I pay her and she gets her purse ready to leave.

"Cool, Ash, and thanks. Even though it didn't end well I enjoyed seeing Ava play."

She looks at Noah, walks over to him and forces a hug. He actually hugs her back lovingly. Naomi looks at him slowly and takes her hands on his face looking directly into his eyes. If I didn't know my own kid I'd say Naomi looked like his mother.

"It's okay, Noah," she says. I can't tell you how many games I lost when I was playing. But the losses honestly helped me get better. You know Michael Jordan says something about failing to succeed, kid, it's true. Take that to heart." They embrace again like it was the only natural thing to do after those words. I watch this from five feet away and can't help but feel jealous. He doesn't have that monotone look he carries with me.

"Thanks Naomi. You're the best," he says back with a voice I hadn't heard before.

"So are you, tiger. Now, go get 'em next time!" she says.

Where in the fuck does she get this energy from I think to myself biting my lip. She turns her mothering eyes to me looking like she had just won a contest.

"Ok Ash, let me know if you need anything. You know I'm always here."

"Yep, got it. See ya later." I pay her while trying hard not to make eye contact. I want this whole Mr. Roger's scene to end so we are able to go on with our day.

Noah and I sit and eat dinner while Ava continues to watch tv. I try and start a conversation like Naomi, but I'm not successful.

"You want to come eat with us and talk about what happened and how we can make it right Ava?"

"Yeah, like you care," she says with her body slumped on the couch.

" I do care Ava. Come talk to us, please," I say in my nicest voice trying to get her to see I do love her deep down. She just is so hard to please. Noah just eats and doesn't say a word. It's silent for a little bit while Noah and I continue to eat.

"When is dad coming home?" she says.

"His flight is coming in at eight or so, but probably won't be home until nine. Why?"

"Why do you think so?" she says with a smartass tone.

"I don't think you should wait for him. You both have homework and need to get to bed after a rough day. He can chat with you in the morning at breakfast, fair?"

Noah doesn't give Ava a chance to respond because he chimes in with, "No, it's not fair."

I am starting to light up inside because I want these two to do their homework and go to bed so I can end this drama. As the minutes go by while all three of us revert to our phones in silence to avert discussions, I can tell the meds are making them feel a little calmer. They will be more apt to listen. They both finally go up to their rooms to do homework, shower, and go to bed. What a long fucking day. I pop the cap off the prescription bottle of Xanax and the cork of wine, and sit down in front of the tv.

I can have a few hours of freedom until Chris arrives, so I find my spot on the couch and watch the Hallmark Channel. If he were here, he would groan about what shit this channel spews out, but I secretly like to pretend I am the main actress living her Barbie-like life. By the time the show is over, I am one bottle of wine in and the problems on the show seemed to have been resolved magically. I need to open another bottle because another show is coming up.

On my way to the refrigerator, I hear the commercial blaring jingle bells and Christmas music. I love when October comes on the Hallmark Channel because they start the countdown to Christmas. Though now as an adult, I hate the hoopla of getting gifts for everyone under the sun, along with hosting Christmas parties and being forced to see family I don't care to see, especially my mother. I sip my wine and think I am going to need to order another case or two of wine in preparation for the holidays coming soon.

I feel a tinge of sadness come over me because I adored Christmas as a child. I loved making ornaments for the tree, the shopping, the Santa Claus pictures, the holiday parties, and the lights that cascaded with a cold breeze of snowflakes. I can't smell cinnamon without thinking of my mom's potpourri pot staining the air ever so lightly as the smell would permeate through the house.

When the lights went up around the neighborhood, inside the houses, and in the towns, I felt full with happiness and good spirit. At no other time in my life, have I achieved that warm feeling. Not even on graduation day, prom night, my wedding day, during the birth of my own children, or Christmas as an adult. My lack of feeling sometimes bothers me because I acknowledge I am a slow-moving creek filled with stones I can see at the bottom, all muddied and rough.

When Christmas would come to a close when I was a kid, seeing the presents unwrapped was like the air being let out of a balloon, all empty and deflated. I looked at the stares of shining faces in my family who went back to clinking glasses and laughing after the presents were opened, while I wondered what to do next with all of the attention off of me, now that the gifts were given. I was like the tree that was tossed to the curb, lying there naked and alone, waiting to be scooped up and taken away to where I didn't know. I was the Christmas tree: once useful and glorious, then cast away with the next week's garbage. The pine tree smell was gone, the lights came down, and the cold winter set in like the sheer darkness of a vast cave.

My most vivid and first memory I can think of goes back to when I was eight years old, and strangely enough when I can trace back the roots of loathing my mother. I remember running down the stairs and quite sure I missed every other step on the way down. It was like I was shot out of a cannon the instant I woke up. I looked at the clock that blared 6:00 AM in bright, big red letters. No alarm, I just woke up instantly, like the dawn of a new day; it just came without any help from anyone.

I burst through the hallway and slammed on my brother's door to get up. He was six years older than me, so waking up as a teenager was somewhat scary, but I didn't care because this day was about me. I then ran to my parents' room and opened their door. I remember wondering about how they looked while sleeping, arms around each other and legs intertwined, like human pretzels. It made me feel warm, yet grossed out at the same time. My brother came out of his room, bed head and all and thumped down the stairs, while my parents followed in the same unison of steps.

When I reached the bottom, what was waiting for me was too much to bear. In front of the blazing fire, in front of the glittering, sparkling lights on the tree, surrounded by tons of other presents, was the Barbie Dream Dollhouse that I always dreamed of. I saw a huge bow at the top, with Barbies set up in different rooms and a red corvette parked outside with a matching bow. A Ken doll was in the driver's seat to complete the setting.

I just started screaming as loud as I could. No one stopped me, but my brother Brett was holding his ears, while Mom rolled her eyes and Dad just beamed.

"Why is she so excited about fake dolls that look scary when we turn off the lights? I don't want to be anywhere near that thing when the lights go out. It gives me the creeps," said Brett.

I could tell my dad was getting ready to yell at Brett for his smart-ass comments, but he didn't want to ruin anything for me. I remembered that Dad spent much of his time yelling at Brett for just about anything. My brother felt like he was never good enough for my dad, so he either discussed with wise-cracks or didn't talk much at all.

Dad was the one that picked the Barbie Dream Dollhouse out. I knew it. Even at this age, I really felt like there was no way there could be a Santa, and surely Santa and his elves didn't build this, but I wasn't going to say anything because I feared I wouldn't get anything if I said I didn't believe. It was easier for me to pretend to believe these lies than admit I knew the truth.

I played with this house every single day. I imagined how wonderful my life would be like Barbie, buying new outfits, feeling pretty, all complete with a perfect body everyone loved. I wanted to live just like this, in a dreamhouse, with a nice car, and man to take care of me.

I already had a huge edge in being blonde, bright blue eyes, with tan skin. My friends said I looked like Barbie. My Dad told me I was the shiniest star in the universe, and some man would be lucky one day to have the pleasure of taking care of me. Every day I looked in the mirror, I was a constant reminder of what I thought was beautiful. I was thrilled to look like my Barbie.

My friend Jenny would come over all the time and we'd play Barbies for hours in my room. We were dressing our Barbies in different outfits and we would pretend they were going out to dance. I remember Jenny saying that she didn't want the husbands to go and that this outing was just for the ladies.

Jenny made Barbie talk and said, "Why don't you take Ken and put him on the elevator and send him upstairs."

I took the Ken doll and got my mean voice on: "You are not coming with us Ken, so get on the elevator and head upstairs now!"

With that statement, I shoved Ken somewhat forcibly into the little yellow elevator and tried to move the elevator up. But a piece of his clothing and hair stopped the elevator and he was stuck. I couldn't get the elevator to move, kind of like when you get your shirt stuck in a zipper and you can't zip it up. I kept pushing at it and edging it in more.

"Come on Ken, get out of here, we want to go," cackled Jenny as she went to push him up too. We got so frustrated eventually with both of us tugging at this that we decided to get my mom.

When my mom came back into my room, she said, "What on earth happened here? How could this doll have gotten stuck? Oh, and it's Ken. Poor Ken, we'll figure out how to help you." she said. My mom tugged at the elevator too, while Jenny and I waited in apprehension. My mom ended up pushing it too hard, so much so that we heard a snap.

"Oh no! This cheap piece of plastic was bound to give some time." The elevator came back down to the ground, complete with Ken completely unharmed, but a broken elevator shaft. The lightheartedness my mom had at first had left her rather suddenly.

"You have to be more careful with your things, Ashley. This is now broken and it won't move up and down anymore. Don't you appreciate anything anyone gives to you? I think it's time Jenny goes home. When you learn to take better care of your things, she can come back."

Jenny got up and cleaned up her Barbies and went home like a dog with her tail between her legs.

Once the door closed, my mom was waiting to talk to me. "Ashley, your father and I are very happy to see you enjoying your Barbies and house so much, but it seems like you are taking them for granted. Do you know what this means?"

"Take what for granted?" I knew a boy named Grant, but what does he have to do this I thought. I knew my dad would never have questioned anything that happened here. He would have fixed this for me and asked if I needed anything else. I wanted to call him and tell him how Mom was being so mean.

Even this young, I looked at my mom questionably, often. I knew she was jealous of me because my dad doted on me a lot, leaving her in the backseat.

I started wondering what she was doing all day long. Our cleaning ladies did all of the chores around the house, but she had limitless time to nitpick, dissect, and needle every single thing we did right down to what we picked out to wear when we weren't wearing school uniforms. Nothing we ever did was good enough for her.

She was not the most affectionate mother either. She loved us, I know that now, but something was lost within her. She had this balancing act of making me a China doll down to what I wore, how I looked, and telling me I was beautiful, to wanting to smash the China Doll into shards of glass, splintering to the floor as I scrambled to put myself back together.

I just stood and stared at her while she explained that taking things for granted meant that I thought I should have everything fixed for me, and that I expected to get everything I wanted. But this is how she lived her life, so why was it not okay for me to live this way?

"So, I think you should go to your room Ashley. I want you to think about all we give to you and why it's important. There are so many kids in this world that don't have what you have, and it bothers me that you don't see it. Don't come downstairs until you have something honest to say, and it better not be an 'I'm sorry' because I know you won't mean it."

I went upstairs thoroughly confused. All I did was get my Ken doll stuck in the elevator. I couldn't figure out why she was making such a big deal about it.

I laid on my bed and stared at the ceiling. I wasn't going to apologize. I wanted to stay in my room all day and wait for Dad to get home. He'd figure a way out of this for me. He would dangle on a star with me while we looked down on the world sparkling below us. He would be my savior, my own Ken doll. Maybe my kids felt like this too. Although I doubt Chris makes them feel the way I do about my dad.

I wake up drowsily and realize I missed the show. I see the clock says ten and no sign of Chris. I go upstairs, wash my face and head to bed. I am barely asleep again when I hear the door open and a beep that follows it. I know he'll be up here soon. I can hear his suitcase rolling across the floor of the dark house. Little fake candles light his way through the darkness. I can hear his footsteps on the stairs and then our door opens. He goes into the bathroom, shuts the door. I can see a sliver of light come through to cast a shadow on a thin line on the bed. The hum of his toothbrush buzzes quite roughly with the water running. He spits. I hear the waterfall of his urine hitting the toilet. Then the sink runs, then quiet. Then the door opens. His shirt and pants come off and I hear them tap the floor lightly. When he opens the covers a breeze of cold air comes in and my nipples instantly get hard. This is good for him because this is a green light for entry. He feels my boobs with his hands and grabs onto them tightly, sucks them kind of forcefully for a few minutes to get me wet. Then he reaches down and pulls off my panties. It was kind of hot at first but my desire dwinds from his lack of affection. I can feel how hard he is within seconds. Then without saying a word he is inside me thrusting back and forth wildly. His face is elsewhere and nowhere near my lips in kissing distance. He lets out a loud scream after a few short minutes. I try to cover his mouth so the kids don't hear but he pulls my hands away. When he is done, he finally kisses my forehead sloppily. "Hey Ash," and then he turns over and is snoring within minutes.

I still have my shirt on but need to find my panties buried under the sheets in the dark with my dignity. I find them and then go to the bathroom to let his drips empty into the toilet. I'll need another drink to be able to go back to sleep.

CHAPTER 9

Tammy

> *"Being alone is scary, but not as scary as being alone in a relationship."*
> - Amelia Earhart

THE crackling of the firepit splits orange and blue bursts of color into sparkles of stars. The stars caress the dark canvas of night and put my mind at ease. The harsh throbs in my skull slow down softly as the fire diminishes to a dull low flame flickering. I fall sound asleep. I am out for what seems like days until I awake sweating from a nightmare I had about my ex-husband Bill. My head is throbbing worse than it was before.

The fire is out now with black ashes that have turned to gray dust. The sun is coming in, sneaking through small slivers of light between the trees. There is a fog on the ground from the humidity as beads of sweat pour down my forehead. My clothes are soaked as if I had jumped in a shower. I am very uncomfortable. I can't get up yet so I sit in my own misery and think about my dream.

This dream was about Bill and I getting back together, and that in and of itself was a nightmare because I never wanted that to happen again. But it got me thinking about a previous dream I had about Bill before we split up. I still remember it very clearly, which I found odd.

Most dreams I forget about but this one still haunts me. I just remember witnessing Bill fall and die right in front of me. It haunted me because I didn't help him when I could have. I remembered after I had the dream that I stumbled through the darkness to the bathroom. Every joint hurt as my foot hit the ground. The pain was so dull, but heavy on my body. I was a lone traveler walking on bumpy terrain in a dark forest. I heard my husband Bill snoring in the near distance and knew that even my elephant-like steps could not wake the dead. I felt this was an epiphany that I no longer loved Bill. I loved him intensely at one time, but I knew over the years that my eating and the way I looked made him fall out of love with me each pound I gained.

At first, I didn't like what happened to my once athletic and strong body, but I got used to a new body. Despite my outward appearance, I was really happy inside: truly happy. I never longed to look like the Barbie image that most men desire, because that meant it was about what a man wants versus what I wanted. However, I'm not an idiot to know what most men like in a woman. They want the gap between our thighs, the round ass, the firm boobs, and how far we can arch our backs so they can enter the Garden of Eden. That's the good stuff and none of which I possessed, so why care about it? I saw the superficiality and let's face it, most men want a warm place to plant their seed in the garden and that's it. This planting process comes with rules of course for most men to fit their internal visual desires. The rows have to be neatly sowed, the soil moist, and the weeds all but gone. I had no resemblance to a garden anymore. There was a drought, the weeds were overgrown, and despite the drought, the seeds would not grow no matter how much I watered them.

I never really dated anyone in high school. I was painfully shy. I played softball and hung out with only those girls on the team. We were like a family and spent much of our time together. We were not interested in what the guys wanted. We were interested in what plays we were going to make, what towns we would get to play in, and winning.

I was a voracious reader and always spent my time reading on the bus between games. I would read anything from Ernest Hemingway, Stephen King, to Judy Bloom, over to Mark Twain and Alice Walker. Many times, there would be laughter and rowdiness on the bus, but it never distracted me. If I got into the right book, it was as if the whole world did not exist.

My friends gave up asking me if I wanted a beer or if I wanted to go to a party. Don't get me wrong, sometimes I did, but it would be on my terms, and they knew this about me and didn't push. That's what made them good teammates.

In addition to my reading, I also started eating a lot more and packing on muscle weight as I settled into my only position as a catcher. I needed to be bigger, and loved to catch, so all of this suited me well.

I met Bill at one of my home soft ball games. He was the same age as me and he was in a few of my classes, so I knew him from afar. The night I met him my team had lost a game pretty badly to a rival high school so I was feeling pretty discouraged. I dragged my bat in the dirt creating a mushroom cloud of dust as I walked into the dugout and that's when I saw him with a group of guys who were watching my teammates. They waited for us to come out of the dugout, and as we did, a young and suave Bill smiled and said hi.

I was attracted to him right away because he gave me a cute nod with his smile that made my stomach flutter. This feeling was as foreign as someone speaking to me in a different language. I had not had a guy look at me that way before. It was almost as if he was intrigued or impressed that we ladies were simply bad asses, not the stick figure Barbie-doll kind of girls. We were muddy, we were untamed, and we could kick ass in a dark alley if we wanted to, and they knew this by watching us play. We were undefeated the whole season until this game and it stung to lose. I was not in the best of moods, and was getting ready to go home, but this time I decided to go out with everyone because Bill was there too. We hit it off perfectly and I remember feeling so good that he liked me.

I had never felt this way before and wasn't sure if a guy would be attracted to me because I never really considered myself attractive, just kind of plain looking. I have lovely green eyes that twinkle when I smile, but I always had that sporty boy look and not at all feminine. Therefore, not many boys gave me a double look, so when Bill took interest in me, it was like a whole new world opened up.

I can still see his jaw tremble a bit with a shaky voice when he asked me how my eyes got as green as the grass of an Irish mountaintop. He had me with that line for sure. We talked for a while at that first game, and as time went on, he was at every game, until we became inseparable for the rest of our senior year.

We went to the senior prom and graduated together. The only thing where we differed was the drive to want to do more. I got accepted into Augustana College in Rock Island and had a softball scholarship, and Bill decided to forego college and go right into the trades because he had no idea what he wanted to do. He was not in any sports or clubs, so he really didn't have a focus, so that seemed to be the next logical step for him. Part of his plan did pose a worry for what would happen when I went off to college and he stayed back at home, but it didn't stop us from spending almost every waking hour together before I left.

We had fooled around a lot after our first meeting, but later we decided to take it a step further. It was a warm June evening when it seemed like the sun would never go down. This was a welcome sight after going through a dark winter and cold spring with little daylight time. When summer approaches in the Midwest the smell leaves its scent in the air, just like a fresh flower getting ready to bloom. Midwesterners have to take advantage of this because they know the flower only blooms for a short time.

We rode like the wind outside of the suburbs to those lonely Illinois cornfield roads that seemed to have no end in sight. It really seemed as if we were traveling to the end of the world. I would look into the farmhouses with one light glowing and wonder how cool it would be to live in such silence, the only sound of birds, and an occasional outsider kicking up the gravel as it stormed on by. I can still hear the bugs and feel the warm wind hitting my face like a blow dryer at a low speed, buzzing and humming as the wheels hit the pavement while The Cure's "Pictures of You" permeated the air.

This was the night I was ready and willing and so was Bill.

We pulled over and parked, hopped into the backseat of Bill's seventy-eight Monte Carlo he earned himself by working his ass off at an auto shop. It was a boat of a car, but the backseat had enough room for a small party. I always joked with Bill to pull the anchor out when he came to a stop, or put the life preserver on when we got in. He always thought it was funny and he would laugh in such a cute way that made me smile from the inside out. Once the nervous giggling stopped, Bill put a blanket down on the seat and we did the deed. Little did I know that the deed would alter the course of our lives because Bill thought he was able to pull out early, but apparently, I placed my vulnerability out on the table. At that moment I was a gambler at a craps table sure we were going to win with this decision. But the dice were not tossed in a way that went in our favor.

Within an eight-week period from that glorious summer night, my dad died suddenly from a heart attack and two weeks after that I found out I was pregnant. The only silver lining in this was that my dad never knew I was pregnant. He was an intelligent, gentle, and kind man. He never raised a hand to me or his voice, but I don't think I could have endured the shame delivered upon me by telling him I was going to have a baby at my age. That would mean he would know what I had done, and this was not something I wanted to share with my dad, even as close as we were. He was so proud of my receiving a scholarship and going to college that the thought of me throwing it away by a five quick minutes in the backseat of a Monte Carlo would have killed him first over the heart attack he suffered.

My Mom was so mentally ensconced dealing with my dad's death that she couldn't even find the time to be upset with me. It was just too exhausting for her. My sister was somewhat helpful and somehow we all managed.

I didn't have time to properly grieve for my dad because I was so worried about being pregnant and I was sick physically and mentally with the hasty decision I made to alter a promising future I had planned on. These feelings would come back to haunt me later because my Dad's death crushed me. I'd eat and eat just to escape the pain I felt when the only man who ever truly loved me was gone.

It wasn't until Alex was born that I felt loved again similar to the way Dad felt for me, but I missed him terribly. Even in pure bliss and joy of delivering Alex, there was still a hollow feeling of craving to see my dad again. This was probably the lowest and greatest time in my life, a very odd juxtaposition to be in for a young woman like me.

Since I found out I was pregnant shortly before going into my first year of college, it ultimately changed the path of the life I once knew. I didn't have to think twice about keeping my baby because I knew I didn't have the heart to terminate a pregnancy. I could not grow a baby and give it away, but I wasn't sure if Bill felt the same way. He was guarded and secretive, and at one time he asked me if I wanted an abortion, or at least give the baby up for adoption. I think he wanted one of these options to happen, but he wimped out and told me that was what his parents kept suggesting. I would break out in tears every time he brought these ideas up, so finally he just stopped talking about it.

So, on a whim and with my convincing Bill, he agreed to get married. I traded in my cleats and scholarship for baby bottles and bibs, while Bill went to trade school for plumbing. We each lived in our own childhood homes for the duration of the pregnancy, and while this was not the path my mom wanted for us, it was a blessing for me to be with her after the loss of my dad. While it was such a blow for me not to play softball in college, I was really glad I was able to be with my mom at the most difficult time of our lives. I don't know how I could have gone to college knowing she would be alone. My sister was still in college, so we would have both been gone, and my mom would have been by herself too soon after Dad died. This was such a confusing time to have an ending and a beginning on the way. It was one of those times when life throws you a shit deal, then you come back, but only to break even. Nonetheless, I took that as a good sign.

While pregnant, I started taking some general education classes at the community college and got a job at the local zoo working in the cafeteria just to make ends meet and save for a place to live once Bill was done with trade school. I really loved working at the zoo. I found myself staying after my shift to roam around the zoo many times pretending to be a zoologist. It was the only time of the day I had to myself. In fact, I would lie and say I was off later just to give myself an hour to walk around.

I was thick from my softball playing and not terribly overweight yet. I really did have every intention to keep my body fit, but it never happened. The only issue with working in the cafeteria is that I was eating more food than I was serving. I just couldn't resist the French fries, hot dogs, and burgers. I tried my best not to eat this way when I was pregnant, but I was trying to cope with being a new mom that was slinging burgers pregnant while I should have been finding new doors to open in college like my teammates, not to mention the stress of losing my father so suddenly. Sometimes the pain of losing my dad would cause such a hollow hole in my stomach that food was a way for me to fill it. Every time I felt sad I just ate. I ate and I ate, even when I was not hungry.

I lost all touch with my teammates when they left for college. They were off on a tour bus around the world. I was the one that got left back at home essentially all alone. But with Bill, he was able to hang with old friends, make new ones, and pursue what he was doing for his next steps in life. He didn't have the same dreams as I to go away to college, so he simply didn't understand or seem to care how my life was going to change. So, I kept all of my feelings inward. Holding these feelings in was like steam getting ready to boil for hot tea. It was bound to come out whistling in a loud, high pitch someday. But once Alex was born, the whistling stopped and the tea was left to remain in a cold kettle on the stove. There were too many other things to focus on being a new mother at my age.

Bill and I had managed to save enough money to move into our own apartment. It was small, but it was our own place. We both had jobs and we were able to make ends meet until Bill finished trade school. Bill wanted me to quit, but I was able to work part-time at the zoo while my mom watched Alex a few days a week. It worked for her because she was terribly lonely with my dad gone, and Alex gave her great joy and took her mind off her loneliness. Those days seemed like a blur to me. I barely had enough time to get out of the house to go to work, let alone make myself a healthy lunch. I only worked part-time, and took some night classes, but not making my own lunch was enough for me to rapidly gain weight, especially after giving birth, and I was always so tired that the thought of working out never even entered my head. It seemed I had morphed into a completely different person physically after Alex was born, but the process was slow. I would go on diets here and there and lose weight up and down, but I always loved to eat in sizable portions and would eat more if I was upset. I guess I was an emotional eater.

Despite the ups and downs of my weight at that time, Bill and I had sex quite often after Alex was born and it used to be somewhat fun. We made sure I went on the pill because we did not want any other children. But when I went on the pill, I started gaining even more weight, and I'd say my eating got worse, and coupled with not losing the baby weight. I just started eating more and then the sex started becoming scarce.

I tried to make friends with moms who had babies in the neighborhood, but many of them were older than me, and I was looked down upon for being a baby mama myself, so friendships didn't happen. It was just me and Alex and my mom. Some days were really hard; other days it was the best thing in the world. But being an employee at the zoo meant a free zoo membership, along with free food from the cafeteria. I would take Alex there often and we would eat at the cafeteria. I had nothing else to do than eat and be a mother, and nothing was more important to me than being with my son.

For Bill, he was really making a name for himself with his career and spent most of his days on jobs and then went out with friends afterwards. He worked for the union, but after a while he started getting the itch to start up his own business, and that was just what he did. For many years we struggled to make ends meet in those early days, but Bill always had a good business mind, and he was able to become quite successful by starting his own company and being able to provide for us consistently. But because he was running his own business, he ended up putting his heart and soul into his work and left us behind. This new found love for his career was similar to falling off a boat and watching the wake. The waves were high at first, but eventually they would get smaller, bubble, and then blend back into the calm water.

Therefore, most of Alex's childhood was me and him. Bill made every excuse to be nonexistent and eventually I just got used to it. That was the new normal, kind of like how the trees lose their leaves every fall, then come back to bloom in the spring. We had settled into our own single paths not noticing the beauty all around us. We stopped laughing together and we completely stopped having sex. We went to bed every night and said "I love you," and then eventually stopped saying this all together because when those words hit the air, they weren't able to survive due to suffocation. We went on like this for almost eighteen long years, with some bursts of sunshine in between, but mostly cloudy days, with me lighting up some sunshine for Alex.

The last time we did have sex was awful. I was surprised Bill even initiated it, but I could tell he was desperate. He didn't even look at me. He just laid his body on top of mine, looked the other way, lifted up my fat to get to the spot he wanted. All I could hear was the slapping of blubber like meat on the counter a butcher was tenderizing. It turned me off completely but I pretended to like it and hoped it would be over soon. I laid there wondering how many women lay down pretending to like this animalistic romp. I realized at that moment my relationship was a ticking time bomb. I was doomed, dead in the water, yet I couldn't bring myself to change my eating style. The more he talked about the way I looked, the more I ate. I would graze during the day at work, but when no one else was around I would consume large portions of food and felt like my appetite would turn ravenous, like a tiger eating for the first time in weeks. I would feel good afterward eating, like I completed my task as a female hunter.

However, despite my outward appearance of the Pillsbury Doughboy, my personality was just as shiny as the ring Bill gave me many moons ago, but he refused to see that light. He only saw my outward appearance of many layers of fat. I think of that song I loved by Ray Charles, "Don't Take My Sunshine," but I wasn't the one who blocked the sunshine; he really was. I should have sung that song to him. I don't like to cast blame; it has honestly never been my style, but I knew for certain Bill burned out the light that was flickering inside me, and I knew I had to replace the bulb. For as much as he talked about how he was going to help me, his negativity and judgment just pushed me further and further away. I often wondered if he was trying to "fix" me to fix things for himself.

Most days it didn't bother me; I just did what I needed to do for Alex's sake while raising him in his primary years. Even into his teenage years, Alex was never once ashamed of me, nor did he ask me to lose weight, or felt the least bit uncomfortable around me. I was always able to be my true authentic self around Alex. I loved him for that more than he could ever know.

When Alex got into his high school years, he was off doing his own thing, and that's when Bill and I created even further distance, as long as the Mississippi River. Alex never asked about our separate lives in our own home because this was all he knew. He may have thought this was how married couples act because he never once questioned us. Sometimes this made me worry about the type of example we were setting for him, but he had friends, was a happy kid, got wonderful grades, excelled in club and sports, and never really gave us problems. As close as Alex and I were, I never asked him what he thought about us, because I didn't find it necessary to drag him into our lack of a marriage. Why inject our toxicity into healthy veins?

The fire pit looks so lonely, so gray and dismal against the fresh bright green grass. I feel the need to get up because I've been sitting too long. Maybe a walk around the grounds will help the pain subside. I wish Alex were here.

CHAPTER 10

Ashley

> *"Anger is an acid that can do more harm to the vessel in which it is stored than to anything on which it is poured."*
> *- Mark Twain*

I hear Chris' alarm clock go off at 5:30 am. I open my eyes but he doesn't see me. I pretend to be asleep. He goes into the bathroom, then comes out with his running gear on. He exits quickly before anyone gets up. I hear the beep on the door slightly downstairs and he's on his way to freedom.

I fall back asleep but then awaken to his voice with the kids downstairs. I don't want to go down there for fear of being attacked when he hears their stories. He will blame how they feel all on me. I just know it. My phone is vibrating. It's Naomi.

"Mornin' Ash. I don't have to go to work until later today. I was just thinking about the kids and wondering if they needed a ride today. I just felt so bad for both of them yesterday. Do you need a hand?" she says so sweetly.

I want so badly to say that I don't need her help. For the first time yesterday I felt overpowered with her parenting my kids like they were her own. I felt like an outsider in my own family. She has to sweep in with her Mr. Rogers quotes and save my family? But with my headache in the forefront again, I decide to speak. I talk quietly. "Hi Naomi. That would be great. I'll tell them you're on your way."

"Great thanks so much Ash.

I have to look for more expensive wine that doesn't give me such a raging headache every day. I fall back asleep. Not long after, Chris is shaking me. His hands feel rough on my shoulder.

"Oh, you're home?" I say sarcastically looking up at him in a daze.

"Very funny dear. You should do stand up. Are you taking the kids to school or staying in bed all day?" he says sarcastically right back.

"Naomi is coming to get the kids to drop them off at school. I'll pick them up today after tennis."

"Oh, you can get to tennis but can't get the kids to school? I thought we were done with Naomi or only using her in a pinch?"

I sit up and pull the covers off abruptly. I stand up and go into the bathroom and walk right past him. I start brushing my teeth. He walks in behind me. I'm not going to escape. He is a racecar driver in my hip pocket waiting to pass me.

"Well? You're just going to ignore me? I was eating breakfast with the kids and they told me about their games yesterday. Ava says she can't talk to you at all because you're a bitch. You let these kids swear now? I come home and it's like I don't know who these kids are. And you? Why can't you get up?"

"Somehow I was useful for you last night," I say after spitting out my toothpaste into the sink, bending over provocatively to throw out my floss.

He pauses for a moment. "That has nothing to do with this and you know it, Ash. I missed you. Is that so bad? You always find something to complain about. You got it so good and you don't even know it."

I stand there. I want badly to say that I didn't enjoy the sex at all last night. I want to say that I felt violated and got nothing out of it. But I say nothing. I just want him to leave so I can go about my day. I had been used to him being gone. He now feels like an intruder in my life. "I don't know what to do with these kids anymore. I try to say something to them but what I say comes out wrong and then they're pissed at me. It's fucking annoying, " I say feeling deflated.

"Alright, I can't talk about this now. I have to get ready for work. We can talk more when I get home. Promise me you'll be picking them up. They need someone to be there for them, Ash." He stands there like my boss asking me to get to work on time.

I don't care for his lack of trust in me that I wouldn't pick up my own kids. What the fuck? "Did you ever think they might need you instead of me?" I say.

He turns away and sighs. "Someone has to work, yes? Don't make me feel bad for providing for my family. That's not fair."

"I don't think it's fair that you don't think I'm capable of picking up my own fucking kids."

"I'll see ya later, Ash. Just pick up the kids, will ya?"

I give him the soldier's salute.

He rolls his eyes and says something under his breath. I hear him go downstairs and finish breakfast with the kids. They are laughing and having a good time while I crawl back into my warm bed that is so cozy and drift off to sleep. I hear Naomi in my twilight sleep with her ear-piercing bubble of a laugh. I grab the pillow and put it over my ears to drown out her optimism.

"See ya Mom!" Noah shouts from the bottom of the stairs.

"Bye Noah, have a good day," I say back. I am not sure if he hears me through the pillow. Not one word from Ava.

I wake up later than I want to but I guess I needed the sleep. I lay in my bed thinking while the house is still like Lake Michigan on a summer night.

When the kids were younger, I took on this new role as mother, and Chris took on the sole financial stability; therefore, I didn't have to worry about anything because Chris made a shit ton of money. I am able to head to my yoga class to calm the chaos, enjoy weekly massages, and receive plenty of Botox injections to keep myself looking young. I am able to get manicures, pedicures, and shop anywhere I like. I can meet my friends anytime I want.

When the kids started school, I volunteered to pass away the time, but my volunteering turned into spying on the other teachers and catching up on the latest gossip from the other moms. I got tired quickly by cutting up the box tops and opening milk cartons at lunch. I had better things to do with my time.

After a while, motherhood was an old shoe that went out of date to the latest fashion. When the kids were infants, I just didn't have any interest in the feedings, picking up toys, coloring and all that stuff Moms should do. I couldn't even remember why I thought it was a good idea to get pregnant. If someone had told me I wouldn't sleep at all after having a baby, I for sure wouldn't have done it. But no one tells anyone this secret because if they did the whole population of the world would come to a screeching halt.

I found out pretty quickly that I was not maternal at all, so when we hired our nanny, Naomi, almost immediately after Noah was born, it was a whole better world for me because someone else picked up all those motherhood responsibilities and I was back to myself.

But there is an unsettling feeling growing inside me again and it scares me. It is not at all that I don't love my children intently; I just love differently than most moms. I lost myself or never knew who I was in the first place, but what I started realizing was that I was not the nicest person.

My mother would tell me at an early age and say, "Think about yourself, Ashley. You are special. You are beautiful. Let no one drag you down in life. You have to rise to the top in this world and if you have to step on others along the way, then so be it. You are the most important one."

This was my dad's mantra, too, and Mom would nod and agree. I can't seem to get my grip on this concept of rising to the top while stepping on everyone else, but it is all I have ever known. I think somewhere deep down I wanted to be a mother who developed a bond with her kids, but I couldn't bring myself to do this. It feels too late to try and swoop in now like Mother Theresa. I have accepted this fate I have been dealt. I just do what I can for my kids and that's where it ends, no more, no less.

Most of the weekends now are spent on soccer fields, baseball and softball diamonds, while standing with blankets in the wet season here and peeling off layers when it is hot. Standing along the sidelines with my red solo cup masking my wine with other moms like me is where I take solace in myself. We aren't fooling anyone with those solo cups. Maybe my red solo cup adorns the sidelines like a red flag.

I am essentially letting everyone know that I am going to get fucked up because this is the reality I fell into and I have to mask it somehow. Some are in it for pure socialization; I for another reason. I found alcohol was the perfect cure for my broken soul, and where the source of my intense drinking started, right there on the little league turf.

Even though the drinking intensified, I did make many good friends on my sports sideline journeys. I shared good times with the other moms while cheering for good plays, cringing at the bad ones, to the spitting sounds of young boys chewing on sunflower seeds. Just like when I was volunteering in the schools, this was a great place to gossip, talk about the other kids and other moms who did not join the solo cup "Clink-Clink club."

Those days made me feel happy like when I was in high school where we would talk about the other girls who didn't fit it. We were the hot moms with the team name printed on our Barbie shirts, complete with glitter melded into the fabric and hats to match. But after a while, the glitter started to fade and I got tired and restless again. That's when I convinced the other moms to join me in a tennis league. So now the kids' games became roadblocks in our way to get to the club.

By the time I get up I notice it's almost 11:30. The whole morning has gone by. I don't care. I check my phone and see Lola called twice. She left a message asking me where I have been. She let me know that if we get into the next tournament we need to practice. She let me know in her second message that I have to learn how to drink like a professional. "Pros don't sleep from a hangover. Hair of the dog Ashley," she said.

I'll call her back later. I decide to go on the treadmill at home, get some more expensive wine than the headache producing shit I was drinking earlier, and then pick up the kids from school at three.

On the way out of the store I notice I'm a little early so I can take my time getting to the school. Coming up to the stop sign, I notice the crossing guard. Because I'm early, everyone is still in school or at work. The crossing guard is punctual and ready to go, always. I drive by a little slowly to get a closer look at her since no one is here. She is sitting on the bench nearby reading a book. Does she stay here all day? She always seems so content. I've seen her reading so many times, her head down and chins flowing underneath her.

I think about pulling over and asking her why she is always smiling. Rain or shine, snow or sleet, she is smiling like fucking Mary Poppins, but a fatter version. I see her car off to the side. It's an old beat-up tan Chevy Cavalier. She has a sheet of plastic and duct tape holding the back driver's side window together. Some days I see her standing and leaning next to the car waiting for people to come by. She drapes her yellow and orange vest over the door like she owns this street. I do think she stands by her car sometimes because she probably gets winded going back and forth all of the time. When she walks across the white lines, I feel she's so huge she could just sink into the street creating a sinkhole for all of us to drive into. The ground would swallow her whole first before we all go tumbling afterwards.

She wears sunglasses, no matter what the weather, and chews gum like a cow chewing on hay, so hard and with purpose. Surprisingly to me, she is really confident, similar to a runway model strutting down the stage. Being as heavy as she is, it seems odd to compare a model to her, but she fascinates me and repulses me at the same time. She is there every day, large and in charge.

I pull into the school feeling a triumphant victory that I'm first in line for pick up. Usually I'm at the end of the line. I have to sit for what seems like hours. Noah comes out first, gets in the car and greets me with a grin.

Ava pops in the backseat minutes afterwards. She shuts the door with a slam to make her presence known. "Where's Dad?" she says.

"Hi to you too darling. Did you have a good day?"

"Is Dad home?" says Noah.

"No, he's at work but will be home for dinner," I say without emotion.

Ava shifts in her seat, clears her throat and says, "Thank God Dad is home now. We had a good talk at breakfast today. He said he is going to call Casey's mom and pay for her doctor appointment because she had to get a cast."

"Oh shit, Ava. Did she break her wrist?"

"Yes Mom, but you don't need to worry about it. Dad is taking care of it."

"Is that so?" I say. "Dad to save the day, that's great."

"Well, you didn't call her Mom, did you?"

"Why should I? This was your fault. You should be calling her and trying to fix how you pitch."

Noah laughs and then chimes in. "Mom, we did have a good talk with Dad. He is going to work with both of us and get us new coaches for private lessons too. It's all gonna be good."

"Okay, whatever Dad thinks is best." Then silence. I sit brewing while they talk about their days. I am not listening to anything they say.

We come to the stop sign with pods of kids crossing. The crossing guard is there smiling at all the kids on their way home. While she smiles, I scowl to myself thinking about what we are going to have for dinner. I hate my life.

Chapter 11

Tammy

> *"Children begin by loving their parents; as they grow older,*
> *they judge them; sometimes they forgive them."*
> *- Oscar Wilde*

It feels good to walk, yet strange at the same time, because I can't seem to recall the last time I got up and walked. I can imagine that walking on the moon felt similar to this. I got used to the bouncy and heavy feeling after some steps. It is quite eerie to see the spot where our home once stood, now just a slab of cement where gravel is sprayed loosely with beautiful wildflowers poking through the concrete. The upside down "U" driveway leading to the house is a path that goes to nowhere. I never really appreciated all the land we had. The mature old oak trees still stand in between the vacancy and an old broken-down fence lines both sides of where the house once stood. The swing set is gone and makes me shiver. Any remnant my dad had his hands on was gone forever.

I feel the pain come back in my head as a dull throbbing. My heart sinks walking down the trails behind the house. I can't find the trailhead because the grass has grown over the dirt paths and it is filled with weeds as far as the eye could see. I hear the hum of a bulldozer and notice that a gigantic house is being built, invading upon peaceful territory. I make my way back to the firepit because I need to sit down again. I think I hear voices behind me because they are getting louder and louder. I need to lie down. I sit in the old chair which was not comfortable at all, but enough to lull me to sleep with voices in the background. I hear my mom and dad's voices through the window. I want to run as fast as I can to see them but my walk zaps me of all energy. I cannot get up even trying, so I sit quietly to listen.

I remember sometimes my mom and dad would drag my sister and me into their arguments when we were kids and it would drive me crazy because I hated having to pick sides. I heard them arguing because the windows were wide open. They didn't argue that often, but when they did it would get ugly. I can remember when I was eight years old a terrible argument my mom had with my dad one night after dinner. I wondered if I was hearing a replay of this night. To this day I don't know what the argument was about, but my dad became livid and unglued with my mom after going round and round in a screaming match. It was not in his character to get riled up but he ended up losing it. He screamed at my mom and called her a bitch, took the keys to the car, and left with a loud slam of the door behind him.

While my sister and I huddled together in her bed crying, we heard another slam from my mom's bedroom door that made us jump. We heard my mom crying through the door and it broke our hearts. To hear a mother crying can make even the most stoic person lose their composure. We felt awful for our mom and the thought of not knowing where Dad was had become equally nerve-wracking.

While we lay there crying, the door opened and a faint beam of light shone into our dark bedroom. Mom heard us crying too and she felt sad watching us.

She sat down on the edge of the bed and sighed. "All parents get in fights girls. Life is not perfect nor will it ever be. Dad will come home and all will be ok."

I believed her, but I was still worried about Dad. I know she saw this concern in my eyes because I still wasn't feeling better after this talk. She went on to tell us that grownups fight and that my Dad had said mean things to her. I remember feeling so uncomfortable because I had not heard her talk bad about my dad before. She said he had no right to leave her and his two daughters at home. She said he was being reckless. Reckless was very far from the truth when describing my dad. He was one of the most hard-working Dads I knew, no joke. He was the dad throwing a ball in the yard with his girls. He taught us how to build a fire. He taught us how to change a tire and how to mow the lawn. He would tell us often there was no reason a man would have to do all those things for us. We were able to make our own way.

I remember feeling really mad at my dad for yelling at my mom and calling her names during the heat of their argument, but now she was trying to get us on her side and I didn't appreciate it all. I was more concerned that Dad was never going to come home. I lay awake for hours after Mom went to her room and my sister fell asleep. I couldn't go to bed until I knew he was home and finally I heard the door slowly creak open downstairs. His footsteps rolled up the stairs. I listened to the low-tone voices of our parents through our bedroom wall and it gave me such comfort.

When I heard my parents speaking through the wall, I could never hear what they were saying. I always tried the old glass to the wall trick, but it never seemed to work. I didn't care that I couldn't hear what they were saying. I was just happy to hear that hum of voices because it put me to sleep so soundly knowing they were there to keep me safe. They weren't yelling either. This sound was as welcome to me as the sound of the birds waking me up on a lovely summer morning.

My sister and I woke up the next day to the smell of French toast coming from the kitchen. When we came downstairs, Dad sat us down at the table and apologized for yelling at my mom and leaving. This was the moment I knew my dad was truly the king of the world in my eyes and he could do no wrong. It takes a big person to admit mistakes and actually try and learn from them.

We told him that we didn't like him yelling at Mom and we were worried that he would not come home. He felt terrible. He took his rough hands, brought them to his face and his eyes became misty, a sight I rarely saw. He told us he was fine and he needed to leave to blow off steam and sometimes that was how people do it. He didn't realize how his leaving abruptly made us feel. He swore he would never leave again, but he couldn't promise he would never argue with Mom again. That's the kind of guy he was: honest.

"Anyone that promises not to argue doesn't have a pulse in their body," he said. "But I won't leave the house again and have you wondering where I am at, I promise."

He kept that promise as good as gold. I wrote a tiny letter to him on a post-it note the night he left. It said, "I am sorry you and Mom are fighting. I love you, come home. Tammy."

It was many years later that I found this note tucked and folded in his dresser drawer next to his bed when we were cleaning out his things after he died. I hadn't seen it in years and forgot I even wrote it. I read this with a single tear streaming down my cheek. Because my dad kept this note, it was even more evidence for me that my dad was a man who loved with his entire soul. He held true to his promise not to leave for the rest of his days because he was a man of integrity. I knew I would never find anyone in my life that could come close to holding a candle to him.

Bill, on the other hand, was the complete opposite of a man compared to my father. He was not a man of integrity at all, and I wish I saw this the day I met him on the ballfield, but there were clouds of dust in the way of seeing things clearly. I would say he was a decent father by way of providing for Alex, but never would Alex feel the least bit comfortable writing a letter to his father or spending time alone with him in a room for more than twenty minutes.

Bill just simply wasn't around because I truly feel like Alex was a reminder of the big mistake he made that he could not undo. During many of our arguments, the subject of keeping Alex would come up and all those negative feelings would come back again. Bill would consistently bring up how life would have been so different if I had the abortion. I think he wanted to throw this back in my face and punish me for wanting to be a mother and dragging him along for the ride. I buried those feelings in the ground and he kept pushing through the soil like a relentless weed with thorns. I couldn't get rid of the roots so the weed kept coming back.

I never once had a thought of terminating my pregnancy, even though I knew if I did, my life's plan would come out the way I wanted it to go, but I just couldn't do it. I pushed worms aside when they were on the sidewalk helping them get back under the slumber of the soil, so how could I harm my own flesh and blood? For me, the guilt would have been too much, but not for Bill. And I believed Bill had held this against Alex subconsciously all of his years growing up.

My hunches were solidified in my mind because Bill didn't even know Alex's friends. He simply never took the time to meet them. He would show up at sports games and clubs that Alex was involved in, but he never seemed to want to be there. He always seemed to have one foot out the door. He would let me know that we would have to take separate cars because he would have to leave early or come later. He wasn't the dad throwing the ball out front; it was me. He would give the orders, expect Alex to know things he had no idea how to do, then berate him for not knowing, leaving Alex feeling conflicted about what he had done to cause such disdain from his father, until finally he just gave up caring about what he thought of him.

I would talk to Bill about this many times, but he would shut me down and say I had no idea how to parent a son. He was right about that because I came from a house of women, but I knew how to love. I knew how to have a kind heart. I knew how to be a mother. Bill would accuse me of being the helicopter parent and that I was doing our son nothing but harm by babying him.

"No boy will turn into a man with his mother following him around," Bill would scold. He was really good at making me feel like a failure and questioning myself. It took me years to figure out he was the one that needed to be questioned, analyzed and prodded at the Spanish Inquisition, not me.

But Bill would never allow that to happen because his heart had turned to stone. His loathing for me turned into jealousy of my relationship with Alex, as well as spite; therefore, he took out even more anger on Alex. I tried to figure out the father-son relationship, but over time I realized this challenge was as complex as reading Tolstoy's *War and Peace*. I fully knew being a helicopter mom would be a detriment to our son, but creating a bond with my child and babying him were two different things. I knew Alex better than Bill ever would, and it was not because Alex picked a favorite. It was because I spent time with Alex. Bill simply did not. He found all Alex's faults, and it was rare when a positive comment came out. After many years of negative comments, a positive comment joined the molecules in the air and remained there: invisible to the eye.

Not once did Alex go on a fishing trip with his father or out to dinner with him. I was always around, and in the rare case I was gone, Alex spent his time looking for me. I just wish Bill knew what a good kid Alex was instead of wishing for him to leave the house because Bill missed his entire childhood.

He missed days at the beach, annual first and last days of school, parent teacher conferences, baseball trips with friends, fun times watching the excitement of the tooth fairy wishes and visits from Santa.

He would scowl as he watched me wrapping presents and hiding things in preparation for Christmas morning. "You happy with yourself lying to your son? I can't wait for him to figure out all of this is not true. Then what are you going to say Tam?" he would comment sarcastically.

"I'll let him know the truth when he is ready to ask," I'd say. "Why would you want to take away a magical time for your son?"

Bill would never have much to say in response. He always sat quiet on Christmas morning. And as much as I would like to say he didn't ruin our fun, he did with his long face, arms folded in judgment.

We knew how he felt.

The whole world knew how he felt.

He was jaded and selfish.

Bill spent so much time wishing for Alex to be an adult so he could rid himself of the chains that held him down for years. I knew when Alex turned eighteen, he was going to break free from those chains and bring him to the top of a mountain, then push him off.

"Go ahead kid, learn to fly!" he would say.

I snap out of this daydream when I hear a stick crack, causing me to jump. The house disappears. My thoughts roam back to Bill. I hold no wishes to be in his presence again, ever. The pain in my temples is grinding my jaw at the thought of Bill. I don't like holding anger inside but I was brewing thinking about the internal pain he has caused me equivalent to the pain I am in now.

When Alex left, I knew he would push me off the mountain too, so I had to plan my strategy before he did.

The game is tied and we're in the bottom of the ninth inning. Bases are loaded with one out. The ball is pulled hard to third base. All I can only hope is that my teammate is going to have the foresight to make the play and throw it home to eliminate a chance of a score.

What happened after that was anyone's game because as the old saying goes, "That's baseball!" Once that play was solidified, no matter what, I was able to walk off that dusty field and never look back.

In the distance and outside of this painting I hear light chatter. I hear beeps again. I want to stay here.

My head swirls with painful sensations.

I close my eyes and fall sound asleep.

Chapter 12

Ashley

> *"God's great cosmic joke on the human race was requiring that men and woman live together in marriage."*
> *- Mark Twain*

WHEN we get home I notice Chris is home early. The kids are excited like they are little children. They practically run into the house. I walk in behind them dragging my feet heavily. I always notice when Chris is home from work because I am able to track his markings: keys on the countertop, rolled up pair of pants on the stairs, shoes off right at the kitchen door so it almost blocked us from walking in. He is sitting on the couch watching the news and the kids have already plopped down next to him. I almost trip over their backpacks.

"I see you're home," I say dryly.

"I'm great too, how are you?" he says sarcastically.

"Well, we are just coming in from running around all day and I suppose I need to get dinner for all of us. It may take me a while to think of something, so I'll let you know when it's ready. Or what about take out?" I shout from the kitchen.

"That's fine Ash; whatever works for you," he says back with a muffled voice over the sounds of the television.

The kids say nothing. I can see them all rolling their eyes at me. Of course, I'm the negative one always being accused of complaining a lot. But if I don't get a ball rolling they will all sit there and starve.

I rarely have the time or energy to cook and have no interest either. Most of our dinners now are take-out. It is just easier that way, and we're lucky if all four of us occupy a room together longer than ten minutes. Dinner usually consists of us all in different locations scrolling on our phones as we eat.

Our conversation was brief due to our argument this morning. This is how we argue. I talk about what I think is important and Chris thinks I turn everything into combat because I like to be miserable. He dictates what he thinks is right and I am supposed to be the little Mrs. with the apron on, but I've never worn an apron in my life. I get so pent up with anger with the way we argue that I just don't give a fuck anymore.

I wish I could dance on my dad's feet in the kitchen because my feet are heavy now. I no longer feel the rhythm of flying over the moon. Sometimes I feel I want to reach out my hand for Chris to take this dance with me, but he walks away most of the time. I can tell he is filled with such disdain for me now. I feel the same way about him.

The silence can only go on for so long though because Chris craves sex and can't go nearly as long as I can go without it. I can easily reel him back in with a quick blowjob or an offer of my ass up in the air. It really doesn't take that much. I take a lot of it for the team honestly; whatever that means. I can't remember the last time I worked on a team. I work alone and I do it well, or at least I think that I do. But I don't even know why I offer that anymore because sex has become a fucking bore and not worth much of my precious time. I would rather sleep. When you are married for over ten years and have a vibrator to finish the job after you have had sex with your husband, what can one conclude? I push this out of my head and move on with my life feeling satisfied as that's all I need: my way, my satisfaction.

As I look for the take-out menus, a merry-go-round in my head is pumping up and down to the cacophony of jilted noises that just won't stop. I am left to wonder when is the right time to jump off, but the ride doesn't slow down enough for me to take the exit. This has been going on for years and years, this feeling of a merry-go-round out of control.

We used to be happy before the kids. Now that the kids are growing up and more challenges are coming our way, we especially don't see eye to eye anymore. Chris likes to leave all the discipline to me because he would rather not deal with it. Therefore, we really don't discipline at all. I am not going to get in my kids' faces like my mom did to me, especially for Ava. I take more of a backseat and let the stars fall where they may. Chris grew up with a Draconian style father and his mother just did what his father said, so he didn't want his kids to endure that wrath either. Therefore, his discipline was no discipline, and then discipline sometimes when he was backed in a corner. It was so fucked up. I guess he felt that he provided the money and that was more than enough. He would volunteer when he could to be an assistant coach for both Noah and Ava, acting like he knew our kids, but his charm was what had everyone fooled.

"I am ordering Mexican, ok?"

"Yeah, that's fine. Whatever you want." he says dryly. The kids don't even look up once. They are sitting next to Chris. All three of them are on their phones while the tv goes on blaring all the stupid shit people have done over the course of the day.

Actually, the fight we had this morning was pretty mild compared to others. The catalyst to exposing the crack in our foundation of parenting was when Noah's pitching fell apart on the mound a week before this past game. Chris was in town then, and when he was around he would help with the coaching. The star pitcher wasn't at the game, so Chris thought it was a good idea to send Noah to the mound, a position he did not like at all. Noah didn't want to pitch, but Chris insisted he try his hand at this. After making many errors while basically falling apart, he decided to yell at Noah in front of everyone because he was embarrassed of how he was becoming unglued, essentially costing them the game.

Noah lashed out by swearing and throwing his mitt at Chris in front of everyone. It was quite embarrassing not for what it did to Noah, but how it made us look in front of all the other parents. I could see the looks, the snickers, and the judgment of our parenting. Suddenly the banner and the fight songs and the glitter lost their sparkle. The noise fizzled out and all I could hear was the sound of bad parenting. On the way home, Noah was bawling in the backseat.

"Quit crying Noah!" shouted Chris. "You're not a little kid anymore! Don't ever embarrass me like that in front of everyone again. You hear me? You have to man-up out there, kid! Your crying sends a signal that you don't have it together!"

Noah wouldn't look up. His baseball hat was covering his face and his ears were all red. I actually felt for him because I knew exactly what this scolding felt like from my mother's antics. I saw how I looked as a kid in my own son and it made me squirm with a painful discomfort similar to being stung by a hornet.

I didn't want my kids to have experiences like I had, not even for a second. And Chris seemed to have transformed into his father for a quick moment, but I am sure he would never admit this. My anger bellowed deep in my belly as the acid started coming up to my mouth. My tongue was left with a sizzling and burning sensation that was hard to halt. It pissed me off to no end that Chris felt he had the right to start disciplining now, at this precise moment. He was too late.

Chris was the dad that would play ball in front with Noah, and softball for Ava, but this was more for show, so that the neighbors would think he was the dad that cared about his kids, not because he wanted them to get better. Chris put on the charm as a career, so he never turned it off with me or the kids. Noah's crying made my heart stand still, and I was quite buzzed from drinking all day. I couldn't hold in that tension anymore, and when my voice hit the air it sounded like I was hooked up to an amplifier.

"You pick the bottom of the ninth with a tie game and our son on the mound to finally be a parent?" I yelled. Chris took a deep breath and inhaled slowly.

"Oh, I suppose you get parent of the year! You don't do shit for these kids. You have other people raise them so you can get what you want for yourself. You now drive them back and forth to school sometimes and you think you deserve a fucking medal? Don't even start judging me because you will fucking lose in a second!" he screamed. I could see the vein pulsing in his right temple. He paused for a moment.

"I do whatever I can to be with other people so I can enjoy my life, not be miserable around you. Maybe you should put your wine down and look around you, you drunk!"

Chris's face was steaming and red like a weightlifter who was lifting three hundred pounds. He dropped the weights, took a long breath again, and looked at me with utter disgust. "You know what? You always tell me how much you hate your mother, but you are just like her. Look in the fucking mirror! You have it all, but you want to be a miserable drunk like her feeling sorry for yourself."

I was thrown completely for a loop. It stopped me dead in my tracks. Was I turning into my mother? I thought to myself.

I lost all of my words.

I tried to turn on the radio but all I got in return was screechy feedback.

The silence on the way home after that rant was deafening, stifling, somewhat like when the cars come to a stop for pedestrians to cross, all of them halted for a peaceful passage, but this gap in time wasn't safe.

The kids both looked up, and I am not sure if they understood what any of this meant, but they knew it wasn't good.

Minutes of silence passed before I reclaimed the voice I had lost.

"Really, that's what you say to me in front of the kids? You yelled at Noah like how your dad would yell at you at your games. You said you hated him for that and now you're doing the same thing!" I shouted back.

"Don't you dare throw this back on me for fuck's sake! You don't parent these kids and they act like assholes. It's that simple and it's all your fault. Are you happy with how you let them behave? Just quit while you're ahead, Ashley or it's not going to be good for anyone," he demanded.

"You are . . .," I started to say but was cut off immediately.

"I said stop now or you'll be sorry Ashley. You got that?" He looked at me and I could see the loathing for me in his eyes again. He could have melted the skin right off my face. I didn't say one more word, and there was complete silence in the car except for the little tinkles coming from Ava's iPad. She hadn't missed a beat in her computer game.

When we pulled up into the driveway, our house looked beautiful on the outside, but broken on the inside. I am sure people walked by and thought that our house was meticulous. Life had to be grand here; it just had to be. The house was big and had a pool. The stained-glass windows let light out to the exquisite landscape and automatic sprinklers. The heavy door was adorned with floral wreaths like something out of a Pottery Barn catalog and a Christmas card yearly to match. We seemingly had it all. The lights were bright and the grass was as green as a fairway. The forced smiles on the Christmas card captured a brief smile in a second, and after the click, the smile lines vanished. And yet no one saw the cracks on the glass windows from the inside out that got larger as the years went on, broken with stains of dysfunction.

We all walked into the house and did our own thing, similar to today's argument. There was cereal to eat, showers to be taken, and then bedtime without the warm and fuzzy "I love you" like you see on the sit-coms. I wish I could say this didn't happen often, but this scene was not the first, and arguments like this seemed to be a habitual act in our household.

I place the order for Mexican food and hit send. I don't think anyone notices me in this kitchen at all. I am just cleaning and daydreaming. I stand there in silence and find myself falling in and out of love with Chris hourly, daily, weekly, and monthly. I pour myself a glass of wine and wash it down with a Xanax. No one looks up to see what I am doing. I'm at a point where I cannot go to bed without taking a pill and finishing a bottle or two of wine because it makes all my thoughts go away and a night of dark sleep.

Fortunately, I used to be able to get up the next day and work it all off, but lately it's been becoming increasingly difficult. I think it's because I find myself drinking during the day now when those troublesome thoughts come back to rear their ugly heads.

"It's just one drink," I say to myself. "It doesn't hurt anyone and no one will know."

But lately one drink has turned into many more, and I can't seem to stop. It's like when I was kid and I never wanted to get out of the pool.

"One more time," I'd shout. "One more time," but it's never the last time and I feel like that again, just falling closer to the bottom of the pool, my breathing laboring, and there is no way to get back up to the top.

Now I know Chris notices these behaviors too. I often wonder when the house of cards will come crashing down.

CHAPTER 13

Tammy

> *"It is better to conquer yourself than to win a thousand battles. Then the victory is yours. It cannot be taken from you, not by angels or by demons, heaven or hell."*
> *- Buddha*

After falling asleep to the hum of the firepit, I wake up in my old bedroom when daylight casts its subtle beams through my window on a brand-new day. I awake to birds singing lightly and a faint sound of beeps I can't place. I feel light again as I marvel at this beautiful world. I feel a slight tickle on my foot and I look down and see a small spider climbing up my leg. It startles me at first, but I brush it off lightly. I know how delicate and important this creature is for the life cycle.

When I was a little girl, I would watch my mom collect spiders from the tub in the bathroom because she refused to kill them.

"Why don't you just step on it? That seems so much easier because those things are so ugly and gross," I said.

"That's what ignorant people think, Tammy," she said. "Did you know that if we removed spiders from the chain of life you would be carried away by insects? We would not be able to walk outside without being attacked by a swarm of bugs. They eat millions of insects, including mosquitos, and for that alone, you should respect what they do, not worry about what they look like. And don't forget that killing a spider is bad luck."

My mother was very superstitious. She was the mom who knocked on wood after a statement she didn't want to come true. She used the phrase "God Forbid" before telling a dramatic story so that story wouldn't turn into her own. She would stay in on Friday the thirteenth, not walk under a ladder, or put shoes on the countertop. She would also go out of her way to trap a spider and set it free from the high porcelain walls of a slippery bathtub because she also believed it was bad luck to kill a spider. I can still hear her while trapping a spider saying, "They have eight legs and can spin a web equivalent to the force of steel, but they can't use them to get out of this tub. No matter what superpower there is, everyone needs help once in a while."

My mom taught me how to be compassionate and how to view the ordinary things in life as extraordinary; like making cookies for girls on the softball team, listening to everyone's problems and not sharing her own. She would give a stranger a compliment at the grocery store. She gave money to homeless people.

I look out the window of my bedroom and see the enormous, beautiful oak tree open to the sky in all its splendor. The leaves move slightly on the branches with the breeze, completely exposed and open to the sun. The oak is an anchor holding down the heavy weight of the leaves and branches, grounded and solid. I can hear the echo of my mom's voice in the hallway outside my bedroom. It sounds so close, yet far away, unreachable.

My mother sees the world differently than most, and for that I will love her to the end of time. My Mom was and still is always able to find a positive about all four seasons, from the coldest day of the year to the hottest day in hell, and she would find something positive to say about the shittiest weather. She embraced life by telling us to marvel at how the snow graces the tree branches, not focus on the gray snow that swept up to the sides of the road from the exhaust. She told us to sit and listen to the cicadas out in the hot and humid summer afternoons because we would long for that sound when we had to suffer the pain of a zero-degree day in the winter. She told us to enjoy the smell of the rain instead of focusing on how it ruined our plans, or to revel in a good thunderstorm because it nourished the plants.

Her very favorite season was autumn. She loved the splendor of the fall leaves, and to this day she still goes on and on about them. Every fall seems like it is her first time she has ever seen this season. I can't go on a walk and smell the crisp autumn air without thinking of her.

When we were kids, we would look for old wasp nests once all the leaves were gone. We would talk about how the tree looked naked and the wasp's secret life was visible as a remnant for everyone to see. She would say, "Look at that incredible architecture? How did something that small make something so strong?" If she was walking on the sidewalk after a rainstorm and saw a worm wriggling on the sidewalk, she would move it to the grass so it wouldn't dry up and die.

I feel so blessed to have had this upbringing, yet other times I felt like it was a curse. I never could find it in me to be mean to anyone, much less kill a spider. I hated anything violent and preferred to surround myself with happy things. Some people in my life viewed this kindness as a weakness and that I was too soft. I became a people pleaser, and that's not always an easy cross to bear because my heart showed on my face. I felt vulnerable to many of those who didn't seem to understand my inquisitive and sympathetic ways.

I think my first awareness of my people pleasing ways came in late elementary school when I was trying to fit in desperately with the cool crowd. Honestly, everything for me was Bambi and butterflies, straight out of a Disney film, until it all came to a screeching halt once I entered fifth grade.

I remember the day my mom and dad got me the Western Cowboy Barbie. I loved this doll and was so excited my parents got it for me. I can still see her white and black cowgirl jumpsuit, complete with red cowboy boots. I played with this doll all through the summer before fifth grade. But when school started, I noticed the girls were consumed with their looks, looking like my Barbie. For a hot minute in time, I wanted my hair to look like the cool girls. They were wearing tight Jordache jeans with a comb in their back pocket to style their feathered bangs like Kristy McNichol. I started feeling like I wanted to look like them and be a part of this group.

This transformation of conformity happened quicker than I thought and I fell into this girl trap. I was the girl at school who never got in trouble until I met the queen bully of the class. Her name was Dana.

Dana was the biggest, selfish bitch now that I think about it, but I didn't see it at the time. She was mean to everyone except a select few. She had this pretty blonde hair, designer clothes, long nails, and she wore make up. She was actually a live version of my Barbie doll. I wanted to be her friend, so I started talking differently, acting differently, even purposely getting in trouble to get the attention of this girl and all the others who blindly followed her like me. Because of my forced trouble-making and new clothes, I made my brief appearance with the cool crowd.

My mom and dad did the best they could to talk me out of wanting to be like Dana. They didn't like what they had heard from stories I told them, but they couldn't change my mind about being with the cool crowd. I know they felt sorry for me because I didn't have a lot of friends, so my mom gave in to my pleas of having her style my hair like Dana's, even though it never came close to looking the same. I was happy back then that I was skinny enough to squeeze into the tight Sergio Valente jeans.

But even with all those ways to make me fit in, I was miserable. I longed to play with my other friends from the neighborhood or other girls who kept to themselves in class. I wanted to play Barbies again, but I wasn't sure I could bring this up to my new friends, and especially Dana. Even so, I decided to take a chance and ask when we were at lunch.

The girls were talking about the new Atari game console, when I sat down to join them. I usually remained quiet until I felt it was a good time to get into the conversation.

When there was a lull I said, "Has anyone seen the new Western Barbie? She looks so cool!"

The lunchroom noise hushed. Their eyes were staring into a slot machine waiting to see if three pictures matched in anticipation of a prize. Then they looked at Dana for her reaction.

"What did you say Tammy?" Dana asked.

I sat bone-quiet because I didn't want more words to fall out of my mouth that weren't acceptable after I saw the shocked faces in front of me. I wanted to pull the other words I said back into my mouth. My face became flushed, and I shook in anticipation of what Dana was about to say in front of everyone.

"You play with Barbies? Really? You are such a baby. No one plays with Barbies. Tammy, c'mon, grow up!"

Everyone laughed and started to make fun of me that I played with Barbies. I was crushed. I tried to make it look like it was a joke. They just moved on to the Atari game they were talking about.

When I got home that day, I found my Barbie and put her in the closet and packed her away and never played with her again. I had buried an old friend. Little did I know I was burying my innocence.

An even bigger wound I felt that day was not telling my mom that I put the Barbies away. I knew she loved to get them for me, and in some way, I felt like I was letting her down. My childhood had been a lovely lit candle in the window with a flickering flame, and Dana just blew it out, smoke wafting up to the ceiling to vanish after a few lingering moments. I went on for months feeling torn about wanting to resurrect the Barbies and keep up my womanly fifth grade appearance at the same time. It was a very conflicting time in my life.

It wasn't until I got invited to a sleepover party a few months later with the cool girls that the charade of myself would end. I remember getting ready for the party and I was in the bathroom with my mother washing my face. As I looked into the mirror, I asked, "Why can't I wear blush Mom? Everyone else is wearing it and I am the only one that can't."

My Mom continued to curl my hair as she sighed. "Please don't ask me again. You are eleven years old and no eleven-year-old girl should be wearing make-up. It is just not proper, that simple. You are lucky that I am even letting you go to the sleepover," she sighed even heavier.

I could tell she didn't approve of these girls, but she didn't forbid me from hanging out with them either.

The slumber party was at Kristin's house. Kristin and some of the other girls going were on my softball team. When I got there, Dana wasn't there yet, so the vibe seemed relaxed. Kristin was nice and all when Dana wasn't around, but as soon as Dana arrived, Kristin did a one-eighty personality change.

While we were waiting for Dana to show up, another girl I knew from the softball team, Kerry, was already there. Even more so than me, she didn't seem at all Dana's type. Kerry had long hair with short sides and was the toughest girl on our team. She was a real jock. We both seemed out of sorts for this crowd, and we often hung together in class. We were fish out of water, new, and not at all comfortable with this new skin.

I remember playing the new Atari Journey video game with her and Kristin, singing like crazy and having a good time until Dana arrived fashionably late, of course. As soon as she got there, the air changed around us. She walked in with a halo of attitude, long nails, a Locker Loot duffle bag, and of course blush on her cheeks to top it all off. We continued the video game until two other girls showed up. Then Dana suggested we walk around the neighborhood since playing video games was boring and something she can do at home by herself. We all went reluctantly, wondering just what it was we were going to do, especially because it was starting to get dark.

The trees lined the street like the suburban houses all falling into place. We sauntered down the sidewalk, and as we were walking, we saw two squirrels chasing each other.

Dana turned to everyone and yelled at us to all get behind the tree. As we were standing there all huddled by the tree she said, "Who wants to throw a rock to see if you can hit a squirrel?"

It got really quiet. No one jumped in and said no because I knew not one of us wanted to do it, especially me.

Kerry spoke up and said, "Why don't you do it?"

I was beaming in my head because I was so happy someone stood up to Dana.

"No way," Dana said. "I asked one of you since you all play softball."

Again, dead silence.

"Ok, shitheads," Dana said. "Since you all are scared, I'll do it."

At this point I wasn't even worried about the squirrel. I just couldn't believe she swore.

She picked up the rock and threw it in the direction of the squirrel. It got nowhere near the animal, bounced off the curb, and into the street.

I sighed and thought in my head, "Thank God she isn't on the team. She throws like a girl."

Kerry, being the biggest jock and being so influenced by Dana, was not going to be shown up by this display of inaccuracy. She bent down, picked up the rock and threw it at the squirrels. It got really close, and one squirrel ran up into the tree while the other one stayed frozen. We were all soldiers hunched in the bunker waiting to strike.

It got eerily quiet again and Dana stared in my direction, did her valley girl eye roll and sighed, "Ok scaredy cat . . . your turn. What are you waiting for?"

I felt like my hand weighed fifty pounds. I, for certain, did not want to hit that squirrel. While I had a good arm, I was not even aiming at the squirrel honestly because my hand was shaking. I loved animals and the last thing I wanted to do was hurt one. This animal was so innocently looking for food, watching its back at every second.

I sat for a moment quietly and thoughts of spiders in bathtubs came to my mind. I thought about how this squirrel didn't have to worry about school, fitting in with the cool crowd, and playing Barbies. Its primary focus was to find food and protect its family.

Dana annoyingly said, "Well, what are you waiting for? Are you out in space you stupid airhead? Stop thinking and just do it already!"

I bent down quickly, picked up the rock and threw it as hard as I could. I tried so hard to miss but I had this awful feeling I was going to be the one that made the shot, and that thought came to fruition.

The rock blasted through the air with a spin, and bam, it nailed the squirrel hard, right directly in its side. I can still remember the sound it made as the squirrel tipped on its side and let out a loud squeal.

At that precise moment, my heart dropped. I lost the air I was breathing and my throat became instantly dry. Dana and the girls jumped up and down laughing and screaming like I just scored the last run in the World Series, patting me on the back. I tried to fake the excitement of my conquest, fighting back the tears.

I was a hero for three seconds only because Dana was on the move for the next shenanigan. No one cared about the squirrel at all. Not one person said a thing, not an, "Awww, I hope it's ok," or "That must have hurt."

Nothing.

All of us just kept going as if it didn't happen. But it didn't end there for me. I felt incredibly guilty and plagued by this emotion. Every step I took pounded in the fact that I just hurt a living thing to bolster my ego and make friends I didn't even like.

Was this who I wanted to be?

As we went on walking, all I could think about was what happened to that squirrel. I wasn't even listening to anything anyone was saying. I kept seeing the squirrel tip over, letting out a squeal. I was a dam holding back the fierce waters. I can't believe the dam didn't explode from the amount of tears I was holding in.

I didn't even know what happened to the squirrel. Did it run up the tree and lie down? Did it make it back to its family? Was it in pain? Would it be injured for the rest of its life? Better yet, what would my mom think if I told her?

We kept walking until we went back to Kristin's house. The plan was to eat pizza, put on our pajamas, and crank call random people and boys from our class. When we sat down to eat, I kept thinking about the squirrel. I wondered if it was able to eat while I was stuffing my face. The more I thought about the squirrel, the more I ate. I wasn't even listening to the girls talk; I just kept inhaling pizza and not even realizing how much I was eating.

"Why don't you save some pizza for us you hog? That's about the thirtieth piece you have had, Tammy, geez!" Dana said with a tone.

"I haven't eaten since lunch," I said sheepishly.

"I've never seen anyone eat like that. You're disgusting," Dana said sarcastically. I said nothing and I put my head down. The other girls said nothing either and they all just went on talking about boys.

After we finished eating, I still could not shake the feeling I had about the squirrel, and the girls making fun of me for eating too much made me feel even worse. I had a terrible stomachache and I knew it wasn't the pizza. I asked Kristin if I could call my mom because I had a stomachache and felt like I was going to throw up. Dana of course made fun of me.

"Ok big baby, you should just go home anyways. You are sick because you ate the whole pizza, stupid. No one wants you here anyways."

Again, the silence.

No one said anything.

They all sat complacent, even Kerry. I and my other so-called friends had every opportunity to stand up to Dana and tell her to go fuck herself, but none of us did. I just didn't have it in me and apparently no one else did either.

I decided to call my mom, and she was there ten minutes later. It was almost like she just stayed in the car awaiting my phone call for a heroic rescue.

I said goodbye to no one because everyone was already downstairs in the basement making prank calls and giggling and having fun. Kristen's Mom waited with me at the door. She felt bad about me leaving. She hollered for Kristin to come up and say goodbye, but Kristen just bellowed up in a half-caring voice, "Bye Tammy."

That was the end of the slumber parties.

That was the end of these "friendships."

The following Monday in school, I was shunned, especially by Dana, and by the other girls. They just blindly followed Dana. They were forced to be circus acts who had to walk over the hot coals, perform tricks and stay in cages. It was as if I didn't even exist. They all just went on and didn't skip a beat.

I was beyond crushed.

I finished the school year pretending like I didn't know those girls either, ate my way through any heartache I felt about fitting in. I did feel much better that I didn't have the pressure of trying to be one of them. I went back to hanging with my neighborhood friends and it felt so refreshing to be myself.

Sometimes I would catch a glimpse of Kerry or Kristin at school or on the softball field. I could tell in their eyes that they were miserable, caught in a net trying to claw their way out. I wanted to set them free, but I gnawed through my net on my own terms. They would have to do that same thing if they wanted to get to the other side. How long they remained in that tangled trap of deception I don't know because I never looked back.

But even now as an adult, when a "Journey" tune comes on, I revert back to those days and feel a slow unsettling feeling in my stomach. Those lazy, innocent happy days shot to pieces in a blink by a gun too big to hold in my hands. I think of what could have been if those friendships had not been severed with a bullet to the heart.

The ups and downs of fitting into middle school and even high school were like waves of nausea for me. It was also another catalyst for my eating issues.

I didn't really need anyone else, especially those who were mean or didn't think the way I did. At this point, I realized I was going to be there for myself. When I sat and ate, it made me feel good. Those friends couldn't make me feel good, but food could. Food gave me life and gave me energy. I knew it was going to fill me up in a way no friend could ever do.

I hear the distance beep in my head again and I start to feel tired. I lie down on my bed and fall into blackness again.

Chapter 14

Ashley

> *"Conquer yourself rather than the world."*
> *- Rene Descartes*

THE Mexican dinner is delivered on time. I eat at the island and the kids eat in front of the tv with Chris. I hear them talking about plans for their sports. But in time, the silence carves the air in the room. Everyone moves on as usual and does their own thing and then to bed. I am left with all the dirty dishes again. Chris walks by me silently before going up to bed. He has nothing to say and neither do I. He doesn't even ask anymore if I am coming with him. Most of the time, I would go back to my Hallmark Channel movies, but I have no inkling to turn on the tv tonight. Our argument is still brewing inside me. I stay up and drink my Pinot Noir. I think my own parents were always in conflict about what was best for me and my brother, but they couldn't even get their own shit together in their marriage, similar to how I am running mine.

Another swig to empty the bottle. I open a new one while thinking about my younger self when I was sixteen and how I used to drink Bartles and James. I've come a long way. Only the good stuff now.

During my senior year of high school, I chose to navigate my path to college somewhat alone, away from the tainted views my mother was offering. I had no academic focus in high school but managed to get A's in every subject. It just came effortlessly for me, and I knew very well how to play the game to get good grades. I joined clubs, I danced on the pom squad, and was even the captain for three years, inducted into the National Honor Society, received an academic scholarship for college, and reigned as homecoming queen for four years in a row, setting a high school record. I ran the roost and had everyone fooled. They all thought I had this passion and direction. I was a fun, goal-driven girl. I was the one everyone wanted to be around: the all-time socialite. No one thought I had any problems. I had any clothes I wanted and got a brand-new car for my sixteenth birthday. I had long, flowing, sculpture-like hair, and because of my body, I had the guys begging at my feet to be at my side.

I loved this control, yet at the same time I wanted to run away from everyone and everything and never come back. One would think that with all this teenage royalty I would have been in heaven. But I was broken with no cracks to be seen on the outside.

I was one of those old farmhouses in the wide-open fields off the interstate. At one time that farmhouse beamed with pride, fields of green against a picturesque sunset, then one day worn out, abandoned and decrepit, and even on the sunniest day the barn looked like it was in a black and white photo. But I read somewhere old barns should never be torn down because it was bad luck to do so.

While I was all the things my parents wanted me to be in high school, they never stopped my selfish behavior, especially when I was mean to other people or made other people feel less than human if I didn't think they were worthy of being in my presence. They were also self-absorbed and wanted to brag about me any chance they got; they ignored my clear disregard for the fellow man.

All I knew was that I certainly couldn't have anyone around me who seemed better or would one-up me in any way. I spent a lot of time carefully crafting who I was going to hang out with, or better yet, who I could manipulate to believe that I would always be the one on top, and I carried this into college. One would be surprised how easily people could be swayed. I was the queen of changing minds for my friends and did it quite well. I just got used to it and I suppose it desensitized me in a way.

But I was left to wonder whether these people I knew were really my friends or my guinea pigs? I got so used to the manipulation that I honestly didn't know if I had true friends or really cared. At the expense of having good character, it just felt too good to be on top; it really did. I built a wall and my heart was a fortress and that didn't allow for compassion or love. I started to learn how to not feel bad for anyone I hurt along the way.

I am out of wine again and not feeling a buzz at all for some reason, and I realize I forgot to take my Xanax to get sleepy. I stumble back into the kitchen and swallow down a pill. I really need to go to sleep to forget about all this shit, but at the same time I hate sleeping because my dreams make me feel guilty about who I have become. I once heard someone say that I should pay attention to dreams because it is the soul talking and that scares the shit of me. I just want to lie down, see nothing, and wake up refreshed.

But lately I am having dreams that I am in high school again, and in all the dreams I am lost, cannot find my locker, and have zombies chasing after me, specifically a girl I used to taunt because she was really fat. Her name was Michelle Larken. There were two hundred and nine graduates in my class and I can still remember her name, her face, and the way she walked. She was grossly overweight, at least two hundred fifty pounds. She wore her hair greasy and short, and she wore smudged glasses way too small for her giant face. She looked as if she grew out of the glasses like an old pair of pants. She had greasy skin tattered with acne and food stuck in the corners of her mouth. She used to walk right by me every day to the last desk in the row and sit right behind me. She was always the last one in class because it would take her longer to walk during passing periods. She reminds me very much of the crossing guard I see every day. I wonder if it's Michelle who has that job.

I would listen to her squeak down the row as her feet would seem like they were going to bust out of her boat shoes. Her heavy panting sounded like she was going to explode, and I could hear the phlegm in her throat rattle as she would prepare for a cough. She would bend down slowly to fit into the desk. Finally, I could hear her drop into her chair like an army tank with a huge sigh, the phlegm rattling a breath at the back of my neck, and then the smell of her fat, sweaty flesh was enough to make me want to vomit. Each day I would watch her in disgust as she would come down that row.

How could she let herself look that way? Better yet, who allowed her to get to that point? I don't think I ever felt bad about anything or anyone, but there was something inside me that made me feel really sorry for her within my disgust.

When she walked by, others around me would shoot glances at each other, trying not to laugh or we would shake our heads in disbelief.

I remember back in high school, a good friend Danny, who was an Eddie Haskell kind of guy, turned to me once and said, "How do you fuck a fat chick? Roll her around in some flour and find the wet spot!"

We laughed and it was obvious that we were laughing at her. I think Danny had a fat chick joke almost every day. I am sure he spent more time looking for fat girl jokes than he spent on his homework.

Like every day before this particular day, she came walking down the row, sat down, sighed and adjusted herself inside the desk, a hunk of Jell-O filling in the mold. She breathed heavily and I felt her labored air on the back of my neck; it repulsed me.

I had enough and couldn't keep my mouth shut anymore. I turned around and just stared at her for what seemed like five minutes. I didn't smile. I gave her a scowl and an eye roll. I had perfected the eye roll and could have received an Emmy award for my valley-girl persona. I had lost it with this pomp and circumstance every day. I wanted her to stop breathing on me.

As I turned around, she smiled very sweetly.

"Well?" I said snottily.

"What's wrong?" she said looking confused.

"I'll tell you what's wrong. Your body is wrong. Everything about you is wrong. How can you live like this? Just stop breathing on me, ok? It's grossing me out!"

She just stared at me. She kind of smiled a little, but her eyes instantly welled up with tears. Before she put her head down on the desk, I saw a tear rolling down her thick cheek. I didn't know what to do because I didn't expect her to start crying, and everyone in our row was looking at me for my reaction.

I suddenly felt bad for a moment that I had crushed this girl with a few words, but I couldn't let anyone else know I was feeling sorry for her. I looked over at another girl sitting next to me who cackled with laughter. She gave me a look of victory. And just like that, my sympathy switched into apathy.

I wanted to be a show-off instead of apologizing for being an asshole. So, I went on while she sat there crying. "Well, you wouldn't be crying if you just went on a diet."

The other people high-fived me for putting it all out there and being the one to say what they wanted to say but didn't have the balls to. I turned back around in my seat like a champion of words.

I never spoke to her again after that day. I would see her in the cafeteria when I walked by with my friends. She would shoot me a glance, then go back to stuffing her face with honey buns and Coca-Cola. She would still come into class every day in the same fashion, but she made sure not to make eye contact with me. But many times I desperately wanted to talk to her, but without the presence of my friends. I really wanted to apologize.

I tried to say sorry one time when I saw her sitting by herself at lunch before my friends got there. She was by herself every time I saw her. I started to make my way over to sit down by her, but one of my friends came to get me and pulled me away. I lost the chance to make amends. I had to let it go and that bothered me, but I would never admit my shame to anyone, not to my friends, and certainly not to my parents.

I have dreams now as an adult that I see Michelle's face wide with sorrow and yet I just bury it in my past continually, but this demon bubbles up to the surface more often than I would like it to. I think it's because that was the last time I felt I had the opportunity to be a good person and I blew it.

But still these dreams always make me wonder whatever happened to Michelle Larken? Did she lose weight? Could she be a model now? Or is she the crossing guard? Maybe I changed her life for the better.

I finish the last drop of wine and start combing through social media to find her. All I end up with is wasted time down a deep black hole of Michelles I don't know and not the one I am looking for. I would have to leave this story in my mind with a fictional ending to take care of my broken soul.

Chapter 15

Tammy

"Sleeping next to someone you are falling out of love with is the biggest distance in this world."
- Anonymous

THE beeps subside and my head starts feeling clear again when I wake up. I find myself in my other bedroom in my house that I had with Bill the whole time we were married. Am I still in the same painting I went into earlier? I don't hear noises in the odorless room now. My settings are morphing into others and I feel compelled to stay in a place that's familiar. I fight the feelings of wanting to flee and go back to the room to hear the chatter. I remember the walls in my bedroom with Bill were painted a dull gray with a little splash of yellow from the curtains. The bed is hard, the pillow is stiff. I feel cold under these thinning and worn-out blankets. I still feel too dizzy to get up and look around, so I lay here thinking about my days in this house.

When I first got married and had Alex, life was water on the move that always made its way back to the waterfall. The water would travel quickly and become frothy and sparkly over the rocks, then blend in with the movement of waves down into a deep pool.

Each day blended into another, but I was happy to be in my own skin even though Bill did not acknowledge me. It was still me inside this bigger body, but he could not find that peace I had within myself. He could chase after his own peace to the ends of the Earth, but he would fall off the edge continuing to look. His love was cold cement on a frozen morning in the winter.

Back then, I almost wished Bill still loved me like he used to before the marriage, but something inside of me felt elated that he was not in love anymore because I was starting to realize I would be much happier without him. He probably thought this way too. I was just not sure why neither of us acted on leaving, but instead we became quietly cold and complacent, each day much like the other.

Bill usually fell asleep downstairs on the couch. He would come into bed at some point, but I didn't even hear him most of the time. I just heard his alarm go off at sixty-thirty in the morning, and I didn't see him again until dinner time. Our relationship reminded me of the song *Angel of Montgomery*: "How the hell can a person go to work in the morning, come home in the evening and have nothing to say."

I first heard this song when I was a kid and loved the melody. I would sing the lyrics of the Bonnie Raitt version and pretend I was her while watching myself sing in the mirror. I never knew what the lyrics meant because I didn't have the experience, but now I lived this song and it unsettled me. "Make me an angel, who flies from Montgomery," buzzing in my head all day long, just like those flies in the kitchen.

I hadn't heard the song in years until one day I heard it on the radio on the way home from my job at the crosswalk. I kept singing it over and over again. The melody lulled me into a sound sleep, until I awoke abruptly in a cold sweat from a nightmare I had about Bill dying right in front of me. My heart was practically thumping through my chest. I was trying everything to get the beats to stop, but my heart was a runaway train coming off the rails. I looked over and saw Bill lying next to me. I watched his chest move up and down in sync with his own heartbeat and wished mine was that content with being miserable.

I remembered that calm face that used to love me. I remembered how we would cuddle in the mornings and not want to get out of bed. I wanted to reach over and hug him, kiss him, and tell him I loved him. But every time I got the inkling to do so, the connection slipped away from me. I was a balloon lost on a windy day, climbing higher through the soft wind until I was no longer visible to anyone.

I glanced at the clock and noticed it was three o'clock in the morning. This time always conveyed mystery, calming silence, and yet eerie tones as well.

When Alex was a baby, I referred to three o'clock in the morning as the "witching hour." This was the time he would wake up crying to eat or if he had a bad dream. But it was also during this time that I felt the most powerful connection with my son. I can remember feeling so tired and wanting to go back to sleep, yet elated to have this precious time together.

In the quiet hours of three o'clock in the morning it also felt like being in a sacred and quiet church. I had the chance to soothe Alex after a bad dream or rub his back if he had a fever. There are no other sweeter moments than this in the many chapters of motherhood. As children grow older, any mother would wish for these times back in a heartbeat instead of watching them drive off in a car for the first time.

If I was sick, either with a stomachache or a fever, inevitably, I would wake up, look at the clock, and then it would say three o'clock. This is the time the phone would ring with an unwanted message, like the call I got at three A.M. from my mom who told me my father had a heart attack. Since that dreaded night, I woke up every night at this time because it took me years to sleep through the night after my father passed.

Because of the nightmare about Bill, I got up and stumbled down the dark hall to the bathroom, one heavy foot after the other. I looked in the mirror at myself while pondering about this nightmare I had. I dreamt that Bill and I were climbing rungs on a ladder attached to a building, and he was behind me. I was sweating profusely and barely made it to the top. When we got to the top, he needed me to get to the final step of our climb. He reached out his hand; but I barely tried to grasp it. I wanted to help him, deep down inside I really wanted to help him. This is the man I fell in love with, the man I married. This was the man who was the father of my only son, but something inside me hated him for how he made me feel.

As he tried to reach for my hand, sweat beaming from his forehead, jaws clenched and pity beaming from his eyes, I let go. I watched him plummet to the ground with a loud thump, and then a peaceful stillness came over me. I saw his body lying there while the air seemed intensely motionless. I was stunned in horror as I looked down.

Once the hushed silence permeated through the thick air, I was amazed actually that Bill got up. He didn't try for the ladder again or even look at me. He just stood up, dusted himself off, and walked away. Watching Bill fall was scary, and yet somehow letting it happen was even more disturbing. But he looked relieved, just silent and determined as he walked and then eventually disappeared into a dark background.

I leaned over the sink, put some cold water on my face and stared at my sad eyes that were staring back at me. It seemed I was no longer looking at myself anymore. I listened intently while the clock downstairs was ticking on the witching hour, and it was then that I knew my time in this relationship was up.

I knew deep down from the hallows of my gut that I didn't need Bill anymore and he didn't need me. We were hanging on the last car in a roller coaster, barely on the tracks and out of control. To some, this was wildly exhilarating, but this car had left the tracks to a deep plummet, and the thrill was all but gone and final. That was the night I decided I was going to pull the trigger on our marriage before he did. I remembered going downstairs in the dark, somewhat on autopilot, and I started looking up online on how to start the process of a divorce.

I lie here thinking about that night and the nightmare I had and how it changed the path of my life. I hear those beeps again returning, the light chatter too, but this time the beeps and chatter is getting louder.

I can't hear myself think.

I look at the time and it says three o'clock. I think I need to go to sleep forever.

CHAPTER 16

Ashley

> *"Lift up your head, princess; if not, the crown falls."*
> *- Anonymous*

I wake up completely dazed and wonder where I am because I already see peeks of sunlight coming in from the front window. The last thing I remember is that it was dark and everyone was in bed for the evening. I guess I fell asleep on the lazy boy chair in the family room scrolling on my phone. I fell down the rabbit hole of social media looking for someone I knew in high school and who haunts my dreams to this day.

I can't go back to sleep again and I have a headache from overdoing the wine last night, so I am content to just lie on the lazy boy chair and relax before the kids get up and my day turns hectic.

The basement door is right next to the family room. It is wide open so all the noise from down below echoes to where I am on the chair in the family room. I hear the loud stomps of Chris's feet on the treadmill slapping down with discipline. He is already up on his daily workout that he never misses. He usually runs outside, but if it is raining or too cold, he retreats to our workout room downstairs. He usually closes the basement door so he doesn't wake everyone up, but today he obviously didn't give a shit. I think he didn't close the door on purpose when he saw me on the couch. I know how he operates and sure his purpose was to wake me up and make me feel like a slouch since I passed out on the couch instead of coming to our bed. I hear sounds of the nineties and it makes me smile wishing for that easier life of makeup, big hair and flannel shirts. I close my eyes and listen to the Counting Crows sing "Round Here" and it reminds me so much of my college days, carefree and easy, no strings attached. Now my strings are tangled and I can't get the knots out because I am forced to be an adult.

I never paid attention to what the song meant until right now. I picture myself in these lyrics and I sing the song softly with my eyes gently closed. I imagine walking away from everything and everyone, like the singer in the song. Still lying on the couch, I think about how it would be liberating to leave everything behind, but it would also entail leaving my old self behind too, and I don't know how to do that. I listen to the Counting Crows blaring from the basement thinking about my younger self in college when I felt free.

I had the best body ever on the day I entered college. I saw the looks I got even with an oversized sweatshirt and leggings. The awful thing was that I did spend too much time covering up that beautiful sculpture of a body with flannels and baggy jeans when the grunge scene came into play. But in typical sorority fashion, the girls in my sorority cut the jeans into shorts where they creeped up our asses because the guys loved it. We hummed along to "Smells Like Teen Spirit" even though we didn't have a clue what Nirvana was saying. The song was what everyone liked so we followed along, sang along, and turned it into our scene. We were clad in ripped-up flannels to expose our cleavage and we unknowingly exposed our ignorance. We followed the movement of pop culture while losing our authenticity in the process.

In order to wear jean shorts we had to know how to cut them. We would cut them short enough to wear where we had some fringe hanging down with the inside part of the white pocket showing on the front of the thigh. I once had a guy tell me he loved the way the jeans seam line split my vagina and told me he loved my "vertical smile." One would think that would cause me to slap him, but it made me feel even hotter. I knew this guy had no mind of his own, just a hard-on waiting to be fucked, and I would be discarded shortly after. It would be a story to tell his friends over quarter beers and later in life sitting around with their fat wives who didn't shave their legs. But even so, I adored this attention I got from the guys. I hated that I liked it.

For the first year I was in college I just partied, made friends with whomever I could, and fucked around with hot guys. Upon meeting my roommate, we got along immediately and pledged to the same sorority. We studied, joined academic clubs, did our homework for our classes, and then went to parties on the weekend. I thought this was truly life.

I rarely went home because of the distance and also had no desire to go back. Going from Illinois to California was like heading into that scene in *Willy Wonka* where the children and their guests find the chocolate river and the Oompa Loompas and candy galore. I was Charlie Bucket on my way to a world that just seemed like pure paradise. I was thrilled to get away from my mom. I had my own life to live, not the one she wanted for me.

The only time I got homesick was when I missed my dad. I would often call him to see how he was doing because the one guilt I had was leaving him home with Mom. Mom was so into herself and I couldn't imagine how he could even live with her. I was hoping he would have the balls to go out and find someone else and dump her ass. My brother was out of college and on his own but checked in once in a while. He and my dad really grew apart over the years before he left. He went to college and never looked back, and that's what I wanted for myself. But just thinking of my dad by himself made me sad. He always sent me care packages, and when they came for parents' weekend, it was usually him that came because my mom always had other plans. I think she came once to visit me during the four years I was in college.

When I went home, I could tell I interrupted their routine. The second I left for college my mom had hired an interior decorator to redo my old room. There wasn't even a bed in there anymore for me when I came back home over break. She gave away all my things and packed everything up in shallow heartless boxes. She took out the nails where my pictures and award plaques were and patched the holes up on the wall. Then she completed the room with a fresh new color of beige and painted me out of her life. When I came back home, I would sleep on a little couch adorned with beaded pillows with empty substance, just like her soul.

Over the years, I would make my time there short and find other places to go. But again, I always felt guilty about leaving my dad. He was too proud of a man to divorce my mother, and he never would. I wanted to tell him so many times he did not have to stay with her because of me or Noah. We had our own lives and didn't need them to stay together for the sake of how we felt, but I never got around to having this conversation with him.

When I went back to college, I started the whole routine up again as if I didn't miss a beat. I went to class and I waited to dress up like Barbie dolls with my friends for the weekend parties. It was nothing short of a miracle that I didn't run into an asshole before I met Chris.

I was never slipped a date rape drug and was never in a precarious situation. Somehow any bad situation took care of itself from the assistance of someone else because I was used to things being taken care of for me. It never phased me that something could go wrong, and if it did, someone would get me out of it: that simple.

That year, I went to yet another frat party, but this was the night I ended up meeting Chris and the path of my new journey began. My life was a stained-glass mosaic vase at that point with one little shattered particle of glass fitting into another, and Chris completed the jagged pieces of the artwork.

The college parties were all the same, and I couldn't even distinguish one of the parties from another over the years. It was the same party scene, with different people, in different settings. On this particular night we were drinking jungle juice, and anyone who had consumed this beverage knew that you can go from sane to crazy in zero to sixty seconds in no time. The inner sex goddess always came out in me when I started drinking, and I couldn't control it, especially hard liquor.

My friends and I were in the middle of the frat house room when "Welcome to the Jungle" came on. Our hair was swinging and our bodies were bending and gyrating wildly. Our hip hugging pants exposed the sheer, tight thong bodysuits we wore showcasing our hourglass waists. We were arching our backs to the sound of the beat as the guys stood off to the side gawking. I had no idea that all those dance routines over the years would come in so handy because we owned the dance floor.

I remembered these feelings all too well on the floor of the gym in high school. Our feet were stomping and echoing through the gym with the bass, our heads were rolling, and we slid with purpose making squeaks across the gym floor with our thighs. That's when the kids would really cheer, and the boys were all on their feet.

There was a balance between dancing for what was in our hearts and feeling confident, versus a show for everyone else at our own expense. But at parties, the dancing was about fun, yet also about attention, and I couldn't get enough.

I was an attention whore.

At one point I looked up and saw a bunch of guys rocking back and forth trying to look like they knew how to dance. This was our show, just like we were back on the gym floor again, yet this time the audience was in grabbing distance. Some of the guys got in the ring. They were just stalking the scene waiting to pounce on the lean and galloping gazelles just minding their own business grazing on the grass.

Then one of those guys came forward outside of the perimeter. He stopped and stood right in front of me. He had wavy dark hair and piercing hazel eyes, and he wasn't waiting for a possible chance when a woman would finally meet his glare. He decided to go right in for the kill, and the confidence he exuded was straight out one of those Hallmark movies I watch now. He felt like Spartacus to me, complete with a shield and sword, ready to take on a victory for all of these men in the name of manhood. I was never nervous around any guy, and always felt I held the cards, but I dropped them all over the floor when I saw Chris.

My heart stopped, the music I heard stopped, and my inner goddess was fading like the bright white shirt I bought that over time turned yellow. I thought I was feeling like this because of the alcohol because no other guy had stopped me in my tracks before. He made me so nervous I wanted to stay there and run at the same time.

At that precise moment I knew I was fucked up and I wasn't sure how to get myself out of this situation of feeling utterly overcome with nausea. I got so dizzy and started sweating intensely. I felt the beads of sweat in the creases of my tight ass jeans, and on my forehead. Chris had to have seen this happening before his eyes, but I think he enjoyed having the control and the upper hand.

He leaned in closely and smelled like a breath of fresh air. "Why did you stop dancing? I was really enjoying the show."

There was something about his eyes that lured me in. I felt sick, like I couldn't breathe, but I didn't want him to know this. I don't even remember what I said next, but my mouth started watering and I could feel the streams of stomach acid getting ready to come out like a volcano, ready to puke. I mumbled in blurred speech while pushing the hair out my eyes, "Sorry, I'll be back," and I left him standing there.

I kept thinking I met this incredible guy and I have to fucking puke? Is this the story I will tell my grandkids and my kids that I ran into their father or grandfather at a party just before I puked from drinking too much? Somehow, I couldn't see myself on the porch sipping a glass of lemonade saying, "Kids, let me tell you a story about how I met your father." I would be forced to lie my entire life.

I had to run as fast as I could down the hallway into the bathroom because the juice was rising out of my jungle, from the forest floor up to the canopy, staining the toilet purple: staining my conscience. It was a horrible feeling to puke like this. The taste it left me with was abhorrent. I wanted to hide in the jungle with my toilet and never come out.

While lying there, I remember a bunch of questions going through my head. Did this guy just walk away? Will I ever see him again? Would I remember this the next day? My world was spinning, my breath was so deluged with fire that it could have harmed someone if they got too close. I had succeeded in making a complete ass out of myself. What was worse is that I didn't feel any better after I was done puking several times, not physically or mentally.

What was I doing with my life?

A couple of my friends knocked on the door to see if I was ok, but I shooed them away and told them I was fine. I wiped the remaining puke off my chin, threw water on my face, washed off the running mascara and managed to somehow piece myself back together, yet still stumbling when I heard another knock at the door.

"Is the dancing queen still in there?" It was Chris coming to check on me. I opened the door and there he was standing there with a smirk, kind of like he knew exactly how things were going to unfold.

He took me back to my dorm, got me something to eat, gave me aspirin and stayed with me all night to make sure I was okay. He was there the next morning and he didn't take advantage of me when he easily could have. He saved me at a vulnerable time in my life so I fell for him immediately.

We spent the better part of our college days together having hot, passionate sex and enjoying each other. We had highs and lows and everything in between. But when we were getting ready to graduate things started falling apart. Our relationship was similar to the joy of throwing confetti up into the air, fun and care-free. But when the confetti pieces came down the fun was gone and the last thing anyone wanted to do was clean it up.

Chris would get jealous of other guys looking at me, and I would get jealous of girls always looking at him. There were lies being told by him because I knew he was cheating on me. Ironically, I was cheating on him too, but the sex always lured us back together. These unhealthy choices continued for a while, only to creep up on us, and eventually it was Chris who decided to end the madness of these mind games.

After yet another argument and just before we were going to graduate, Chris asked me to meet him at one of our favorite cafes that we would go to all of the time. We used to sip coffee here trying to nurse hangovers. We would act like adults and do our homework here. We would make up here from many of our fights and then go have make up sex afterwards.

I thought this was going to be just like all the times before, but little did I know this time would be different. I decided to walk over and clear my head before I got there. This cafe always felt like a warm and welcoming home I never had, so I absolutely loved to go there. I had no idea he wanted to torch the place up in flames and walk away from the only place where I ever felt like I belonged.

When I arrived fashionably late, Chris was already there waiting for me outside on the patio. I smiled pretty and sat down. He glared over with a partial grin. I could tell he was irritated that I was late. We sat in awkward silence for a bit while the waiter filled our mugs with hot coffee. He drank his coffee black with no cream or sugar. He blew on the cup, took a sip and set it down. He breathed in deeply, grabbed my hands from across the table, and looked at me directly into my eyes. He simply told me I was not in his master plan after graduation. I don't even remember the exact words he used to sever the ties, but I remember the utter shock I felt as my eyes widened and I sat up straighter. My coffee got cold instantly and my stomach ached. I had no idea this was coming.

I watched the gorgeous palm tree sway in the warm sun after he uttered his words so matter-of-factly. The breeze hit the palms and they flapped in the delicate wind under the heat. I no longer viewed them as pretty. Instead, I saw them turn into big giant sticks making clunking noises that made me want to scream out loud.

Tears rolled down my cheeks and I threw out offers of how I would change and that he should give me time, and maybe we could work it out. None of these pleas worked. He said he would always love me, but he needed to end things and start clean. Chris is a serious person so when he made his mind up, that was it for him. He was not budging on this decision he made and I knew this was the end.

I felt like I barely sat down. I needed to digest this but he wanted to get out of there as soon as he could. He didn't like drama. He didn't like too many words. He got up from the table to give me a hug and say goodbye. It took everything in me not to grab onto him and beg for him to stay. I couldn't believe he didn't offer to at least drive me back to my place. He said he had to be somewhere and walked out of my life.

I took the breakup very hard, but I wanted to act like it was no big deal. I even told people I was the one who broke it off with Chris. After some time, I actually started believing my own lies and felt better about the ending. I went out with other guys and made it look like I was the one who came out on top. I had some pride left so I wasn't going to go crawling back to Chris. I listened to "I Will Survive" every night by myself like countless other dejected women and picked up the pieces with some help of self-medicating. This helped me finish college and graduate.

I would talk with my dad about the breakup and he was the one who talked me into staying in California and starting a new chapter without Chris. He did everything he could to divert me from spending energy thinking about the breakup. He got me an interview from a client he knew and I landed my first job right out of college.

"Round Here" is fading out now and I think about my strength at that time in my life. Like the singer, I can't see anything around here but misery. Counting Crows stops and it is silent. Chris appears through the basement door, his face sweaty and flushed in a way that makes him look healthy and alive.

He wipes his head with a towel and says, " I just ran six miles and you are still passed out like you're in college again."

I smile because I am too exhausted to continue to fight with this man.

"Yep, just like in college. This is what I did when you broke up with me. I guess nothing has changed," I say sarcastically.

"Seriously? Why do you wallow in the past? We are married, aren't we? So, are we going to talk or what? Or are you still going to play these fucking games? I thought I was done with that. I have to go work to pay for you to live in luxury."

"Well, if you have one foot out the door, why bother talking?" I say.

He sighs heavily. "I know we have problems, Ash, but I don't want to argue in front of the kids anymore. They didn't need to be a part of that in the car. It's just not right."

"They don't fucking care or even know what's going on," I say as I wave my hand like that would make all the wrongs go away like magic.

"Don't justify it Ash. I talked to Noah before I went to bed last night and Ava too. Noah just shrugged his shoulders but Ava started crying and said she is worried we are going to get a divorce. You might know how they feel if you took the time to talk to them instead of pawning them off to other people and places."

"Oh, I get it. You should get Dad-of-the year." I shake my head.

"This is not about me, Ash. It's about you and me together. Stop fucking feeling sorry for yourself and we can talk more when I get home later." Then he stands there staring at me. He has that look of "let's have make-up sex."

"Why don't you come upstairs with me in the shower and we can talk more about it there?"

I smile slowly and flirtingly because out of nowhere I start to feel like I wanted sex again. "Only if you wash my back first."

We both got really good over the years of luring each other into forgetting about the shit we had laid down.

"Deal," he says and grabs my hand.

CHAPTER 17

Tammy

> *"Do ye not comprehend that we are worms born to bring forth the angelic butterfly that flieth unto judgement without screen."*
> *- Dante Alighieri*

I thought I had been sleeping forever because I hear nothing for what seems like days. The faint beeping wakes me up again and I can't get this annoying noise out of my head. I am not in my bedroom anymore. My childhood backyard is before me; it's openness and comfort make me feel great peace. The sound of the leaves blowing from the trees takes my mind off the incessant beeps.

Our house was very spacious with a lot of land and trees. In the sea of trees, there stood the big oak tree outside by the bedroom window. Because I coveted her the most, I named her Dryad. I loved reading Greek mythology as a kid so this is where I came up with the name for the tree. The dryad is a nature spirit said to originally have lived in oak trees. The dryads took the shape of a woman, which is why I refer to the tree as she. I marvel at her majestic beauty before me. It feels so good to see her yet again. The beeps are nowhere to be heard, just the silent stillness of her presence. Her towering limbs still full of leaves create an enormous umbrella to shield me from the bright sun. She will always be my North Star.

My Dad built our house around the trees. He was very proud of his accomplishment of providing a shelter of love for his family and preserving the beauty of the outside world. The only downfall the house had was that it was on a busy street and set back in the woods, so it didn't have a typical suburban neighborhood feel because the houses were spread far apart. But over the years I would come to realize this setup was not a bad thing at all. We became friends with the neighbors despite the distance between houses because of the secret path. The path was our own adventure trail through a secret neighborhood, unlike the cookie cutter subdivisions that popped up quickly nearby, just kernels in a popper.

My parents grew up on the south side of Chicago, so coming out to this open land not far from the city was the best of all worlds for them. They loved the city and they were able to get to it quickly, but it afforded them the space they so desired after living in close quarters for much of their lives. When I got older and moved to a place of my own, I realized that humans are kernels popping up and spraying out of the pot wherever we landed. For us, perhaps the exodus from the city was indeed white flight just disguised in a safe little haven free from the chaos of a city. While I adored my childhood home, I couldn't deny that I lived a sheltered childhood.

I lie on the grass and stare up into the vastness of Dryad. She still stands untouched, but what happened to my childhood friends? I thought about the games we used to play and the ups and downs of this time period. Looking back, I can see that I morphed into different shapes during this time of my life. I started out innocent and round in form, circular with notions of original perfection with no angles or sides. Over time I settled into becoming a square, unified, exact and civilized.

When I start thinking of childhood memories now my shapes change yet again, not equal in sides or angles, but in a form that is not definitive in nature. I hadn't talked to my friends from my neighborhood in years, yet they helped me become who I am because they were with me during this pinnacle time of my life during the metamorphosis of shape building from straight lines to uneven sides and zig zags.

One of my favorite games I played with my sister and my friends was *Charlie's Angels*. We would pretend we were the investigators trying to find the clues to the murder mystery. My sister was always Kate Jackson, our friend Jenny was Jacklyn Smith, and I wanted to be Farrah Fawcett. I wanted to wear that red bathing suit, tilt my head back, and flash a toothy smile as big as the sun, complete with pointy nipples to top it all off. I think I wanted to be Farrah because I knew I had the brains, but never, ever, would I look like that. People who look that good are truly born that way and live a whole different life than most.

We would find our other friends to play too, which were mostly girls. But there was one boy who was a little older than us. His name was Denny, and he was a skinny and gangly looking kid with a high voice. He always seemed aloof and not able to fit in with other boys. We took him into our brood and declared his character as Mr. Bosley. He seemed to be okay with this for a little while, but even when he was in character as Mr. Bosley, I had this sense that he was uncomfortable being the man. He always wanted to switch roles with us and we would never let him. When Cheryl Ladd replaced Farrah Fawcett, he desperately wanted to be her character, Chris. Being all girls, we took such issue with this, and me especially because I wanted to remain as Farrah Fawcett. But once her new replacement Cheryl Ladd came, I wanted to be her instead. She was equally beautiful and seemed to have a bit more in the brains department, so that worked out even better for me. There was no way I was going to let Denny acquire that role as a boy, especially how Denny looked. Plus, we didn't understand why he wanted to be a girl, when he was clearly a boy. To act like a girl when he was a boy was just not acceptable when I was growing up. Our ignorance back then of not understanding him went along with the narrow mindedness of the time. This action was viewed as being weird, and then it prompted us to ask questions about why he didn't want to be Mr. Bosley. We probed further and asked Denny why he wasn't playing with the boys. He never gave us a clear answer. He would just shake his head and utter that they were boring and he didn't like playing sports.

I recall many times seeing Denny run from the neighborhood boys as they were chasing him with sticks. It reminded me a bit of an antelope that would run like the wind to get away from the lions, get scratched and pulled, but always found a way to be free, yet not free of an open wound. Part of me felt sorry for him, but I was more concerned about how I was going to play the role I wanted in our game. I think he got tired of the abuse from us so he gave up, quit asking to be someone else, and continued to play Mr. Bosley.

After a while though, he just stopped coming down the secret path through the forest. We would wait for him to come over the clearing, but he never returned. We knocked on his door, rang his doorbell day after day. We tried to call his house, but his mom always said he wasn't home. After a while, it wasn't even about having a Mr. Bosley in the group because ironically one of my girlfriends ended up taking that role and we never blinked an eye about it. Now looking back, I know what a huge mistake we made by not letting him play a woman's part. But ironically, this is where my square seemed to lose the same length in sides.

My shape was changing.

Yet something still made me question why Denny would stop coming over after playing for such a long time. I remembered how my sister and Denny would come to blows over various issues so I thought I could go talk to her. I recalled seeing her many times bossing Denny around over the years and saying mean things to him like calling him an oddball or a weirdo. Even when we would switch gears and play softball, Denny would agree to play, but we would throw the ball too hard for him, or pitch too fast and he would strike out. If he did make it to a base, he would run in a straight path without even lifting his knees. "Pick your knees up you pansy!" We would scream back.

"You guys are already on a team, so how can I keep up?" he would moan. "I'm going home."

This was always a guarantee how every game would come to a screeching halt, but he would always say yes to play and every time he quit, and no one would go get him to come back. He was just an old punching bag that would wear out one day, but it was always satisfying to give it a hard kick because we had power over him.

Night after night I would harass my sister Dawn about Denny, trying to figure out why he would sometimes play with us now and sometimes not, or leave early.

She said to me one night very frankly, "I was talking to Jim and Tommy today and they both said that we shouldn't play with Denny anymore, so just shut up about it already. Why do you care if he doesn't come to play with us? Maybe he'll find some other weirdo girls to hang out with and play with their dolls or something."

"Alright fine," I said and hesitated a moment. "But I like when Denny plays with us, that's all."

"Well, get over it already Tammy. He's just a faggot," she said.

"What's a faggot?" I asked.

"It's when two guys like each other," Dawn said.

My mind went blank and I made a face similar to when the smell of dog poop appeared on the bottom of a favorite shoe. "That's disgusting!" I moaned. "How can he like another boy?" I asked.

"I don't know," said Dawn. "And I sure as hell don't want to figure it out, and neither should you. The word is gay when two boys like each other. Just stay away from him, that's all." She turned off the light and went to bed.

I lay there feeling so confused as to why Denny wouldn't play with us anymore and what it meant to be gay. I wanted to ask my mom but I was afraid. So I just let it go.

Denny didn't come back again that summer while we went on slip and slides, bike rides, nature hunts, wargames, Dungeons and Dragons, gymnastics on the swing set, pick up softball games, and scheduled house league games. I don't know if he didn't come back because he outgrew our childish games or if he realized he wasn't like us, but now I know it was the latter.

I have that crushing feeling in my chest again that I hate because it brings on a sense of doom within me. Just then I see a butterfly land softly in a branch above me taking a silent rest. I watch the wings stop, then flutter a few times before it takes off again. I hear distant noises of kids laughing on the secret path while the earth crunches under their feet. Is there any sound as magical?

Chapter 18

Ashley

> *"We should consider every day lost on which we have not danced at least once."*
> *- Friedrich Wilhelm Nietzsche*

Makeup sex with Chris is refreshing. My body is finally nourished and I have the itch to do a dance routine again like when I was a kid. Chris leaves for work, and after I drop the kids off at school, I decide to skip tennis and come home and try to remember some of my old dance routines.

I started dancing at the age of three up into adulthood so there were so many routines I have done over the years. I think for a while about this one while I start to set the scene. I walk into our family room with moveable furniture and a throw rug. I move it all to the side and before me lies a bare wooden floor like a dance studio. I can catch my reflection in the large picture window that overlooks the backyard and pool. I find *Upside Down* by Dianna Ross and chuckle thinking about how this song is perfect for where I am in my life right now. It just pops into my head serendipitously. I turn up the sound on the speakers as loud as I can in my makeshift dance studio.

As the music starts to play, I am in utter shock how the moves just float back into my life so easily after so many years. I see myself in the reflection of the patio door. I watch my hips moving back and forth with an attitude so mindlessly without effort. I remember that each dancer in this routine had to do somersaults over each other and cartwheels, round and round to the words of the song. I haven't done diving somersaults in years, so I quickly erase that idea. But being in shape, I think I can manage a cartwheel for sure and am willing to give it a try.

When the music pours out of the speakers, my mind reverts back instantly to the Candlelight Dinner Playhouse in Chicago. I saw a low-lit room with bright lights on a stage. I wore a black leotard, sparkling white fringe, and white go-go boots. I see the stage that was set above dinner tables. I can almost hear the glasses clinking, the chatter of families, and the smell of Italian lasagna being served to the audience who was getting ready to view our energy. I feel a tinge of sadness because The Candlelight Dinner Playhouse is nothing now but a memory leveled to the ground that made room for a hot dog stand.

I stand humming and moving my hips to the beat. I actually smile thinking of my mom because she was my coach during my early years of dance at the age of three up to middle school. She had a dance studio in our basement where we practiced our routines together. At one time our two bodies were musical notes on a staff measure creating a pretty melody. Then one day the same notes no longer played a beautiful song. They just fell off the measures into a miserable dark pile of dots out of tune.

My mom was a dancer as a child herself, which is why she drilled dance into me at an early age. She moved all the way to the top to become a professional dancer, and any chance she got she let everyone know. If we were at a wedding, she would show off on the dance floor, making others feel like they had two left feet. If her favorite song came on in the car, she would move along to the beat as she drove. Any party we were at, she made sure a dance party started at some point. She craved the attention, not the freeness of the soul which dancing does for the mind; her dancing was soulless and attention seeking in her hollow body. She reminded me of a diamond once so bright, only to become dull, losing its shine over the years.

I used to look at her pictures, outfits, and shoes with envy. At one point in my life, she was a special queen to me. I thought I wanted to be a professional dancer like her. I dressed up in her shoes, her clothes, and watched her routines on tape and found her routines mesmerizing.

Until one day when I was in eighth grade, I lost the dream of being a professional dancer because all my mom did was criticize, not teach. I questioned if she wanted me to dance for me, or for her. This is when I began to look at her skeptically when we would work on my routines together. At one time in my life, I watched her every move with wide eyes and wonder. But as time kept passing, I longed for her to leave me alone. I wanted to learn to dance from somebody other than my mother. I remember dreaming that she was a giant ocean liner that I would watch sink along the horizon. Before she went down, I pictured myself staring into the vast dark sea in her eyes lingering for a few long moments. I wanted to witness with my own eyes her bow sinking as water engulfed the tip of the boat. I was relieved to watch the boat finally disappear quietly, buried underwater for no one to see anymore. I didn't want her to come up for air. Here and there and over the years, the remains of her wreckage would be exposed and brought back up to the surface from time to time because even as an adult, I still don't ever feel gone from her grip.

As I get older, I actually feel sorry for her because she was a product of her parents' Draconian ways of forcing lessons on her with practice until her toes were bleeding, knee surgeries and a back injury where it all came to a halt. Fortunately, my dad came along to save her. He was enticed by her dancer moves and body, enthralled with the idea of being by a professional dancer's side, not noticing the tragic trap that he would end up in for the rest of his life. She really was the washed-up treasure that came to the surface nowhere near as bright as it used to be.

When I started high school, I started taking notice that my mom was a lost soul. I started going out with my friends more often and not wanting to be around her as much. When I would walk in from school or out with my friends, my mother could often be found sitting in her armchair with a crestfallen look on her face as she stared off into the distance. I would break the awkward silence, ask if she was ok. But she would always reply with, "I was in another place darling. I am glad you are home." What place was she in I would wonder as I went upstairs. I could hear my dad's television blaring the theme song from *Mash* as I walked into my room. I guess this is how they lived while my brother and I were gone. They were like two dolls in a dollhouse, set in separate rooms once moving from the children moving them, but when the lights went out, they were alone and stuck in their spots, lifeless.

Her critique of how I did in my dance competitions continued to go on throughout middle school. I was told what I did wrong, what I could do better, and how I should look. At this age, she even started critiquing my weight. She told me if I lost five pounds, I would have been able to make the tuck and roll somersault at the end of the routine. But because I didn't lose the five pounds, the part had been bestowed upon a lighter dancer. The weight comments were the catalyst that created a crack as wide as the San Andreas fault.

Nothing I did was ever good enough for her.

When I got to high school, I remember getting ready to try out for the dance squad, when I overheard my dad talking to my mom before the tryouts. He told her to not talk to me about my dancing and that it may be a good idea for her not to be my coach anymore.

"Of course, darling, I get all that."

But deep down she wasn't ready to let go yet. Reluctantly, she agreed to have someone else coach me, but she still found ways to interject her thoughts and critiques. She was never truly gone from the picture. Being around my mother was like one of those horror movies where one thinks the bad guy is dead, only to resurrect again and again.

Even after working with another dance coach, my mom still found ways to inject her venom. I started to learn to let her criticisms go in one ear and out the other. I tried to completely shut her out of my life as much as I could. This was the time of my life where I felt myself turning into a great white shark, solitary and disoriented if trapped, not at all acquiescing to captivity. I wanted to desperately break out of the cage to devour the scientist who was carefully watching me, because there was no way she could ever tame me.

Upside Down fades out like the eighties and I can't believe I remember all the moves. I actually feel happy for the first time in a while. I hit play again and attempt a cartwheel and into a somersault. I actually land it!

This show of display leaves me spinning with the same short-lived giddiness I remember as a child. I wish I filmed it or had an audience.

Chapter 19

Tammy

> *"Every man is guilty of all the good he did not do."*
> *- Voltaire*

As I sit in the backyard, the sounds of children laughing hush while the bright daylight colors transform into a low orange sun kissing everyone goodnight. This low glowing light reminds me how dusk in the summer will always remain my favorite time of the day. The dusk sky mirrors the colors of a fire followed by the vibrations of night insects. I can smell the air of a humid evening and view the countless lightning bugs flickering over and over. When the sun sinks off the horizon, I peer out into the forest of lightning bugs. I feel like I am watching a fireworks display without the noise and smell of gunpowder in the air.

I can see myself as a little girl picking weeds with my mother and watching those lightning bugs. I used to look at my mom while weeding and think about how I never wanted to leave her side. When I see that first lightning bug softly glow at dusk, it feels like a reminder of my mom's presence, so kind and soft, hovering on a slight summer wind.

I feel right at home and elated to Mom again. I move in closer to touch her, but I hear those beeps again and my head pounds. I am grounded where I am at and need to sit and take some deep breaths from the pain. The lightning bugs find their mate and then their lights dim. It is pitch black out now. I wish my head would stop pounding, but all I feel is pain with no light. And in this darkness, my mind shifts back to thinking about Denny again.

I think about the other boys we used to play with on the trails behind my house. I wonder if there were any boys in our neighborhood that acted like Denny. We all played outdoors all summer long until the days started to get short and the sounds of back-to-school commercials brought us to a screeching halt. The summer always seemed to pass like the smell of fresh baked cookies. This sweet fragrance permeated the air, but in no time that same glorious smell was gone leaving the air stale again.

I can remember seeing Denny when we went back to school occasionally walking through the halls. Our eyes would make contact, then we would both quickly shift our gaze downwards toward the floor. I wanted so much to reach out to him, but I just didn't have the courage to speak to him. It ended up that the whole school year went by and I never found the courage to make contact with Denny.

It wasn't until the following summer after sixth grade that I saw Denny again on the trail. I went down the path to get my friend Jenny. On the way over I heard boys' voices and sticks crackling and echoing to where I was standing. I stopped and stood there and waited for a little bit to see if I could hear what kind of action was going to happen.

I heard, "Stop running, you stupid fag!" It sounded like Jim's voice, but I wasn't entirely sure. Jim and Tommy hung out all the time. They were the all-American boys, athletic and rugged outdoor kids. They were the kids that came home with their clothes all muddied and stories that made the hair on their mom's necks stand up. When they weren't adorning their summer uniforms, their time was spent running through the woods and fishing in the creek that ran alongside the trail. They were also the boys who swiped their parents' cigarettes and Playboy magazines. They would find a place to take puffs in the woods while perusing the pages thinking the blonde bombshells were the only kind of women they needed to be with in their lives.

My friends and I really just did our best to stay out of their way as much as we could, although we did have a connection with the sports. Granted, their intent was not to connect with us, because they made it a point consistently to tell us that softball was nowhere near as hard as hitting a baseball. They would humor us when we played a pick-up game, but secretly I knew they were really shocked at how fast we could pitch the ball and hit. However, they would never admit that. It usually turned into an ego-ridden game of we can hit farther, we can pitch faster, and no way you throw farther than me bullshit.

On many instances the game ended with them saying, "Forget it. We got better things to do. Go home and put your tampons in," and they would leave chuckling.

They would make me so mad, so when I saw Denny running by me and Jim and Tommy on his tail, it startled me for a bit, but I was intrigued, which is why I made the split decision to run with them.

"Get in this chase, Tammy! We are going to catch this faggot!" yelled Tommy.

I had heard that word before and I wanted to chase after the meaning that I had been trying to figure out for so long. I ran like I have never run before. I wasn't even sure where I was going. Part of me wanted to prove to myself that I was capable of keeping up with them, yet also find out why he was running away from boys if he indeed liked boys.

The trail was not an easy path to run on, but I knew it like the back of my hand. Over the years I had learned the ups and downs, where the holes were at, the parts that were gravel, and sharp rocks sticking up around the twists and turns. The path was dry that day as it hadn't rained in weeks, so my feet were sliding on the dust a bit as we rounded turns, but I stayed right on their heels.

I knew eventually the path would lead out into an open meadow and I wasn't sure at this point if I was going to be able to keep up if they had intended to run through that whole area, especially in tall grass. I think back about how fit I was at this time in my life. Wow, it would be great to feel like that again. I remember my mind was racing like I was in a maze. I wasn't sure where the ending was or what was going to happen when we got there. My quickness on my feet was being supplied by sheer adrenaline pumping through my veins. I was moving my feet one after the other faster than I have ever gone. For one hot minute I thought I could easily make the track team if I kept up this stamina.

Up ahead of Jim, I was able to see Denny running as fast as he could, but he started to slow down. As the path moved uphill, I saw Denny get to the top, then trip on a tree root that was poking out of the ground. The root was there like a snake making its appearance to strike at precisely the wrong time.

We all made our way to where he was lying on the ground. I stopped for a minute to catch my breath as I was gasping for air, my heart beating a million times a minute. I slowly walked to the tip of the clearing and Jim and Tommy already had Denny on the ground. I moved in closely so I could hear what was going on.

Denny was thrashing and screaming for them to get off of him. "Get off of me you stupid dipshits! My dad has a gun to shoot both of you if you think you can beat me up!" he wailed.

"Oh, please man, shut the fuck up. Your Dad is a faggot just like you! He would have to use a gun cause he's a pussy and has no idea how to throw a punch!" said Tommy.

Denny had a lot of adrenaline running through him too, but he had no chance in hell to break away from these two.

At this moment I knew this was not a good situation. I immediately began to second guess this decision to follow these assholes. But I was in a pickle. I grappled there thinking about turning around and going back home, but that meant that I would have to leave Denny there to get the shit kicked out of him. I also just ran a flipping half mile at racehorse speed and I couldn't let that all go to waste; plus, I was dying to know why Denny didn't hang with us anymore. I had so many questions. We were all leaning over him while Jim grabbed one arm and Tommy grabbed the other. They pinned him to the ground and put their knees on his arms. He was lying flat on his back breathing heavily, his eyes scrunched, and sweat was dripping from his forehead. This all happened so fast I had no time to take in all of what was happening.

"Let me go! Tammy, tell them to get off of me!" he screamed. "Tell em Tammy; tell em to get off me!" he pleaded again.

Jim and Tommy looked back at me somewhat in disbelief that I was still there.

I could barely catch my breath, but I found a small voice that was cracking with fear. "Let him go guys," I managed to get out meekly.

"What did you just say? Fucking speak louder!" said Tommy.

"Let him go," I said in a soft monotone voice.

"Well, that doesn't sound convincing at all, Tammy. You sure you want us to let him go?"

Tommy looked at Jim with a smirk and they both chuckled mischievously while Denny lay on his back still squirming. Denny was dead in the water. I wasn't sure I could save him. He started to kick his legs and tried to break loose, but he was so skinny that even his legs didn't have enough torque to get his body to move. He was pinned down from the weight of the muscular bodies of Jim and Tommy.

Jim was panting heavily, too. He turned and looked at me with laser-focused eyes. "Tammy, I'll bet you could beat up this faggot," he said snottily. "Even a girl can kick your ass, you faggot gay-boy. What do you think of that?"

There were those "gay" and "faggot" words I kept hearing. They sounded so ugly coming out of their mouths.

At this point I knew I was in a situation that was wrong because now they were asking me to do something I really didn't want to do, but I had not been making clear decisions once my shoe hit the ground in the foot chase following blindly. I never thought I would wind up there, but that's what happens when you follow others blindly searching for answers that would not get answered. Denny was still trying to get away and Jim and Tommy were growing impatient with me because they had to keep their bodies down on Denny to keep him in place.

"Hit him!" shouted Jim at me with saliva spewing out of his mouth.

"Hit him!" shouted Tommy even louder. "Hit him because he's a fag! He needs to be taught how to be a man!"

I shook my head no, and no words came out. How could I hit him?

"Get them off me Tammy . . . they're hurting me!" Denny kept wriggling his body in an attempt to get away, but every time he squirmed, they sat down on him harder. Denny's voice screamed pure desperation. These screams split my eardrums in half along with my sinking heart. His voice was a squealing puppy far from its mother.

I wanted this all to end, and something in me had me believe if I just hit him then I could end this nightmare. I didn't see any other way out of it. I walked over to the ground and looked over at Denny lying pitifully on the ground. My heart was beating and my hands were sweaty.

I wanted to make this all go away, so I bent down and with all my might I punched Denny in the stomach as hard as I could.

I heard him wince in pain and try to catch his breath while Jim and Tom kept holding him down. I then slapped his face two times, balled up my fist and punched him across the jaw as hard as I could. I saw the blood spray from his lip and land all over my hands.

I wiped the blood off on my shorts, trying to wipe this from my conscience. I really don't know where that hateful energy came from because it certainly didn't come from my parents. The moment my fist left Denny's face I knew my parents would be so disappointed in me. The thought of my parents knowing what I did made me cry in my sleep many nights from the crushing guilt. I could still hear the noises Denny made when I hit him. To this day I still feel conflicted as to what I had done. I catered in to peer pressure and wish I could take it all back.

The boys screeched and laughed and shouted, "What a fag! Getting beat up by a girl! What a fag!" laughing and shrieking the whole time. I had to stop after the last punch because the breath left my body. I had a horrible feeling of despair that made my body tremble all over.

I wanted to instantly clean up his wounds and take care of him. I wanted to make this right, but the boys were cheering me on and giving me high fives like I had done something good. I stood there bewildered just wanting the boys to let Denny go.

Somehow between their gallant and superficial cheers, I managed to find my backbone and screamed with conviction, "Let him go!"

I saw the blood coming out of Denny's nose now mixing with the tears that were running down his cheeks. I felt an inferno inside me brewing until it all came out with rage so loud that tears bled out of my eyes. I thought I blew out my vocal cords. That's how loud my voice shrieked when I said it. I said it again louder, "Let him fucking go!!" That was the first time in my life that I swore.

This inferno shocked the boys because they looked up at me like I had two heads. There was silence for what seemed like an hour. I wasn't sure what Jim and Tommy were going to do next, but I had my fists balled ready to kick their asses because they should have been the ones getting the shit kicked out of them.

"Ok, Tammy, relax already! You just beat someone up and you want to act like a pussy too, then go ahead and hang out with your puss, gay, faggot boy. Go ahead you stupid bitch!"

Then Jim and Tommy loosened their grip and they released Denny.

I have never seen someone spring up from the ground so fast. Denny grabbed his nose and sprinted back into the woods like a rabbit fleeing from danger. He never looked at me. I didn't have a chance to say sorry because I was still in shock at what had just transpired.

The boys looked past me and screamed at Denny, "Go ahead and run you pussy!" Then they watched him run back into the woods until their gaze met upon me.

I was relieved that they didn't go and chase him again, but I was terrified at what their reaction was going to be towards me who was still left standing in a sea of chaos.

I didn't know what Jim and Tommy were capable of or how they would react by not having declared this whole show a victory.

I felt myself backing up slowly as more sweat started to bead on my forehead. I thought for sure they could see my shirt moving from my heart pounding through the cloth on my chest because I knew I was in trouble now, not Denny. Suddenly, I was that spider in the bathtub, pretending to play dead. I hoped I would get a break from the giants standing above me.

I felt so insignificant in an enormous world.

I made no sudden movements to agitate or provoke Jim and Tommy though. I remembered how my dad taught me to act around boys. He told me not to be pushed around, stand up for myself, but also to know my place in time, as well as not put myself in situations where there was no way out. I had done the opposite, reacted quickly, and this is where I ended up. I wanted my dad to come save me, but I had no choice but to figure my way out of this danger on my own.

Jim and Tommy had a look of pure disdain on their faces. Just minutes earlier they looked at me as their equal, and now seconds later I was their enemy.

I didn't care for the way they were looking at my body and it made me shiver. I stood there longer thinking of my exit plan because I knew I had to get out of there. I looked down at my feet because I wanted to run just like Denny, but I wasn't sure if they would start chasing me so I stood there.

Jim broke the silence and turned to Tommy and said, "Maybe Tammy should be taught a lesson to mind her own fucking business. What do you think Tommy?" He paused for a second with a nasty smirk. Tommy said nothing, so he went on. "Why did you follow, Tammy, if you weren't going to help us out by teaching Denny a lesson about being a man?"

I wanted with all my might to punch Jim right in the face, but I knew my opponents and there was no way I would be able to beat off the two of them, let alone one.

Jim stood there looking like a salivating dog. I was so uneasy with the way he was looking at me, but to my surprise, and relief, Tommy came towards me smiling and reached out for a high five.

"That was awesome, Tammy. You kicked ass," Tommy said. It made me very nervous that he got that close to me.

I half slapped his hand in disbelief at what I had done and pissed at myself that I even was able to do something so horribly mean. But this gesture by Tommy was my get of jail free card. I had to take advantage of it. At least Tommy had somewhat of a conscience. I was not at all sure what Jim was capable of for sure. I breathed in heavily and knew that my only way out was to leave immediately.

"I gotta go," and with a quick pivot, I ran back home just as quickly as Denny did.

I was trying so hard to run fast not only to get away from Jim and Tommy, but also to catch up with Denny if I could. Each step was like cement planting a guilty print into the ground, but I kept running until I got to the bottom of the path towards my house. Denny was nowhere to be found. I stopped and looked around to make sure the boys weren't on my tail. There was no sign of them either, so I stood still for a moment trying to take it all in under the quiet hush of the trees. I took in some deep breaths and sat down on the ground. The tears just started flowing. I knew I couldn't undo anything that just happened. It physically made my insides crawl. I leaned over and started vomiting there on the dry ground.

While I lay there crying, gagging and sobbing, I looked up and saw a little caterpillar on the ground. It looked like it had just made its way out of its egg. All this chaos and a little caterpillar peacefully left his warm shelter. Every little step was an obstacle for this tiny little creature. It looked like it was making its way over to the tree nearby, but it had such a far way to go. There were so many variables that could have ended up killing this little guy unintentionally. I started to think about this journey and how it would be awful to just be born and then die right away because of something bigger, something with a little more clout or someone not paying attention to the world around them.

How many caterpillars did I run over on my way up to the meadow today? How many have I stepped on unknowingly over the years of playing in this forest? I wanted to give this caterpillar a safe gap to make up for the torture I just delivered. I suddenly felt the need to redeem myself for the actions I had taken. I very lightly laid the back of my hand down on the ground and grabbed a small twig. I used the twig to gently move the caterpillar onto the palm of my hand. It felt soft and tickly. I almost dropped it.

I walked it over to the tree and put it right on the bark so it could climb out to the leaves and prepare to eat. I watched the caterpillar for a while before it took on the task of eating itself until oblivion before turning itself into a chrysalis. One day that safe space of the chrysalis where it was kept quiet and reflective would ultimately be too tight, too constraining, and it would have to bust out. Its wings would be wet for a bit, before completely morphing into a butterfly. It would fly away quietly without anyone noticing on a warm summer day under the scorching hot sun. I found great peace watching this caterpillar. I laid there for a while savoring these precious minutes until the stench of my own vomit dragged me right back into reality.

I got up, covered my vomit with dirt and made my way home. When I got close to the house, I could smell the barbeque going. Dad was making burgers and corn on the cob. With every ounce of my being, I wanted to eat this dinner. It was one of my favorite summer meals, but I knew for sure I wasn't going to be able to eat. For once, I had lost my appetite. I also knew that I was not ever going to be able to tell this story to anyone. I just couldn't, and that about ate me alive, but over the years I learned to bury it within me.

As I made my way up the path to the back yard, my dad greeted me with his signature phrase, "Hey slugger, whatcha been up to?"

"Oh nothing," I said as a matter of fact, with my heart still beating out of my chest.

"Well, go let Mom know you're home because she was worried about you. She wanted me to get the sniffing dogs out after you," he chuckled.

"Why would Mom be so worried?" I asked.

"Well, Jenny called her and said you were supposed to be coming over, and when you didn't show she got concerned so she called Mom."

With all that had happened I completely forgot I was setting off to go to Jenny's.

I went into the kitchen and found Mom finishing the coleslaw for dinner. I opened the screen door and then it smack-shut behind me. Mom said she always loved that sound of the screen door opening because it was the sound of those she loved the most coming home.

"Oh, I am so glad to see you! When Jenny called and said you didn't show up, I got concerned," Mom said.

"I see. It looks like you were worried," I said sarcastically.

"Well, little missy. I am glad to see you, but why weren't you at Jenny's? And if you weren't there, then where were you?" Mom said.

"I, um, I just didn't feel like going there, so I decided just to go on a nature walk instead," I lied.

I realized I acted violently and now I was lying to my mother as well. I wondered what kind of person I was becoming. I had become a hater and liar and I loathed feeling like this about myself.

"That sounds strange honey, are you ok?"

"Fine Mom. Sometimes I just want to be by myself. Is that a problem?" More lies.

"No, of course not. I guess you are just getting older now and things are changing," Mom said with a smile and she tapped me on the head. She handed me the plates and told me to set the table.

Upon walking to the table, I started thinking about that caterpillar. That little insect will go through massive changes in a very short time. I wanted to tell my mom what happened but I was too ashamed. I couldn't even tell my sister and I certainly wasn't going to tell my dad. What would they think of me? Would they ever look at me the same way again? Just the mere thought of them looking at me in horror was enough to keep this secret locked inside forever.

During our campfires out in the backyard there always seemed to be such ease of being genuine. This is where we spent our time talking about the events of the day. I always felt this was the absolute safest place on Earth to unleash a secret. But even that night after dinner when we went to sit outside by the fire and listened to the snaps of embers along with Mom's stories, I knew for certain I had to let this secret burn into ashes when the fire was put out for the evening. The thought of interrupting such a sacred time with the atrocity I was part of would have created a chasm in the backyard and in our family.

The pressure in my head starts to build and I don't make any sudden movements because I feel my head could easily explode. I look out at the sky and see the sun getting ready to push its way off the horizon. Darkness settles in as I sit alone in the backyard. The silence spread before me was as big as a crater that I created on that day many years ago.

Chapter 20

Ashley

> *"Familiarity breeds contempt – and children."*
> *-Mark Twain*

It feels so good to dance again so I keep going after "Upside Down." I do one routine after the other. I can't believe how most of the moves just flow right back into my body.

I feel wildly free for the first time in a long while.

I don't care about my emails, tennis club, texts, or social media. I am dancing right here in my living room like it is my own private stage. It isn't until I go into the kitchen to fill up my water bottle that I notice the clock. Apparently, I have been dancing for hours and I've lost track of the time in the presence of my own rhythm.

I start to scramble because I have to get to my spa appointment. My weekly massages are not something I need to be late for. The spa isn't close, so I have to hurry to get there. I quickly get into the shower and leave with my wet hair in a ponytail.

When I get into the car, Queen's "Crazy Little Thing Called Love" comes on. This was another routine song I danced to. This song can make anyone's heart sing, but not mine because it makes me think of my mom and how she ruined my last dancing routine in high school.

She was even capable of stripping the love out of one of the happiest songs written. Then, like at any point I think of my mother, the air flow leaves every crevice of space in my car. I have to open the window to let more air in. It's incredible how a song can take me back to a time and place, or even a smell or a setting, good or bad.

I should change the station, but I listen anyway to try and make peace with my love-hate relationship with this song. I try to focus on the road, but I can't help replaying my senior year dance routine in my head and how my mother ruined something so sacred to me.

My release of captivity from my mother's love forced its appearance at my very last competition at the end of my senior year of high school. In poms, dancers were considered a squad, where everyone needed to be on with each other at all times. We were constantly counting fours and eights over and over in our heads, while gathering feel, placing our hands and feet correctly, coming in at solo jumps or acrobatics at the precise beat to a song and looking peripherally to make sure we were on target with the people around us. So, if we were even a second off in competition, it showed. This was the only time in my life where my mind was set on discipline and feel. I have been searching for that inner peace I felt with squad dancing ever since. I came close to that peace while dancing by myself today.

I try to get happy and switch my thoughts to my dad instead. I think about how he made ninety-five percent of my performances and took pride in coming. The only time he missed was when he had to be out of town for work. My dad came because he knew how much it meant to me, because I am sure he had other things he wanted to do than watch teenagers dance, but he was always there with a smiling face in the crowd of madness. I know sometimes he did not like particular moves or thought they were too provocative, but he never said anything. He just grinned, kept quiet, and for as long as I can remember, he always brought me flowers afterwards, no matter what, always. When he wasn't there, it honestly felt like there was a lag in the music.

My thoughts quickly move back to my mom, who was at every one of my performances from age three up to my last routine of my high school career. It was rare when she threw out a compliment, and she never got me flowers. It was always her passing the flowers from my father and saying, "Daddy got your these for you sweetie." Just once I wanted her to say they were from her too, but I never had the courage to speak back to her.

My mom was also a "yeah butter." She was one of those people that started off with a good thing to say, yet placed a "but" after the good thing, thus negating the good. She would say things like, "You really looked lovely sweetie, but I wish we left your hair down instead of up." Or, "Your outfit was so pretty, but your strap was hanging off your shoulder." It was never just, "I thought you did well!"

The older I got, she became the Charlie Brown adult voice droning on and on, not at all understandable. I would purposely not look for her in the audience and pretend she wasn't there. If I spotted her at any moment, I knew my body would feel like the releasing of the air out of a beautiful hot air balloon that just took flight on a warm, pastel painted Arizona evening.

Bright red brake lights flash into my vision and knock me into reality as I slam on my brakes. My heart quickly shifts from a beat to pounding thumps. I am two inches from the bumper in front of me at the stoplight. I quickly look in my rear-view mirror and hear the brakes screech from the person behind me. I didn't even realize I was coming to the stoplight. The Queen song ends and I ignore the beeping from behind me. Not my fault. That guy behind me should have been paying attention. Good thing he didn't hit my car or I'd be even later than I am right now.

My heartbeat subsides and I realize that even in my own thoughts my mother haunts every aspect of my being. The light turns green and I start thinking how I love Queen, but my mom ruined their vibe for me since my dance team did a Queen medley for our final senior competition. I start thinking of that day, replaying it still, over and over. I can't remember when my anniversary is, but I can remember every detail of that day.

When I was dancing when I was little, I loved getting the flowers, putting makeup on, the rehearsals, the costumes, and getting my hair done. My mom would put sponge rollers in my hair the night before a performance. I felt like a little beauty queen when I woke up and unrolled the roller for lovely locks of golden bounce. My mom would put me in front of her lightbulb vanity making me feel like a movie star. This was the time I enjoyed with my mother because she pampered me and gave me attention. She would fix my hair, adjust my outfit, and put make-up on me. I always loved the finishing touch of the lip gloss, as well. I was able to taste the strawberries of the balm cascade over my lips like dew drops dancing on a leaf on a fresh spring morning. I felt alive; I felt like a young adult. This was the only time I felt loved by my mother. She wanted me to feel good before I performed, so she told me how pretty I was, how I was chosen to be in the front because I worked the hardest. It wasn't until I got into middle school that her harsh critiques after performances destroyed my bouncy curls. My blush was no longer a vibrant red, and the strawberry lip gloss was sloppy mud on tires instead of moisture from dew drops.

Therefore, by the time I got into high school, I didn't want my mom anywhere near me when I was getting ready. She was flat out a nuisance with her, "Darling, you should wear your hair up," or, "Let me put a darker eyeshadow on with glitter so your eyes pop," and on and on. I would close the door of the bathroom. There were vanity lights, but the glass popped from the bulbs leaving chards of unhappy remnants on the cold tile floor. I needed my own light, my own way.

As I was getting ready for my last routine of my high school career, my mom knocked on my door. "Do you want me to check the back of your hair and leotard to make sure everything looks ok?"

"No, I got it Mom."

I was ready to come out so I had to open the door, but I knew she would be waiting for me on the other side. There was no way one giant piece of wood between us could keep her away. I opened the door, and there she was standing there with this cynical look on her face. I felt similar to how one would stand in front of a judge waiting for my verdict, except twelve people weren't deciding my fate; it was one lone, loud juror.

"Are you sure that is the right eye shadow for that outfit? I was thinking that pink glitter eyeshadow would accent the black leotard, that's all."

"Is that all?" I said snottily.

"No, actually it is not," my mom proceeded on. "Dad is coming, but he has to come right from work so he will meet us there. I'll be heading up there on my own unless you want me to drive you," she said.

"No, thanks Mom, I'll just see you there," I said as I continued to stand and stare pretending to be happy while not showing any feelings on my face. I didn't feel like arguing with her on this day of all days. I rushed by her so she couldn't get another glimpse of me to critique.

"How are you getting there?" Mom said.

"Liz is coming to get me and she'll be here in ten minutes, so I have to get moving here," I said rifling through my bag to make sure I had everything I needed.

She followed me to my room. Her presence was making me so nervous.

"Ok, that's fine, but are you sure you have the right eyeshadow on for that outfit?"

"Yes, I am sure Mom." I sighed quietly. I so desperately wanted to say, "Whose day is it, mine or yours?" But I bit my tongue and stayed quiet.

Thinking back, I should have blown up before I left, because in my head my mind was spinning with how much I loathed this woman instead of remembering my steps, direction, and being in the moment.

I finished gathering my stuff, trying so hard to avoid speaking to her. I got all my things together, walked past her, ran downstairs and went to the living room by the open window overlooking the driveway. I waited patiently for Liz to come while going over the counts in my head to get into my mental zone.

Liz was one of my best friends growing up. Her parents had a ton of money, like us, but they moved from their house next door to an even larger house in the next town over. She was beautiful, smart, and a hell of a dancer. We really were a team in creating the center of attention around us at all times. I always felt like she was my twin sister.

But her one flaw was that she was notoriously late. Of all days, I wanted her to for once show up on time; she didn't. I was running over the routines waiting by the front door when my mom came downstairs. Nails on a chalkboard was an understatement for her wretched voice. The sound waves of her voice made their way to my ears and it made the little hairs on my neck stand up. No matter how hard she tried, she just couldn't leave me alone.

"Liz is always late, you know," she said with a judgmental tone. "Are you sure she remembered that she has to pick you up? I can take you sweetie if you would rather get there on time. You know this is a big day."

"Of course, I know mom, really," I said with a terse voice. As I finished that sentence Liz came in on two wheels, a wing, and a prayer. "All good Mom; no need to worry," I said. I gave a half smile, blew a kiss, and ran out of there as fast as I could so she wasn't able to have the last word.

I got in the car and Liz was all dolled up, ready to go. She looked as if she had the best night's sleep, all put together neatly like a package under the tree on Christmas morning. She was one of those gifts so nicely wrapped tight that no one wants to open because it's too pretty. Her mom was always there at our performances with flowers and a smile, complete with hugs and positive words always, and not only towards her daughter, but all of us on the team. She went out of her way to make us feel appreciated.

Liz was the one who seemed to have it all together more than me. However, I found out later she had her fair share of skeletons. Turns out her mom gave her all the praise she needed because her father was never around. The rumor was that her dad was sleeping with everyone but her mom, and this caused considerable stress on Liz. She always seemed to appear like she had it all, but I knew deep down she was a delicate flower on the verge of wilting. I knew that even though she was running late on such a big day, she would manage to create the scene to look calm as ever because this is how her mom handled her marriage. Like her mother, Liz was Miss-All-Put-Together and a train wreck under all the veneer of paint shellacked on her face, complete with Vaseline on her teeth to keep the smile wide.

"What?" she said nonchalantly.

"You already put the Vaseline on your teeth?" I snarled.

"Yes; gotta be the best dear," she bragged. "What's with you? This is our last routine together and may be our last one ever, so quit your fucking whining you little bitch," she said laughing.

She always looked so cool. I can see her face now in my head, the sun filtering off her neon Ray Bans. Her teeth were pearly white and her gum chewing jaws moved up and down to the beat of Def Leppard's *Love Bites*. I wanted to be like her, so polished and relaxed, but I let my mom seep into my core, a nail driving into a board, smacked hard into place. I braced for impact. I was polished for sure, but nowhere near as cool and relaxed as Liz. I wanted to trade places with her.

"My Mom was all over my case this morning and she pissed me off," I said. "I think she does it on purpose, you know, just to fuck with my head."

"Well, it sounds like it's working, so cut it out already. Don't let her fuck up our routine. Just flush it."

I always hated when Liz said that. All I pictured was a big piece of shit that wouldn't go down and clog the toilet. "Well, that's easy for you to say Liz, because your mom isn't up your ass like my mom. I was running over steps in my head and she knocked me out of my concentration. I had to spend the extra time I had coming up with schemes to keep her the fuck away from me."

"Where was your dad?" Liz said. "He is usually good about distracting your mom.

"He is working and coming later, thank God. Everything's better when he's around," I said instantly, making me feel better.

"At least you have your dad around. God only knows where my dad was last night, or any other night for that matter," Liz said flippantly.

I ignored her comment because I had my own baggage to deal with. I didn't feel like opening her suitcase to see if she had brought everything with her. I knew she liked my dad because she always saw him as encouraging to me. She also saw how my dad doted all over my mom. I knew she wished her dad would do the same for her mom.

Def Leppard was in the background shouting out the tragic ballad, "love bites . . . love bleeds."

"Forget it, I don't want to waste any more time on my mom," I droned. I reached into my purse and pulled out the Queen medley tape for the routine. "Can I put this in to listen to it on the way there,"

I motioned to Liz while dangling the tape like a piece of meat in front of a tiger.

"Come on now Ash, I think you have heard it ten thousand times for fuck's sake," she snickered.

"You can't turn Def Leppard off now? Come on!" I sighed and looked out the window. "Ok, fuck it then, you're right. I am so psyched to dance. I am not even going to look at her. I just hope my dad shows up."

When we got close to McCormick Place in the city, we came up along Interstate fifty-five. The highway curves along the bend and there in all her glory is the aquamarine and serene Lake Michigan. It's like coursing up a mountaintop to the summit to say, "Ah."

As a kid, I used to love riding in the car and getting to this point in the drive downtown. After sitting in traffic and finally as far East as the highway could go to hit Lake Michigan, it felt like reaching the promised land. It didn't matter what the temperature was or the elements, I would, like clockwork, crack the window a bit to take in the fresh water smell. As a kid, my parents would yell and scream for me to roll the window up, but over time it turned into a secret family laughter. I would roll my window down at the precise time Lake Michigan came into view and say, "Ah."

Only my family knew about my fetish whenever we came around this bend. I couldn't explain this to anyone, and after I cracked the window open and said "Ah," I looked at Liz to see if she noticed.

She did look over, but all she said was, "Roll the window up for fuck's sake. It's going to ruin our hair!"

I smiled to myself thinking of one of the good old times with my family. There was something so settling in that view of Lake Michigan to me, like a place in my heart I always knew as home, yet it meant absolutely nothing to Liz which in a strange way made my heart wince a little, longing for my childhood with a family I once loved.

Knowing I am going to be late for the spa, I come up to the same bend and see Lake Michigan snapping me out of the daydreaming mode I was in.

"It's always good to see you," I say to myself and roll down the window. I say, "Ah . . . " It never gets old today to say this but today my "Ah" feeling feels heavy, like the choppy waves in front of me waiting to swallow me whole. My mind shifts back to the dance competition as I pass McCormick Place, which is a large black building with wide open spaces for expos.

When we got to the competition at McCormick Place, we made our way down what seemed like mile-long tunnels to reach our destination. The place was filled with signs pointing to our school and girls just hustling and moving fast to get to our spots with our teammates. As we were walking, I was able to see some of the parents trying to keep up with their kids, some hovering and doting. It made me feel nauseous because I felt for those girls. I was thrilled not to be followed, but it made me think of my mom and how I knew she would desperately want to be here for this part following me.

It's hard to describe the exact feelings before getting ready to perform, but the easiest way to describe it is like the nervousness felt while standing in line to get on a scary rollercoaster. There's some heart pounding and a longing for escape, but once the ride is underway there is no turning back and a wanting for more. This is always how I felt at every competition. Even if I was scared, I sure as hell wasn't going to let anyone see it.

My favorite time before the dance was our group huddle. I went to a private school, so we always started out with a prayer. I didn't think too much about the prayers because they never made much sense in a modern world. The huddle to me was based more on the way others looked, so solemn and calm, not necessarily about the words themselves. Were we really thinking God was going to get us a number one trophy here just because we were from a private school?

Weren't there more pressing things going on in the world God needed to attend to? I went through the motions anyways because I did what everyone else was doing because we were a team. My skill was not really based on my faith in God. Sure, I went to a private school, took religion classes, but my parents were drive-by Catholics. They were the ones who sent us to Catholic schools, put us through the rituals but never explained why they wanted us to go down this path.

My brother and I would ask questions, but my parents never came back with anything substantial but to say, "We did this as kids so you will too," and that was all we were given and no questions encouraged. We were the Chreasters, the ones who went to church only at school and hated every minute of the boring, droning priest, and then adorned the church walls on the holidays like we were a holy rolling family.

The worst was how my mom thought she owned the place when we would enter the mass on Easter or Christmas. She used the middle row between the pews as a red-carpet runway for her to show off her latest outfit and gorgeous figure at her age. Her jaunt down the aisle was more like a tightrope walk, so balanced, so fragile with one foot after another, hoping not to fall in front of the eying parishioners watching her every move.

My dad was at her side like Prince Charming, looking dapper and always together. These people all knew about this phony pomp and circumstance my parents put on. I was surprised a bolt of lightning never came down to strike them up into a mushroom cloud of hypocritical smoke. Yet all those other people praying would sit in judgment themselves. I was quite sure coffee time after church was spent desecrating my mother. Religion was all a game of who was better than who, and I always found the people at church displayed a surface level of humanity.

Back in my last huddle of my time in dance, our coach started off with a prayer of a Hail Mary, proceeded by our daily pep talk about how we work hard, we drill hard, we play hard, and none of it was hard anymore because we owned that floor! Our hands were down, clasped all together and hands up and out as we shouted, "Go Saints Go!!!"

I will always remember that moment, the smell of wanting to win, the nerves in my stomach, the excitement, all of it. And then we ran off in full steam to our positions, like gazelles coming to a standstill in the savannah; we stopped, we waited, we moved in sync. The lights were out and our heads were down, our chests moved in and out as the pulses of our heartbeats made it look like waves of beads moving on our chests. I was able to hear us all breathing, and Liz, who was my dancer to the right, breathed out a sigh and said, "Last dance lady, last dance." I smiled with my head down and closed my eyes deeply.

Once the music started and the lights hit our bodies, that was my cue to breathe deep as the bass from Queen's "Another One Bites the Dust" set the rhythm. I felt myself come out of my shell. I was a turtle feeling the warm sun after spending its time in chilly water all day. The bass drove the song and it was the catalyst for the movement in all of our songs in the Queen medley. I rarely looked out into the audience when I was dancing, but something pulled me away from my focus and count. I was able to feel it. "Don't look up," I said to myself. But I made the move and looked out into the audience and this proved to be a fatal mistake. I immediately saw my mom front and center, and then my dad hurrying in fashionably late and frenzied as he hopped over people to take his seat.

From the stage I was able to see my mom's disgusted look at my dad that he was late. If someone didn't rise to her occasion, the world would end for her, pure and simple, and she let you know it. I let her presence seep into my mind and felt her heat, and then I was out of my zone, that quickly. I was off and behind the beat by a fraction of a second. This caused me to miss a move to keep in sync with the others.

I was trying desperately to keep up with Liz and make up for the time I lost. It was not easy to jump back up into the time when it's lost, but I also knew it could be done with the amount of practice I had endured over the years.

I had lost the beat and gotten back to the rhythm many times over the years, but this time it wasn't my physicality, it was a total breach of my mental capacity. The dominoes went down and I couldn't stop what was going to happen next.

Because I was off and behind, I went out for my running cartwheel, into a round off, and back flip seconds off where it should have been, thus all the girls behind me that needed to do the same thing were late, then it wasn't synchronized to the beat after doing that dance hundreds of times. My team didn't even have to say anything because I could feel their heat, like the sun beating down on a hot black car. But in typical me-fashion, I didn't make eye contact with anyone. I wasn't going to admit I was off or even say anything. I felt if I ignored it then it simply didn't happen. I was just too embarrassed and pissed that I had been the one to mess this up for everyone and it was all because of my mother.

Once this song ended, we went right into the other Queen songs for the medley and I was able to get back on time, but not before making several more fatal errors. At one point I was ready to commit the cardinal sin in dancing: just stop and leave the stage. But that was not ever an option, and especially not in the final competition.

I felt a sudden urge to throw up. I was not enjoying myself at all on my last performance possibly ever, and that is what didn't sit well with me. I tried so hard to fight my mind and enjoy the music, but I couldn't. I remember thinking that this would be the last time I could ever listen to Queen again. Like today, whenever it comes on the radio or anywhere it sends a shiver to my body, a constant reminder of my negligence but mostly disdain for my mother.

While it seemed like time had stood still, I made it through the rest of the dance. At the end, our bodies fell to the floor with a dramatic hair sweep with our heads flopping down to the ground in a split. I felt like I could stay there forever with my scissored legs and my chest wide open along with a split heart for everyone to see. I can't remember a time in my life where I felt this uncomfortable with thoughts of anger, disappointment, shock, and bitterness all wrapped up into one. I was able to feel myself getting ready to explode, like the fizzle after a firecracker is lit. The crackle is heard, a sizzle pops, and the smell of smoke and the anticipation of the sparkles pierce ears with a giant burst of flames.

I picked my head up and tried so hard not to cry or show any emotion, but that was like being a bull tiptoeing through a China shop. I was usually good at keeping a poker face and made damn sure I did exactly that upon standing up. I held my head up and smiled over my greasy lips and held the fake smile like a creepy doll from a toy store. When I looked out into the crowd, my dad was standing and his face gave me a slight glimmer of comfort. I didn't want to do it, but my eyes were drawn to my mom. I had so much fury inside me because without a question of a doubt this was her fault. I caught a terse glance at my mom for a split second and it felt like I had seen the flame of Mordor. Not only did my mom not get up from her seat, but she was just sitting there cold as a statue, arms crossed with no emotion. I was staring at her failure. She fucked this up, not me.

I swerve up into the spa like Jeff Gordan. I don't remember most of the ride here. The valet greets me by my name, which knocks me into reality, takes my keys and I head inside to unwind. I fucking hate my mom. She is the reason my whole life is fucked up. I need a drink and a massage, that fucking bitch.

Chapter 21

Tammy

> *"The more you know yourself, the more you forgive yourself."*
> *-Confucius*

ONE thing in life is a guarantee: The sun always rises, then sets no matter what happens in the busyness of the day. A glimmer of light comes peeking through the top of the chasm after the hours of darkness overnight. I am in my childhood backyard again because I haven't found a reason to leave. There is light chatter in the background, but I have a strong longing to stay here. Ahead of me in eye distance lies a hammock my dad tied to two trees many years ago.

It is a lovely surprise to me that it is still there, unkept, yet welcoming. Walking over I slowly sit down. The cloth sinks into my heavy body and encompasses me. I am almost touching the ground because I have become quite large since I last lay here many years ago, but something inside tells me it won't break due to the solid construction from my father. I lie here in complete bliss. Now I know what it feels like to be a butterfly. This warm blanket will shield me from the world before getting ready to stretch out and fly to other places. I feel the tranquility immediately with slight apprehension for what lies ahead. The rocking motion back and forth reminds me of my mother's arms and it takes some of the pressure off of my throbbing head for now. But that warmth leaves me quickly as I feel a damp breeze with some cold raindrops falling on my face. It sends a shiver down my spine as the hammock stops swaying. I gaze out in front of me and now my backyard looks like an eerie maze. I look up at the sky to divert my attention to my uneasiness that came over me. The clouds change shape above the treetops.

I start swaying back and forth again. But even the peacefulness of this cradle can't subdue the demons that creep into my mind about a dark memory that happened here in my backyard. I start to think about my younger self going through the kitchen door after that horrible day of beating up Denny so many years ago.

On that day when I beat up Denny, my mom had so many questions about where I was. I knew where I was, but I didn't tell her I was out in the meadow beating up Denny while Jim and Tommy watched. I also remember being out of breath in the kitchen telling one lie after the other while she was cooking dinner.

I don't know what was worse, making up the lies to my mom for covering my actions, or the actual physical and mental damage I caused Denny. I can't believe I never had the courage to talk about Denny with even the most trusted people in my life around the most comfortable setting in front of the fire pit. If I had just spoken up, I wouldn't have hidden this experience so deep within me all of these years. I would be able to sway back and forth in soft silence on the hammock, my mind not so filled with clutter.

This story was a sunken boat, hidden with the weight of the water above it for years until my son Alex unknowingly hoisted the boat back up to the surface. I start to cry thinking about how much I miss seeing my son Alex every day. Just thinking of his electric smile and laugh makes me grin, and all the pain in my head subsides until all I can hear is a moderate wind moving the hammock side to side. I wish he would come to me now, tell me everything is going to be okay, and that I will find my way.

I sway and grin thinking back to the early teenage years when Alex and I were in the car and he was learning how to drive. This is when the story of Denny came out because I found that my most profound conversations with my son were in the car, shoulder to shoulder. We would go for miles and miles practicing, and finally he got better and was able to drive and tell stories. On one of those drives he started talking about his good friend of his who just came out as being gay. As the years passed, stories of acceptance, struggle and protests changed the landscape I once knew. Over space and time, the plates shifted underground and the tide changed. In this metamorphosis of the Earth, the secret I held buried under those plates surfaced to the top in the newly formed landscape sticking out as a sharp jagged rock.

As we were driving, I would catch a glance at Alex and sit in disbelief that he was driving me around instead of the opposite, so sometimes I would get lost in those mom thoughts and half-listened to his stories. But this particular time in the car, he caught my attention immediately as if someone had punched me in the stomach. My story about Denny had lain dormant, deprived of air, and now there it was right in our car breathing again. All of a sudden, I felt the seatbelt crushing my guilt heavy on my chest.

Alex spoke so nonchalantly with his hands lined on the wheel at ten and two. "So, one of my friends told me today he is gay."

I sat up straight and felt the seatbelt pull tighter to my chest as thoughts of Denny instantly popped into my head. A car stopped abruptly before us, red brake lights flashing at my instantaneous shame. I threw my hand out instinctively across Alex's chest and pressed the imaginary brake on the passenger side down with my foot so hard I let out a shriek.

"Mom, don't do that, please," snapped Alex. "I had more than enough time to stop. You make me nervous when you do that!"

I remember my heart beating fast while beads of sweat started to form. I couldn't handle this new territory of no control and the dread of my story at the same time. I tried to act calm and just dismissed my overreaction on the passenger side.

"Oh really, who told you they were gay?" I said.

"Cade," said Alex.

"Oh, wow, how did this all come about?" I inquired.

"Pretty simple actually. We were all playing football and when we sat down on the grass to have a drink he just blurted out, 'Guys, I'm gay.' There were like three seconds and Nico asked him why it took him so long to tell us. Then I said, 'Is that why you suck at football?' We all started laughing and went on to the next thing. I could tell he was so relieved."

"And that was it?" I said.

"Yup, that was it. We figured if any of the other guys didn't like it, they sure the hell weren't going to say anything, and if they did, we'd have to kick their ass," he said without a flinch.

I sat looking at him in disbelief for a while. This is not at all how any of this would have gone down with my group of girlfriends or my sister Dawn. There might have been tears, shrieks, judgment, or flat-out gossip. I wasn't surprised at Alex's response though because he was always mature before his age. I just marveled at the open acceptance I had not known as a child.

"Boy, we've come a long way," I said, shaking my head. "I know when I was younger, being gay came up in class or anywhere I would hear things like it's Adam and Eve not Adam and Steve."

"Oh my gosh Mom, that's horrible. What the hell?"

"I know," I said. "I am embarrassed to admit this but I laughed and agreed with that statement at one point in my life. I just went with what others thought and the whole thing of a guy being with a guy or woman with a woman was so foreign to me that I viewed it as weird. It wasn't until I got older and started reading more that I knew I acted like an ignorant fool. It made me think about how dumb I sounded, not to mention who I hurt in the process feeling that way. You young kids now just have so much more open-minded views and that's awesome. I think about my childhood and how being gay was viewed, and it was simply not acceptable."

My son just sat quietly, shook his head and said, "That sucks."

"I know." I paused for a second, my whole body feeling all of the senses back to the day when I chastised Denny. I suddenly felt a powerful urge to relinquish this story to someone I completely trusted: my son.

"You know what? I never told anyone this story, but I am going to tell you," I sighed. I told the story with all of its detail and emotion as if I was reliving it again, right there with my son, shoulder to shoulder. I never looked him in the eye as I was telling it. Alex was driving with his face contorted in a way that resembled him smelling something really bad. I sat zombie-like, stared out the window and told the story that hadn't hit open air since it happened. It was like I was retelling it in slow motion and it made me feel very nervous and shaky. Only the animals heard Denny's frightful echoes on that day reverberating off the trees. Many years later, the story stained the air with a horrid aroma. Every single one of my senses was heightened just as the day it all happened, like how I wanted to vomit again, my insides all tangled. When I got to the end of the story, I was sweating again while a tear started rolling down my thick cheek. I hadn't expected to get this emotional this many years later. I had my head down, my voice was trailing off into the distance.

Alex had pulled the car over to the end of our driveway, idling softly while he put the car in park. I felt him turn to look at me. I had to face the music and look at him too. The stare he gave me was the look I envisioned my family giving me if I had told them, and it felt worse to have my own son look at me like this. I instantly started regretting telling him this deep and guarded secret.

He didn't say anything for a moment and then he spoke with a serious voice. "Mom, Cade is one of my good friends. Can you imagine someone doing this to him?" he said sadly.

"No, I can't, and I am sorry that I was that someone at one point in my life."

"Did you ever tell your parents, or Auntie Dawn? I just can't believe you of all people would do something like that," he said.

That statement crushed me right in half. I hoped he didn't think less of me because I couldn't go to sleep knowing that Alex was ashamed of his own mother.

"No, this is the first time I have ever talked about this out loud because I buried it so deeply," I said, shaking my head.

I wanted to tell him about the caterpillar I saved that day. Somehow that small act made me feel like I could make up for the pain I had caused to get rid of the guilt, but I left that part out because I was not even sure if he would believe me. Maybe he would think I inserted a Disney-like scene here to make up for the shitstorm I created.

"You know I don't feel this way now, of course, and if I could take it back from time, it would be the first memory I would erase." Suddenly I was even more ashamed than the day it happened. I started crying again, but this time I started sobbing.

"That's a really bad story, Mom, but you're not bad. You know, just like you tell me. You made a mistake so please stop crying because that makes me sad," he said as he reached in for a hug. "You can't continue to beat yourself up, right? You know you could see if you can find Denny on Facebook," he suggested.

I wiped my eyes with the sleeve of my shirt, wiping my conscience. "You're right, I could, but I doubt he would want to be friends with me after all these years. Would you?" I said inquisitively.

"I don't know, but an apology might go somewhere, ya never know."

I thought about Alex's suggestion. When we got inside, Alex went to make himself something to eat. I plopped onto the couch, took out my phone, and started a virtual manhunt for Denny. One link led me to another, then down into a black hole that got me absolutely nowhere.

"Where could he be? Did he ever find a safe haven?" All I wanted to do was apologize, but I had to accept the fact that this may never happen. I had to make this peace within myself, and I felt like just the mere fact of vocalizing this story to my son was a step in the right direction of chipping away at the iceberg of guilt I had felt all of those years.

My head pounds now with pulses of rhythm that circulate through my temples to the swaying of the hammock. I want to fall asleep again. I want to go back to a chrysalis because my wings are still wet. I need to be ready to wake up with dry wings, stretch, and push out of the warmth into a new spring-like current. Being in the chrysalis wasn't the end of me. I had crawled all over and searched for food to eat for survival. When I wake from slumber, I have a world to see when I morph into a beautiful butterfly.

Chapter 22

Ashley

> *"Truths and roses have thorns about them."*
> *- Henry David Thoreau*

I half-run into the building and I am greeted by Nancy, the pleasant receptionist. She is always the first person I see. Each time I see her she nauseates me because she is always so damn happy. I don't know what she looks like without a smile because she is always smiling. I'd like to knock that fucking grin right off her pink-hued cheeks. How can someone be this pleasant all the time, especially being a receptionist? How much could she possibly get paid? I smirk at her suspiciously, while I eye her up and down focusing in on the veneer smile. There seems to be minutes that pass while we both stare at each other. She is smiling, I am not. I wonder if she is so happy because she gets laid every day. What else can make someone this happy? She is still smiling while handing me a glass of cucumber water. I take the glass from her hastily and a few drops spill out dropping on her paperwork. This bitch is still smiling. It's now actually creepy.

"It's ok, no big deal Ashley. The papers will dry," she says as she makes a cute giggle noise that makes me want to vomit. I lift my eyes up to the ceiling. I think about torching this place with oil and a match right under her fucking desk. Then would she still continue to smile? There is nothing but space and air while she waits patiently to respond.

"Ashley," she says calmly with a pretty little grin that makes the dimple crease in her cheek. "I tried to call you to tell you to come in later, but you didn't answer. Did you get my voicemail?"

"Well, if I am standing in front of you now, I obviously didn't get your message now, did I? I think you called too late, Naaa-ncy." I stretch out her name for dramatic affect.

I wait again before speaking so I can rattle her enough to wipe off her smile. "I was too busy to look at my phone before I left. So, I rushed to get here, really? So no, I didn't get the message. So now what? Does someone else have an opening for me? I am not canceling and coming back so, you need to find someone to give me my massage. I really need it today. Not to mention that this is a terrible inconvenience for me because my whole day is stacked with appointments," I say, which is a lie.

I just had tennis and then needed to be back to get the kids from school. I stand there waiting for that fucking smile to leave her face. But no. She is still smiling at me.

What the fuck? I mumble in my head. She takes a slow, calm breath and continues to smile. She looks like those monks clad in orange robes with not one care in the world with all that peace and love shit.

"The point of coming here is to relax my friend," she says, very Zen-like. "Now take a sip and head into the powder room to change. I'll rearrange things so you can see Brooke shortly, then you will have some time to unwind." She turns again and flashes a serene smile.

Maybe it's not sex at all keeping her happy because I am eyeing Nancy up and down before I head to the powder room as she calls it. What is this, the fifties? I can't imagine Nancy is having sex at all by the way she keeps herself. She has a middle-aged dough look like a circle Mom, complete with no nail polish and barely any make-up on, and her hair tied up in a ponytail with pieces hanging out of place. I can't believe this spa would hire someone who can't take care of their own basic needs. Maybe it's all this meditative music that's piped through here that gives her this permanent grin because it sure isn't how she looks. I continue to stare daggers at her.

I finish the water quickly like I am downing a shot of Jack Daniels. I refuse to smile at her, but she refuses to stop smiling at me. This pisses me off, so I sigh and huff, then leave my glass with her and walk into the powder room. Fuck that stupid game, I've had enough stress already this morning.

I take off my clothes, put them in the locker and sit in my panties and robe. I am bored and annoyed that I had to rush here just to sit and wait. I scroll through Facebook waiting for Brooke. The same music that is being played out in front is playing here too. I try to relax, but I always feel like my brain is a motor on the run and in constant need of fuel.

I look up from my phone for a split second and notice a painting that catches my eye. It's a beautiful rosebush glistening in a gorgeous oil painting. All these years coming, I never noticed this painting until right now. The petals are a perfect shade of pink, the leaves so green, and the thorns so realistic that if I got close to the painting, I would feel their pain. The thought of touching that thorn reminds me of my mother. And just like that, that fucking bitch is back in my head here while I am trying to relax after my run-in with fluffy Nancy. When my mother's withered claws seep into my mind I try to divert to thoughts of my dad. I stare at the painting in a trance and take in some essential oil-filled air. My dad loved the rose bushes that decorated the entrance of my childhood home which was pure and mighty, just like this painting.

I start to daydream about gardening as a child with my dad. His friends never believed that he liked to garden, but he did at one very brief time in his life. Gardening gave my dad great joy before his job robbed him of burying his hands in the earth. After the age of seven, I never once saw my dad's hands dirty again. To this day, he has well-manicured hands that feel soft as a rose petal. He passed the spade to the landscaper when he started making really big money and became an outsider to his own hobby.

Even though my dad wasn't around to plant anymore, I still loved the flowers. I wanted to plant them, water them, and tend to them. I once found it fascinating to watch a seed transform into immense beauty. But my mom couldn't understand why I was so interested in this process. She thwarted my passion and discouraged me from wanting to do something someone else could do. "Cut out the middleman Ashley," she would say. This was her motto for living a life of watching everyone else work hard to keep her occupied and content.

This may have been my first outright defiance of my mom's ways because when I was little, I started to help the gardeners take care of the roses despite her telling me to keep away. I couldn't help it. I was enamored by the rosebush's majestic beauty. When I heard the truck pull up, the sound of the lawnmower starting, I would drop everything I was doing. When the landscapers were at the house, I would sneak out and shadow them. I did this for a while because my mom was always preoccupied with whatever it was she was doing. But one day she happened to be present in what I was up to. She demanded I stop working with the gardener because she found it embarrassing that I wanted to work with the hired help. But I still found ways to sneak around without her knowing. She didn't know that I loved Molly the gardener more than I loved her. Molly loved her job and loved teaching me all about nature. Her hands were dirty and her smile was wide, nothing at all like my mother. She taught me all about those rose bushes that lined the sidewalk before entering my home.

Roses didn't allow you to get too close with the thorns, but what I was really intrigued by was the sucker cane. This is a long stem that shoots out of the rose bush taking on its own personality in an attempt to suffocate the rosebush. Molly taught me how to look for them and get rid of them as soon as possible. A sucker cane will, if left to grow, suck the majority of nutrients necessary for good growth and performance from their counterparts, weakening the upper part of the bush. If left to grow, many times the upper portion of the bush dies. This is why Molly told me removing rose suckers as they sprout was important. Sucker canes will usually take on a totally different growth habit from the rest of the rose bush, which I found fascinating. They will grow tall and a bit wild, much like an untrained climbing rose, but not have the actual flower attached. The leaves on the sucker canes will differ from the leaf structure and sometimes vary a bit in coloration too, with few to no leaves. Rose bush suckers typically will not set buds or bloom, at least in the first year of their growth. Even to the untrained eye, one can pick a blood sucker out immediately.

I think about my dad again while staring at this painting. I know he knew about the bloodsuckers because sometimes I would catch him snipping a few here and there if ever he had a free moment on the weekend. But if he knew about this bloodsucker, then I wondered why he stayed with my mother all of these years? I look at the painting and now I know why my mom didn't want me to take part in the landscaping. This woman who brought me into this garden found out she didn't want to share her beauty. She couldn't have me overtaking her beauty, so she grew her own thorns. She had morphed into the sucker cane to deprive me of the nutrients I needed because she wasn't happy with her own.

I look up again at the painting. I don't see a sucker cane, but now this painting seems darker than when I first walked in as if the sucker cane was there, permeating with its presence, shielding these roses from their natural beauty. I am tempted to rip the painting off the wall now.

I sigh deeply and try to relax. I go back on my phone sighing over the people acting like they're happy on Facebook. How can someone love their kids that much? This one is going to an Ivy League college, this one just got the state trophy for volleyball, smiling faces over a melting butter sunset on a dream vacation. My own kids annoy the fuck out of me. If I posted pictures of my kids it would be a photo of my son playing video games, or my daughter pretending to act like she likes sports, but instead throwing pitches that break bones. I'm so fucking bored. The whole world is out there enjoying it and I am just sitting here waiting for a massage. I have been here over ten minutes and still no Brooke yet. I want to get up and complain, but this painting draws my attention once again.

In this trance my mind shifts back to my thoughts in the car when I heard the Queen song being played. I think about the evening of my last dance competition in high school when I made such atrocious mistakes that cost us winning the title. I remember when the music stopped playing there was a silent stillness. We all left the stage and came down to our huddle and waited. We had to watch one more routine before announcements would be made on who held the state title.

Normally, we would congratulate each other, talk about what went well, what didn't, and sit with nervous excitement while our stomachs turned the size of our bellowing backflips across the stage. This was the time where we would hug and hold each other's hands. We sat deathly quiet on this last leg of our journey, because deep down we knew we weren't going to be on the top, and much of it had to do with my performance. The only person I looked at was Liz. She had a sallow look on her face, took a big sigh, and grabbed my hand. I remember her hand feeling cold and clammy instead of warm.

"It's alright," she whispered. "What will be will be, that's all. But what happened to you out there? I am not trying to make you feel bad, it is just you seemed off in another place. I was trying to give you some of my energy, but you didn't take the bait," she said.

I was slightly annoyed with her what-will-be-will-be bullshit, which was a stupid thing to say. Basically, these words showed me that she didn't have the balls to tell me she was mad at me, and she had no idea how to process this mess. Therefore, she just filled the air with useless words that hung in the balance taking up space. I think people fill space with clichés because they don't have to dive too deep to just blurt out what they are really thinking. I hear it all the time. It drives me nuts. Just don't talk.

"I don't know what happened either," I lied as the words barely came out of my mouth.

"It was your mom, wasn't it," said Liz.

I just shook my head and turned the other way squeezing her hand. She squeezed my hand back. This is exactly what it was but I didn't want to say it out loud.

The last team to perform was the best I have ever seen. Every girl was smiling and every girl was on. They had their routine nailed down from the beginning to the end. They embraced every beat, style, and showcased positive energy. They took the wind right out of our sails.

This deep and visceral jealousy cut through my veins coursing poison throughout my body. We waited for what seemed like an eternity to hear the judges call. When they announced our nemesis had won first place, I felt like my heart was in my mouth. Our heads went down and the tears flowed as fast as the Mississippi River made its way to the gulf. I knew deep down it wasn't just my performance, but I also couldn't deny a good deal of it was me. I just chose to ignore the mistakes the best I could and not discuss it with anyone. We ended up taking third place, which was not bad at all, considering the numerous teams we were up against, but it didn't sit well with any of us, including the coach. She gave us her same speech and prayer as she always did with a loss, but it didn't nearly have the faith it did as when we won. I think she wanted this more than we did. She certainly wasn't going to come over to me and console just me. She just kind of winced, sighed and came over to each of us with half-baited energy.

There is nothing worse than disappointing a coach besides your parents, and that is what happened. The coach fell silent as a church mouse for a few aching minutes in anticipated silence. She never raised her voice because she didn't have to. She said calmly, "We were not the best tonight. We just weren't and there is no way around that. I won't sugar coat anything. Am I disappointed? Yes, because I know you are the first-place team. I know our seniors on the team are upset, however, this is life and life is full of just as many disappointments than our celebrations." A tear moved down her cheek as she gave us all hugs. She walked over to each girl and said something.

I waited there, similar to waiting for a doctor to announce a diagnosis. When it was my turn, she gave me a heartfelt hug from the back of my collar bone to the ends of my toes. It felt like the world was putting a blanket over me. I have never felt this warmth before like I felt from her. She whispered in my ear, "Don't beat yourself up over this. We all make mistakes and sometimes do this at the worst times, but in the end, you always gave it your all. It just wasn't your night tonight for a small moment in time. Think of all the wonderful moments over the years and be proud of your many accomplishments."

All I could do was feel her embrace and hug her tighter. I had no words for my sheer disappointment. My competitive nature was ugly, and for once in my life I could not retaliate with yelling, but just stand there limp in her arms. After our embrace, she grabbed my face and put both of her hands on my cheeks. She reached in and her nose touched mine. She grinned and breathed life into me. She moved on with the utmost class as always and hugged all the other girls. I saw her whispering in everyone's ear with her loving embrace. I longed for her to be my mother. I am sure she was saying something different to everyone because she knew each and every one of us from the beads on the leotard to the tips of our hair. She was what I have always wanted in a mother. She took a piece of my heart with her as she walked away from me forever.

She called us one last time in our huddle in a sea of tears and she ended our season with a prayer and a good wish. I won't forget that quiet stillness of peace we all felt in our huddle, stained with a tinge of sourness upon losing. We wiped away tears, consoled each other and went on stage for our third-place medals. It felt okay to medal, but it was so difficult to be there with the first-place winners. I wanted to be happy for them, but I couldn't get myself to feel peace in my competitive side just yet. There was a lion leashed inside my head. I felt a powerful urge inside my body to take the medals on those first-place girls and wrap them around their necks suffocating them right there on the spot.

But somehow I maintained my composure and walked off the stage for the last time. I remember those steps passing the curtain, slowing down and looking back one more time, my insides filled with rage. I mourned the loss of that stage because it was always my place to shine, my place to own, my place to be free of anything anyone thought was good for me. I felt as if I had left a blue-sky sunlit day to enter a deluge of black clouds along the horizon.

When we got back to the long hallway, our parents were standing there. Some parents had purchased balloons with all the senior's names on them. There were flowers, flashes of light that seemed to hold their light too long, and claps as we came down the corridor. I did not want to see my mother, but fortunately I saw my dad right away holding a beautiful bouquet of pink roses. Next to him was my brother Brett. He gave me a big hug and I started bawling. I had been holding this inferno in like a cloud holding too much rain. I never had a close relationship with Brett, but it moved me that my brother came to see my last competition. My dance recitals were not something he willingly wanted to come to over the years. I could tell by the look on his face that he wanted to be there for me. I had taken him aback at my outburst of tears. He looked surprised but he let me cry it out. "I'm proud of you Ashley," he said, holding my face.

"I can't believe you came home just to see this," I said crying. I had no idea he was coming. He instantly took away all the pain I felt holding a third-place medal.

"There is life after high school. It's an even better place to be sis, trust me, but enjoy this now even with a loss. You looked like a star up there Ash, you always do."

I think that was the sweetest thing he ever said to me and for a quick moment, I felt alright again. But a magnet pulled through the air and my gaze fell upon my mother. The pink roses that I saw my Dad carrying lost all their beauty because I saw a vision of the sucker cane.

She came walking over heavily, as if each step weighed a hundred pounds. "What can you do, sugar? It just wasn't your night."

She pulled me in for a hug but it was like hugging a mop that had been drenched in water all sloppy and mushy. I breathed in heavily and felt I could exhale fire. I pulled away sharply.

I looked up at Brett and he gave me that smirk we would both have on our faces when Mom would offer her shitty advice. We both felt the wrath of her no matter how near or far she was to us. I walked away quickly to escape to be with my friends and take pictures. We stayed there for a while hanging in a potpourri of voices that saturated those gray cement cinder blocks in the room until we all knew it was time to leave.

Liz came up to me and asked me if I wanted a ride. I asked my folks if I could go home with her but my mother snapped right away with, "No, you will come home with us darling."

My brother got a ride there, so he asked to take my dad's car home since he was meeting a friend, which meant the three of us would end up in Mom' car.

Brett gave me a big, long hug. In my ear he whispered, "Don't let Mom ruin this moment for you."

"She already did," I said softly and hugged him even tighter.

He let go, looked at me, and smiled that Brett-dazzling smile. He told me with his eyes to let it go as he gave Mom and Dad a hug then sifted through the crowd out of sight.

I watched him walk away for a moment so tall and confident. I wish I had his class; his ability to let it all go.

Liz stood watching this transpire. She gave me a longing pity-like look and said, "See you later. Don't sweat it tonight. At least we got some hardware!" She always saw the glass half full even in the worst of times.

When we got into the car, it took my mom one second to start her bullshit after the door slammed. She started unloading on every single fault and some things I didn't even notice or anyone else for that matter, including my coach. My dad kept trying to interject and at one point he raised his voice and told my mom that this was not her journey, but mine. Then like clockwork, the two of them started arguing about dance scholarships, colleges, dance schools, and basically how to plan my life and I lost it.

I didn't want anything to do with dance schools and this was not the time to talk about it. I was in the backseat and wild horses came out of me with a running gallop of fury. I was infuriated and it all spilled out of the top of my lungs. "Shut the fuck up! Just shut the fuck up!" I screamed this with all the might I could because I had been holding this in for years.

In my eighteen years on this planet, I was never allowed to swear or talk back to my parents, but I had cracked under this pressure. My outrage was similar to a levy that broke. The water went rushing about finding any space it could to devour, to ruin.

My parents stopped talking. They sat in disbelief. The silence radiated through the car viciously swirling in the open space, then my mother said mightily, "How dare you talk to us like that after all we have done for you?"

"All you have done for me!" I screamed back. "All you have done for me has made me miserable! I am not you Mom! I will never be you! I don't want to be you! My coach is more like a mother to me than you will ever be. You don't know anything about me or who I am. You fucked up that dance for tonight. You . . . fucking you!"

"Stop swearing Ashley, right now!" Dad demanded. "You will not talk to your mother like that!"

I had never heard my dad raise his voice to me, ever. His tone and pitch stung me to the core. I needed an escape. I couldn't understand why he would defend such a heartless woman.

"Pull the car over!" I yelled. "I want out. I am not going to dinner to talk or celebrate! You ruined my last dance recital, are you happy? You ruined my life, you crazy bitch!"

I knew I shouldn't have gone this far, but I did. When this sentence hit the air there was no going back. My mother took off her seatbelt very calmly. I can still hear that click as it felt like a time bomb about ready to go off. Three, two, one . . . she reached around from the front seat and slapped my face as hard as she could muster. It hit with such a hated blow that the sting stayed with me like little needles piercing my cheek. My dad did not stop her and did not say a word. This about killed me. He always came to my rescue, but not then. He watched me struggle. He didn't throw me a rope.

"Pull over or I am going to jump out!" I screamed as hard as I could through the tears. I wanted to run as fast as I could away from the misery. "I am quite sure no other mother I know is slapping their daughter for messing up in the recital. You did this to me you bitch! It's you!"

My Dad pulled over abruptly, put the car in park and pleaded. "Honey, we can go talk about this over dinner. Come on now."

He had decided to throw out the rope. I felt his rescue voice, finally, but it was too late. I got out of the car and slammed the door as hard as I could. The sound reverberated through the air like a castle door being pulled up to lock the fortress with a crack of doom. I looked up and shot my mother a death stare while they proceeded to drive away slowly. I walked home with my duffle bag draped over my back. My ego and my dance shoes were wrapped up tightly inside. From that precise moment while I walked down the gravel along the shoulder of the neat suburban streets, I never let my ego out of that bag again. It was left there, trapped with little to no air waiting to come out one day. As I walked down the street to my house, it was lit up like a Christmas tree. I could see my parents pacing back and forth wondering if I was going to come home. As I walked up the long driveway adorned with rose bushes, I marveled at their majestic fuchsia colors just as lovely as could be.

My eye caught a cane sucker and I winced. "How could this beautiful plant allow something to take it down?" I walked into the house, said not one word as I walked past my parents, grabbed the scissors, and went back out to the front again. I snipped the cane sucker. The click of the snip did wonders for my soul.

I exhaled loudly.

The sucker cane fell to the ground without a sound. I decided to leave it there and not pick it up. Even the sucker cane has so many thorns that it took a skilled hand to not get stuck by one. I felt it better to let it lie there and decompose into the ground. This was the epiphany; the turning point in my life. I could be my own self and live only for me.

When I walked back into the house, my parents were as cold as the granite island they were standing against. I could tell they were ready to jump right back into the ring punching, but I had no energy left to bring to this arena, including my ability to speak. I looked them both in the eyes with all the dismay and discontent I could muster. And before they could sneak in a word edgewise, I kept my silence. I tried to walk away like Brett, all tall and confident but I didn't look like him at all. I ran upstairs to my bedroom, slammed the door, then locked it. I plopped down on my bed, just exhausted. Many moons later I remember waking up to the sound of loud knocking on my door.

"Ashley, are you up yet?" Then silence.

Her voice made my skin crawl. I was a new person overnight, refreshed and ready to start new, without the constraints of the prison I was living in. Maybe this is how Brett felt the moment he left for college and didn't have Mom and Dad breathing down his back anymore.

The knocking seemed a bit more intense with each moment littered with tones of worry. "Ashley?" her voice shrill a little while continuing to knock.

I liked that I had her worried. She just kept knocking. I fell back into a deep slumber of freedom.

But later on everyone just moved on as if nothing had happened. No one said a word.

On that day, I was a new person no longer giving a fuck what my mom thought of me. But I could still hear that knocking on my door and it kept getting louder until it startled me awake. "Ashley? Are you okay?"

It is the veneer smile on Nancy's face that snaps me back to reality. "Brooke is ready for you. My apologies for the mix-up and the time you had to spend waiting," she says, not letting go of that smile for nothing. I am half out of it from daydreaming. I want to check my phone before I go into the massage because I feel like I've been waiting way too long. I don't answer Nancy at all. I open my locker to look for my phone. I can feel Nancy's presence behind me, just a blob of space.

There are several texts on my phone, of course. The first one is Chris telling me he has to leave for New York tomorrow unexpectedly. He is asking for me to be home for dinner with the kids. Then he asks if I want to join him there at some point for a quick weekend just like "old times." He drops this bomb then ends it with his famous we-can-talk-when-he gets home shit.

I text back quickly with an "ok." Of course, gotta jump when he says go. I shake my head. Nancy is still waiting behind me. I can still feel her presence judging.

"Is everything ok," she says inquisitively.

I am going to make her wait like she did to me so I don't say a word back. I check the next text and it's Lola. She is wondering if I'm coming to the tennis club today. I decide to ignore the text because she could pair up with anyone else. I don't fucking care. The next text is my mom. Fuck. How interesting that she texts me when I am sitting here thinking about what a bitch she is. She wants to know if she and Dad can come see the kids this weekend. Fuck no I'm not answering that one right now. I can tell Nancy wants to say something while keeping that artificial grin. I hear her sigh a little, trying not to act pissed off that she is now waiting like I was. I think for sure the smile will leave her face, but no.

"That painting is pretty, isn't it? I noticed you looking at it deep in thought when I came in to get you. It brings me great joy," Nancy says smiling. I put my phone back.

"Well it made me feel fucking miserable," I say walking past her without another word.

CHAPTER 23

Tammy

"Our value lies in what we are and what we have been, not in our ability to recite the recent past."
– Homer

I wake up gently from dozing on my hammock in the backyard. I don't know how long I have been out, but it feels like days. I had a dream that I was a monarch butterfly. I enjoyed the splendor of the spring and summer flying from flower-to-flower laying eggs everywhere in my path. And then one day the pleasant air vanished into a crisp fall air weakening my strength. It was then I knew it was time to find my way to a warmer climate. The journey was not an easy one. I felt myself feeling weak many times wondering if I was going to make it. I stopped. I rested. I thought. I followed the others. Some made it, some simply didn't. I had to let that go and move on. Miles of cold air made this plight even worse and then somehow my wings started to relax. The pleasant air had arrived.

I feel a bead of sweat run from my forehead, and that is what wakes me up. I try to go back to sleep to fly again through that pleasant air, feel the wind on my wings and follow my friends. I desperately want to see where I would end up on that journey as a butterfly, but I guess I never will. I stare up at the blue sky watching white clouds burn off as they pass by in slow motion. I wake up from my dream thinking of my childhood again when everything was so simple. I don't have the strength to get up from the hammock because I know that would be a chore like moving a beached whale off the shore. I lie here daydreaming and it reminds me of how I used to watch clouds as a kid.

When I was little and at my grandparents' house, I would lie in their backyard and stare off into the sky and look intently at the cloud formations. My grandma would ask me to guess what the clouds looked like. I would pretend the clouds were animals, or objects and watch them float by and take different shapes quickly as they disappeared off into the horizon. I can see my sister Dawn lying next to me, and even my Grandma at times. I sigh happily just thinking of how great it would be to transport myself back to my grandparents' house. Guessing the clouds was just one of the many lovely things we did when we were at my grandparents' house. They had a small bungalow in the south side of Chicago about forty minutes east of our home in the suburbs. It really felt like going over to another world when we went there. The houses were very close together all laid out on a square grid. There was always a lot of commotion of people on foot, in cars and buses. The best was seeing the neighbors cooking dinner right through the kitchen window. My childhood house was just the opposite with wide open spaces, campfires, and imagination.

One of the best memories I have from my grandparent's house was being able to eat anything we wanted in any size portion. Food was at the center of all of our activities. Dawn and I loved that we could eat anything we wanted because even though my mom came from the same family, we were not able to eat junk food at home. My mom also watched our portion sizes like a hawk. We were never allowed to go into the pantry and help ourselves. So having a free-for-all at my grandparents was something I really looked forward to.

Now for my sister, a free-for-all was fine because somehow she always knew when to stop. For me, I found ways to eat gigantic portions, succumb to a stomachache, then find a way to eat even more. All I had to do was take my grandpa's baking soda and water concoction that he dubbed the "thirty second belcher." It would work every time. I would slam it down because Grandpa would say, "It has to go down in one swoop! No baby bottle here . . . just do it!" Sure enough, thirty seconds later, I let out an enormous burp while my sister would giggle to the high heavens. I instantly felt better. This quick remedy paved the way for more food. It also started my long battle with my weight because I always viewed food as a contest to see who could eat the most. And for me, food makes me happy. Eating makes me feel safe like a child.

"How can you even think of having more?" said Dawn.

I would shrug my shoulders playing ignorance. When we were finished eating, my sister and I would get a whole cold glass bottle of coke. My grandma would twist off the cap and put a straw in the top.

She would set the bottle down at our eyesight and whisper softly as if she was telling a secret to the FBI. "Now don't tell your parents. This is our little secret."

Just like not going into the pantry, my parents didn't allow soda in our house, so this was another royal treatment. The best part of finishing the coke bottle was taking a walk a few city blocks over to Bibi's dime store to return the bottle. Money was given back for each bottle that was turned in. Grandma would give us the coins earned to get gumballs in the gumball machine. Talk about a sugar rush! The clink of the noise going round on the dial of the machine would create a buzz inside of us, heavy with anticipation of the clink at the bottom. We were then left wondering what flavor gumball we were going to get.

The burst of sugar flavor going in was entertainment for our mouths for a brief, few moments. Before long, the taste would fizzle out like the quiet hum of the foam from the wave that breaks at the shore slowly, then bubbling back serenely into the deep blue sea.

After all the eating and the thrills of the day, we never argued about going to bed like we did when we were at home because we ended up with a sugar crash ready to hit the sack. Before bed, my grandmother would tell us *The Three Bears* as a bedtime story. Her voice was the most soothing and loving voice I have ever heard.

As I lie on the hammock swaying slowly, I can still hear her voice echo and bounce sound waves to the inner parts of my heart.

I think about my sister now wishing we were little girls again, so sweet and innocent. I wish I still had a relationship with my sister. Our connection went away gradually the way a turtle comes out of an egg searching for the water, maybe to live fully or succumb to darkness soon at some point. The hammock sways slowly.

I remember our guest room so vividly. There were two beds across from each other. I would lie on one bed and Dawn on the other one. There was a little dresser in between us with a glass nightlight in the shape of what looked like a crystal ball. My sister and I used to pretend it was magical. We made three wishes as soon as we put our suitcases down in the guest room. When Grandma turned off the lights, you would hear the tick of the crystal ball light go on, which cast diamond-shaped shadows on the wall. At that very moment the shapes hit the wall, we were safe. I wish I had that nightlight now to keep as a North Star.

I lie here thinking about what a starry sky looks like. All my life I never managed to locate any stars that were bright enough. The needles in my temple start up again, so I try to go back to the guest room at my grandparents in my mind. The room comes into view.

As my grandmother told the bedtime story, I would see the characters in my head and become so relaxed. Because grandma's voice was like velvet, it sent me into the deepest of all calming sleeps. I would awaken the next day asking Dawn what happened to

Goldilocks because without fail I would miss the ending of that story every time. But Grandma would always tell me the ending at breakfast because we would rise to the aroma of buttered pancakes and coffee.

I can still remember opening the bedroom door to see Grandpa cooking up his magical breakfast with a jovial, "Good morning sun shines. A wonderful thing happened to us today . . . we woke up."

We would smile and give him a big hug. That hug was the warm sun over a glorious blue sea.

I lie here thinking how I would give anything in the world to feel those moments in person just one more time, but then a million times wouldn't be enough either. For a moment I drift off thinking of these visits of checkers, hide and seek, picking vegetables in the garden, and watching the *Carol Burnett Show* on Friday nights. Those were days I looked forward to. Those were days I wish I had back right now.

My hammock swings back and forth. I am not really sure why my hammock continues to move because there is no breeze now, but it soothes the needles poking at my temple. Maybe the hammock is moving from the gravitational pull from the moon similar to the tides that move the water in the ocean. The rocking of this hammock reminds me of the rocker Dawn and I would sit on in our grandparents' den.

The hammock shifts back and forth with a lull of comfort, yet there is still something unsettling like the dull pain I'm feeling in my temples. This slow sway back and forth reminds me of the day I swayed gently on the rocker and heard the bad news.

My grandparents had a small glass clock that sat above the television. It had little chimes that were the shape of golden balls that would twist halfway circular, then back the other way circular. The den was always the first place we would run to when we arrived at their house so we could sit and stare at the clock while bouncing on the rocker. My sister and I would fight over the rocker, but we would eventually squeeze in together and rock slowly in unison.

Back and forth the clock would move to the same beat as the rocker lulling us in a euphoric state. For me, the clock was like a magnet drawing me into its sweet trance. My sister would inevitably jump off and find something else to do after a few minutes. She was what my mom called a "fart in a barrel." She couldn't sit still real long.

For me, I loved to relax. I loved staring at that clock. I never once knew what time it was when I came in to look at the clock. It didn't matter and that was the best part. Time always stood still when I entered my grandparents' home. But on this particular day I remembered the time. The clock said two thirty-four and I watched that clock as a tear ran down my cheek while rocking back and forth on the rocker. I overheard my parents in the kitchen discussing my grandmother's illness of Alzheimer's. I had no idea what that meant or how to pronounce that word, but I knew by the seriousness in tone that it wasn't good. Little did I know that this disease was on its way to strip all life from my absolutely glorious grandmother.

Watching someone go through Alzheimer's is similar to leaving a trail of footprints on the dark orange sand. Each foot would glide down and land gently, one foot in front of the other. One could look back and see those slender prints prominent for a bit until high tide would come in. The water swirled smoothly over the top of the footprints creating a slow diminish of the print, distorting it, yet still an impression the eye was able to see. Slowly with each tide the print would morph into another shape until eventually it would vanish completely. How small and impermanent we all are on this Earth. We share the time with nature and we eventually succumb to our demise, yet the Earth prevails taking on new movement, new tides, new shapes. We are just a grain of sand in a vast mound of particles.

There were gradual signs leading up to my grandmother's illness, but being a kid, I did not necessarily take this into consideration until it was pointed out to me by my mother.

My grandmother started to lose her memory and had to ask us over and over again who we were. Then she would get frustrated and apologize. She would start telling us a bedtime story, forget what she was saying, then ramble on about something else that had nothing to do with the story.

One time when this happened, she got up abruptly, ran out of the room, and started crying. I heard her muffled tones outside of the bedroom and my grandfather's deep voice shushing her and telling her it would all be okay. My sister and I were so confused. This was not like my grandmother at all to leave details behind. She was a woman who always wanted to give, who always wanted to feel loved and be loved. It pained us to see her this way.

While Dawn and I would lie in bed talking and staring at the diamond shaped shadows, we would make wishes into our crystal magic night light that grandma would turn back into herself. Perhaps we shouldn't have vocalized our wishes out loud because those wishes never came to fruition. The magic light lost its light eventually and the diamond shadows on the ceiling had faded. The only glimmer would be when the door would open slowly. A small piece of light would find its way into the bedroom like a searchlight from a lighthouse over a dark ocean.

"It will be okay, girls. Grandma is just not feeling like herself and she needs to rest. Where was she in the story? I can finish off for you, girlies," Grandpa said as his voice sounded different than usual.

While my grandpa did his best to tell the rest of the story, something about it wasn't the same. We knew something was wrong, but we didn't want to upset him more by asking questions. We just preferred silence on this subject because we had a sense that he needed the silence too.

From that time on, a piece of our grandma died every time we saw her, like that footprint losing its shape slowly in the sand. She slowly left herself behind and reverted backwards in her life until not only did she not know us, but everyone else in our family, including my parents, specifically my mother.

My mom never spoke of this pain but I can only imagine the grief she went through before her mom even died. My grandma didn't even know her own husband after a while, who by the way was the absolute love of her life. How incredibly sad to lose the feeling of true love. Their true love was tossed overboard. It careened over the waves and melted into foam bubbles before disappearing over the sand out of reach.

Eventually, Grandma's condition got so bad that my grandpa couldn't do all the care taking because he couldn't leave her by herself anymore. It took the convincing strength of an army to get my grandpa to see that he needed outside help, but he made a promise to my grandma that he would not put her in a nursing home. Every bone in his body was held together with promise and conviction, so there was no way he was going to break that bond to his true love. This was admirable actually, yet frustrating at the same time because he had to continue to work, had to keep his social ties, but his drinking got heavier with each passing day. This was the only way he found where he could survive. But eventually though and without much choice, he surrendered to at least having someone come in and help, even though for him it was an intrusion of everything he knew in his life.

Because of Grandma's rapid decline, our visits became more frequent. That antique clock on the television I held dear to my heart began to tick with a heavier weight. It was always a peacefully quiet clock, but I started hearing the ticks for the first time as they wound back and forth almost in a nervous kind of way. My sister and I would go to my grandparents' house every Monday, Wednesday, and Friday in the summer with my mom and spend the day with

Grandma, taking care of her, painting her nails, and keeping her looking pretty. As sick as she was, it was important for her to still feel like a woman. We would take turns styling her hair, shopping for pretty blouses and skirts, and putting on her make-up. My Mom would prepare her meals while the radio above the refrigerator played the oldies of the good-old-days. My grandma, always looking pretty, would rock monotonously as the wind from the trees outside the window caressed the house wanting to get in through any open cracks. The sun would rise over the horizon each day and set on a new day chipping away one cell at a time.

As the years went on, time changed the tide. We would no longer be able to spend a ton of time at my grandparents' house due to school and activities. Mom and her sister would go together or take turns going while we were in school until even that wasn't enough. Another chapter started and a full-time caregiver took the place of the love matched between my grandparents. But because of the caretaker, my grandpa was able to work and somehow make a new life stumbling in the dark to find a new light.

As for Dawn and me, we turned into the weekly Saturday or Sunday morning visitors, then down to twice a month or whenever we could get there. Eventually these visits would turn into visits with Grandpa. Every Saturday we would arrive to find doughnuts, the smell of coffee, and great conversations.

In the midst of this circle of life, Grandma would be in the background, almost deafeningly silent. She reminded me of an old banyan tree alive with wonder, girth and size, making her presence known even though we couldn't see the process of what was going on inside her to keep her alive. At one time we climbed her branches, listened to the rain slide off her leaves, and relaxed under her umbrella of shade. She was a tree we walked by on the street and marveled at how her eyes had so many days before ours. For many years we watched the beauty and splendor of this tree until one day the branches lay barren, then empty on a dark and cold night. We watched a quick flash of lightning take down a huge branch to leave an open wound. The noise of severed wood would ring harsh upon the air. The smell of sawdust created a plume of dust particles that blew through the air to vanish into time. The roots too deep and intertwined in the dirt left a stump still there rooted and grounded without the majestic canopy overhead. She was one with the earth. That wide stump left in the ground was a welcome respite for a short rest on a long haul.

I sat on that stump for a long time on the day my grandmother died. I found myself in quiet meditation of peace and hope for her no longer suffering, but I had a selfish and unsettling feeling of melancholy thoughts. This death forced me to see my childhood drift out of sight. During my grandmother's illness, her damaged brain took her backwards through her childhood. She would sit and laugh and recount the joys of innocence like a young child laughing on the playground.

For me I cried as I have never cried before because I was moving forward away from my childhood. From my eyes the deluge of salt water formed a tide pool for small creatures to live in for a short time until the sun's strong rays dried up the hole. Nothing would ever be the same again setting me on a different path. I was on the crossroads into adulthood and I couldn't go back the way I had come.

My stomach is unsettled because I've lain in this hammock all day. Darkness sets in again, blending one day into another. I am still swaying back and forth. This dreaded headache is starting up again. It starts slowly like a little needle inside my temple. I think of death when it gets dark. These thoughts begin to fill me with dread, but this makes my head hurt even more. In an attempt to stop this pain, I drape my hand over my forehead. It feels good. I wish there were someone to put their hand on my head. Why am I alone? Death brings on a dark heavy blanket for many days before being able to climb out from under it, stand up, wash the blanket, fold it and put it away for another day.

I think about my Grandpa who had to pick up the pieces and move on with his life after Grandma died. He spent many of those dark days by himself, and we, as much as we could, would visit and reminisce, try to solve the world's problems right there in his kitchen. I would look out the window and watch the train blister by as we were talking.

"Who wants to guess the color of the caboose like we used to?" Grandpa would say. "Whoever guesses right, gets ten dollars!"

Even in our intelligent conversations, Grandpa always made me feel care-free like an innocent child, even after I thought for sure I had gone to the other side of adulthood. I cherished these child-like moments with him all the way up until his death came roaring in unannounced three years after my grandma.

Unlike my grandma, he died all on his own, not with one person in front of him. The thought of him dying alone haunted me for a long time, but he was too proud of a man to even die in front of anyone. He wouldn't want to bother anyone with dying because that is the man that he was. He was always put together on the outside, always. But on the inside, he was lost and scared, similar to a lion cub scrambling to find his mother in the thick grassland.

My head starts to subside just a little. The sky is so dark now and I can't recall how long I have been lying here with no inkling to move.

My eyes saw a love story, and I searched everywhere in the hopes to find this too. I wish I had this story to tell. I wish I had someone to grow old with, but this great honor was not to be bestowed upon me.

I sway back and forth alone and feel the needles in my temple ticking slightly, like the movement of my grandparents' clock.

I remember Grandpa's soft words before bedtime. He said that life is a struggle, life is ordinary, but any time spent loving is extraordinary. I remember this every single day. I remember the day

I walked around my grandparents' house collecting artifacts of my childhood I could cling on to for dear life. I got some jewelry, dinner plates, my grandpa's hairbrush and favorite little trinkets. Somehow, I could not find the coveted nightlight, but I managed to get the clock.

For a moment the dull ticks in my head stop because the clock had stopped ticking, like an old heart that lost its beat. I want to go see the clock that sits on my mantle above my fireplace. I never once tried to fix it. It always said two-thirty-four.

And then I fall sound asleep into deep darkness.

When my eyes open, I see a blue sky with puffy clouds. Like a kid again, the passing of these clouds make me feel so small in such a big world. The needles in my head are dull now, but still ever present. I still can't get myself to get out of this hammock. I feel a breeze blowing a lonely balloon from a far-away place. I wonder where it comes from and how long it has been this lone traveler. How long will it be able to keep itself safe from the elements? Who is the owner of the balloon? Are they down below feeling sad that this object floated away without their permission? The balloon will travel up and up and around, possibly over oceans without losing distance as it goes, until it loses the air and balance it once had, shriveling slowly back down to the ground. Will it be litter on the shore, life in another place, or a choking hazard for birds? We are all just balloons floating to an unknown place.

The needles in my head get sharper. I feel pain against my skin that I can't stop.

I want to go back to the room because I hear familiar voices but I can't escape.

I hope that someone is here to pick me up and fill me with air again.

Chapter 24

Ashley

"Beauty is power; a smile is its sword."
- John Ray

BROOK is apologetic when I walk into the room. She can tell by my disgruntled look that I am pissed I had to wait this long for her. I notice her hair is a little disheveled with pieces out of place, and not tied back neatly in a bun like always. She appears out of breath like she just ended a workout.

"I'm so sorry you had to wait, Ashley. I asked Nancy if you could come in later because I am just overbooked today."

I'm a little pissed at how Brook is acting because it is making me feel uneasy, and all I want is my massage, not her fucking excuses as to why she is fucking late. She looks like she could use a massage instead of me. It's pissing me off. I take a breath of annoyance as she drones on.

"I had a new client that went overtime. I'm also covering for Lana, who called in sick today. I have not had a moment to get a bite to eat or use the bathroom. It is just one of those days, so again, sorry to make you wait," she says, making one excuse after the next.

"Well, my hamstrings are really tight from running, so it would be great if you can focus a little more there today with my massage," I say, getting right to the point so I don't have more of my time wasted.

"Of course." Brook grins. "Lie down and I'll get right to work." She starts the music and I can feel her preparing her hands with oil. The first touch of her hands makes me jump a little.

"All ok?" she says.

"Any chance you can warm the oil a bit. Your hands are cold and it startled me."

"Why yes, of course," she says.

I hear her hands rubbing together to create friction. The warm oil drips over my body with pleasure the minute it touches my skin. I sigh heavily and start thinking about Chris. He always says that there is no way a massage can't turn sexual. But even as exotic as this is, I don't want to have sex with Brook, but perhaps it might be different if there was a hot man rubbing every crevice of my naked body.

This massage is so soothing, but I don't want to fall asleep because then I won't enjoy it. As each drop of oil pierces my skin so softly, thoughts of this guy I see at the tennis club pop into my head, not Chris. This guy is equally as hot as Chris, but I think of him more often. He has dark brown eyes like chocolate and his forearms are thick. I catch him checking me out a lot when we are in the middle of matches. He smiles at me when I walk by, but it has never gone anywhere else. I catch myself thinking of him now, wishing it were his hands touching me all over.

Part of me wishes I were thinking of Chris, but it's almost like I forget he exists sometimes because he travels for his job for much of his life. This means I'm without him more than I am with him. What am I supposed to do when I get lonely? A vibrator only goes so far. I worry my fantasizing of other men will be destructive at some point, but what harm is it if it's only in my mind? I'll just stick to fantasizing and a vibrator for now because I have it way too good to fuck this up. More drops of oil glide over my skin. It makes me wince. My mind drifts back to Chris again. Maybe New York could be fun. We haven't traveled together alone for a while like we used to before the kids.

Chris is the CFO of a posh hotel chain. This job of course has many perks, like staying at hotels anywhere in the world for free. This part of my marriage has been incredible I must say because it really does fit perfectly with my Barbie way of life, specifically before kids. We never have to pay for a hotel anywhere we travel. Chris travels so often that there is no way I could go with him all the time with our family, so I just got used to spending a lot of time by myself.

But when we were first married without kids, Chris and I would find time to get away. I was able to take time off from work and join him on his business trips, which were spread all over the globe. We would always have fun and the sex was great, but even back in our early days of marriage, there always seemed to be something missing, even with all this money. I was never able to put my finger on it. It was almost like he married me to shut me up or show me off as his little trophy he could brag about, then place me on the shelf when he went off to do something else, leaving me to collect dust.

I thought we had fallen in love pretty quickly, but I was too heart-first and not thinking clearly, caught up in what I thought I should be doing with my life and what came next in sequential order. Kind of like that song we used to sing as tweens, *Jim and Sue, sitting in a tree, k-i-s-s-i-n-g, first comes love, then comes marriage, then comes a baby in the baby carriage.*

I thought these steps were the natural chain of events and I didn't want to veer from that path. I remember vividly Chris telling me that I was the girl he had been looking for all his life, even though he was scared to let himself go because he knew there was no way out once he fell in. Once he met me he was in quicksand grasping for a while to get air, but ultimately he was going to go down.

For me, I felt like Alice staring at that hole under the tree questioning whether or not I should dive down. Of course, I was enticed rolling down that rabbit hole.

Here I am now though, hot oil being poured down my back while visualizing myself riding the tennis player in a charismatic frenzy. Then quickly thoughts shift back to Chris and his pitch of going to New York for a short weekend.

I decide I am going to find that spark again because all too often my thoughts of many other men besides the tennis guy are prominent in my mind. Maybe going to New York might be a way to find our relationship again now that the kids are getting a little older.

Brook adds a new coat of oil on my lower back. I try not to sigh out loud, but I can't help it because it feels so good. As Brook's hands course into my aching muscles, I think about falling in love with someone at first sight. I really felt this happened when I first laid my eyes on Chris. But then, is it possible to fall out of love with that same person after love fades over time?

As the warm oil oozes down by back, I can feel it trickle down off my sides and onto the freshly cleaned sheets. The sheer warmth of Brook's hands spiraling in and out of deep tissue moves me into a trance.

I have a dream that I am a cicada, lying in the ground dormant for years. I forge through the cold ground to get to the warmth and follow the way. I feel alive, ready to see the world, but before I embark on my journey, I stop and find a place for my wings to dry. I meditate for only a few minutes on the sun sparkling on the fence post I am on. I watch all the other insects move about in search of their mate and food. I admire them and their splendor as I continue to wait for my wings to dry. This respite is a gift of silence. I'm ready to make the metamorphosis into a fully ready cicada flying to my mate. I wait for his loud shrieking calls on a hot summer day with all the trees alive busting with a cacophony of ear-piercing noises. Once I make that journey, I am flying from tree to tree in search of the right buzz. Not even a zephyr on this hot summer night can relieve the humid air that stifles the stillness under my wings. I search for the precise right call that will turn me whole, give me purpose for leaving the damp, dark and cold earth after all these years while I lie waiting for my chance. I hear his buzz among the lovely summer branches, following his vibration. But then I feel a smack, and then a gulp, as I land in the mouth of a ravenous bird. Just like that I leave this world as quickly as I entered, my heart broken in half. My body twitches hard as I feel the gulp.

Brook gasped. "Oh no Ashley, did I do something wrong?"

"Yes, I felt a twinge near my chest weirdly enough. Did you press too hard on a nerve?" I can't believe I fell asleep and then dreamt about a fucking insect instead of a hot guy. What the fuck?

"I don't think so, Ashley. Perhaps you were dreaming about something and this caused an involuntary response?" she says so scientifically.

I have never believed in tarot card reading, or that palm reading psychological bullshit, but I feel this dream is a bad omen for what was about to happen on my trip to New York. I don't like this feeling at all. Now I am rethinking going, but don't know how I am going to get out of it either. Oh fuck that stupid dream. I make the decision to go. This whole fucking appointment agitates me and now I am leaving feeling the same way. This is not how I am supposed to feel after a massage. No fucking happy ending.

"Well, our time's up Ashley. I hope I was able to relieve some of your pressure today so you are ready for your next tennis match."

I lie still on the bed quietly, half out of it from this dream. I intend to open my eyes and say something, but I can't find the words in my anger. It feels better to not say a fucking word to her, especially after she made me wait so long for a stressed massage. I can hear Brook cleaning up as little clanks behind me pierce the air in awkward silence.

It seems like hours before she says goodbye and closes the door softly. I feel the oil dripping off the back of my neck as I sit up and stare at another painting of roses. This painting has beautiful red roses standing majestically without thorns in a prominent vase. What the fuck is with all these rose paintings? I wonder why I had not noticed these before. The more I think about those roses, the more pissed I become. I can't even relax without my mother intruding hot oil into every pore. I grab my robe and head back towards the dressing room where I was before. I try not to glance at the painting I was staring at before because it would just stir up even more bad memories.

I get dressed quickly because I need to get to my tennis match before getting the kids from school, because this whole day is running away from me at full speed. I walk back through the lobby. I see Nancy sitting there still with that fucking smile on her face. I see the tip envelopes, but I decided fuck that, no tip today for making me wait. I don't want to say a word to Nancy either, so I keep my head down and my pace steady.

But then I hear Mary fucking Poppins say, "Same time next week Ashley dear?"

"Of course, but write the time down correctly this time Naaancy. I can't say her name in two crisp syllables. Her name comes out naturally to me in an elongated way similar to how her annoying presence lingers on me. "I don't care to wait when I have a scheduled time. If it happens again, I am going somewhere else. This was not at all relaxing today," I say.

I have one foot out the door as I hear her say, "Ok, Ashley and make it a good one, darling."

I want to say, "Make what a good one?" but I bit my lip in a halt to thwart my sarcasm. I have had quite enough of that bitch today. Her persistence in engaging with me in a superficial fashion reminds me of my mother's bloodsucker cane.

Chapter 25

Tammy

> *"I remember my mother's prayers, and they have always followed me."*
> *- Abraham Lincoln*

I want to get up and move so badly but the throbbing in my head is a relentless pain that won't go away. In brief moments of respite, a kaleidoscope of colors shifts in and out of my brain. I stream along through time and space similar to the movement from the bottom to the top of a Ferris wheel. I start the slow climb from the bottom then over the top feeling the wind in my hair, along with a stomach drop on the way down.

It's during that drop that I lie here on this hammock thinking about all the things in my life that I would have changed. Suddenly the butterflies in my stomach allow me to feel alive again. Round and round I go over the top and back to the bottom feeling the wind move my hair softly. Everything around me looks so small from the top then back to normal as I get closer to the ground. The wheel in my mind swirls with dizzy delight. I don't want to stop because this feeling makes me a child again. But as all innocence ends, inevitably the ride ends. The car swings back and forth a little until it loses its sway. The bar over me lifts quite abruptly but I am not ready to jump off the seat. I am dizzy from lying so long in this hammock in my backyard for what seems like forever with no time in existence. I start to move very slowly and notice that my legs feel like I'm walking in cement.

As each foot sinks into the grass, I wonder what life would have looked like if my dad hadn't died so young. He would have been the best grandfather anyone could ask for and Alex would have been his best buddy. We would have been sitting around many more campfires that were tragically cut short. My Dad would have seen Alex off to school and been so proud. I think of what would have happened if I had gone to college and played softball, found my passion and met someone other than Bill.

The course of my life turned upside down and every which way on small decisions, big decisions, and many decisions in between. No one escapes this road of circumstances. At some point in life, innocence stays on the sticky cotton candy seats of the Ferris Wheel. Once off the magical sway of a circular motion the path leads down to the unsettling funhouse, face to face with life, and there won't be an easy way out. The funhouse is dark and there are twists and turns, loud noises, bouncing floors, complete with jump scares and a skinny and fat mirror distorting all familiar images of the self. I want to run back to the Ferris Wheel but finding the way out of the funhouse is a monumental task. There is no turning back. All that is left is the sweet smell of popcorn and funnel cakes permeating through the air.

I see the lights fade away on the Ferris Wheel as I make my way over to the fire pit. I feel as though someone let the air out of me. I need to sit down. There is an old and tattered wooden patio chair that calls my name. I sit down and it creaks and wobbles a bit but I manage to sit somewhat comfortably. The throbbing in my head increases because of this short walk to the fire pit but it is worth it to finally get up and move. Like a Jedi in training, I try to focus on something else to retrain the pain I feel everywhere. I start the fire just like Dad taught me. I sit back and think of Alex because no one else in my life can take my mind off of my anguish but him. I can see his face in front of me smiling, laughing, and raising his eyebrow ever so slightly when he tells me an exciting story. I miss his stories so much it hurts as much as my throbbing head.

When Alex left for college I thought my heart was going to explode out of my chest. I have that same feeling now thinking of him where all the memories bubble up in my throat forming a lump making it hard to breathe. The way I feel at this moment is the exact same way I felt the day before Alex left for college.

I remember looking at the clock, listening to its chimes set each hour all that day wishing it to cease quietly, just as it did on my grandparents' clock many moons earlier. I lean back on the chair and stare at the fire pit here under a blue sky. The sun feels good on my face and I close my eyes.

I wanted Alex to go to college, it was just that he is always my lifeline and with him moving far away, I was forced to put one foot in front of the other, similar to what my mom had to do when my dad died. I remember her using the word, "readjust" over and over again. She always said nothing in this life is permanent. These thoughts would haunt me at the worst times, but I had to force myself to push them aside. I had to refocus and think about how I was not the only one in the world whose child left for college. Countless mothers were going to sleep just like me overthinking and not getting a wink of sleep while the significant others slept like bears. I knew countless generations of mothers before me let their kids go out of the nest for whatever the path was, but it didn't help the crushing feeling in my chest. I knew I was also not the only one with marital problems. I was not the only one who was overweight, or whose father died way too young. I knew that living with what I had right now was the path I should take for myself, not watch the derailing train I could not save from its demise. I would find nothing but self-pity and heartache at a train wreckage. What I needed most was to cope, not arrive at an accident I couldn't clean up.

But as I sit here now thinking about Alex, my heart feels so heavy without him here. I wish he could hold my hand and tell me this pain in my head would go away and everything would be alright. I feel somewhat content to be back clinging to my roots of home, but strangely enough, none of this feels right with no one else here but me. I must try and think about something that gives me joy to feel alive again and back to my own world, not here by myself.

My Alex.

I hear his deep voice in a hushed pitch lightly filling the air. He is talking low so as to not disturb the restful state I was in. He always knows what is best for me. I wonder if he can see me in the painting on the wall.

I dive in deeper and think about my feelings of pride that Alex had received an academic scholarship to Georgia Tech. He worked diligently to attain this goal and most of it was done all on his own, with some guidance from my family of course. Bill's parents were older and so involved in their own lives that they really didn't know Alex, nor did he know them. Their relationship was cordial with no bitterness, just no bond. I can count on one hand how many times his parents were at my house for a birthday or graduation. Just like Bill, they weren't present.

Bill didn't really care either about whether or not he saw his family. In his mind he had moved on. He had become a man of his own and needed no one else to live his life for him or give him the stamp of approval of how to live his life. I also thought he was embarrassed of me and my weight and how I had come to look different than what they remembered in his young bride. In many ways I always found this admirable to not be concerned about what his family thought. But yet to me, family is the glue that holds culture together and should be passed on to the next generation.

If it weren't for me, I am quite sure Bill would have rarely talked to his parents again. He always said, "My parents are here and they know I am here. Why do I need to call them? What am I going to say?" I would just shake my head perplexed.

My Mom always said, "You can lead a horse to water, but you can't make him drink."

Oh, she was filled with wisdom from all her quotes. My mother's sayings have helped me in so many situations. I just found it sad that Bill was not connected to his family but there won't be any love loss for either of us anyways, so I gave up trying to hold up the house of cards when I knew they would blow down with the slightest bit of movement.

My Mom, on the other hand, took the place of all the grandparents and then some. She was always there for Alex his whole life all the way up through the process of looking for colleges and even offered to go with and view them, make a travel weekend out of it, and that we did do, which was a great experience. She was forever encouraging. I think deep down she was thrilled to see her grandson go to college since my admission to college was halted. I was ecstatic she was getting to see his success now.

I try to push certain memories out of my throbbing head but my brain won't let me forget. Sitting here on this hard chair, I shift uncomfortably, stoke the fire, then think of the day Alex left for college. It was so terribly bittersweet, even though I felt that whoever has sent their pride and joy off to an unknown land in an unknown world knows the hollow pain in your gut that won't go away even with a drip filled with morphine. I can't believe I thought dropping off Alex for kindergarten was bad. I thought childbirth labor was horrible. Those events were nothing compared to this pain.

With lots of time to think in between these headaches, I know I would, with a hundred percent certainty, love to go back in time to spend more time with Alex.

I could have left the dishes in the sink longer, postponed the visit to the grocery store, or waited to go fold laundry. I fell in love with the mundanity of Alex coming home at three o'clock starving as if he had never eaten before. I would watch him fall asleep under the stars I pasted on the top of his ceiling that stuck there from when he was five years old. I can still hear him say, "Love you to the stars Mom," each night after the sun had made its glorious disappearance and it was the moon's turn to shine.

I would read a book to him and tell stories. When I would turn off the light, the stars on the ceiling would glow. We would sit in silence before I would shut his door and hum the song, *What a Wonderful World*.

It was on the day Alex was packing that he told me he loved falling asleep to the quiet glow of the stars on his ceiling after I left from reading a book to him. I felt my heart turn to butter when he said this. That butter, so warm that it soothes my aching head even right now as I sit here on this old chair.

He peeled a few stars off the ceiling and put them in a baggie in his suitcase. It took everything within me not to burst out sobbing as he was doing this, so I just touched his shoulder and grinned and let him be. When he came downstairs after packing he set his phone down on the table. I saw that he had put one of those stars on his phone cover. My mind felt calm knowing I gave Alex a loving childhood, yet a hollowing sadness from deep down swirled inside of me at the same time. Depressing as it was for Alex to leave, I took comfort knowing that a piece of his childhood innocence would be a North Star on his new path.

The clock in our kitchen chimed on the hour. I counted all those chimes as they struck twelve. Each sound lightly touched the air to count the routines of the day, but on the day Alex left, the sounds were a reminder that the peaceful noise would end.

I'd be left with silence.

The next time the chimes would sound, Alex would be gone. And that house that was everything to us as a family would fall to ruins the minute my men decided to leave me all alone. I knew the glow of those stars in Alex's room would dim, then fall from the sky leaving a quick flash of light behind. The walls of that house of loneliness would eat me alive. I also felt right then and there that the house had to be sold immediately. I unplugged the clock no longer wanting to hear the sweet sounds of the chimes with Alex not there.

Out of pure desperation not to sit and cry all day, I decided my room and Alex's room needed to be painted before selling. I brought a ladder to Alex's room and made the climb to the ceiling. This was no easy task for me at all and quite dangerous as heavy as I was, but I was determined to do this myself. Part of me was not concerned about a fall, but another part of me hoped it would happen to put me out of my misery.

The first thing I had to do was take the stars off the ceiling. By the time I got to the top of the ladder I was already out of breath. I stood there trying my best to balance my overweight body and my head filled with the water weight of tears.

My head hurts the same now as I remember this day as if it was happening to me all over. The pain seeps into my temple side by side with this memory. I have to hold my hands against my temple to stop the pounding.

I reached up carefully to the ceiling and peeled all the stars down slowly one by one. Some dropped into a baggie I had, and some of them fell with a light clink to the ground. This sound of the plastic star hitting the ground left stardust trailing behind it. Each star that fell was a memory from childhood. I take those stars in a baggie with me wherever I go. I took a star out of the baggie and added it to my phone cover like Alex did. I needed that North Star too.

Tears roll down my cheeks mixing with the throbbing. I feel a sharp pain below my ribcage.

I really want to forget about the past, I really do. I read self-help books, quotes and all the advice of moving forward is so very true, but I can't ignore that the past shapes who you become in the present. And while sitting here in pain seemingly stuck in my mind, all I have is time to go back and replay these events that shaped me to who I am now.

When packing was complete and we were getting into the car, the door shut, then it was the official cutting of the cord. I could only hope all the things that were taught to Alex in the last eighteen years sunk in. He was Frodo on the shire, and there was no way I could protect him from any of the obstacles he would see along the way. Maybe he would find his "Sam Gamgee" to walk along the journey, but at one point he would be alone to navigate as a man. He would have to know how to overcome obstacles with his sword, use the knowledge he gained, demonstrate his pride with actions, and always understand the heavy cost of carrying a ring too close to his heart.

I always told Alex two things in life, almost daily, and especially through the trying middle school and high school years. I said, "Do the right thing, and be a good person." Moving on, I am sure the last bits of the cord would fall away out of the belly button. He could tend to the protruding cord by adding rubbing alcohol to reveal a new opening without an attachment to another human being.

Alex was such an independent soul and avoided unneeded stress when he could. He was very logical and smart this way. He already had a job lined up at school so he needed to leave a few weeks early before school started. I secretly wished he would have begun when everyone else did because then I would be able to buy more time with him, but I also had to get used to the time without him in a new way. I was sure there would be breaks and holidays where I would see him, but it wouldn't be the same and I had to get used to this new way, kind of like ripping the band aid off quickly. It would not do him good to have a mother hovering like a helicopter. The helicopter noise was riveting, and it blew too much wind for him to stand still. He would eventually run, never looking back. That's not what I wanted for him.

I did do a lot for Alex, don't get me wrong, and Bill would accuse me of doing too much sometimes. I would get mad at Bill, but I really needed this reality check and that is one thing I do thank Bill for. I think mothers just want the best for their children, but if you hover too much, it's eerily similar to keeping a bird in the cage to bite the wires desperately trying to get out. If that bird is kept caged too long, it falters, and gives into the beck and call of the owner while remaining motionless and compliant, caged, and never able to fly.

I see these moms like lawnmowers or even worse, the snow blower. They pave the path and they only want what is best for their kids, but they cause a damaging wake in their path. I don't see the need for the magnetized bumper sticker on the minivan to let the world know we need to be patient because of a student driver. These parents should just create a new slogan that reads, "Watch out, my child is traveling in a bubble."

When I saw stickers like that I tried not to let it irritate me, but it made me feel cognizant not to behave like this for my son because I wanted him to become a man of independence. With the money Alex made in his first few weeks at school, he furnished his dorm. Not only was he logical and well read, but also a minimalist. He didn't want to take much of anything with him because he said he wanted to start a new life. Therefore, he was able to fly to his new destination with very little but his suitcase and his dignity. I envied these qualities in him. He packed his clothes, plastic stars, books, belongings, and we got him a one-way ticket to his new chapter in life.

Gosh this chair is uncomfortable. I don't like sitting by a fire during the day, but I love to hear the crackle of a fire. I had this one going well just like Dad showed me. I hear the pops, then lean back and stare into the flames again.

Bill comes to mind upon this heat rising in front of me. The crackle and pop of the fire bends my mind towards the day we took Alex to the airport. By nothing short of a miracle, Bill was able to go with us to the airport on the day Alex was to leave. I remember feeling really good about that. I was surprised and Alex was taken aback because Bill rarely was a part of our lives because he was always somewhere else. So even though I felt he was too late, it felt good for him to come on this important day. Alex didn't want a fan fair coming into the airport, but he wanted us to drop him off and we both agreed. I remembered thinking on that day that that ride may have been the last time the three of us would be in a car driving anywhere together. I was feeling I needed to be present because nothing about that trip was about me or Bill, just Alex.

On the way there, I sat quietly while Bill drove. I looked out the window and wondered how all this time went by so fast. I wore dark sunglasses so as to not reveal the tears streaming down my face uncontrollably. The tears seeped out of the sides of my glasses like a slow trickle from a constantly moving waterfall. I felt the years of baby bottles, late night feedings, first days of school, vacations, graduations, dances, braces appointments, broken bones, and all the in-betweens played by me like a movie that was in fast forward. These memories moved about the same speed of our car rolling down the highway at seventy-five miles an hour.

While I like to answer the question of "Where did the time go?" with my answer of, "In my heart," it still didn't make me feel better at all. Each bump we hit was a reminder, like a kick in the gut that I was going to be alone, really alone especially because I didn't have a spouse to share this pain with. I was hoping for traffic, for an accident, for even a little slow down to get any extra minute I could. But I caught a glimpse of Alex's face in the rear-view mirror and he didn't look nervous at all. He was a young man with a look of freedom in his eyes. There was a calmness on his slightly grinning lips. That was the only thing that brought on a slight relief similar to a Tums soothing a severe stomachache.

We sat in silence until we pulled up in front of the airport. Bill got out first and went to get the suitcase from the trunk. By the time I got out, because it takes me a little bit with my weight, I walked around back to find Alex and Bill in a tight embrace. Bill's face flushed with actual tears. Could this man have loved our son? Had I been wrong about him this whole time? Strange how poignant moments like these can break down a wall as strong as a Roman pillar. They embraced for a long time, and this embrace was encompassing and heartfelt. This sight brought me to an all-out sob as quiet as I could make it. Alex pulled away after a bit, some tears from him too.

"Love you Dad. I'll be fine," he said sniffling.

"I know you will," said Bill. "Just be a man and take on all the responsibilities given to you and more and you will be successful." He turned and looked me in the eyes for what seemed like the first time in years, smiled softly and got back into the car.

Any mother knows that your baby is your baby forever no matter how big they become or how old. No one can take that bond away, not a gale wind, nor a flood or a tsunami wave.

The air was calm.

I was left to stand there with my only son, my baby whom I loved more than myself for the last eighteen years unconditionally. I had to cut the pacifier, pack away the onesies, hand him the keys to a new journey. This was a tough pill to swallow. I took a deep breath and tried to hold it together. A gentle August breeze moved suddenly with traces of humidity, yet tones of the turn of the season left me standing there speechless and hollow, waiting to embrace the frigid cold air moving in soon.

What do you say? Like every parent who has had to do this in some way, be it college, job, military, or even death, we lose the young mother that was once in our hearts when we wave goodbye and bid farewell. We mothers would have to wait to be filled again with a new beginning of a fresh mother's love, just in a different way now.

Alex's voice was trembling. "Will you be okay Mom?"

"Of course, I will honey. You know I am a warrior. Nothing knocks me down easily because no one can at this weight." It both sent us into a giant laugh.

Alex has the best sense of humor. He was able to laugh at himself, just like I could and not skip a beat even when we were feeling our absolute worst.

"Maybe the next time you see me, I will look different. I am going to try my best to go on a diet. I want to live long to see you do all the things you are going to accomplish in life." And with that, the tears couldn't be held back. I felt like I couldn't stop the liquid, like the levees breaking during Hurricane Katrina.

We stayed there for a little while until the airport attendant came over to tell us we had to move the car. She had been watching this whole thing.

She came up to me with tears in her eyes. "I see a ton of these goodbyes everyday here and I guess at what kind of goodbyes these are and then move on. But something about this parting made me cry. Thanks for passing on the love. It's so hard to be a mother, isn't it? I hate to tell you to move darlin', but it's my job. You've been here too long," she said with a smile.

I nodded understandably with a quiet grin from mother to mother. Sometimes the humanity in life's moments make me feel there is no hatred in the world. I loved that feeling.

I was glad this mother intervened because I would have clung on to Alex and never let go, but the hum of the helicopter gave me a signal to vacate the area, along with the horn beep from Bill.

I grabbed Alex's hand one last time and gave him my Dr. Seuss line of moving mountains.

Alex giggled as a tear rolled down his cheek. "You always quote Dr. Seuss Mom or anyone for that matter. Do you have any words of your own, you literary slacker?"

We both laughed again.

"You had to make me cry, didn't you?" he said. He picked up his suitcase and backpack, held my hand tightly one more second, smiled and waved to Bill sitting in the car.

As I watched him turn away, I took a mental note in my head to remember all my senses at this time of our parting. I watched him walk through the doors that close like the official ending of a chapter. I could see him snake in the lines until he disappeared, just like the sun melting down quietly on the horizon over another beautifully brilliant day.

When I got back into the car Bill took my hand, squeezed it, and we drove off in silence back home to the emptiness. Neither of us said a word the whole ride home. There was just sheer, dead, silence. Something about the air we were breathing seemed unsettling, so I had to crack a window to get some relief to breathe clearly. The air dove into the car madly. It created a pressure that hurt our ears. Bill had to crack his window open to balance the unsettled pressure of parenthood. My heart felt as hollow as the remnants of a spider web that decorated a once lit window on a humid night. The temperature lowered, the leaves fell off, the spider left for warmer days. All that remained were stringy lifeless lines. LandSlide played softly on the radio and I told Bill he had to turn it off or I would never stop crying.

When we pulled up into the driveway and went into the house, I noticed another suitcase that brought me to a halt. "Oh no, did Alex forget this?" I said with a worried voice only a mother can project. I turned around to look at Bill and he just stood there stoically.

"It's mine Tammy. Please tell me you knew this was coming," Bill said calmly.

The suitcase was Bill's. He had beat me to the punch. Once Alex was on his flight cruising at an altitude of thirty-two thousand feet, Bill told me he was moving into his own apartment and wanted to separate. Of course, I knew this was coming, but something in me wanted me to be the one to do this first and not directly after we dropped Alex off at the airport. I felt blind-sided, but at that point it didn't matter who started what first. He was just not wasting any time starting his new life as well.

I needed to start my new life right then and there. I didn't say one word, but I walked over and gave him a hug. It felt somewhat superficial this time, yet apropos for the moment. He let go rather quickly as he could barely get his arms all the way around me. I know this bothered him to the core because I felt his disappointment and smelled his shame in our quick embrace.

He kissed the top of my forehead and said, "I never fell out of love with the girl you once were," then he walked out the door.

I heard the car start and pull away as the motor muffled against the wind. I knew at that moment I hadn't changed, he had. This farewell was a dagger to my heart.

Staring into this fire is supposed to be meditative, not tearful. My head throbs worse when I cry. This is the last thing I want to do right now is lose tears over Bill. Crying over Alex is always worth it but not Bill. I didn't think I had any tears to waste on that man anymore. I'm pissed at myself for allowing Bill to seep into my life especially in this pain I am in, but I can't help replaying what happened after he walked out the door.

I stoke the fire and make sure I give it more air so I can continue to hear the pops. I replay the events after Bill walked out the door. I remember that I walked into the dark kitchen without turning on the light to get something to eat after he left. Walking to the kitchen was always my way out in times of trouble. I knew every step to the food trail, similar to a bloodhound tracking a murder victim. I stood in front of the refrigerator as the only light that illuminated was when the door opened. It arose immediately like the lights people see at the end of the tunnel upon coming to their death. The light was so bright, beckoning me to come that way, but something in me made me turn away. I had no inkling to grab food for the first time in my life.

And then I saw the bottle of wine someone gave me a while ago. I thought about drinking the whole thing down. I shifted my thought of self-medicating, while letting the light almost sting my eyes again with the darkness all around me. I felt like I was on a small boat floating on the gentle waves with my feet dangling off the edge of the world. I could float away for a little while, but eventually I would have to dock the boat because a storm was coming. I had to prepare and batten down the hatches to protect all of my valuables. I closed the refrigerator door. The light left again in a quick flash moving away suddenly and without warning. I desperately wanted to open it again and I did, and I did, and I did again until my hands left the refrigerator handle finally. On the last time I let go of that handle I looked down and saw a plastic star on the ground. It glowed so brightly in the dark kitchen illuminating my new path out of the past.

The fire is close to dying out. It is getting dark again because there is now a small glow of black ashes still clinging on to the air.

I still hear Alex's voice but I can't make out what he's saying.

I feel my Mom is nearby, silent with thoughts of encouragement.

I think of my dad.

He will guide me on what I should do next in my life.

I feel so lost without him.

Chapter 26

Ashley

> *"Watch the little things; a small leak will sink a great ship."*
> -Benjamin Franklin

I ended up getting out of the massage later than expected so no way I was going to make tennis. My phone started buzzing with texts from Lola and Chris as soon as I put the car in drive. Apparently my text of "ok" was taken as I was being a bitch. He told me he really wanted me to come to New York and also to make sure I was home for dinner later.

I text him back with a "Got it." He also expected me to tell the kids that he was leaving for New York on the way home from school today so I could lessen the boom for him.

Of course, why would he tell them? He was supposed to be their savior. He was supposed to make all their problems go away by throwing a ball around the backyard for ten minutes. He probably already hired a coach to pick up his slack.

Lola was looking for me because I blew off tennis today. She could be a nagging bitch when she wanted to be. I almost drive off the road texting her back. The tires skid off the road kicking up gravel. I have to swerve the car to get back on the pavement. I am texting her back when the phone starts ringing. Lola's name flashes across the screen on the dash. I decide not to answer it. I am sure by this time she's found someone else to hit with her. I let it go to voicemail because I don't feel like hearing her shit. At the light, I finish my text to her, saying I'm not feeling well and that I would text her in the morning. All she comes back with is a middle finger emoji.

    I pull up into the circus line at school. Noah gets in the car right away but we wait for Ava, who is always fashionably late. She is walking briskly when she comes out the front door, which is a giant arch adorned with a glorious cross. She sees my car then all of a sudden walks very slowly like a cat just waking up from a nap.

    "Well, hi to you too, Noah," I finally say because it seemed like a contest of who was going to say hello first.

    "Hey," he says without any hint of emotion.

    Ava enters the car with her presence. I can feel the drama getting ready to showcase itself like we are an audience at a play.

    "Will Dad be home when we get home?" she says.

    Oh shit. I don't want to tell her and Noah that Chris would be leaving again so soon. My muscles are already tensing up after a massage. She barely gives me a minute to choose what I am going to say. Ava monopolizes the oxygen with her poisonous gases permeating the space.

    "Well hi to you, too," I say annoyed. Do these kids give a fuck if I even show up?

    "Dad told Noah and me that we can practice today after school," she says excitedly. She is acting like she has never seen the man before. I have to blurt it out.

    "Oh, that's good. But I hate to tell ya that he won't be around for the next game because he is leaving for New York tomorrow morning. I plan on going out there at the end of the trip. He says he may have to be gone longer than usual, possibly two to three weeks. He has a big project he is working on. He needs to be there."

"What?" says Ava who is already starting to cry.

Oh fuck, I don't hear her bullshit. She could cry at the drop of a hat. The crying always goes right through me.

"Really Mom? That's not what he told us last night," Noah chimes in.

"I know, I just heard today guys. Stop crying Ava because there is nothing you can do. Crying just makes things worse in life. You should learn this now, missy. Plans change quickly in business. I can't tell him not to go so you can both throw the ball around with him in the backyard. He is the one paying for all these things you all have. We'll have dinner tonight before he leaves tomorrow," I say, sounding like a parent.

"How long will he be gone?" says Noah again with no emotion in his voice. He is looking out the window straight ahead, not looking in my direction at all.

"I'm not sure because I haven't seen him yet. His text was short. I am sure he is getting a new coach for both of you, so don't worry," I say, trying to make up for the fact that he'll be gone again. I am shocked at their sudden need to be around Chris.

"Is he going to get us a coach then?" Ava says in her bitchiest voice. She has stopped crying because she knows it isn't going to get her anywhere. She sounds pissed now. It is loud and clear to me at this point. She doesn't give one fuck about her dad. Ava just wants to get what works for her. What a little bitch.

"I am sure he already has people on it, Ava. You'll get someone that will help you be able to get the ball over the plate." I can't help being sarcastic because her selfish comment pisses me off.

"Please Mom. Have you ever thrown a pitch? You just danced so you have no idea what you're talking about. Dad gets it," she says proudly in her snarky response.

This is where I end it and let Chris take over before he leaves. If I go further I'll just end up slapping her.

I can tell Noah gives a shit that Chris will be gone again because I catch a glimpse of him when I turn my head. He looks sad as he sits pensively staring out the window. I take my eyes off him because I have to hit the brakes fast. The car in front of me stops sooner than I realize. I instinctually throw my hands out in front of Noah quite dramatically. I shock myself at this touch of motherhood. I didn't think I had it in me.

"Wow Mom! Why did you do that? I have my seatbelt on, geez! You scared me," he yells.

I am surprised he got that upset. It is like he is mad that I physically touched him. His emotion takes me off guard but I think his anger is about Chris, not me.

"Guess it was just mother's instinct babe. Sorry to startle ya," I say defensively.

Everyone gets quiet again. It seems like we can't have a normal conversation without someone whining or getting annoyed. Here comes the crossing guard. We all sit staring at the herd of people crossing the street. Some people are walking. Some kids are running, parents talking, and there is the big lady. She looks even bigger to me today. She is lagging behind everyone because her stomach is sagging over her saggy thighs. She has saddlebags that are almost touching the ground. Her arm is up high with the stop sign. Layers of fat sag down over her raised arm. She looks strained holding this one-pound sign for God's sake. She is out of breath. All the people clear off the white lines. The cars move forward while she stays on that side. I drive past looking right at her to see that she is wildly chewing her gum. She grins as I ride by with a friendly nod making direct eye contact with me.

I look away.

I want to roll the window down and tell her to check out Weight Watchers but I drive away with a cold stare out the window.

In the silence that was still lingering in the car, I think about this New York trip with Chris. Even though the kids are older now, I still am not able to leave them alone just yet. It is pretty easy to plan though because I figure I will just ask Naomi to come stay with the kids. I am quite sure she will want to come stay at the house, eat my food, and drive my car. She will pretty much pretend to be me. If Naomi can't help, I'll ask my parents, but they would be the last resort.

Sometimes in my life I feel like a tightrope walker who carelessly floats on the wire. But when I lose my balance, I know I am able to fall into a delicate net that will cradle my fragile ego. I get up, dust myself off and move on to the next thing without a thought. I've always had someone to take care of my plans.

At the next light I text Naomi. Within a millisecond, the response is a yes. This woman has no life of her own.

Ava and Noah remain silent in the car, headphones go on and they are in their own little worlds. I start to feel myself getting excited about this trip. We haven't gone on a trip, just us, in a while. It feels good to want to be with Chris again because day by day lately, I have seemed to lose my interest in sex. I felt my sex drive changing slowly over time a few years ago. I have always been known as the sex vixen, even at a young age because I bloomed well before my years. But now, I am getting worried about my libido because it seems to be losing air like a slow leaking tire. What is worse is I have to hide my lack of appetite for sex because this has been my image for as long as I can remember.

Sex was what landed Chris.

I have to sustain this ride or it will start going down the tubes. Our relationship has been about wild sex right from the start, but now it is not easy to keep up with, especially at my age. Therefore, I have kept up the way I look with my body, my whole being, even if it is at the expense of me not always enjoying our intimacy. Over the last few years I have had to fake orgasms more than I have them. I have been prescribed hormone options by my doctor, but it has done little to gain back what I had back in college. I am willing to give it a shot to keep my marriage together. I guess hormone shots, Botox shots, breast lifts, liposuction, electrolysis, waxing, and soothing jelly will be the glue holding my relationship in somewhat one piece.

But when Chris was gone on his trips, I got into my own routine because I simply did everything without him. I was able to be at home, shop, work out, see my friends, enjoy my own orgasms that required a fantasy, no pressure, a few minutes, then peace. I basically got to do whatever I wanted to do, whenever I wanted to do it, without having to worry what he was doing or having to put out for his obsession with sex. It was exhausting as he was ready to go twenty-four seven.

There have been many times I feel like I'm just a high-class call girl. Sometimes I miss our old days of being obsessed with each other but it just kept fading like the intensity of my orgasms. When he was gone, we would talk a few times a week, text daily and sometimes facetime, but most of these conversations were short, non-authentic, or just check-ins to see how the kids were doing. I thought the kids got really used to him being gone as well, especially Noah because he didn't have someone riding his ass all the time. But I'm not so sure anymore because of his outburst. Ava on the other hand, was a big drama queen. She was Daddy's girl when she was younger, especially at bedtime. I can remember almost every night she would cry before going to bed when Chris was gone. I would feel her climb into my bed at three am to find comfort. I usually let her stay because sometimes I secretly welcomed it, for I felt alone too at night sometimes, so having her there was a nice security blanket for me as well. That chapter of Daddy's girl ended abruptly, though, when she figured out her phone was a better replacement for her dad, and me too.

I read once that you need thirty days to establish new routines, and we have moved past that mark. It is clear that this mundanity is our life. The good thing with Chris gone though is that he is paying the bills. Therefore, I do not have to burden myself with expenses. The money is rolling in and plentiful. I've become used to this lifestyle so I can't imagine having to go to work again. Therefore, I deal with the mundanity.

The kids do, too.

This little trip to New York will going to interfere with my routine, but I feel ready and willing to go. Maybe this will be a good time to rekindle the flame. Maybe it will help our kids? I keep thinking of Noah's sad face in the car.

Our flame was on low for a while but now needs more oxygen. I am not talking about the robust flame with sparks because I know that will take way more than I have in me, but having some oxygen to create a moderate fire is all I am asking for. It's what we need.

We pull into the driveway. Chris is not home yet.

We walk in and move our separate ways.

Chapter 27

Tammy

> *"Life did not stop, and one had to live."*
> *- Leo Tolstoy*

Even though the flames have gone down in the fire pit, the hot coals scintillate with an orange glow against the now dark sky. I don't know how long I have been sitting here. There are no chimes, no clocks, and no numbers dictating what I should do next. It feels good for once. The glimmer of the fire light makes me feel warm all over with thoughts of my dad.

His family was so much different than my mom's but I loved them all the same. I really enjoyed my visits to the city to visit both sets of grandparents. Our house wasn't far away from where my dad grew up on the south side of Chicago, which is where most of my relatives had set their anchors to stay.

My dad's parents had a house that sat right on the flight path a stone's throw away from the short runways at Chicago's Midway Airport. To the outside visitor, the sound and sight of the airplanes could send people running to seek shelter. That's how close the planes would fly over my grandparents' house when they were coming in for a landing. From my grandparents' porch, anyone could wave to the pilot and passengers as the plane rumbled by shaking the house. I got used to it after a while, but I can remember the first time visitors would hold their ears to cover up the noise. When the planes flew over us we didn't miss a beat chatting while eating Grandma's homemade Italian meals.

Friday nights were always something to look forward to when I was growing up because Dawn and I loved to go to Dad's softball games in his old neighborhood. We would stop off at grandma and grandpa's house before the game to enjoy their company. Sometimes they would come too to watch the "glory days." My dad played sixteen-inch softball using no mitt with his old high school buddies, most of whom he also went to Vietnam with as well. It baffled me to see the men trying to catch this big ball pummeling off the bat, shooting out like a cannon. This is why Dad had band-aids on almost every finger, in addition to being a carpenter. No sixteen-inch player or tradesman had hands that looked like someone who worked in an office. My dad's hands were calloused, white-taped, and swollen from becoming jammed, but the game went on. This is where my love of softball started.

What didn't occur to me as a kid was how important these softball games were for my dad because they sealed lasting bonds with his friends. To have a solid core group of friends you knew from grade school, high school, or both was unique. Most of them were also drafted at age nineteen spending their youth in Vietnam. They were shipped to a country on the other side of the world where they did not understand what they were being asked to do or for what cause. Amazingly, most of my Dad's friends came back from the war, somewhat in one piece, and continued to keep their forever lasting bond. I grew up with these men as role models but felt I took their relationships for granted. I was too young to understand what they had to endure and how it shaped who they had become.

My dad was a private man, so he rarely talked about his experiences in Vietnam. As a kid, I just didn't understand what it meant to go to war or even what war was, but my sister, being older than me, was always intrigued about his experiences because she was learning about wars at school. Many times she would ask questions at dinner, or when we were sitting around the fire pit. I could tell Dad was guarded, but mom would jump in with a light-hearted story if she could because she also went through an experience in a different way of course.

I hear my mom's infectious laugh on a lower volume from a distance in the cold room. It makes me smile.

The fire pit glows so low now but the coals are still bright orange and red, stained with some light illuminating. I want this fire to remain warm as I longed to hear my Dad's voice again and feel my mom's arms around me. I put another log on the fire to keep the flame going.

I would give anything to hear one more story of his around this fire. I wish I had asked him more questions about Vietnam when he would talk about it. I always felt fearful of making him talk about something he wanted to bury. My sister had no problem extracting stories from Dad's vault though because she was the complete opposite of me with her directness.

The fire glows and the heat warms my skin so gently.

I feel Dawn's hand on mine.

I remember very distinctly a time when Dawn was doing a research project on the Vietnam War. Each night at dinner she would ask dad questions about his experiences to learn more. In her words, she said she wanted to capture the "human side of war" in her paper. I could tell at times my dad would squirm in his seat when she would start talking about protests and Kent State. Or when she would start stating facts that she read about that she thought were true. My dad would shake his head saying her teacher was wrong about events. I remember seeing him get defensive, trying not to raise his voice but I knew he wanted to. I knew he had stories he wanted to tell but couldn't. I knew he couldn't give any answers to the question we all wanted to ask. I don't think he would be able to let the truth out into the open air for fear of retaliation, guilt, and sin. He was a very religious man, so both Dawn and I respected anything he said about Vietnam or what he didn't want to say.

I knew that what the teachers told my sister from hearsay and history books couldn't hold a candle to dad's stories. He didn't read about the journey; he lived the journey. Some of his stories were funny, but most of them were serious. He told these stories on his terms, not anyone else's. So when he spoke, we listened. For some of the stories he would say he needed to talk to my sister privately because he didn't want me to hear, so he would sit with her and talk in the family room. I wanted desperately to be part of the conversation, but I was told Dawn was older so she was mature enough to hear them. I always saw my dad as a superhero, someone not at all insecure or vulnerable. But when he would relinquish some of the stories he had, I sensed instability and a visceral anger within him, and it unsettled me.

On the last day of the war unit in Dawn's class, the teacher showed a movie when all the research papers were turned in. My sister thought she learned all she needed to know about the war, but even dad's stories didn't prepare her for what she saw in this movie. Dawn was always so put together similar to soldiers preparing for war, stoic, hard-nosed, and ready for battle. So it shocked me at dinner when she burst into tears when she started telling us about watching the movie *Born on the Fourth of July* by Oliver Stone.

Quite suddenly Dawn got worked up as her voice started shaking. She said, "Dad, I had no idea what you had to go through in Vietnam, especially when you came home. I can't believe people hated you and spit at the soldiers after all you did to help." She sobbed again in between the sobbing, " How could they? Thank you. I've never said it before but thank you Daddy," and tears started flowing down her cheeks.

Her voice had an intensity I had never heard from her mouth before. And then she started sobbing. She got up and gave my dad a heart-wrenching hug. She wasn't letting him go. I was confused. I was unglued watching her because I had never seen her act like this. It was like an alien had dropped in for dinner and I was trying to figure out where she came from. She was crying so hard that it made me cry. My gaze fell off her and onto my parents. My dad was holding my sister.

My Mom got up from the table and joined in the hug. This was all so perplexing that I didn't know if I should join the hug party. I saw my Dad's shoulders shaking up and down. He was crying too, so was Mom. He grabbed the napkin and covered his face. When he took the napkin away his eyes were stained red with Vietnam. The color of his face lost its hue, and he had this faraway look like he had been possessed. He looked like a stranger to me for the first time in my life. Then it got awkwardly silent. I wanted this to end. I wanted my sister to sit back down and stop talking so we could get back to the fun stories we would tell. I had seen my mom cry before but not my dad. All of a sudden I lost my appetite.

I was uncomfortable in a way similar to losing a favorite teddy bear.

All sense of belonging and safety left my body and I got nervous. Dawn was crying for what she saw because these were experiences our dad lived. My dad looked at me because he sensed my being uncomfortable. He rose from his chair and gave me a hug. This broke the tension a little but I didn't know what to say, so I said nothing. I could tell he was concerned about my tears, and my look of sheer confusion. He held me tightly so I could try and figure out just why I was crying too. I finally found my words.

"What is Dawn talking about that people would spit at soldiers at a welcome home parade?" I asked, trying to break this awkward silence.

Mom tried to explain but Dawn cut her off before she could launch into a Vietnam War history lesson. "Did you get spit at Dad?" Dawn asked.

Before he could answer I said, "Dad, did you ever hurt?"

But I got cut off by Mom rather abruptly. "Sweetie, there are things you can't ask a veteran and that's one of them, ok?"

Dad didn't answer. He just sat quietly and cried, his hands covering his face again. Mom was patting his back trying to console him. He had trauma packed from the barracks that needed to be purged.

He never unpacked his suitcase.

I never asked that question again.

I know Dad did not like his vulnerability on display for his girls so he interrupted the uncomfortable situation. "I didn't go to any parade, girls. My parents and mom's parents put up a banner on their windows. With tension back here at home, we didn't want to draw attention to the fact that I was a Vietnam Veteran. We had a welcome back party with our own family, not a parade," he said matter of factly.

At that point I was interested more in why someone would spit at soldiers at a parade, not what my dad went through. Even at a young age, I have always been inquisitive, so I figured out this topic was much more complicated based on how this dinner automatically shifted from jovial to heart-attack serious in seconds. But I didn't want to see my dad in this situation again. He was vulnerable and I didn't like any part of it. I sat quietly not knowing what to do. I really didn't have any more questions.

I was pissed at my sister for making my dad feel this way. Dawn had really struck a nerve to break my Dad's soul wide open. I held this against her for many years even though she didn't know it.

It wasn't until after Dad died that I fully understood why Dawn got so emotional that night at dinner. I saw the movie with Bill years later because I could never bring myself to watch it, especially after Dad died. Bill sat unaffected while I bawled my eyes out throughout the entire film. I finally understood Dawn's outburst years before. I wanted so badly to give my dad a hug like she did, tell him thank you for all of his honor. I sat silently at dinner that night because I didn't want to see my dad lose his strength. But I failed to see that his tears were his strength.

The coals are almost out of heat. The orange and red flames are low, turning to black. The heat is low but still present in front of me. I shift uncomfortably because my headache is coming back. I get up from the chair and find my way back to the hammock. I sink in slowly. I cover my face the way my dad did years ago at the dinner table. I think of the stories they told us and it makes me smile.

My parents always stuck with the same theme that Dad's experience from Vietnam was the worst time in their life. They thanked God they were young when this happened. Whenever stressful moments arose in life, they would say to themselves that if they got through that time, any time forward would be a piece of cake. All of this was good for me to see because what my dad and mom did was establish a core group of friends that would stick with them all the way to the end of the road.

I would think about these friendships even deeper as I sat at Dad's funeral when they folded the flag and let out the military salute. I thought about how he could survive such an atrocity, then die of a heart attack at age forty-one. The doctors tried to save him. He hung on for some days until he had no more left to give. My mom never left his side for a minute. Watching her was even more tortuous than watching my dad die. He had given more than enough in our book, but it didn't extinguish the excruciating pain we all felt.

None of this seemed right to me.

I watched his dear friends one by one, men who fought in Vietnam weep with such sorrow as they wore white gloves to hold the weight of my dad's casket. These grown men survived a war. They were the toughest men I knew and to see them weep forced my soul to weep with grief. I heard stories I hadn't heard, some I had, but mostly the theme was about my dad's strong conviction to his friends and family, not to mention the loyalty to his country. Don't get me wrong, he told us how he had thought about fleeing to Canada upon getting drafted. My mom's father had political connections and could have gotten my dad out of the draft, but my dad said no because he felt an obligation to serve his country. He was a man of integrity and character, even as a nineteen-year-old young man.

I always felt Dawn knew more about my dad's plight, but he did start telling me more the older I got. I lie here now thinking of his low voice in the peaceful darkness because I feel like I haven't heard his voice in a hundred years.

When I was entering high school I felt very nervous. He told me he grew up very quickly because he had no other choice and that this was how I needed to view this new step. His statement stuck with me. I knew exactly what he meant when I took my first step into a long and crowded high school hallway. This was the time of my life when he would tell stories that I could apply to my own journey. I can see him sitting at the fire giving me a speech when my sister had gone off to college. I felt lost and empty without her in the house. He started out with how he was drafted and how he was beyond worried. He was a troublemaker in high school, but after graduation he knew he needed to make a living. He thought about college, but his parents couldn't afford it, so he started trade school after high school and shortly after he married my mom. He was feeling right with his path in life and in love, then the draft. It hung heavy over him like a stratus cloud filled with precipitation. Right before he was to leave for boot camp, he found out Mom was pregnant with Dawn. This threw even more chaos into the mix and everyone in the family scrambled trying to get him out of going. While he had already been enrolled in trade school, the government didn't feel that was as important as going to college. The government also didn't care that he was expecting a baby either. "They needed nineteen-year-old men to be pawns in their political games," Dad would say.

He taught me the word "brainwash" during this conversation and how he learned quickly how to read people. My Dad had to undergo intense training, leave his family, travel to far-away places, separate from his friends not knowing whether they were dead or alive, and sleep with a millipede a foot long crawling out of his backpack.

The fear of almost being killed daily put a heavier strain on him than the backpack he was carrying. He told me how he listened to *The Doors* for hours on end, dreaming of going home, back to his wife, his family, and his friends. What he wouldn't give for an Italian dinner at his mom and dad's house in their tiny kitchen. He would have even gone back to my grandmother launching coke bottles at his head when he failed to come home one night at the age of sixteen. He wanted to hear those planes roaring overhead, until the sound of a chopper would jolt him back into the reality of where he was really at, left to wonder if would ever see his old life again. Suddenly, I didn't feel so bad that my sister left for college. I felt it was my time to receive all my dad's attention. I knew I could overcome any obstacle if he was able to do all of these things.

I shift to adjust my head in the hammock. I sway comfortably thinking about my dad's incredible journey. It has always been at the forefront of my life as a guiding light. What led my dad back home after a year in Vietnam was nothing short of fate, faith and timing.

Before my dad left, my mom's aunt, who was a Catholic nun, gave him a St. Joseph's prayer card. She said for him to keep it on him every single day. He did this faithfully. Part of the prayer card describes that holding this card about you would cause you never to die in the hands of the enemy or be burned in any fire.

On the very St. Joseph's Day, my dad and another young soldier were in an LST naval type tank waiting to cross a river. They flipped coins to see who would drive. My dad won the toss so he got to drive. A few moments later, a bomb hit the back end of the tank and blew up on the passenger side.

When the bomb exploded and the dust settled, my dad was lying on the ground severely injured. He received a tracheotomy right there in the field along with substantial head injuries. He vaguely remembered the details after the bomb hit, but he remembered the trauma and noises of what ensued. He was in a coma.

He woke up a month later in a Japanese hospital to find out his soldier friend had died in this accident. Additionally, he found out he was now a new father with the birth of my sister Dawn. He had not been there to see this take place, not to mention the incredible guilt he had of surviving over his buddy in the passenger seat. He had been blind for a few weeks, and he shattered just about every bone in his face. He had received several plastic surgeries to put his face back together, complete with plastic cheek bones that he sometimes would push to scare my sister and me. The plastic would stick out towards the corner of his eye. He would show us this to freak us out when we were little, but we never knew why he had this. He would just tell us he got hurt when we were younger, but as we matured, we finally knew the real story behind the moving cheekbone. We also always carried around a St. Joseph card faithfully in honor of Dad.

I honestly don't know how my mom survived. While my dad was injured, she had no way of knowing whether Dad was alive or not. These life and death circumstances were all communicated through telegrams, with weeks in between each report. My mom didn't feel better until she started receiving letters not in Dad's handwriting, but from the nurse who would scribe for my dad. My Mom still has the telegraphs and the little red, white, and blue striped letters that chronicle the plight of emotion of this intense love story. When mom would tell us stories her eyes would drift to a far distant universe. She was gone in time for moments while speaking. She showed us the telegrams and said she might let us read some letters when we were older, but I always felt this was an invasion of privacy. I felt their story was preserved beautifully, sealed, and stored away in the attic.

It was months of recovery before my dad was sent home to somehow put the pieces back together of the life he once knew. In just over a year, his eyes had seen more than most in a single lifetime, if ever at all.

I can still see my dad at the fire pit talking.

"Just think," my dad said over the crackling of the fire casting an orange glow on his face. "A coin flip decided my fate and my buddy. If I lost the coin toss, I wouldn't be here and neither would you, Tammy. In that one flip, the course of our lives changed for the better, and not in a good way for my buddy who died," and he sighed.

This is the second time I saw him cry. He stopped and hung his head bringing his hands to his face again to hide his shame. I could feel the guilt oozing out of his pores. Even though I was older I still didn't get up to give him a hug or thank him for his service. I don't know why I didn't, and it bothers me to this day. I had a second opportunity to tell him how I felt but I blew it.

I shift quietly again as my thoughts move back to this story. I hear my dad speaking again.

"I was never able to tell my buddy's parents that their son had asked to trade seats. I didn't tell them that I had the St. Joseph's card, not him. I didn't find it necessary to expose them to even more anguish on one small decision. They would play the game over and over again of 'What if?' I play this game all the time and eats away at me when life is quiet. I just didn't feel it was right for them to live like this, but I have taken on and owned that guilt every day of my life. I ask myself often, why was I spared? What can I do to live this life to the fullest because I was granted this tremendous gift?" He took a deep breath, grabbed my mom's hand with love.

We sat quietly listening to the sudden cracks of sticks popping from the heat. I wished my sister was there because maybe she would have gotten up from her chair to give another hug, prompting me to do this because I always wanted to be like her.

I take a deep breath. I think I hear one last pop on the fire I made, but I think it was something else because it is dark again.

My dad sure did live and lead by example, by being an extraordinary father, husband, and dedicated friend to all who knew him. He really truly was my one and only hero. I wish I had found the words to tell him that when he was alive right in front of me.

I fall sound asleep again with the dark ashes of war no longer smoldering, but destruction around every corner.

Chapter 28

Ashley

> *"What happens is not as important as how you react to what happens."*
> *- Ellen Glasgow*

By some miracle, school schedules align, events are taken care of, and all goes off without a hitch. I am on my way to New York City. Chris would be in a meeting when I am scheduled to land so he arranged for a car service to pick me up at the airport and take me to the hotel.

The New York skyline is somewhat nice, but nowhere near as neat and streamlined like the skyline of Chicago. I see my chaos locked into the New York skyline, kind of spread thin with lights not as twinkly. There is a dark ring of haze slowly circling around the busy people with harsh faces, garbage piled on filthy streets with loud horns beeping. New York City is nothing like where I would go to stay with my grandparents at the Hampton's, but it is a change of scenery at least from my suburban prison, so I am happy to make the break. Chris isn't going to be at the hotel until at least five so I have some time to kill.

I vacillate between going for a walk or getting a drink fifteen feet away at the hotel bar. I choose the latter because I figure I can go relax, text my kids and let them know I arrived, see how they were doing, check my emails, scroll through Facebook, judge everyone, and just chill.

I've been to New York several times and grew kind of tired of it. There will be plenty of time for leisurely walks with Chris later anyways. The bar is a happier place for me to be. I saunter over to have a liquid lunch with a shot of Xanax to take the edge off from traveling. This is not an uncommon practice because I am finding lately that many of my days turn into liquid lunches and a pill, but it is nice to change up the setting for something different.

The bar in the lobby is very bright and has fancy modern orange chairs that are really comfortable. Each end of the bar has these magnificent floral arrangements done in yellow and red to counterbalance the orange chairs. There is an older couple sitting chatting quietly. I notice that they looked very keen on each other. To the right of them is a man sitting at the corner of the bar ensconced in his laptop.

I sit down at the other end of the bar in the comfortable modern chairs. I take my phone out and text Noah and Ava to let them know I had arrived in New York. They both text back almost instantly with emojis. This is how we communicate these days, but nonetheless, they are all right. Neither of them text back about their games or anything. They have settled into the fact that Chris won't be there this weekend for the games. He had gotten them each a coach to work with while we are gone. Naomi is taking them to school and to their games. They are content so I don't have to deal with their drama, at least for this weekend. It feels freeing.

I make eye contact with the bartender coming towards me. He has a confident walk and broad shoulders that catches my attention right away. He kind of eyes me up and down, probably wondering why I am by myself in the middle of the day. I'm used to men staring at me, trying to initiate shallow conversations for a way to get into my pants.

I'm not an idiot, and I know where all the angles are instead of the genuine conversations. I must note though that he is absolutely adorable. He is way too young for me, but I don't think he would care either way. He has this sexy jaw. His sleeves are rolled up to his biceps so I can see his thick forearms painted with detailed tattoos. He is a badass with a swagger that turns me on instantly. He wears a tight white dress shirt with black pants rolled at the bottom with Doc Marten black boots. He sports a black beaded chain that hangs around his thick neck that lands so nicely on his tan skin. He wears a mala on one wrist and the other wrist bares a tattoo of three birds wrapping around the script that said, "Let it Be."

I wonder if he is a musician. Yeah, I can see him playing the guitar. I bet he has more tattoos hiding under his clothes. I can see him on stage rocking out with his guitar, hanging over the stage trying to rattle up the roadies. Lots of blowjobs behind the stage and parties, you know, sex drugs and rock and roll and all that shit.

He has really good hands. I always look at a man's hands and their forearms. My friends always laugh when I tell them this, but it's true for me. Some men's hands are so ugly with hair and bitten down nails that repulse me. I like a man's hands that look like they work, play the guitar, that look like they can grab a hammer and fix something, or put that hand around your waist, even hold your child tightly while throwing them up in the air at the pool. And the forearms have to be thick, like a drummer or a baseball player. Just thinking about it pulls me out of my perimenopause dryness. This guy has the whole package and has those masculine, nice hands I can visualize touching me. I sit there staring. I've already had sex with him.

"Hi," he says.

"Can I get you something to drink?" he smiles with a little boy charm.

I smile back coyly. I want to give a stare before I start speaking just to make a point. "I'll have a gin and tonic please with two limes."

He nods, turns around, and goes to work. I know many women look at a man's ass. I do not even look in that direction because most of the time a man's pants hangs off his ass because he doesn't have one. Everything about a man's ass repulses me, to be honest, all smelly and hairy. I know, it sounds weird, but that's how I feel. I can hear my mother-in-law in my head talking about Neil Diamond's buns. She would get crazy when she saw him in concert and talk about how she and her girlfriends would make their hands look like they were squeezing his butt. They were just nutty about Neil Diamond's tight-fitting suits.

"Oh, those buns!" my mother-in-law would say.

I would ask, "Did you like the music?"

"Of course, but look at those buns!" I would shake my head and wonder what the fascination was. But my mother-in-law was the best. She was filled with life. I loved her more than my own mother.

But a part of a man that makes me feel even more turned on besides forearms and shoulders, is a man's back. I watch the bartender move to get my drink and my eyes never leave his back. I can make out his muscles under his white shirt. I listen to the sound of the ice hitting the glass , the carbonation popping over the ice, the fizz, and the squeeze of the limes from his hands. He walks back slowly as if in slow motion. I watch his hand grip my glass as he lays it down softly on a napkin. He grabs a straw and slips it slowly into my gin with a slight turn of the liquid.

He has curly blonde hair that rolls to the side so effortlessly. He keeps pushing the hair out of his eyes with this head roll, kind of like he just got off a surfboard getting the sand out. Maybe he isn't a musician, but a surfer who moved to New York to try a new and different landscape. I visualize him as one of those guys who drifts in and out, tries out new places, stays there for a little while and moves on, kind of like a beatnik. His blue eyes match the ocean he is swimming in, and for a moment when we make eye contact, I feel like jumping in. He is leaning on the bar with a very confident what-have-you-got-going-on look. I am there, lost in a moment of sexual bliss and then, he opens his mouth. The water I am getting ready to jump into is cold. It is salty, stings my eyes, goes down my throat, and makes me choke. I had forgotten he had to talk.

"Sweetheart, I can tell you're not from New York. You must be from Chicago."

First of all, he calls me sweetheart. My dad calls me sweetheart. Where would any other man get off calling me that? One word and he ruins everything I am thinking about him. I am sure his name is Cooper or Cash, or maybe Austin. I don't know because I don't bother to ask, instead I sit there again for a long, flirty moment.

"If you knew me well, you would not think I was a sweetheart," I say.

"Oh wow, sorry to throw something nice out there in this wild world we live in." He has this thick New York accent and even though he calls me sweetheart, I kind of feel attracted to him in an unusual way.

It is kind of like when there is a scene in a movie where you know something bad is going to happen and you want to cover your eyes, but you just can't.

I can teach this guy a lot of things I think. Then suddenly my mind goes in a direction where I start visualizing him taking my clothes off and him kissing me intensely. I look at his lips. They are subtle and soft.

"Well, are you okay or should I leave you alone?" he says.

"Forget that, okay. Just tell me how you figured out I'm from Chicago by knowing me one minute while ordering a drink." Talking is part of this, so I need to play the game.

"I can tell by your accent. You said, 'Can I have a gin and tonic?' and he stressed the o in tonic. He continues, "You Chicago-ins say your o's so hard. So, I knew right away you were from Chicago."

He grins and of course he has this cute little dimple that fits his adorable smile. Those lips, my word.

"Really?" I say. "By one word, you know where I am from?"

"Yes, I do. Go ahead and say this word and he spelled it out, C-A-T."

I say, "cat."

"See, you said caaaat." and he moves his mouth accenting the sound. I really see his teeth when he does this, so prominent with a devilish smile that melts hearts. I think it is a bit dramatic to be truthful, but nonetheless it is a small conversation to strike up this love-hate fuckable brief encounter, but I am feeling enticed at the moment.

"I just don't see how you can take two words and make a decision on where I am from. That just seems presumptuous, that's all." I can't believe what comes out of my mouth. I am a walking contradiction and I am aware of it.

He barely speaks and I think I have his whole life story down and yet I am questioning why he thinks he knows where I was from. I guess there is a Chicago accent.

"Well," he says. "I am a hotel bartender in New York where many people come in from all over the world, so I think this makes me highly qualified in this department if I must say so myself." As he says this, he towels off the wet glasses he rinsed. His hands move around the glasses tightly picking up every last drop before he places them above the bar in a rack of neatly hanging glasses.

His hands land flush on the bar.

He moves in a little closer where I am able to smell him.

I start to get nervous because he looks directly into my eyes, similar to the nervous feeling I had when I first met Chris. I haven't felt this way in many years and it kind of feels good again. There they are again, those pools of blue. I stand with one toe in the water and check it out. The water slides over my toes and my feet are submerged. Do I go in deeper? I try not to glance away, but those eyes go right through me. I feel the gin mixing with my pill and it goes to my head. I think I appear flushed. I pick up my drink and sip it to divert the attention of this eye fuck that's happening in front of me. I need not to look like a schoolgirl lost in a craze of puppy love. I have to be in control with confidence as mighty as Katherine Hepburn.

"Okay," he says really slowly and closely. "I have one more word play I am going to throw out and it will be my final clue that you are from Chicago." He chuckles.

"Alright, go ahead," I say while rolling an ice cube around in my mouth very slowly and sexy.

See, this is my problem. I know that if I fucked this bartender that it would be really stupid, but something inside me wants to fuck him very badly, and not out of love, but out of pure lust and conquest. I mean flat out sex, no talking, just sex, and when it is done, we wouldn't sit there and cuddle. Somehow I am able to get in the mood. I visualize the crazy sex like when I was in college. Afterwards we would be able to just move on. I wouldn't even need to know his name. After sex we would put our clothes back on, give each other a kiss and move on with our lives before it got too complicated.

But then something stops me again. It isn't even for Chris's sake and the deception it would cause. I haven't once thought about how my action would affect my kids either until just now and even if I do, I don't think they fit in this equation. No one would know if I threw him down on this bar right now. It could be my little secret. Maybe this is what I need. Maybe this would make me a bad Mom. Maybe this would make me a bad wife. Maybe it would make me a jaded person but I need to be thinking about myself for once.

But I am not going to pull the trigger with this conquest because I don't want to deal with the backlash my infidelity would cause for me. There would be questioning, anger, and interrogation. Would I have to go get a job again? I simply don't want to deal with that. So, I flirt, and I flirt endlessly because I can. I guess I like it when a man is attracted to me. I know I can't have him and he can't have me, it just turns me on because I am receiving the attention I love.

The attention I have received from Chris has fizzled out like a carbonated soda that was left out for hours. There is no more fizz and no more bubbles, just a flat bland taste that makes your face move in an ugly way. Therefore, I like these mind games I play and I love the power they offer. It makes a man even more attractive to me if that makes sense. I can then make fantasies up in my head that belong to me. There is no questioning, there is no interrogation from anyone. There are absolutely no strings but my own thoughts.

I can tell Surfer Boy is watching me roll the cubes around in my mouth like a tiger getting ready to pounce. He sighs, wipes his forehead, then leans in closely.

I can smell him again. He has an aroma of charm, sweet sweat, and lust.

"Tell me what the word is for a pair of something for your feet that you wear to work out in."

I am now biting the ice that has melted, as I take another sip slowly making sure he can see my tongue caress the lime soaked with gin. "Gym shoes."

"That's it! You are from Chicago for sure!" He is acting like he just won the fucking lotto.

"New Yorkers say sneakers. You say gym shoes."

"Well, guess what? You're right. I am from Chicago . . . impressive. So what? Do I owe you something now?" I raise my eyebrows and bite my lip seductively.

"Well, we can see what can be arranged," he says right back without blinking an eye. He is right there with me on top of it all.

"So, is this really the only way you knew I was from Chicago? Tell me more," I say. Tell me more, tell me more, I sing in my head like Rizzo from the Pink Ladies.

"I'm from upstate New York, but I went to school at the University of Columbia in Chicago and spent many nights drinking with my friends. We always talked about the Chicago-New York competition shit. I found it funny that they said gym shoes and they would bust my balls and laugh when I said sneakers. It was a topic we always joked about. I was studying film and acting there. I auditioned for many commercials and was in plays since I'm an actor, so I know how to change accents depending on what I am acting in. I moved back to New York a few years ago to get into the Broadway Theater scene. I started taking more classes and networking. It ain't easy though, so I'm bartending on the side to pay my rent." He smiles with that dimple again.

Without much effort, he floats back around the bar to take care of others. The guy on the laptop hasn't looked up one time even when ordering another beer. The couple not far from me starts kissing. This is intriguing. They're hooked like a beer pretzel all salty and hot.

I keep staring at them. Everyone has a story.

"Good," I think to myself. Because he walked away so casually, this is going nowhere and not worth the time I'm spending on this worthless endeavor. I have this surfer-musician boy all wrong. It is a good thing I didn't jump in the water. Boy, I'm a good judge of character. Don't put me on a jury bench. I really had intended on sitting alone and not saying a fucking thing, but then some guy comes in and pierces the serene, calm air with needless words. But then again, what else do I have to do? I have a lot of hours on my hands. I think a good way out of this conversation if he comes back is simply pull out my phone and scroll through Facebook.

I swipe my screen of images of seemingly happy people or folks just trying to correct all the injustices of the world. Some of these pictures showcase gorgeous children with cascading hair on beaches clad all in white, posed family portraits, snow filled mountain tops on skis, anniversary cheers combined with political jargon, opinionated bullshit, and some strong but mostly weak arguments.

Most people just need an audience for their day-to-day existence. I don't post or hit likes. I just scroll. I wish there was a fuck you button, or a dislike button. Then I would hit it. I guess many of us feel the need to be acknowledged. But everyone knows that person who has to photograph everything in their life. Do we need to see the pasta dish you made? Do we need to see every single day and minute of your tropical vacation? It's always the good parts that are shown. Do we see you shitting in the bathroom after you had too many tequila drinks paired with a cheese burrito? Do we see your whiny three-year-old having a tantrum on the floor in the middle of paradise? What about your sassy teenager telling you to go fuck yourself? Now that would be entertaining. I know for sure behind most of those small moments on Facebook that people appear happy on the outside, but broken on the inside, just like me.

I wonder if people see through me like looking through a clean windshield, or is it foggy, not yet defrosted. I used to be good at hiding these things, but lately I feel as if I am losing my touch. I wonder if there could be a filter Facebook could use that shows shards of glass on most of these photos I see to capture what is really going on. No one wants to post their dirty laundry?

But I continue to scroll.

I am bored wishing Surfer Boy would come back. I can play hard-to-get like a scene from Three's Company at the Regal Beagle. If he sees me on my phone, that would indicate that I look busy and not want to engage with him anymore. Surely, he could pick up on that hint if he knows I am from Chicago.

Here he comes again for another drink, another seduction act. He had forgotten about me for a while and weirdly I was feeling left out.

"You need another one?"

"No, I don't *need* another one, I *want* another one."

"Ok," he smiles sweetly back at me. Oh my, those eyes. That dimple.

"I'll get right on top of that."

"I bet you will," I say. He turns and looks at me a little surprised at my comment. He smiles. No words, but I can tell he loves my comeback. He strolls back with the drink and leans in again closer and starts whispering this time. I feel butterflies inside.

He smells even better this time.

"You want to go out after my shift? It's almost over. We can go talk about our Chicago-New York connection," he says grinning with that dimple again.

I lead this conversation here full well knowing nothing will happen, but I cannot stop myself.

"Did you notice I had a ring on?" I say.

"Yeah, I noticed, but why would you be in this conversation so deeply if you were a happy woman?" He looks at me again with this eye fuck stare like he knows so much about me.

It pisses me off, yet I am enticed at the same time. I think this stupid little jerk sees right through me more than Chris has ever have picked up on.

"Listen, I'm not going to be your Mrs. Robinson." I smile thinking I've pulled one on him, but I had forgotten with all the gin that was rolling around in my brain that I am talking to a graduate of film from Columbia.

"Ha, that is one of my favorite films! Judging by the way that movie ended, I'd say it's best you go on your way and I go on mine, right?" He starts laughing at his own joke. He is not an idiot. I kinda like that about him too. He is quick-witted in a naughty, flirtatious way. I am squirming a little, feeling steamy down below.

"But you never did tell me about why you are here. Where is your husband? Do you have kids?" he says.

"You didn't ask why I was here prior to any of this conversation," I say.

"Well, I'm asking now," he says. "Does it really matter at this point?"

"No, I guess it doesn't." I say irritated. I have met my match with this flirting competition. Now I am going to lose.

I hate to lose.

He leans in again closer this time almost inches within my ear. I can feel his lips on my jaw, his breath asking for my permission to give in to his conquest. He is the quintessence of masculinity. After his face leaves mine he stands erect waiting for my voice to leave my throat but it is stuck, all lumpy and muddled. He gives me a pensive stare that goes right through my soul.

I shiver all over. Suddenly, I want to run because I am in too deep. I start to get up and leave but he grabs my wrist. I think walking away would end this, but every time he touches me I feel a warm IV of liquid saturate my veins. I keep craving more.

"I hope you have a good stay with your husband," he says with a smirk. But take my number just in case." He writes his number down, folds it, then opens my hand to put it in my palm. Again, his fingers touching mine lets a warm rush of an IV injecting a stronger dose. He gives me one last look to let me know he has had the last word. His eyes tell a story.

He wins. This stings because I want to jump right in but can't. I wonder when Chris will get here. I look at my phone to see if he texted but nothing. He will be here soon at the time he said. I am looking forward to Chris getting me out of this. I can't do it alone.

And with business as usual, Surfer Boy asks the couple sitting next to me if he could get them a drink while flashing me one more dimpled smile. The couple are sitting even closer to each other than before. I think they might fuck right then and there. I wonder if they are married or am I witnessing infidelity? I sit there with six drinks in, along with a bruised ego. I go up to the desk and ask if I can get into the room. To my dismay the answer is no because they are cleaning it and I had to wait.

I think about going back to the bar to get a drink but choose the cushy chairs in the lobby, not too far from the bar just in case. I look at the napkin. The numbers are scratched and slanted in a flirty way complete with a little heart. I put the napkin in my purse. I lay my drunken head back on the cushion thinking about all the times I have been lost and rescued. I need Chris to get his ass back here as soon as possible so I can escape this maze in my mind.

CHAPTER 29

Tammy

> *"Not until we are lost do we begin to understand ourselves."*
> *- Henry David Thoreau*

I wake up again to bright daylight. The birds are singing in great fervor to seize the new day. I hear a dog barking in the distance. I had dreams all night about my Dad. In my dreams I was watching my dad and his friends play softball, getting candy from the concession stand, and hearing the sound of the cantaloupe-type ball crunching off the bat with sounds of cheers in the background. It made me smile upon waking. I want to continue this dream. It saddened me to wake up, so I lay quietly to daydream thinking about those days.

There was a park located right near the field for Dawn and me to go play if we got bored during the game. Our cousins would meet us there too. But the best part was going to The Red Barrel restaurant after the game. Upon walking into the restaurant, there was a potpourri smell of warm hot buttered popcorn mixed with cigarette smoke and Old Style beer. It was the most unusual of smells, but very distinctive nonetheless. This was the trademark aroma of the south side of Chicago. My feet would crunch over peanut shells when I walked in and it looked like the place hadn't been cleaned in months.

Dad would sit with his friends in the high-top barrel chairs and lament over plays and strategize for the next game. My sister and I and our cousins would run to the popcorn machine, grab the little red and white paper baskets and fill them to our heart's content. I would eat most of the cousins under the table. I was a bottomless pit as they called me.

My dad always got us a kiddy table in the middle of the restaurant that had a courtyard, where we would gorge on peanuts and popcorn fighting over seconds being poured from the pitchers of Coca Cola. There was a courtyard where pet rabbits each had their own pen. They were running free and wild, yet caged in a small area where all the customers could see them. If we liked, we could venture out there as well to pet them. There were always carrot chips and seeds you could buy for a quarter, so you were able to go feed the rabbits, too. It was a child's paradise for sure. I really can't recall Mom frequenting weekly with us because she had her own bowling league on Friday nights with her friends, and that was not nearly as entertaining as going to the game at the Red Barrel. We always ended up going with Dad for pure entertainment. Plus, after dad had a few beers we were able to get anything we wanted.

One particular day, a rain-out game had been rescheduled for a late Saturday morning. Mom was invited to a baby shower nearby so we all went together. Mom dropped Dad, Dawn, and me off at the game. My uncle was meeting us there with my cousins. He was supposed to be keeping an eye on us while the men were playing. Because none of the ladies went to the games all the time, the team would choose one guy, who when sitting out, went back and forth to the park to check on the kids, as we were somewhat little all the ages of five to age ten.

But as the men got involved in the game, the babysitting seemed to play second fiddle. I can remember my dad saying to Dawn and me that we had to look out for each other instead of relying on the players. We always knew where the other one was. This little lecture always took place in the car before we got there. It was usually short and sweet and more directed at Dawn since she was older. But with my mom in the car this time the lecture turned into a town hall discussion about safety at the park. We were happy when she dumped us off and went on our way because she worried too much. We were fine. Sometimes my mother could drone on and on and go way overboard. She always thought of scenarios that could go wrong and quiz you on how to react. Well, this was one of the times I wished I had heard her whole speech because I then would have known what to do in a situation.

Shortly after Mom pulled up to the ball field, we were like *Lord of the Flies*, just thrown into an unknown world and left to fend for ourselves. We found this wildly invigorating because we were free from our parents to play what we wanted.

This time, Uncle Paulie was supposed to be watching us, but when I heard this story told to me later as a young adult, Uncle Paulie said he wasn't put in charge, and that it was someone else's job. It seemed like a clear example of miscommunication. But the result was that Dawn and I and our few cousins were left at the park with no one in charge. What is funny is that none of us were alarmed by this because that is how it was at most of the games. The dads would come over after the game ended and ask who was there watching us. "No one was here to watch us," we would laugh. You would hear groans from them indicating in their minds that this was not true. But it was. They didn't watch us like our moms did, that simple. They were laissez-faire because there was no problem until there was a problem.

I clearly remember that I walked far away from the park because I had quickly lost my bearings on where I was during our game of hide and seek. Even at age five, I was pretty good in nature, being able to play with my friends in our backyard trails and passages, but that was one thing. To be in the city was a whole different setting. Each house looked the same, maybe different paint color, or painted railings, or flowers planted or hung in different spots. The setting was very similar to Campbell's cans of soup on a grocery shelf. There were all different flavors, but the labels looked the same. You had to lean in closely to tell what was what.

Before I knew it, I was far away from the park and lost. I called out for Dawn and my cousins, but no one heard me. I am not even sure why I wandered so far to be honest. I kept moving, not standing still trying my best to trust that I knew what I was doing. I was lost like my dad in the jungles of Vietnam trying to grip the wet mud without falling. I had to keep watching my back for any crackle or snap of a branch. An airplane charged through the sky with such a fierce noise that I felt the breeze come off my face. I kept walking to see if any of the houses looked like my grandparents' or see if I could find someone to help me find the park. It felt like I was the only one walking down this desolate street, broad daylight feeling helpless and vulnerable, like a duckling looking for its mother.

I started to cry. I remember calling out names. "Dad!" "Dawn!" Over and over again until my voice was hoarse. I kept walking and an old man saw me. I can remember it being hot and he was watering his lawn. He had a large belly with a white t-shirt and loose shorts. He had gray hair that loosely was swept over his balding head. Years later I would see my Dad watching Benny Hill and think that he looked just like the guy on the show, which is kind of creepy in a way. I do remember tones of feeling very uneasy approaching this man. I walked up to him because he was the only person in sight. I was desperate. My mom always told me to look for a lady who looked like a mom. I did listen to her advice but it didn't work because there were no women around. I had no choice, so I told him I was lost. I am sure he asked me a barrage of questions, but I don't recall what he asked. I do remember that he took my hand and pointed at each house on the street of neatly trimmed houses.

"Is this your grandma's house?"

"No, I would say."

"Is this your grandma's house?"

We walked like this for house after house. It seemed like we walked for hours because according to my mom, who came back to the park after the shower to get me was horrified to see the whole softball team not playing the game, but frantically looking for me. She sensed something was terribly wrong and she ran out to the park frantically. "What's going on?" with a frightened voice.

"We can't find Tammy," Dad said.

"What?!" my mom screamed. Her worst scenario had come true.

"I thought someone was watching the kids!" Mom said.

"We thought someone was too, but Dawn came to tell us that they were playing hide and seek and they couldn't find Tammy and got scared," Dad said.

From the many retells of the story over the years, Mom said Dad looked even more frightened than the day he left for Vietnam when she pulled up to the park.

Meanwhile, the wind was gently moving the leaves on a summer Saturday morning. Kids were selling lemonade, lawns were being mowed, and laundry was hanging on lines swaying under humid air.

I moved with the old man from house after house. I kept crying. He kept telling me everything would be all right. It felt like a dream. Hours of my life here are unaccounted for because I just can't remember all the details, just bits and pieces, like putting together a puzzle for days while missing several pieces to make it complete. I've pondered many times over my life to recall the events of my being lost to no avail, similar to trying to find a dream to chase, always a step out of reach. After all, I was only five.

I know those memories of being lost went deep into my conscience. The scare and fragmented details of that day would be displayed in my dreams from faraway places with people I didn't know. I have never fully pieced it all together. I lie here on the hammock now still haunted in a cavernous cave of thoughts of what happened that day.

I still feel lost.

Each day of my life someone walked me to a strange place. "Is this your house?" I could never answer the question because nothing ever felt like home when I left my childhood.

I turn over slowly trying to rest my head but my head stings with pain. I stay where I'm at, uncomfortable in my heaviness. I try so hard to recover from the events so I keep stretching my brain.

I go back in time.

After scoping out many houses on an adventure hunt, eventually the old man somehow got out of me that I was at the park with my cousins, so that's where he took me. When I got back to the park, everyone had divided up into teams looking for me. I don't remember everyone running towards me hugging me and crying when they saw me coming over the hill to the park either. I don't remember the embrace of my mom finding me or my dad.

I shift uncomfortably in the hammock again. I need to sit up. My head feels dizzy so I just sit here for a bit thinking.

How can I not remember the joyous part of this story? Was fear so vast that it overtook the feeling of joy? Fear is a drape closing off the sun from the outside apparently. I find my lack of memory here especially strange because my mom was my right arm. I do remember that when I was lost all I wanted was my mom. It plagues me that I don't remember the bliss of being reunited with her after such a fright. This is why I had her tell me the story many times over. I only knew the ending to this story because of what my mom witnessed on this day. My mom said she won't forget the torturous moments of losing me, nor the sheer euphoric feeling of finding me. She said she was bawling while hugging me tightly because she thought she had lost me for good because I was gone for so long. Maybe I buried the idea of my mom bawling. I had to settle into the fact that it all remains a mystery of my lost hours.

While we all sat at the Red Barrel that night going over the details of "The Lost Story" because it would be retold many times over the years, I do start to remember my mom's tight grip around me while I sat on her lap at the restaurant after it was all over. She wouldn't let me go play with the bunnies on my own with my sister and cousins. She was glued to my side.

I strain my memory so much my head hurts but I want to feel the closeness of my mom after being found. I fall into a soft sleep. I hear voices of laughter in the distance. I can feel myself sitting with my mom at the Red Barrel.

I was content as we sat around in a circle telling stories. I remember looking out the window at the summer sky. I saw the lightning bugs gracefully exuding their glow.

I now feel an inner peace overcome me somewhat like an epiphany. I see myself lying in bed. My mom is here next to me, holding my hand. I sit here on the hammock like I am sitting on my mom's lap. I know at this moment I never want to be lost again without at least telling someone about my path first.

CHAPTER 30

Ashley

"But it is the same with man as with the tree. The more he seeks to rise into the height and light, the more vigorously do his roots struggle earthward, downward, into the dark, the deep - into evil."
- Friedrich Nietzsche

My drunken head leads me to thinking about my childhood. I close my eyes with my head leaned back. This couch feels like a bed. I can hear the clinking of glasses at the bar with light useless conversations in the background. I slip into a dreamlike state that leads the way to my hometown.

The old trees adorned the streets of my neighborhood like a fortress built around castles, complete with moats to keep anyone out who was not supposed to come in. The entrance of our house was grand. There were two long and wide sidewalks painted by red rose bushes complete with a small fountain in the middle. The entrance of the driveway led to two white pillars with beige brick of a stately and strong house. It screamed, "Come in only if invited."

Even deliveries of any kind were pointed to the side of the house on a golden plate on the front gate. I liked this gold plate because it made me feel safe. No one was allowed in our house without going through the alarmed gate and intercom system. I used to pretend I was the munchkin guarding the Land of Oz when someone rang the doorbell. "Who goes there?" I would say. I would give a little bit of grief to whomever it was, then with a chuckle, I would allow them to enter the threshold or go to the side gate.

My mom would get mad and yell at me for doing this. "You can't just let anybody in this house. It is not your decision to make Ashley, so you are not allowed to answer the door anymore."

I would ask why I couldn't answer the door, but she never gave me an answer. I was fucking Rapunzel locked in the castle. I had no choice but to do what she said. I wanted so badly to break free of her shackles.

My body wakes slightly out of a dream while I turn over to readjust to get comfortable. I open my eyes slightly. I can feel Surfer Boy behind me in the distance. He is free. I close my eyes again.

Sometimes when I am lying in my own bed now as an adult, I think about my old room. It was clad all in pink. The walls looked like someone came in and sprayed Pepto Bismol all over them. I wanted badly to change the color over the years but Mom would never let me.

After a while the walls became a dingy tone of red stained from my passage into womanhood. But my mom insisted on keeping the color pink because she was a professional ballerina. The color of my room was called "ballerina slippers." She sure had the feet to prove it too. My mom's body was perfect in every way even at her older age, but you wouldn't want to get a glance at her feet. She had calluses, corns, hammer toes, and broken nails with a broken soul. She would get her feet pedicured diligently, but it really was always like polishing a turd. I don't even know why she got her feet done because she went out of her way to hide them from the world. Her bare feet would never grace the sand at a beach or run through a field of grass. She wasn't free at all even though she wanted to be. I could tell she longed to be someone else but she was too jaded to let it all go. Instead, she spent much of her time decorating, buying things, and micromanaging my every move to take her mind off her own pain. She had my whole room done up with matching bedspreads, pillow cases, drapery, and the rug, too. My bed had a huge canopy that was sprayed with pink polka dots. She even had a loft built for me with a ladder that led to nowhere, each rung was a step away from her. I would play with my Barbie dolls up in the loft pretending to escape the grips of a broken ballerina. I had it all at my fingertips, and whatever I wanted I got. At one point I relished in being the queen of the castle, but day by day my tiara became tarnished.

Our town was a well-known wealthy area rooted with history just some twenty-three miles from Chicago. It was a stone's throw in a car from the city, and even faster bellowing down the tracks right from the train station to our town, which was a twenty-two-minute ride on the express train. The streets were heavy with mom and pop stores, medical buildings, coffee shops, fancy boutiques, some commercial stores, but mostly owners of small specialty shops. We had the staple bakery that everyone loved, and the boutiques were always stocked with the latest styles of clothing that were one of a kind, not mass produced. The clothes were also extremely expensive, so no one else was going to have the same outfit. That would be extremely embarrassing.

For kids and teens, the downtown area was the place to be in the summer with friends. These were the good-ole-days of riding our bikes to the pool, eating lunch, then walking around downtown.

Everyone knew each other and one looked much like the other.

It was very easy to pick out an outsider. If we met anyone at the pool we didn't know, no matter what they looked like, we would make sure we gave him or her the test. The test came with a standard question. "What does your dad do?" Inevitably the answer would come back as a doctor, a lawyer, CEO, stockbroker, car dealership owner, and other jobs I didn't even know existed. However, someone who didn't know what their dad did would simply say, "My dad makes a lot of money because we have a big house," or "We have an expensive car," or "We have a cleaning lady." Those answers would always suffice for someone who looked like we did.

My dream funnels deeper into the day a new girl showed up at the pool. I haven't thought about her in years. She seemed a bit rough around the edges and not all dressed nicely. In order to protect the pride, it was necessary to see who she was and why she was there.

My friends Liz and Jenny were with me sitting on beach chairs circling the prey. Our predator gene kicked in and we were stalking the weak link. The girl's mom was with her, and she also looked out of place. The girl had a towel with a slight tear in it along with a worn-out bag that said "Beach Life" enhancing the faded letters and stains. Her Mom's hair was long and brown, striped with some gray, pulled back half-heartedly with messy strands hanging down. She looked like she just woke up. Her bathing suit was an ugly green one-piece that hung off her as if it had been worn way too many times, complete with chipped red nail polish on her feet and toes. She looked nothing like our moms looked. My mom wouldn't even dress like that for bed, let alone walk outside looking like this woman.

We circled the girl where she was sitting by the pool. Her feet were dangling in a pool of dark secrets. The girl told us she lived in Chicago for a while. Her parents said they wanted to get her out of the school in the city and have her go to a nicer school. She reminded me of Pig Pen in Charlie Brown. She had dirt under her fingernails, scabs on her knees, and she just looked kind of rickety, but she was willing to join in our conversation. I could tell she desperately wanted to make friends but yet was somewhat guarded. She had no idea that she had to pass our test before joining our club, that is, if we let her join. We just didn't let anyone in. We certainly wouldn't allow the sympathy card either, that's for sure.

So we decided to hang out with her before leading her to the kill. She was trying too hard to fit in all day and her actions really seemed forced. We were also not used to someone who didn't look like us. She told us her name was Maria. She had dark beautiful skin, jet-black hair, with deep stunning chocolate melting eyes that seemed to have looked right through you. I wasn't going to admit it, but she made me a little apprehensive because I wasn't sure she was going to buy into my need to be the boss. The longer we talked to her, the more we noticed she was smart with common sense. Her looks were absolutely striking under her mess of an appearance. Anyone could see that. I was jealous because she seemed prettier than me with even more confidence to match. Many of the boys that walked by checked her out with more than second glances, and not because she was an outsider, but because she truly was beautiful.

I hated that the boys were not looking at me.

She told us she spoke Spanish too, and when we asked her to say a sentence we gave her in English, she translated it immediately. She was not only beautiful, but smart, too. She was a direct threat. All of these qualities should have been impressive, but Liz shouted out, "That's weird, Maria. You shouldn't speak Spanish here because no one will know what you are saying," she said high-and-mighty.

Maria just didn't fit in.

"That's the point," said Maria with a sarcastic charm.

She had the brains and the beauty, but that wasn't going to be enough. We had to find the weak spot to break her down. And we knew where we could break down that wall of confidence.

It came crashing down quickly after the standard club question of, "What does your dad do?"

She stood for a moment puzzled. She carefully looked us all over before firing an answer out. "What?" she said looking confused at the question.

I think she was stalling.

"You heard me," I said with all the confidence of a prize fighter. Suddenly, I shifted back into feeling confident again. I had played this game more than once with others. I was determined to come out on top. "Well, you heard me. Or, do we need to translate this one?" I said rudely with conviction. I asked again and this time louder with more force. "What does your dad do?"

She looked back at me with those chocolate eyes piercing through me. She stood up straighter.

"What does your dad do blondie?" She threw it back at me! I wasn't expecting this as no one stood up to me like this before. It really, really pissed me off.

"My dad makes a lot of money. He is a corporate lawyer. We live in one of the biggest houses up on that hill. Can you see it?" I pointed in the direction of my house.

The pool was set at the bottom of the hill in the town, and from that point of view there was a steady climb of houses with a lot of trees in the way. But if you looked close enough, you could see our house standing majestically on top of the hill. My Dad was very proud of buying a house on a hill. He was able to see clearly over everyone with great views.

"Big deal," she said.

Jenny and Liz chimed in with what their dads did and then asked her again. This conversation turned from phony to fierce within minutes.

"Are you going to answer or what?" Liz said.

"Why does it matter what my dad does?" Maria said. "He's not even here."

"Because we have a club, and if you want to be in this club, we need to know what your dad does. It's that simple. So put up or shut up," I said as astutely as that phrase could sound.

After looking up to the sky, I could tell she didn't want to let this out, but she didn't know what to do either.

With the force of the sun melting butter on a hot day she said, "Okay fine already. My dad is a truck driver, are you okay with that?"

There was silence for what seemed like hours, then shrieking laughter from all of us.

"A truck driver, really?" I laughed the hardest out of everyone. I interrupted anyone who was going to talk because this was my conquest to knock this girl down. "How could you possibly have a house here? There is no way you live here or can come to this pool. Do you have a guest pass?" I looked down at her wristband and noticed it indeed was a guest pass.

When people come with someone else, or they inquire about the club, they are entitled to one free pass. This was an exclusive pool club so it wasn't often outsiders tried to come in. Maria knew she was an alien being dropped into a new galaxy, foreign and unknown and we all knew it too. We circled around again to be intimidating in our stance.

"My mom took me here today so we could see if we like the pool, so yes, we are guests today. You got a problem with that blondie?" she said trying so hard to act cool but her voice was shaking. She wasn't as calm as she was minutes earlier.

"Yes, I do," I said, "and stop calling me Blondie!"

Jenny and Liz stood there not saying anything, but backing me up nonetheless. They usually let me do the talking because I was the most quick witted.

But Jenny decided to chime in as well. "So, what does your house look like if your dad is a truck driver? What does he do, drive around, hot dogs?" she said with a giggle.

We all started laughing loudly.

"No, you jerks, he drives food to grocery stores. If he didn't do this, you people wouldn't eat!" she retaliated back thinking she had the upper hand.

"So, he drives around hot dogs? We don't eat hot dogs here! Hot dogs are for fat people."

We all started laughing even harder this time all in unison.

"I am not going to tell you where I live, you spoiled brats. Just leave me alone. I can find other people here to hang out with!" she barked back at us. Her chocolate eyes were melting. She had beads of sweat dripping off her forehead that dripped slowly.

"Who are you going to hang out with Maria, the cleaning staff?" I went on driving the nail harder. "Because that's about the only people that will hang with you. Your dad doesn't make money driving around hot dogs, so you should just find another place to go."

With that, we all turned around and started walking away. There was no way we were going to hang with her. She just didn't fit in. But as we turned around to walk away, I felt something hit my head. I shrieked, grabbed the back of my head, and we all turned around. Maria went and got her sandal and whipped it with anger at the back of my head. And then she went even further as if the sandal throwing wasn't bad enough. She was filled with rage brewing inside her unleashing a volatile eruption.

"You can't tell me to leave, you little bitch! This is public property and it's a free world!"

She had her hands on her hips and a determined look on her face to kick my ass. Those chocolate eyes had now come back to life with visceral anger. We were now on a dusty road in a small town face to face in a Western movie. I looked right back at her and found my inner Clint Eastwood. Who was going to fire first? It was my turn to pull the trigger. I could hear the music rolling in my head for this confrontation.

"You think throwing things and swearing at people is a good idea? That is not something we do here." I got closer to her, but not too close because I had never been in a fist fight before. I didn't even know what to do, and I wasn't sure what she was capable of since she launched a shoe at my head. I certainly didn't want her to hit me in front of everyone. I was feeling very nervous that this was going to happen. I didn't expect it to go this way at all. I had to come out on top because there were several boys waiting with their mouths open to watch chicks fight. Did they think we would end up in a wrestling match on the ground clawing each other's clothes off? Then they would get a free peek at our bodies? What savages. There was a long pregnant pause as to who was going to draw their guns next.

Then I spoke up loudly so everyone that was watching could hear. "Maybe you should go back and hang around with your gangs in Chicago because that's where you fit in, certainly not here!" I shouted not getting too close.

My pitch startled her a bit because she looked worried. I took advantage and moved closer to her, almost inches from her. If she threw a punch I'd block it. I was prepared to do this because I suddenly felt a rush of adrenaline from down below creating my saliva to fly out of my mouth with such force that it was difficult to stop. I was two inches in front of her now. We were blue eyes wide with fury to chocolate eyes ready to melt again.

"You know what? I think I know where you live. You probably live in those little apartments on the other side of the tracks, don't you? My dad is on the village board and they are trying very hard to get them knocked down. He says apartment buildings don't look good in this town. And we certainly don't want people like you coming to live here." Jenny and Liz were right next to me, one on either side. They had my back.

"So, I hope you like living there now. Don't get too used to it because there's going to be a wrecking ball coming through it soon," Liz chimed in perfectly.

"Oh yeah," said Jenny. "I know where those apartments are. Some kids in our class call it "Little Mexico." We all started laughing again. Maria just stood there in silence. I was shocked she didn't throw a punch for how angry she looked, but she let her guard down. For a quick second I felt sorry for her, but she fucked with the wrong person.

"You're going to talk in Spanish so we don't understand, comprender, right?" Liz said with a mocked Spanish accent.

She continued to stand there, lifeless and alone.

"Where are your amigas now, Maria?" I said standing there with my hands on my hips, too.

She was scaring me the way she wouldn't move. This wasn't over because Maria was Medusa complete with a steady force. She had found her breath. "You all think you're better than everyone else, don't you?" She took her gaze off me.

I felt some relief that I wasn't completely on the hot seat. Maria turned to Liz with a quick piercing jerk with her finger in Liz's face.

She was not backing down. "And don't talk my language you white shithead because you aren't saying it right because you're too stupid to say it correctly!" Her voice was booming louder at this point.

There was enough noise to attract the attention of my mother, who happened to be sitting with my grandmother not too far away. Maria's mother was on the other side of the pool, oblivious to what was going on. At one point, she lowered her sunglasses, looked up and smiled thinking this was a pleasant atmosphere then went back to reading her trashy magazine about celebrities because she had no life of her own obviously.

The boys started chanting "Chick fight, chick fight, chick fight!" While their interference pissed me off, it did relieve pressure on what to do next because then my mom and my grandmother came walking over. As soon as the boys saw this they scattered like flies. What pussies I thought.

My Mom in her slim build, black one-piece suit complete with a high brim black hat, and closed black heels, strolled forward with all the movement of a queen. My grandmother, who was exactly the same and also in the same attire, walked alongside her gracefully and slowly. They were both like royal blood entering a palace. Their long-manicured fingers went to their chins at this spectacle.

"And what do we have going on Ashley? Do you wish to introduce your new friend to us?"

She looked down at Maria who finally backed away from me. She was standing by herself and all of us were in a group. My mother was staring at Maria from head to toe. Then she held out her long delicate hand to shake Maria's hand. "How do you do, young lady?"

Maria refused to shake my mom's hand. My Mom was insulted. My mom could have melted like the wicked witch of the west getting water thrown on her. She was shocked with the lack of manners because she was a woman of uppity class.

So, my grandmother, being the know it all she is, thought she would be able to get somewhere since her daughter clearly failed. She uttered almost the same words, like two robots trying to rectify a human problem. It was actually humorous to watch them struggle a bit. From the little time I knew Maria, what I noticed was that she wasn't going to let her guard down, even with adults. I was still afraid that she would make me look like a fool in front of everyone. Being made a fool was as foreign to me as going to a country where I spoke not one word of the language. For a split second I wished I never talked to Maria because no matter what happened now, I looked like a fool.

"Well, well, well," my grandmother said with a snarky tone, "What is the problem here young lady? Are you being mean to my granddaughter?"

"No!" shouted Maria. "Your granddaughter is a total jerk. I don't like her and I don't like either of you. You better not tear down the apartment where we live or my family won't have a place to live!"

This was a perfect segue for my last word. "See, you just admitted it. I was right. I knew you lived in the apartments!" I screamed out just hoping to get the gun out of my holster and shoot her dead right there.

"Okay girls, that is enough from all of you. Is your mother here darling? I am thinking you should go over by her and not come by my daughter and her friends anymore. We just don't want mischief of any kind," my mother said in her fakest voice.

"Yes, my mom is here. She is right there on the other side of the pool, but she wouldn't want to talk to you," Maria said with her arms folded.

She didn't want to look like a fool either. This meeting was beyond uncomfortable. I couldn't believe this whole time that Maria's Mom never even looked up. Her daughter could have been drowning and she wouldn't have been any the wiser. My mom aggravated me a lot but at least she stuck up for me, good or bad. Maria's mother had her head buried in the wet celebrity sand.

"I think it is time for you all to part ways and that's it. You go back to your side, and the girls will stay here. After all, they are members. Do you get what I am saying here little girl?"

Maria stared back at my grandmother with those piercing chocolate eyes, stuck her tongue at her, gave all of us the finger, and walked away.

"That's it!" my grandmother said. I don't recall seeing my grandmother so furious. I couldn't tell if she forgot her sunblock because she had all the makings of someone who sat out in the sun too long. The shades of red matched her sleek black attire. Now she was the fool but at least it took the gaping pressure off of me. "All of you ladies go get your things, pack up, and meet us out in front in five minutes. We will not stay here with this little brat. I plan on reporting her at the front desk."

We gave Maria one more death stare on the way out as we walked by her with snotty giggles. Her mother still did not look up.

The boys cheered halfheartedly while we flipped them off. But we looked like the victorious ones and that's all that counted.

"We got out of that one," I said to my friends.

"It doesn't matter. We won't see her again more than likely," said Jenny.

"Those kids in the apartments don't stay here long," said Liz. "How can she stay here with her dad driving hot dogs around all day," she snorted while making pig noises. We all laughed before going into the locker room.

Meanwhile, Maria stared back at us from her seat across the pool. She stood intently with those chocolate eyes at both my mom and my grandma. She gave them the finger one more time, then dove into the pool without saying a word. My mom and grandma looked at each other in horror. I wanted to laugh because I have always wanted to flip these women off but couldn't do it. I never had the balls too, but Maria did.

"If Ashley ever talked like that to anyone she would be in the house for a year," my mother scowled. "No way any daughter of mine would talk like that to her elders."

"I would certainly hope not," said my grandmother. They walked past Maria's mother. They decided not to say a thing because she was oblivious to the whole event. So, they just went to talk to the office manager about Maria. Mom and my grandmother were gone just a short while. We saw them making gestures and shaking their heads talking through the glass office. What happened next was quick and easy. With a tear of a check from my grandmother, the problem was solved. We never saw Maria there again.

What sucked about leaving that day was I wasn't allowed to walk home or ride my bike with Jenny or Liz. When my grandma came to visit, my mom wanted me to bond with her. But bonding with her was like bonding with my mother. It was like trying to become friends with a cobra. I mostly just sat far away from her and kept quiet, for fear of her lashing out quickly with a deadly venomous bite. She and my grandfather were the equivalent to talking at statues. They really had no idea how to talk to me or my brother so there was a lot of forced talk. We just simply didn't know them. I truly don't think they wanted to get to know us. They were busy traveling the world and attending galas and fundraisers. Even at their funerals as an adult, I shed not one tear when they died. The world just moved on for me. They were a presence here at one time, leaving all their money behind for us to have. That's all they did was buy stuff for us the whole time I was growing up. The only time I came close to touching either of them was when our hands accidentally made contact when they were handing us money when they were leaving, one foot out the door most of the time. I really didn't know anything about them but that they were filthy rich. Every time I saw them, I expected something.

As the door shut in the car upon leaving the pool, my mother asked what happened. Naturally, I made it look like this whole situation was all Maria's fault.

"Is that girl a friend or someone you know Ashley? How did she get into the pool without being a member?" my grandmother asked.

"Well, you can come as a guest I think," I said back rather nervously.

"When I saw her throw her sandal at your head Ashley, I thought that this was not good at all. I couldn't believe her mother didn't see it or try to help in any way. We were left there to deal with this riff raff coming to our pool and she clearly didn't belong there," my mother said. But she was more upset that she looked like an idiot for sure.

"Well, you don't have to worry about it now because it has all been taken care of," my grandmother said. She looked at my mother with a glance of she had it covered.

"You better talk to that husband of yours darling so he can clear this up with the board. You don't want this town turning into a melting pot, do you?" she said. My mom nodded in agreement. I'm sure she would give Dad a blow-by-blow description.

"No, I don't want that Mom. I promise you this town won't turn into a melting pot," she said sternly. I can still see the air conditioning blowing my mom's brim hat ever so gently with her look of victory as she drove up the hill of our driveway. The car halted rather abruptly at the top of the world, instantly waking me up.

It is a little louder now at the bar and the air is still lingering with the useless conversations. I turn around and notice the couple at the bar is gone. They probably took their hot love and went to a room. The guy on his laptop is still there gazing into the light like a zombie.

Surfer boy is there now leaning in towards two young, sexy ladies who were giggling with delight. I can see his dimples from where I am sitting.

My head starts to hurt. Where the fuck is Chris? I stand up to go to the front desk to throw my weight around since Chris is still not here. I glance over at the Surfer boy on the way over to the front desk. He looks up over the sexy girls and flashes a wink of satisfaction. I look away. I don't want to be a fool again.

Just then, I see Chris walking through the lobby in a rush. Oh finally, I am being rescued from this sinking ship in the deep blue ocean. I run to him, throwing my arms around him like I've never seen him before. I want Surfer boy to see that I indeed am not the fool.

CHAPTER 31

Tammy

> *"Either define the moment, or the moment will define you."*
> *- Walt Whitman*

I reflect here on the hammock thinking about how I love getting up early, but not today because that throbbing in my head is back with a vengeance. I feel very alone, so the only way out of this is to think back because it's all I have. I wish I could go back to my old life.

Mornings always filled me with the promise of a new day. I used to sit on my porch at dawn before I left for work every day. I watched the world go by in front of me with my coffee and a doughnut. This was how I chose to start my new solo journey in my new place once Alex and Bill left, minus the donut. I felt like Amelia Earhart flying on her solo mission over the Atlantic, with feelings of exuberance and bravery, yet anxiety for what was to come. I just hoped my ending turned out better than hers, but I'm not so sure it did now that I'm stuck in daydreams of the past But no one can take away that Amelia Earhart made the move to independence single handedly paving the way for all of us trailblazers living in a male dominated society. I felt like her for a brief moment and it felt really good.

I was listening to the sound of the birds one morning when I saw a hornet fly into an unknown spider web in the corner. I hated to see this struggle in front of me. I got up and moved closer and watched the hornet furiously try to get out of this mess. On the other hand, I marveled at the pure genius of the spider who trapped its meals by preying on those who travel in haste, not observing their surroundings.

I thought about getting a stick to help the hornet break free from this entrapment. But in my ear, I heard Alex saying, "Don't intervene in nature. It's not your place." I guess he was right. I watched this hornet's legs feverishly try and untwist in this silk of steel. In a few moments, the hornet actually broke free. I was shocked because I thought for sure it was a goner. It made me think about how the hornet felt, scared and trapped, seemingly thinking it was the end, only to find out it had broken free and was able to fly on to its intended destination. It gave me hope that I would do the very same thing with my life.

While Bill took his things and hit the road, I was left to deal with all the divorce proceedings since I did call a lawyer before I knew he was going to "get the hell out of dodge" without making legal plans to end this chapter of my life. I knew I didn't want a trial separation or counseling. We both agreed we wanted the divorce done quickly before there was a chance of a rekindling of this relationship if I lost a couple hundred pounds and Bill fell in love with me again.

The damage was done.

I did the research on divorce and sent him the information on an uncontested divorce. If he agreed to this, it would be inexpensive and painless. We would split our assets equally, no trial, no lawyer, and we would walk away as if we had never met. We would be set free from the chains that shackled us together.

I tried to call Bill after seeing that hornet break free. He didn't pick up, so I left a voicemail telling him to look for an email I was sending with information about uncontested divorces. I hoped he would not want to go the lawyer route due to the business because then I would be an insect in a web who couldn't get out. It was solidified before Bill left that we were both in agreement to help Alex where we could each on our own, but I was concerned about his business. I didn't want him to fight me on getting any of the profits. I am not the kind of person to take every penny from Bill, but my mom suggested that I should at least get something since we were married with a child. I also helped out a lot with Bill getting his business off the ground. I was running it behind the scenes until he was able to hire other people. That should really count for something, not to mention pretty much raising our son as a single mother.

Right before going on my crossing guard duty at lunch, I happened to look at my phone to see what the time was before going out to the crosswalk when I saw a voicemail from Bill. His voice sounded heartless, like I was some shitty salesperson asking him a question. We had a life together. We share a son.

"Alex hasn't been gone forty-eight hours but I guess you aren't wasting any time either." He said. "Fine with me. We can meet and talk it all over. I like the sound of the uncontested divorce. I'm prepared to do what I can Tammy so I can start a new life. Call me later so we can meet up to get this done."

I did everything I could not to cry right there. I don't cry easily, but this message took my breath away. I wanted this divorce and I made the final move for checkmate, but to hear my almost eighteen years of marriage sound like it was just another errand to get done was a whole other ballgame. I wiped away the tears, put on my gear because it would be chaos on that corner if I neglected to get out there due to my own self-pity. That was the very last time I shed a tear over Bill, and vowed it was to be my last.

Because Alex was gone the divorce was pretty easy. In a short time it all ended with signatures on a paper and an uneventful farewell. Bill and I split everything down the middle, so I was able to live comfortably within my means. Bill and I agreed to put the house up for sale and split the profit. Once that was done, I moved to a two-bedroom condo closer to the school where I worked. There were too many memories there at that house, some good and some bad, but if I was starting over, I had to do it right with a whole cleansing of the past.

The condo was perfect for me. It was within walking distance to the school I was working at in the hopes that I would walk there every day to start losing weight. I made a promise to Alex that I would work on my health before I saw him for family weekend.

The timing of all of these new events was perfect because I ended up getting a job at the school where I was a crossing guard. The school needed a teacher's aide to help in kindergarten. I found myself giddy everyday working with the minds of five-year old children, plus I would be making more money than just the crossing guard duty. It made me very happy that I had a place to go in between my crossing guard duties. I even started taking education classes since I had finished my general education classes. I had started a while back and never got to finish in between all of my mom roles. I wanted to become a teacher and was going to do whatever I could to achieve the goal. I know many people looked at me as the overweight and lonely crossing guard. I could hear them saying, "What does she do that she can come out here at odd times each day. She must be one of those people who collects a disability check." I was actually asked that question before, which I found a deeply personal question to ask. I felt the judgment from people when they looked at me. So many people wore pity for me on their sleeves.

I wanted to be treated as a human no matter how much I weighed. I wanted to wear a sign on my shirt that read "Heavy people lead lives too." We laugh and live like everyone else. I don't need anyone thinking that I needed to be rescued.

I knew who I was.

I know who I am.

I am a happy person despite my outward appearance and making changes for me. I wish I could give a speech about my mantra on a crowded stage. It would appear like a public service announcement.

But my feet won't move so here I sit on this hammock. I am left with my thoughts hammering into my head throughout the dull pain.

Things were moving along quite smoothly until I started to make plans to go see Alex for a family weekend in mid-October. I had lost twenty pounds since Alex left, but I was still rather large to say the very least. It would take a lot more pounds for someone to note the difference, but I started feeling it and that's what counted. What would be difficult was flying to see Alex because I hadn't seen him physically in months. But what was holding me back was the fear of getting into an airplane seat. I was so big and wide, that I just didn't want to suffer the embarrassment of people watching me try to squeeze into the seat like a pair of jeans you can't get into. The thing is that I was able to squeeze into a pair of jeans within the privacy of my own home, but on the plane, I would be on display for everyone to see, and let's face it, people are cruel when it comes to critiquing overweight people.

I wanted to drive to see Alex, but it was such a long ride on my own because I knew I would have a hard time sitting that long. I hoped I could get my mom to come with me. I had all the determination of a matador at a bullfight, so I convinced her to come with me. My mom had gone back to work when my dad died, so she was pretty busy, plus in between working she loved to be with her various friends. Unlike me, she was a social butterfly. I wished I was like her. She was in a golf league and loved to travel. She was active because she really knew how to live life. Over the years in her subtle ways, she had let me know that I needed to be healthier and that I had a choice of how I looked , but she never harped on me over it. I kind of wish she had because maybe I'd be in a better place. But I now know as a mother there are things that happen as a parent where your child will criticize you for past doings. You are damned if you do and damned if you don't. This parenting thing didn't come with a rule book.

But now that I was starting a clean slate, it was time to make some necessary changes. Her discipline is what I admired about her the most. If anything, I wanted to make her proud, and Alex too. I started walking every day because Mom told me this was the best way to start good habits. My Mom works out every day in some fashion. She never misses a walk in rain, shine, or snow three-hundred and sixty-five days a year. She told me she walks every day after being inspired by Anne frank who said that nature takes care of all troubles. This inspired me all over again.

I sway on the hammock. I can see my mom gardening here, tending to all the needs of this household while talking about her favorite books.

I never fully knew how much she did until I became a mother. My Mom gave birth to Dawn and me in her early twenties, so she was still quite the young mother, and grandmother, but she kept that youthful glow in sparkles of sunshine, even after Dad died.

She still jokes today how it was such a curse to have the title "Grandma" at age forty and that no woman should have to bear that title before the gray hair set in. But titles aside, she was the best grandmother anyone could ask for. Even though my mother had a tight network of friends and always had plans at bay, without one ounce of hesitation, she went with me on the journey to see Alex. Turns out I didn't have to convince her at all to come with me.

Mom and I were able to take turns driving on the journey. It was good to have Mom with me because we spent much of the drive discussing small talk and how things were going—like my job, going back to school, being an empty nester, and more importantly my divorce.

My mom and I always had a good relationship but it got even stronger when Dad died and I had Alex. The lights went out suddenly over our lives as we were left stumbling in a pitch-black night. She lit the candle that cast the light for us to see what was in front of us. I've been even closer to her ever since because we had each other to navigate that darkness.

During one of our stops at the rest area, we got some snacks at the vending machine. I went over to the picnic table to sit under a lovely shady elm tree. I nicknamed the tree Treebeard and smiled saying that Dad would love the reference to *Lord of the Rings* since he read the whole novel aloud to me and my sister.

Mom's smile diminished slowly and she said, "Boy I still miss him. Most of my days go by and I enjoy them, but there is not one day that goes by all these years that I don't think of Dad." she lamented. She breathed deeply, found a smile, but it seemed like she had to force her lips to go upwards.

I could read her like a book. She was concerned for me. She always grinned slightly and exhaled a little when something heavy was weighing on her mind.

She spoke slowly and said, "Are you sure this was the right decision Tammy? Just because this is not only about you, but what Alex will think. I worry about him too. He is gone on his own now, but what about when he comes home? Why haven't you shared this with him yet?"

I breathed heavily too, but my breathing was more about the lack of oxygen in hot weather. I had started noticing how my weight was affecting my breathing and it was starting to scare me. I should not have breathing issues at my age, which was one of the fuels for me to drop weight. "There just didn't seem to be a right time Mom. I didn't want to tell him over the phone or on Facetime. It just seemed so impersonal, plus I didn't want him to worry about me while he was gone and feel obligated to come home and take care of me. I know Bill hasn't said anything because he has barely talked to Alex but for texting occasionally."

My mom looked a little perturbed. She shook her head a little. "So, you think telling him on family weekend is a good time?"

"I do Mom," I said back. "I can talk to him about this over dinner with you there and let him know that it is done and over with. I will let him know I sold the house, got a condo, started exercising to lose weight, and that I am working full-time. I think he will take it better knowing that I have all my ducks in a row. He'll be happy for me," I said confidently.

Mom turned sideways and took another breath in like she was blowing up a balloon. "So, you think having me here will lessen the boom? Just because he's eighteen and on his own doesn't mean he won't react in a bad way. You have basically eradicated his childhood in one sweep. Most kids deal with the fact that their bedrooms have been turned into offices or a spare room after they leave, not a whole new life when both the parents aren't in it." She seemed disappointed in me.

I hated that feeling. When your mom is disappointed, the whole world is disappointed. "Mom, I didn't see any other way, and I don't have Bill's support at all. I never had Bill's support. That has been most of our problems over the years. You don't get that because you never had this problem with Dad. What's done is done and Alex can't change anything now. He will have to learn how to accept or reject this divorce. I'm hoping he goes with accepting, but I will give him time to take it all in. I guess you will have too as well."

Mom looked at me for a moment before speaking. "I know you're right Tammy. I was just hoping you really are happy and content with the decisions you made. If you are, then I have no other choice but to be accepting. I don't like to see you unhappy. I feel like your appearance shows how unhappy you have been for many years. I am hoping this is the beginning of the new you," she said, grabbing my hand.

I can almost feel her hand on mine sitting here on the hammock. I sway back and forth slowly. The breeze feels so nice. My headache has started going away thinking about the trip to see Alex. I feel no pain in this daydream. I try hard to remember every detail.

I was sure Alex was thrilled that we were coming, while Bill made excuses as to why he could not visit. Bill made it known that he was very busy at work and couldn't get away for family weekend. He also made it known that flying to see Alex was not going to be something he would readily do since he hated flying. He lacked the time to drive when he was busy working. I was happy about him not coming though because he would have ruined this time for Alex, and I didn't want that. He was used to him not being there for him, what would change this now? Alex said he had been corresponding with Bill via text and an occasional Facetime, so that made me feel good for Alex, because while I held disdain for Bill, Alex always looked for Bill's approval. This approval Alex was seeking always set a lump in my throat because I knew no matter what Alex did, it would never be good enough for Bill because nothing ever was. I just didn't want to be the one to tell Alex this. It certainly wasn't my place anymore now that our vows disintegrated into thin air.

When we arrived at Alex's dorm, I texted him to let him know I was there and that I had a surprise. He didn't know Mom was coming. When he came out of the door it was as if I was looking at a stranger. This young boy had turned into a grown man. It seemingly happened over night. I was watching him come closer to the car and thought about how that was the age I had brought him into this world never to see what he was seeing on a college campus. The dream I chased ran away from me. My world had changed overnight, but his has just started. I was truly happy that he got to experience what I didn't get. Somehow watching him made me not regret one thing that happened on my path. I didn't want to cry because no son wanted to stand outside their dorm and watch their mom cry.

He came walking up slowly to greet us, calm and collected. "Grandma, I didn't know you were coming," he said, cracking a smile and giving her a hug.

He reached in for me with his warmth and charm. I had never felt so embraced with love when I felt his heart beating with this hug. I think this was the longest time I have ever spent away from him, and it was not easy to get used to, so to be with him again in person made me feel a hundred pounds lighter. He was my grown son now, yet always my little baby whom I nurtured into who he is now. I couldn't help but see flashes of nap times, trips to the zoo, books on my lap, skinned knees, cheers from the sidelines, his shadow playing hot crossed buns on the cello, braces, getting a driver's license, parties, and all these scenes playing like the flashing credits at the end of a movie leaving a need for more, or a sequel at the very least.

"So good to see you Mom!"

I pulled back and stared at him right in those dreamy green eyes. "Oh Alex, you are a sight for sore eyes." I had to give one of my sayings.

"I miss your sayings Mom."

And then like a kid leading us through a toy store, we were almost instantly following him into his dorm room. As soon as we walked in, the smell was quite direct. There was no mistaking that this building was filled with a lot of young men.

Alex's room was just the way I had pictured it to be. He had posters of the Golden Gate Bridge, the Guggenheim Museum, and other unique pieces of architecture sprinkled with his favorite sports figures. He was enthralled with architecture and wanted to be a part of something big and unique like the pieces displayed on his wall. He showed us around to the common room where many others started saying hello as he passed. He was like a celebrity strolling through the halls as we were introduced to many people. I got used to that bewildered look people would give me as Alex was very muscular and fit from all of his athletics over the years. He did not gain an ounce of the "freshman fifteen." He was active in club sports. I am sure these people were thinking how could someone this fit have a mother that was so big. I felt for Alex because as many of the parents were buzzing by, it was taking me longer just to keep up. I could not believe how winded I was feeling. I didn't want to embarrass Alex so I did what I do best—smile and show my friendly ways like I do at my job.

I was not at all surprised though that Alex had settled in right away. I always called him the mixer. Being an only child, he always craved companionship. He gave up asking Bill and me for a brother or sister, so he would actively seek out friends to play with whenever he had a chance. He spent much of his childhood making connections with all different groups of kids and throughout high school. He was voted "Most Charming" in high school after all. Apparently, he carried that with him here at his new school.

The rest of the day was filled with community meetings, a football game, and dinner plans. We were going to have Alex give us a tour the next day, have lunch, and then head back home.

Mom and I went back to the hotel while he went to the game with his friends. I was not sure I would be able to handle the stands in a game, the seating size again, and just wanted to avoid all that embarrassment for everyone. Alex understood, and said he would meet us for dinner afterwards. Mom and I sat in the lobby and ordered some tea at the bar. Streams of parents were coming in and out. It was a good place for people watching. Mom and I just watched the people scattering this way and that way.

"Did I miss the memo? Should we have worn our Georgia Tech shirts?" Mom said, rolling her eyes. "Look at these people," she said. "They are all walking around with their Georgia Tech gear like they go here. Is this experience for them or the kids?"

My mom was as lovely as a flower just making its bloom, but I noticed the older she got the more she critiqued the world. I felt like she had the right being my elder, and you know what? She was right . . . she was always right. I rarely get nauseated, but these people made me want to throw up, literally. I got so sick of watching these robots traipsing around with their Georgia Tech gear like they were walking advertisements. It was okay to be proud, don't get me wrong. But this display reminded me of those people who put bumper stickers on their cars showcasing their honor students. These parents were all life size walking bumper stickers. Then came the posting of the college family visits on Instagram and Facebook so the whole world knows you somehow did your job as a parent because you bought an overpriced eighty-five-dollar sweatshirt, complete with a banner to hang in your office, along with an anchor on your bank account so you couldn't retire until age eighty. But you get the badge of honor of putting it on Facebook.

I told my mom about a teacher at my school who had a son who went to Notre Dame. The classroom had hints of the Fighting Irish all over the place. There was a sticker here, a coffee cup there, and incessant posts and conversations of football games and family visits, only to be stripped from the walls the following year when her son couldn't handle the pressure. I suppose he was an athlete no longer the star of the school in a sea of many other stars in the galaxy. The star lost its light. The sweatshirt was packed away never to be brought out again for fear of sheer embarrassment. It was easier to not say a word, take the posts down and move on with life while the child struggled like a mouse caught in a sticky trap. His legs got stuck, he tried ferociously to get out and then gave up in the end. The "Fighting Irishman" lost that fight. I didn't want this to happen to Alex so I let him find his own way in the way he thought best.

My mom listened to that whole story and sighed. I notice she sighs a lot. "This whole scene is tough to watch, all I am going to say on that topic."

"Don't worry about me, Mom. I don't need to jump on that crazy train and neither do you. Alex knows we are not morons like this. He wouldn't dare expect us to act like sheep this way."

"You are right. Okay, Tammy." She sat quietly for a moment. Her Mom lens was on. "Did you ever think this could have been you? Or what did I miss?"

"Yes, I lay in bed many nights crying for what I thought I would have had. I spent too many nights thinking about it until my brain hurt, but looking at what I see now, I wish I could take all those nights back thinking about what my friends were doing, what I would be doing and all of that." I sighed too. Maybe this comes with age. "Now that I am older and here, there's a part of me that does feel that hole in my stomach I felt almost eighteen years ago wishing I had this experience." I stopped for a moment and almost started crying, but I held it together.

My mom reached over and grabbed my hand. I guess I was holding those tears in for a long time. They were dead weight and too heavy. I felt lighter. "You did the right thing honey and I will always love you for it, and so does Alex."

"Thanks Mom," I said. "And I know another thing, too. I am quite certain I couldn't have done it without you. I wouldn't change one event that led me to having Alex, even being unhappy in my marriage. I have finally found peace. This is what I hope to tell Alex tonight at dinner."

"It will all be okay," Mom said while grabbing my hand again.

I feel her hand again on mine through the pain increasing in my head.

And when she said those words, I felt the safest and most loved I've ever felt.

I feel the same way now.

The swaying of the hammock stops when I can no longer hear her voice. I go to sleep to try and dream of her again.

CHAPTER 32

Ashley

> *"A person can't have everything in this world; and it was a little unreasonable for her to expect it."*
> *- Kate Chopin*

I remember the first time I saw Chris on the dance floor. Seeing him now reminds me of that very night. All my thoughts of the crazy ass bartender go out the window. I shift my thinking about how Chris looks at this moment, with the haze of gin circling my mind. My mind is always wide open when I drink.

Chris has a commanding presence, a look in his eye that makes people feel somewhat vulnerable. His striking dark hair and jawline set below his deep, dark hazel eyes glancing in my direction is enough to make little beads of sweat bubble up behind my neck. He still looks like he did the first day I met him. Here he is again to rescue me from a drunken haze at the grips of another man behind the bar.

To be truthful, Chris looks better with age, still taut and splendidly in shape. He works out all the time, even on business trips and vacations. The man doesn't miss a day. Most ladies probably think I am out of my mind for not being completely smitten with his charm and his money. But they don't know the Chris I know at home underneath the shine on the outside.

The Chris that pulled up on his horse the night I met him kept me on horseback for a while, but he let me fall off as time marched on. I got dragged through the mud gasping for air trying to hang on while the dust flew up in my face.

People think I have it all, they really do. I take advantage of Chris always being there for me, always having money and getting what I want. But at this moment, I strangely have that "butterfly feeling" I had when I first saw Chris.

I start confusing my feelings for the bartender with Chris and I am drunk. I actually feel myself going warm with a tinkle of moisture between my legs. Is it the booze? What is happening to me? This is the father of my children. This is the man who loves me.

I talk to myself a lot, especially when I've been drinking. And like a record on repeat a million questions pop into my head. "Did he let me fall off the horse or did I jump off on my own accord? How did I lose this feeling of love for him already? How in God's name do people celebrate their fiftieth anniversary? I can't even fathom what one has to deal with to lead that far into life with the same person. Are they really happy or am I just a selfish fuck?

Well, this is my chance to make up for lost time I guess. I quickly grab the drink I brought with me to the couch because I need one more swig to keep the buzz going after sleeping. As Chris came closer, a wave of Prada lingered in the air. I can place that smell anywhere and think of him.

"Hey Ash!" He hugs me so tightly that I am able to feel his chest and shoulders just take over. I lean into it, drunk, but delighted to feel this warmth. It has been a long time since we embraced each other like this. He grabs my hand and walks over to the corner of the bar to get a glass of the fancy fruited water. I don't want to go back to the bar but I can't stop him. I watch his forearms and hands grasp the glass. I want those familiar hands and those arms to feel me all over. I don't want to see Surfer Boy so I keep my head hanging low. I want to whisk Chris upstairs like one of those trashy romance novels, take all his clothes off, whip off mine with my sexy lingerie and ride him all night long into the early hours of the morning.

But then my self-doubt kicks in. I can feel Surfer Boy watching us, but I dare not make eye contact. I want to get the hell out of there as quickly as we can, but Chris pulls a seat up to the bar. He nods his head for me to sit down. He wants to lament about his day.

"Let's get a drink, yes? Then we can go up to the room."

I didn't say anything.

"What time did you get here? Or better yet, how long have you been drinking?"

"It's good to see you too," I reply sarcastically with a wet gin kiss.

And just like that, his one smartass sentence brings me down. I'm not sure how to get back up. He thinks my drinking is more important than him, I can tell. Why the fuck does he say this? I think he is worried about my drinking, but I have this under control. He leans over, takes the glass out of my hand and lays it back on the bar with a sigh.

Surfer Boy is pouring a drink for a new guy who walked up to the bar before us. Chris stares at the bartender for a bit longer. Then he looks at me. At this moment I wonder if Chris is even more perceptive than I thought. I can't tell if it is my buzz messing me up or if surfer boy and Chris know me more then I know myself.

They are both looking at my lens under a microscope.

"I see you found yourself a spot to cozy up to ha, Ash?" Chris says. He keeps looking at Surfer Boy staring him down like he is ready to take his front teeth out. He turns his glance back at me. He has lost the excitement he had when he walked into the lobby.

"You know I've been staying here, Ash. I don't think I have sat at this bar more than two times. You come here for a few hours and I have the feeling that you own the place," he says with a tone. He takes another glance in the direction of Surfer Boy.

I fight my words before speaking. I take a deep breath and try not to roll my eyes.

I had even said to myself out loud in the car ride here, "Don't pick a fight. This will not be the time or the place. Don't say anything stupid. This could be a great time between us, so don't blow it."

I'm sure the driver thought I was crazy talking to myself like that, but the older I get the more I find talking to myself is helpful. But I do admit that I usually say horrible things in the midst of my anger, especially when I am drinking. Arguing and drinking is like throwing oil into a fire. There is an awareness of the destruction that could happen by mixing these elements along with the impossibility of making it stop once it has started.

I decide to move Chris away from the bar into the lobby by the couches to avoid a volatile mixture of elements. This was the only way out of this. "Let's go upstairs Chris. We can order room service and be alone."

Chris eyes up the bartender one more time for what seems like days. But he finally agrees and we start to get up. I can tell Chris doesn't want to let go of what happened at the bar, but I realize I hadn't paid for any of the drinks. Shit.

Then I hear Surfer Boy calling. "Hey, just so you know I'm gonna need your room number for the drinks today."

"Room 716," Chris yells out loudly.

The guy on the laptop all day looks up.

"Okay, cool, thanks," says Surfer Boy. "Have a great evening." He smiles.

Chris turns and flashes him a dirty look. I keep my head down pretending not to have even laid eyes on him but my head gravitates up because secretly I don't want to leave him. I see him shake his head when he sees me holding hands with Chris.

I get my suitcase from the concierge and we are on our way up. When we get on the elevator Chris looks at me deeply. Oh, those eyes, they are so hypnotizing. They are the color of fresh cut grass and then the color of night, mysterious and yet able to see what I am thinking most of the time. His eyes are the exact opposite color of the pool I was diving into earlier. It drives me crazy when Chris stares and doesn't say anything. There are a thousand seconds in between breaths, like when you wait to jump into cold water thinking about it carefully before taking the plunge.

"Are we done arguing now?" he says.

"I didn't know we were arguing?" I say right back.

"I'm waiting for a kiss from my wife."

"Well, what were you expecting? Want me to drop down right here, give you a blow job like the video *Love in an Elevator*?" I say flirtingly.

"Well, if you must, let's take this party upstairs," he says as his hand slips down my back and he squeezes my ass.

It's just like us to spin a possible fight and lure each other into sex. He was an expert at this when we first met and now he has me hook, line and sinker all over again. When he has my attention sexually, he knows just how to compliment and seduce at the right moment.

"Looks like you have been working out darling, you can bounce a quarter off this," he says looking down at me with a sinister smile.

He leans in to kiss me again. This time it is a wet and hot kiss. I haven't felt a kiss like that in a long time. It is one of those kisses that make me forget who I am for a moment even while standing in the largest city in the United States. All these people in this city and I can't hear them. It almost feels like we are in college again. He kisses my neck, which leaves me without any more words. We start making out all the way up in the elevator. I feel like I am in a White Snake video, you know, Tawny Kitaen-like rolling my hair along as my back is being pushed in the back of the elevator.

I will be the star of the show if I can just pull off a front walkover and into the splits, my white sheer blouse flapping in a breeze like a veil over a virginal young bride. But that ship has sailed, better yet, it makes a slow descent to the bottom of the sea. So of course, this love scene isn't going to end up like a music video but I am determined to try and make my inner sex appeal reappear again. The elevator door stops, opens and in walks a family of four. I am trying to sober up a little, and not look so flustered, but I know they can tell what we are doing.

It feels like hours waiting to get to our floor. We scoot out rather briskly laughing as Chris finds the room and he fumbles to get the door open. Once we enter, we are taking each other's clothes off piece by piece. I am on the bed and he gets on top of me, but I roll him back over so I can get on top. I am feeling the need to be in the driver's seat. This doesn't last long because I can feel Chris steering me over to my back shortly after I climb on top. The beautiful sun blinds the view until there is nothing to see but a sliver of light, and feelings of thankfulness set in to leave the glare in the rear-view mirror. I feel his need for control when he lays his hot sweaty body on top of mine. He smells so good; he feels so good. I roll with it.

I am finally feeling totally awake at the moment.

I rarely admit this, but I like this take-charge-of-me way sometimes. I feel it here. But as we start getting into the act, I can tell he is not all the way there in his mind with me again. His hands are around the side of me, not physically on my body. He doesn't look me in the eye at this point or kiss me. It is like he is putting all of his energy into getting this charade over with, somehow to appease me, yet he isn't directly concerned about whether I come or not, because all of a sudden, and to my shock, he is done. I let it happen, just like I let everything happen in this marriage. Then I choose not to say anything to cover it up, acting all rough and tough on the exterior, but the interior is a mess. When he is done, he kisses the top of my head.

"That was wild shit, babe, yeah?" he says feeling totally relaxed.

That was wild shit babe? I say to myself. I go on in my head. Holy shit, really? For who? I was about to get off myself but it was cut short. All this way for this? I could have had a better time at home, or better yet, I should have fucked Surfer Boy.

Now I am thinking only of him.

"Yeah, that was wild alright," I say with no emotion.

We lie next to each other taking deep breaths from our romp. I am inclined to smoke a cigarette like I see those phonies do on the tv screen or in a cheesy movie.

I remember that those sex parts in the movies made me feel hot and bothered, yet shy at the same time. I always wondered if the sex I saw would really be like that in real life. The people always looked so satisfied when they were done. What a perfect time to light a cigarette. That way the focus was on the shit that was going into their mouths instead. The smoke would blow out, and deep breaths would permeate the air so as to not focus on the person lying next to you.

What bothers me is that Chris doesn't even ask me if I came. I find this odd because he used to ask me all of the time. I know he asked not because he really cared, but more about the fact that his making me cum was somehow a little trophy he needed to polish so he could stroke his ego. Maybe some of the times he really did care, but I would put money down that it was more about him than me. But I am suspicious of him not asking at all if I came.

For Chris and me, sex was just not something we analyzed in our years of marriage. We just did it. Sometimes it was great, sometimes it was bad, and sometimes it was just something I engaged in because I knew if I didn't there would be problems.

The older I got, the less sex I craved. I love looking sexy and acting sexy, but I didn't find the need to be screwed all the time anymore. I honestly would rather drink myself to sleep and take my pills so I can fall into a slumber of relaxation. When Chris was gone on his trips, I was relieved I didn't need to put out because sex was a full-time job with him. I felt obliged because of what he did for me and for the kids. But I had no problem not having sex when he was gone because Chris was a sex fiend. When he was at home, he scheduled sex times with me, no joke. So, Monday, Wednesday, Friday and Saturday are a guarantee and I had to be ready when he was ready. There was no spontaneity, just bare bones and we got it on. I have been in more positions than an Olympic gymnast. And after years of these romps, any longer than seven minutes and I was lost waiting to get it over with.

So while I am lying in bed, I start to question how Chris had been on trips for a while without the physical act of sex. Hell, I was in the lobby for two hours and could have fucked that guy through the bar, but I at least have some kind of control. I start to wonder what he does with all of his time by the way he was just acting when we were together. With having sex this much, of course it can get stale, but something was different this time. I feel a dull ache like a root decaying under a molar. I am thinking deeply when Chris fell asleep on top of me.

He is suffocating me.

How can someone fall asleep that fast? I have no chance to even discuss this distance with him, and have no idea how to even bring it up. I get up and pick up my clothes. I decide to get dressed and go back downstairs to the bar to see if Surfer boy is there, but then I think about how that would all look. I talk myself right out of that one. What pisses me off is that for once I was actually feeling sexual and he missed it. The only way to get a great night's sleep would be to masturbate, but I don't feel like doing that with him in bed, even though I have done it many times before. But my mind is clouded and I can't even take care of myself. I get up and I stumble in the dark to the bathroom. I just can't lie in bed and try to figure this relationship out anymore.

Deep down I know I am unhappy.

I didn't come to New York to pick a fight. I really had the best of intentions, but now none of this seems right at all. I know if I say anything to Chris, I will ruin this trip. Perhaps I am just overthinking. I think about calling my friend Lola. I think about calling my cousin. I think about this for a long while until my stomach is sick. I feel this warm feeling in my belly. I am getting ready to throw up.

Holy shit, not now, I say to myself, but here it comes. It is all the gin because I haven't eaten anything since eight in the morning. I get this over with and to me it sounds loud, but Chris doesn't even wake up. He has been dealing with me puking since the minute I met him so if he did hear it, I am sure it was like second nature to him.

No way he would get up to see if I was alright. I brush my teeth and try to collect my dignity. I open the door quietly, but there he is snoring. I close the door and pick up my phone to call Lola, but all I see was Chris bashing. That isn't going to help me, especially if things get better. In the end she won't be of any help. She will just have a jaded view of Chris. No way, I would rather deal with my own affairs.

The only way I am able to calm my restless mind is with more gin because it went down easy and it doesn't talk back. I have Xanax too so think I will wash that down with gin. I sit at the hotel desk in the room in the dark to think about this because I will have to go back to the bar to get the gin. Out of my peripheral vision a small light keeps shining on the ceiling along with a faint buzzing. I turn to look and saw it was Chris's phone on the nightstand next to the bed. It keeps buzzing over and over. I keep thinking about who would be texting so much. I start to get nervous and think it might be the kids, especially Ava being a worry wart, so I get up and check my phone. Neither Ava nor Noah had called or texted.

My head is heavy and my eyes are so droopy. I am feeling really out of it from the combination of traveling, the Xanax, and the gin and everything seems to be a haze like walking through dense fog. I go over and pickup Chris' phone. He never lets me have his code to enter, but I once saw him put it in and memorized it. I plug in the code and find out quickly the texts aren't from the kids. It starts with a few threads.

"Where are you?" and "I can't wait to see you next." Then a picture pops up of an absolutely gorgeous woman complete with her mountain of cleavage, but way too much make-up, I might add.

Next text: "When does your wife leave? I don't know if I can take it with you after this long."

Then there is silence for five minutes as my blood pressure is rising like bread with too much yeast.

"Are you there? Check this out. It should wake you up XOXO!" On this text, there was a picture of this drop-dead gorgeous brunette. Her back was at the camera and she had arched so you can see the small of her back leading into her round and voluptuous ass cheeks. "Don't you want to lick all of me Chris?"

I feel like I am in a ring with Mike Tyson. This is one punch and I am down for the count, lights out. I get up from the ring and stumble trying to get a hold of myself. I hear the coach shouting at me to get back up. "Don't take this shit lying down, now get back in there!" I get back up. I huff and puff and breathe while Chris lies in a dream-like state. I look at him like a king cobra would look before the kill, and then I look at the phone just awaiting the next text that will light up the dark room.

There are decisions to be made and I don't know which way to go.

I stand in the dark and in the silence and listen to myself breathe. A warm sensation goes all over my body. I am completely in control. The gin and the Xanax together equal a powerful elixir for me. I can't imagine how I would have reacted to this news sober.

I suddenly start feeling relieved that I can walk away from this motherfucker and take him for all he had to his name. I know now for certain I am not a happy woman in this marriage. I am no longer staying quiet to not ruin this trip. And also, another part of me is furious that he has been lying to me for God knows how long.

Part of me is pissed that I gave up many opportunities to be with others because I made a commitment to him. I still love him in a strange way though, and something in me will not allow my eyes to shed a tear because I don't feel the betrayal like I should, and then I ask myself why. All these feelings I have but none of them are sadness, more anger that I have been hanging on like the little Mrs. who waited for her husband to do everything, not to mention being his sex slave.

I don't know what to do, or where to go though, so I continue to stand in silence for a bit, staring at the phone. I am watching Chris' chest move up and down so peacefully and melodically.

Fifteen minutes goes by and the next text buzz shocks me back into reality.

"Well . . . send me a picture of you Chris. Then I can at least look at you to get myself off. I'll start by getting myself juicy wet, press my nipples, then finger myself and call out your name. You hear me?"

I turn and look at Chris who is now snoring loudly. I take a picture of him with his mouth wide open, drooling, looking like a drunken sailor who was out all night fucking a bunch of whores. Chris looks great all the time, but he is the ugliest he ever is when he is sleeping. Without a hesitation or thought on what will happen next, I text the picture of Chris sleeping. I start writing like I was writing the best essay for a college assignment.

"I can't lick anything, baby, because I've been out all night with my wife. We fucked for hours on end and I never thought of you once. Why don't you get fucked by someone else tonight you stupid little slut. By the way, your boobs look droopy. Try doing some editing next time, okay honey? I don't want to lick those fat ass cheeks either. Think about losing 10 pounds yet?"

My next picture to her is me, sexy in a t-shirt hanging off my shoulder, hair messy, but makeup flawless. I proudly have my middle finger sticking up with blowjob lips. I laugh and think this is an incredible way to shoot my wicked thoughts through sound waves over time.

I imagine her face when she sees the pictures and the words. Maybe her jaw drops. I wonder how big her jaw is. Is her jaw big enough to wrap around Chris's dick? I was sure she has a big mouth because any woman knows how easy it is to lure a man by simply saying she'll give a blowjob. I am sure this is how she lured Chris.

I start thinking about how many women he has been sleeping with. Then I start thinking about my health and go into panic mode. I noticed the Xanax hadn't blocked this emotion because I have to worry about an STD and that really sets me off. I want so badly to kick him in the balls right now so he is able to feel what I feel. The rage I feel is trapped from the slow pace in my blood of Xanax and gin.

Meanwhile, the airwaves on the phone are dead. There is no light and no buzz. This bimbo is dead in the water. I dive into her perspective to see what she will come back with on text. Maybe she will send back a picture of her pussy because that is what she is right now with no text back yet for a cross examination. There is an angered hush in the air. I wait for the text to light up the ceiling while Chris is in a lovely meditative slumber. Then it comes, like a flash of lighting before the thunder crashes. I am shocked it doesn't wake Chris.

"Oh my, I am sorry. I think I have the wrong number. My apologies."

What in the actual fuck? This is how she responds? I angle the camera down at myself and take my shirt off this time so only my black bra straps are showing my cut shoulders and nice cleavage. I know exactly how to angle myself for film just like this bitch. I then take off my black panties and lay them on the white countertop.

I take a picture of them as a still life shot. I send both these pictures to her. "You don't have the wrong number bitch. This is Chris's wife Ashley. He is not married to some fat, ugly, hag. I'm hot and there is no reason for him to hunt for pussy elsewhere. He's been fed the entrée and dessert here. Your sex romps are now over. You were just a shitty appetizer. You may want to invest in a vibrator sweetie because he took my panties off with his teeth. I wore his ass out and he can't even see straight. You may want to lose his number because I am blocking your ass. No more gravy train sister. Get your own man!"

Almost instantaneously another text shoots back through the dark evening. "I don't know what you are talking about. I said this is the wrong number. Have a blessed day now, ok?"

I am tired of this charade. She knows she was caught but too much of a pussy to even admit it. I call her number hoping to talk to her but she doesn't pick up. It goes right to voicemail so I hang up. I am dealing with a spineless wench, and if she were in front of me, I would have hit her with all the force I could muster, but I don't want to waste more time than I've already wasted. I start thinking instantly of Surfer Boy again. Maybe this was a chance not to pass up on.

I text her again. My fingers get heavier with each sentence I write with fury. "You will be blocked, you stupid cunt. Go get fucked by someone else. By the way, you have a blessed day!"

I block her number. Oh, Chris will love that. He will act like a heroin addict trying to hunt down another fix.

This is not how I envisioned our first night together. I don't even care about these Barbie fairytales I make up in my head. All I want to do is go home.

I remember the dream I had before coming here. I could feel that I was that cicada getting ready to be gulped up in a hungry bird's mouth, but with all my might I fought this exchange. I had spent more time under the ground than on top. I needed to stay in the warm air that gave me light instead of below in sheer darkness.

The dirt was heavy and I needed to be free.

I turn Chris' phone off and put it face down on his nightstand. I take a super quick shower to wash off the sex and the smell of infidelity, put on a new pair of sexy panties with no bra. I start getting wet just thinking about Surfer Boy. This incredible urge of what he could do to me has me moving quickly. Without another thought, I ride the elevator down to the lobby. I head right towards the bar. Surfer boy is just getting ready to leave. I stop, turn on the allure and stare, saying nothing. He has his backpack on the bar and is grabbing his keys when he catches my eye. He looks intrigued and bewildered at the same time.

"Oh Chicago, what's the story?" he says with a look of I-knew-you'd-be-back."

I just smile.

"Did you drive here?" I say.

"Yeah, I actually did. I borrowed my roommate's car. "Why?"

I stare as sultry as I could and lower my voice to a whisper for effect just like he did when he was leaning in close to me at the bar. "I thought maybe we could go for a ride? What do you think?"

He stops for a moment with a skeptical look on his face. It takes him a little bit to find some words. "Of course, I can show you the town, but what will Mr. Hot Shot think?"

I laugh because that was pretty funny. I am glad he finds a comeback. "He had other plans, no need to worry about him." I say.

And that was his green light. He grabs my hand so fast that I find my feet aren't even hitting the sidewalk as we sprint to his car. By the time we get into the front seat, clothes are ripped off in a steaming wave of frenzy. I am on top of him in a New York minute. He keeps talking and telling me how hot I am.

He lets me stay on top.

I feel his strong hands guiding me up and down his warm mountain. We are on a climb to the top. "Your pussy is so wet and I'm rock hard, yes!"

He keeps grabbing and sucking on my boobs. My gosh does this feel fantastic. I can't remember being so excited.

"Oh, your tits are the best, let me see them bounce up and down like a cowgirl! You're so fucking beautiful. I wanted to fuck you the second I saw you. I know every guy that sees you thinks the same thing. You love this, yeah? Come on, fuck me harder, fuck me harder, yeah, yeah, yeah."

It is hot and all, but I just want him to shut the fuck up already. What is this, a porn? I don't need dialogue to fulfill a fantasy on a shady video on the internet. All of this talk is interfering with my mission, but I don't want him to stop though because it feels so fucking good, all warm and tingly. It feels wildly freeing to be with someone who knows not one thing about me except where I am from.

He doesn't know my name. I don't know his name.

While I continue to rock up and down all over him, I finally put my finger to his lips to get him to slow his roll and quiet him down. It is like this was his first rodeo and I don't just want to be the girl with her tits bouncing all around.

I want to be in charge.

This was my mission, not his.

"Let me take control here, ok?"

This turns him on even more and he starts to talk again until I put my hand forcefully over his mouth this time, but I am still able to hear the grunts and heavy breathing. He finally gets quiet. I reach down to feel his broad shoulders, touch his biceps. His hands are circling my waist moving me around in a circular motion. I am riding the waves on this ocean. It is as smooth as glass, salty and serene all at once from the top of my head to the bottoms of my toes. I honestly don't even know if he came, and I don't care because I am riding the oxytocin wave of glory.

But I think he did cum because he made this crazy loud noise after I came and then he lay limply afterwards, silent and breathing heavily.

I'd feel the remnants of him dripping out of me later when I shower him and Chris off. What a great seven-minute sex romp and right up my alley for a timeline. The last thing I want is to be vaggravated.

He isn't sure if he should speak, but I know he is dying to say something. He is sweating and still panting while zipping up his pants. "Wow, that was intense, Chicago. Don't you think I should know your name after that?"

"No," I say softly.

"And I don't want to know yours. You did me a favor tonight darling, and I'll remember it always," I say. "Hope you catch a big break. I can say I knew ya when . . . "

I put on my clothes, breathe a little sigh of calmness, lean over and give him a kiss.

"That's it?" he says, confused.

I chuckle to myself because he looks like a little lost puppy needing help finding his owner. I have seen this look many times in my life from men I have fucked around with who wanted more after I was already done and putting my clothes back on in a hurry.

"No number? Want to go out while you are here and get dinner?"

"Oh no," I say, chuckling softly. "This is the end of the movie."

He rolls his eyes before talking. He caresses some bangs that fall softly near my eyes. He tucks the strands behind my ears, leans over and kisses my forehead ever so gently. It is very sweet. I almost fall in love for a moment, but that's not what I need.

I already got what I need.

"I want you to know that you are absolutely stunning. Can I at least walk you back into the hotel?" he coos.

Damn those puppy dog eyes. I do fall for this shit sometimes. I am feeling a little uneasy about walking through an alley at night in New York City anyways. So, I let him walk me back to the lobby.

He kisses me one more time when we get there. "You all good to go up now sweetheart? Is it okay to call you that now since I know you intimately?" he says laughing.

"It's all good. I am a grown woman and can handle going back upstairs by myself. But what you saw back there was not a sweetheart, but a horny housewife." I laugh kind of pathetically realizing what I have just done. "But I am not in need of rescuing, really," I say.

I can tell that he thinks this statement is not at all that convincing. I know it isn't true either, but the last thing I want is for him to come out on top here.

"You could have fooled me darling," he says, frowning and shaking his head a little back and forth. "Just don't get lost, ok? It's a big city and it will be hard to find your way around." He gives me one more sexy, sultry kiss. "Why in the fuck would your husband not be fucking you every night? I don't get it. He looks like he's got it all. What's the fucking problem?" he asks.

"It's late and you should be going. I won't waste any more of your time."

He kisses my forehead lightly complete with a tap on my ass. He just smiles. As he walks away, I get lost staring at his confident stride, along with his muscular back that slips into darkness. I watch the brake lights of his car slowly fade away into the dirty air. I walk back into the hotel and ride the elevator up to the room.

When I get back, Chris is still in the same position I left him in. I pick up the phone to see if there are many more text threads, but mine was the last text that was sent. I get in the shower again and let the warm water run all over me. I am able to feel the water in every groove and crevice. It is soothing as the water beads roll off my body like a waterfall in a Japanese garden. This water smells pure, but it is tainted with poisonous organisms, yet at the same time it feels like a renewal at a christening. I had walked into an ocean, shallow at first, but now am submerged underwater in the deep blue part, no bottom to feel grounded.

When I get out of the shower, I am heavy with heartache and climb back into bed and wonder what tomorrow will bring on this trip. Chris lets out a loud snore when I get into the bed, turns over and puts his arm around me. It takes everything in me not to rip his arm right off his body.

Chapter 33

Tammy

> *"A journey of a thousand miles begins with a single step."*
> *- Lao Tzu*

A heavy wind blows the hammock. I am awakened by this movement but want to continue thinking about my time with Alex at family weekend. I have a lot of time so I am retraining my mind now how to dream as if I am in control. It is working and it's the only thing that will take the head pain away.

Alex texted us when he got back from the football game and asked that we pick him up at his dorm for dinner. He looked freshly showered while jogging lightly down the building stairs, almost a spring in his step. When he got into the car, the whole space smelled like a single's bar. It made me smile because as a mom of a son, I was thrilled he brushed his hair and teeth for the occasion. He actually didn't smell like the high school gym locker. There was hope after all. He really seemed to look at home here and that thrilled me to no end. I just hoped in my head that telling him the news tonight about me and Bill would not cause him to lose a step. I got that nervous feeling in my stomach but tried to focus on being present in the moment. Mom chimed in and asked how the game was sensing my apprehension. She really was a master at timing.

"Oh, it was great. I wish you guys came because it really was so entertaining. I would have been able to introduce you to my friends. That's okay, though. There is one more thing for parents tomorrow before you leave so I can have you meet them then."

"Oh, that's good," I said.

And then Alex became our personal tour guide on the way to the restaurant. He showed us all the halls, dorms, frats, sororities, the quad, and his whole new city he calls home and even a place called the "freshman hill."

In the middle of this tour his phone started buzzing. "Hang on, gotta answer this." He sounded so professional that it made me chuckle. We heard a few ah-ha's and yeses.

"So that was Ryan, my roommate. It looks like his parents aren't going to make it and he has no plans. Would it be okay if he joins us for dinner?"

Mom looked over at me, and I looked over at her. I was thinking that this was not a good idea because I didn't want to tell Alex the news with a perfect stranger. I also didn't want to wait to tell Alex either. I knew it would be awkward for his roommate to hear this news, but I also didn't want his roommate alone either on parents' weekend.

I motioned into the back seat. "Does he need us to turn around and go get him?

"No, he says he has to shower and he'll get a ride over a little later after our reservation."

I sighed a breath of relief. I had a timeline. I could not blow this off because my window was small.

Alex continued on with his tour until we arrived at the restaurant. Of course, Alex picked his favorite Italian restaurant to eat at because he loved specialty pizzas.

"Thanks for taking me here, Mom. I don't go out to restaurants much, so this is a nice treat," he said.

"Have you eaten here before Alex?" Grandma said.

"No, funny enough I have not. But I asked around and people said this was the best Italian restaurant so thought it was a good place to come."

When Alex was happy telling stories, he always raised his right eyebrow a little while speaking. I know he didn't even know he was doing this. This observation was something only a mom could pick out. It always made my heart sing. He has been doing this as far back as I can recall.

"I'm really happy you came too, Grandma. I know that was a long drive for Mom to drive by herself. What do you think of the campus?"

"I must say it is quite impressive, don't you think Tammy?" She motioned over to me and I agreed.

I was half in the conversation just staring at Alex still finding this all still like some kind of dream. How can he be talking about his new home? How does he live this far away from me? There was a strong pull on an undertow pulling me back in time all of a sudden. I would go back and relive my life all over again, but this time do it even better. I had more to give, but my time ran out. I saw an egg timer lying in front of me. The tiny grains of sand slipped through the glass without a sound landing ever so gently. If I had to tip it over and start again, I don't know if I could watch those grains of sand slip away again, silent and permanent.

"Mom. Where did you go? Earth to Mom," Alex said as he noticed me slipping into a different world.

"Oh Alex, I am sorry. I think the campus here is really something. I can totally see why you love it so much. There is no reason at all to be homesick that's for sure." I beamed.

"You're right Mom. But I would be lying if I didn't say I was homesick. Remember those first few weeks I kept calling asking for little things here and there? It just felt good to hear your voice, that's all. But once I started to find my way around, it got easier not to think about home because I was too busy trying to figure everything out here."

Mom looked at me and smiled.

"Yes, that's life, Alex. Don't get used to anything being permanent, but be grateful for what you have in life," I said.

Mom looked at me and kind of gave me the eye to tell Alex about Bill and me before Ryan got there. I gave her the okay-I-got-it-look.

The waitress came at the precise moment I was going to say something, but after we put our order in, I just dove in.

"So, Alex. I have something to tell you. It's not terrible and it's not the best news," I said with my voice trembling a bit. "There really wasn't any good way to tell you, so I will just say it." I sighed, but before I could get the next sentence out Alex interrupted me saving me from saying this out loud.

"Is this about you and Dad? Because if it is, I already know what you're going to say," he said. "I heard you got a divorce."

If all the air could be sucked out of a room in a second it would have been right there. I felt myself starting to choke and gasp for the air that was leaving the room. The look on my mom's face was one of shock and disbelief, but she remained quiet. I had to pick my jaw up from the table.

"Alex, how could you possibly have known this news? I have been brooding and thinking about this for a while, along with subjecting Grandma to this the whole ride here and figuring out how and when to tell you. Then you just blurt it out like it's yesterday's news?"

I all of a sudden started feeling a bit pissed off that I was not the one to tell Alex this news. I didn't like his laissez-faire attitude, but this was how Alex rolled. He was very carefree and logical. I wanted to be like him but I was from a different mold.

"So be it," he said nonchalantly.

Why I was so nervous to tell him I don't know. Perhaps it was more about me than him. "So, are you going to tell me how you know this, how long you've known, and why you haven't said anything to me?"

He looked at me kind of funny and surprised at my reaction. "I suppose I could ask the same thing of you, Mom."

I sat for a minute with this comment before responding. "Well, Alex, this is not the easiest thing to tell your child because essentially I am admitting to you that I have failed in keeping a marriage together. I failed at being a parent that kept her family together and that's not an easy pill to swallow. There was no right time for me to tell you this, so I sat on it for a bit to get a grip on my own feelings."

I could feel the tears welling up and my voice starting to shake. I took a drink of water and Mom grabbed hold of my thick arm. I looked down and noticed her hand couldn't wrap around my wrist. It startled me. What have I become? I had to shift and refocus.

"Well, now that this is out there, obviously Dad told you, but when? I would be lying if I said I wasn't completely shocked at this one, Alex. Since when did Dad all of a sudden take an interest in how anything might affect you?"

I was staring at him with anguished eyes, but he sat there not knowing what to say. I stepped in for him.

"I didn't want to tell you right away, Alex, because I didn't want to burden you with our marital problems while you were at school trying to adjust to a whole new life. Then your father had to go and spill that one out there for you to sit and dwell in?"

"I haven't been dwelling on this mom. You speak for me sometimes and you just did that now. You are guessing how I would feel without even knowing how I actually feel."

I stopped for a moment to take that all in. I guess I did do this a lot. "All I can say is that I am sorry, Alex. I wish things would have gone in a different direction. Sometimes you can fall completely in love with a person and yet fall completely out of love on the other end. This is the worst kind of feeling I wouldn't wish on anyone, especially my child, but I can't go back and undo anything now." I felt the shame and disappointment of admitting failure, especially to my son.

"I know," Alex said. Dad and I had a good talk about this. It was pretty simple. You guys just weren't in love anymore, so why should you stay together? I get that. I just wonder why now? Did you stay together unhappy just for me? Because you could have done it earlier. I told Dad this same thing and he kind of laughed thinking who am I to tell you guys what to do in your marriage. But really, why did you stay together?"

"Well, truth be told, Alex, we did it for you. We never talked about it honestly, we just lived together and that worked fine for when you were at home. So, when you moved out, that's when we both decided it was time to start different lives as you were starting your own too."

We sat in uncomfortable silence while the bus boy came to fill up our water glasses. I was thinking about asking him for more air, but I was certain that wasn't on the menu.

"Mom," Alex sighed. "I didn't know about the divorce that long if that makes you feel better. Dad called a few weeks ago to tell me he was not able to make parents' weekend, but that he was going to be in Tallahassee with some friends on a fishing trip last week. They drove, and he said he was going to stop here on his way back from Tallahassee because it is just about four and half hours away from here."

All I could think of when Alex was explaining this trip was that Bill was able to go on a fishing trip with his friends, but not one time ever took his son when he was growing up or anywhere for that matter. I had to try and clear that anger from my mind, but it wasn't working. I was getting hostile within my head. I breathed deeply and angrily a few times.

"So, he actually showed up here?"

Alex nodded. "Yeah, he did and it was nice. I got to show him around. He met some of my friends. He took me out to dinner and we had a long talk about everything." His eyebrow was raising and he looked thrilled to be talking about his dad.

I wanted to be happy but my blood was boiling. Suddenly his eyebrow raising wasn't cute anymore. While he was talking, I was doing everything to constrain my hostile jealousy.

"Dad told me a lot about his family and stories I had never heard before. That's when he told me that you guys got divorced and why. He basically said the same thing you did and that he had fallen out of love with who you once were."

"He said that Alex? Who I once was?"

Alex looked a little uncomfortable because he was not used to seeing me agitated, but clearly he struck a nerve. Mom just sat. She didn't have much to say. They were both waiting on what I was going to say next. But I had to sit a moment and talk in my head so as to not hurt Alex anymore than I already had. That alone would kill me. I was still the same person, just heavier. Who was he kidding? Did he have the balls to tell Alex he treated me like shit because I got fat? I am sure he didn't, because he had no backbone. I wanted to excuse myself, to call Bill and ream him into an asshole because he deserved it. I could feel heat rising in me. Sweat beads were forming on my forehead and around the collar of my neck. I am not sure if they noticed. I get hives when I am uncomfortable in situations. I was able to feel red hot dots forming on my neck like the bubbling of hot lava ready to spill out of the Earth's crust.

Then Alex broke the silence. "Mom, I can see you are getting upset and I don't want you to be because I'm not upset about this. I am just telling you what Dad said to me and sounded just like what you said. So, you shouldn't be getting mad. You wanted a divorce too, right? Dad said you were both in agreement and why it happened so fast because you split everything down the middle. You and Dad haven't gotten along in years, right? Do you think I didn't notice? You and I did almost everything separately. It was rare when the three of us were together, come on now Mom. It was just something I got used to and never really questioned. I thought this was how Moms and Dads were until I saw some of my friends' parents together. Then I thought their family was just weird and different. But I never really wanted that for me because it didn't seem to be a problem in our house. There was never any yelling or screaming, or crying, or at least none that I saw, and you guys never talked about each other, so I thought it was all fine. I just did everything with you and Grandma too."

I couldn't believe it. He was trying to console me instead of me consoling him. This is not the way I wanted this to go. I cooled down a bit. "While I am happy to hear this, Alex, I hope you are not just saying this to blow smoke up my butt. You know I don't like anything sugar-coated. I hope that is not what you are doing now to lessen the boom."

Alex chuckled a little and then the smile faded. "Alright, to be honest, I used to get upset sometimes that Dad really never did much with me, but again, I didn't know anything different and you guys never really talked about it. Remember how some of the dads in the neighborhood used to go on a camping trip every year? Dad didn't care for some of the neighborhood dads and I remember how you used to try to get Dad to go and get upset. Dad even went with me a few times, but I could tell he didn't want to be there. Why did you force him to be someone he was not? That's a problem Mom, don't you think?" he said and went on. "I admit I used to get upset about Dad not coming too, but after a while, it just didn't phase me anymore, like all the other things he wasn't around for. It was fine just the way it was. I think maybe you felt worse about it than me."

I had not wanted to cry, but I couldn't help being overwhelmed with emotions. A trail of tears was upon me. I had lost my voice and couldn't speak.

So, my mom chimed in at this point. I knew she wouldn't be able to stay out of this one this long. "Alex, all your mom did was love you from the very first minute she knew she was having you. She missed a chance at a softball scholarship and college. She tried her very best to deal with being a mother at the age of eighteen while all of her friends went to start their new lives. She was stuck at home and forced to become an adult overnight. She and your father really were in love at one point, they really were, even at their young age." She took a short breath with a sigh.

" Your Dad had to do all the providing at his young age, too, and none of it was easy. But what was easy was loving you. So, while your dad was not the encouraging type or always the present kind of father, he still loves you and always wanted the best for you. I just don't think he knew how to show it, that's all," and then she stepped off the stage as gracefully as she had entered.

It was her last curtain call and she delivered it well. My mom knew exactly what to say at precisely the right time. Sometimes I would lie in bed and thank my lucky stars and wonder just what the hell I would do without her.

"Oh Alex, I am so sorry. I only want the best for you, you know that, right?"

He shook his head yes. His eyes were also filled with tears. I pulled myself together. "You still have us as parents, always. We are now able to live out the rest of our lives trying to find who we are because I think we lost that many years ago. But none of this is your fault, you have to believe that. I hope you can believe that," I pleaded. "I know we have to give you time to process this all, and you have every right to feel lost, mad or even just sad, or nothing at all. I just want you to know that our divorce does not change the love we feel for you. Does this make sense?"

"It does Mom. I actually had a good visit with Dad. It was the first time in a very long time that we talked just me and him without you. It seemed a bit unnatural at first, but as we got talking, it really felt good to talk to him. He told me you guys sold the house and he found a nice condo and liked where he lived. He said you got a condo too. Good thing I got all my stuff out before you signed the closing papers. Some kids have their rooms remodeled, you guys sold my childhood instead," and he laughed.

"Alex, you sure know how to make a mom feel bad! Come on now. I did save things that were still yours and brought it to the condo, which is less than a mile from the old house by the way. When you want to come back, you can stay at either place. I have two bedrooms."

It seemed so odd to be talking about this and I was still trying to figure out if it was really my life that I was talking about. "It really is great Alex. I love my walk to work, and I really enjoy working with the kindergarten kids now. I lost twenty pounds and I'm on my way to losing more. I am finally in a good place in my life, taking classes and comfortable where I am at."

"Mom, that makes me happy. I can't wait to see the condo," he said so sincerely. "You know what Mom? Dad actually told me he was proud of me. I was shocked."

I kind of half chuckled. As pissed as I was at Bill for telling Alex first, I guess it was a good thing and who knows, maybe it was the start of a relationship, finally. One could hope.

It was all good timing because Ryan showed up just as we were finishing our talk so we had to end the conversation. Alex gave me one of his it-will-all-be okay looks and somehow, I knew he would be fine. We finished out the evening making Ryan feel comfortable. Each of the boys told us stories about their paths and how they came to become good friends in a few short months. I noticed Alex's eyebrow raising again with each story he told. This time it gave me more joy than he can ever know.

I remembered that the next day was filled with fun as Mom and I got to meet more of Alex's friends, see more sights, and set out for the drive home. The clock kept ticking making me feel like the Cinderella carriage was getting ready to morph back into a pumpkin. I felt myself not wanting to leave Alex there, similar to how I felt when we dropped him off at the airport, but I knew the next time I would see him he would be even more mature than he was right now. This made me feel better leaving him.

As Alex gave me a hug goodbye, he said, "Mom, are you going to be okay by yourself?"

"Alex, I will be just fine, don't worry about me. We all have a blank canvas, and we have to paint it now, right?"

"Yep, love you." He walked over towards Mom. "I love you too Grandma and thanks for coming."

She smiled her infectious smile. "I wouldn't have missed it, although you could have picked a closer place to go to school, kid, I'm getting old!"

We all laughed. Leave it to my mom to keep us all from crying.

As we drove out of the campus, I got to thinking about how Bill, myself and Alex all had a bond together in starting our new lives. It made me smile because we were all finally free to live this new chapter. As we were pulling out, I was able to see Alex in the rear-view mirror walking away with his friends. He had his head held high walking proudly with broad shoulders, ready to conquer the world. I held that image in my head most of the ride home, all eleven and a half hours of it.

The wind sways gently. I want to dream of nothing but silence, so I do.

Chapter 34

Ashley

"Beauty is not caused. It is."
- Emily Dickinson

I am lying in bed while Chris is snoring so loudly that I punch him to get him to move away from him. I don't want his arms around me. He turns over and breathes his dragon breath the other way. It feels good to hit him. What in the fuck have I just done? I became a sex object for man's conquest, or was it for me? I honestly don't know. I am a pawn in the game, the middleman.

What the fuck am I doing with my life? I cannot sleep one wink. I just lie here brooding about my marriage and my relationships with men. I haven't thought about my first sexual experience in years. But lying here now I get to thinking about the first guy I was with. Strangely, Surfer Boy reminds me of him. I feel like I was a young teenager tonight fucking in a car. This makes me smile. I turn away from Chris to drift back into time.

When I turned thirteen I was the first girl in my neighborhood to start blossoming. I was the envy of both the boys and the girls. I must say I enjoyed every bit of the attention I received. Because of this new-found attention, my mom took me for my first bra. I remember feeling so grown up and ready to show off the blessings I had been bestowed. I even went so far as to wear light colored shirts so that everyone could see I indeed was wearing a bra. Prior to this new bra, I wore tight t-shirts, but my boobs had grown so quickly, it wasn't a good plan to not wear a bra because when I got measured, I was already in a C cup. I don't know why my mom waited so long to take me. To accompany these new-found pleasures on the top half of my body was my long wavy blonde hair. My thick hair was light from the sun in the summer, almost bleach blonde. Throw in the boobs and my slender dancing legs and I knew I was a force to be reckoned with. I let all the boys know this and the girls too. My Dad would tell me I belonged in California running on the beach, not roaming the streets in our town, yet also he warned me of boys who would only look at me in one way.

"Oh Daddy," I'd say whining. "I don't know what you're talking about."

"Well, I do because I'm a man. I am sure your mother will be talking to you soon, but in the meantime, promise me you won't grow up and leave me, my sunshine." And he tussled my hair a bit.

"Of course, Daddy," I said as I hugged him back.

In my head I knew I couldn't keep this promise, but I didn't want to break his heart. I fed into this claim that I'd stay around forever. Little did he know that each day I was moving farther away from him by finding my womanhood.

Interestingly enough, my mom never came to me to have the old birds and the bees talk on her own accord. She felt getting me a bra explained it all. My mom had a private dressing consultant so she made an appointment for me and off we went. Her approach on this next rite of passage was pure and simple. She felt there was no need to get weepy or sappy.

The consultant took measurements and we got the bras and had them fitted. "How does it fit darling?" she said.

"Feels great," I said, beaming and turning in the three-way mirror admiring my body.

My mom motioned to the dressing consultant, "Ok, we will have five of those in different colors."

We waited together silently sipping tea while the bras were being packaged up in lovely lacy pink dainty boxes. So, the actual talk of the birds and bees didn't happen because she barely said a word about me and my experience. She mostly talked about her first bra and what she went through with her mother. We went out for lunch and then it was done.

It wasn't long before my new-found bra wearing days were noticed. There was a rowdy bunch of boys that all hung together in our neighborhood. Some were cute, and some were not, but they all seemed to hang together and ride their bikes past my house, or we would see them out on the baseball fields, at the pool, or on the tennis courts. One boy named Jeff was beyond adorable with curly brown hair. He was the alpha male of the group. Mike, another cute boy with blonde hair, was always trying to take Jeff's spot. He spent a lot of time trying to make it happen, while the other boys just followed along like sheep. It remains a mystery, but I guess the news got out somehow that I had started wearing a bra or perhaps they saw it through my shirt.

One day, Liz, Jenny, and I were out riding bikes when the boys were coming from the opposite direction. They formed a blockade to stop us from going through. I had on a white tank top with pink shorts. The straps stuck out a little where the tank top didn't cover, so it was crystal clear that I had been wearing a bra.

Jeff started the conversation first. "Hey Ashley, heard you got a bra. I thought it was just a rumor, but I can clearly see it now."

The boys started laughing and cackling while we all stood still on our bikes.

Then Mike chimed in and turned to Liz and Jenny. "I hope you two didn't go running out to get a bra like Ashley. Your parents will just waste their money. You two have chests like an airplane runway . . . flat and smooth." He patted his chest in a smug way.

"Oh, that's a good one, real original," Liz said. "You wouldn't even know how to get it off if you tried anyway you jerk, so cram it." She felt proud of herself for getting better at retaliating.

"I don't have to take one off of you because you ain't got one on, stupid," Mike said. "That probably won't happen for a while!"

They all started laughing at the same time. I could tell that Jeff was getting irritated by all this because he kept staring at me and told everyone to shut up. Clearly, he was the leader so when he told everyone to shut up rather forcefully, they all scattered like flies.

While these jackasses had no right to taunt us like they did, they were observant. My boobs were a good size C and getting bigger every day. They were quite perky, so I did stand out from the rest of the girls for sure.

Jeff just stood there staring at me. With this early phenomenon of control I seemed to magically possess, I had the upper hand and I felt it. Jeff was still standing there looking at me. I had never been looked at in this way before. I wasn't sure if it was creepy or if it turned me on. I started feeling a little hot. I could feel a tingling and warmness down under. I couldn't tell if this warm feeling was from how I was sitting on the bike or if it was the way Jeff was looking at me, or both. I wondered if these two mountains on my chest could simply be a way to reign like a monarchy? I wasn't sure, so we all started riding away after this long stare.

As we started to ride past him, Jeff stopped me with his tire. He liked that he had stopped me in my tracks, I could tell. "Want to meet me by the bleachers at the baseball field at four o'clock today? I'd like to talk to you."

He had an edge to him and he was really cute and quite convincing. I got these butterflies in my stomach. I wasn't sure what to say, but out came the word rather quietly, "Yes."

We all rode away giggling.

When we got back to my house Liz and Jenny and I went up to my room and closed the door behind us to chat about what was going to happen.

"How did you get these boobs, Ashley? Did your mom give you some kind of medicine? The boys are fascinated with you, especially Jeff. What are you going to do at the park?" Jenny said.

"I don't know," I said. "But when he reached in to talk to me, I felt his breath in my ear and made my vagina warm."

With this we all started giggling as hard as we could. They were looking up at me as I was staring at myself in the mirror like they hadn't known me, or that I had arrived from another planet.

Liz and Jenny have been my friends since kindergarten. Jenny lived across the street and Liz lived next door until she moved a little further in town when we were in high school. But as we got older, I could tell that three of us together became an issue. Two scenarios would happen: Jenny would get mad at me and Liz, then she would stay away. Or Liz would get at me, and Jenny and I would hang. I was never really left out all but maybe one time, and it wasn't long before they both came to knock on my door to make up. But I felt like at one point someone was going to jump ship. I just didn't know who it was going to be. If I had to guess before this event happened, I would have said Jenny. She was her own person and had already started hanging out with some other girls. I just didn't feel like they were my type, but I still wanted to hang out with her since I had known her since kindergarten.

Back at the mirror, Liz and Jenny were hanging on every word I said with questions and giggling. "I think Jeff loves your boobs, Ashley. I can tell by the way he was staring," Jenny said.

"They were all staring at you!" Liz said.

I looked up at the ceiling like I had found my answer up there. "Yes, I saw the way they were staring, sillies. I'm not an idiot."

"Well, are you going to let him touch your boobs?" Liz asked.

"Should I?" I said back.

"No way!" said Jenny. "What's he going to do with them anyways?" she retorted.

"I don't know. I think he wants to touch them," I said.

"Of course, he does silly!" said Liz. Liz was more of the advanced one of all of extended friends, even though she hadn't done anything with a boy yet. She had an older brother who would swipe his dad's Playboy and Hustler magazines. He used to bring them into the forest preserve close by. One time we found a bunch of magazines that he had left behind. We picked them up and rifled through the pictures. We saw things we had never seen before. We wanted to close it and walk away, but we just couldn't get ourselves to leave, our mouths hanging open, then a look of horror at some of the more detailed images. Playboy had just nude pictures, but in Hustler there was a lot more interaction. In the magazine I had, there was a picture of a guy licking a lady's boobs. At first it took me aback and I actually gasped. But now just thinking of this image made my vagina get that same warm feeling I had today when Jeff leaned into me whispering in my ear. That warm feeling kept luring me back in to want more. I kept wondering where it came from because it felt so darn good.

"Well maybe it feels good for someone to touch them," I said. "You know, like in the magazine. You know we couldn't stop looking at it," I reminded them.

"Yeah, I remember that," said Jenny. "So what? How gross is that? It's like the lady was a monkey giving milk to a baby. Are you going to let Jeff do that?"

"I might," I said. "Why not? I want to see if it feels good. I am getting these things now so I might as well use them."

We all started laughing again, but I could tell Jenny was not comfortable with much of this topic, but she joined in nonetheless.

"Oh my gosh, Ashley, are you going to let him touch your vagina then too?" Jenny said inquisitively.

"Ah no, one thing at a time."

"You mean two things at a time!" said Liz, which sent us into a louder laugh.

Jenny sighed and wanted to change the subject. "So, why don't you show us the bra? What does it look like?"

"Are you sure you want to see it?" I asked.

"Won't this be weird?" Jenny said.

"No, it won't be, " said Liz excitedly. " I want to see your new bra and your boobs. I am so jealous!"

I thought for a quick second, then I took off my shirt and showed them my bra. It was white with a little pink bow splitting my cleavage like two perfect hemispheres.

"Oh my God, that is so cute. Is it comfortable?" Liz inquired.

"Yes, it is," I said.

"Now they are not rubbing against my t-shirt and bouncing all over the place," I said, like I'd been wearing a bra for years.

"Turn around," said Liz. "I want to know if he is going to be able to get that thing off!" she said.

"I suppose I could help him," I suggested.

"Oh my gosh, are you supposed to do that?" Jenny asked.

"I don't know," I said. "Maybe he has never had to do this. I guess we'll see. Let's see how hard it is to get off. Liz, pretend you are Jeff and try to get it off."

I was standing in front of the full-length mirror with Liz and Jenny by my side in just my bra and my pink shorts. Jenny found the hook and the eye closures. Jenny sounded like a professional.

"Well, he will have to kind of push the two pieces together until the hook comes off the closure," I said.

"Or he could pull the straps down with his teeth!" shrieked Liz.

"That's gross, stop it," said Jenny.

I just stood there while my friends tried to unhook the bra. I was like a guinea pig, being poked and prodded, but I felt better that they were doing this first before I let Jeff try it. It kind of made me feel a little prepared for what was coming.

The girls tugged a little but seemed to get the hang of it pretty easily and out appeared my boobs. I was left standing there in the mirror while we were all staring at this new metamorphosis. I knew they were in awe, because over the years we had seen each other naked on many occasions, like at slumber parties and changing in the locker room at the pool. Our boobs all looked the same as little girls. We looked just like the boys did without their tops on. We had the same flat chest and protruding nipples that we never gave a second glance at. But my chest was something completely foreign to us now and quite shocking. This transformation was like watching a caterpillar turn into a butterfly, or a tadpole into a frog. I had completely morphed into someone else and they didn't know what to make of it. I stood there for what seemed like an eternity and then I spoke first.

"Well, what are you just staring at?" I said, waiting for someone to speak.

"I can't get over how big they are and so round! Your nipples look so small against all the puffiness. They're like two big bowling balls, Wow!" Liz giggled.

"They look like the ladies in the magazines," said Jenny.

"Mine don't look like that at all," said Liz frowning and looking at her flat chest.

"Me either," said Jenny looking at her flat chest too.

I didn't say anything to them because they were right. My boobs were two perfect pieces of art complete with little quarter sized pink nipples that immediately peaked when the air hit them once the bra came off. I actually started getting that warm feeling again with them being out in the open, but I stayed quiet about this.

"Okay," Liz said, "I know this is weird, but I have to touch them."

"What, are you nuts?" said Jenny.

I puckered up my face thinking about whether Liz should touch them.

"Okay, I won't touch them in a way that's weird," said Liz. "I just want to feel them so I know what it will be like when I get them."

"That may never happen for us, Ashley," Jenny said looking down again at her chest. Her face looked hopeless.

"Plus, don't you want to know what it feels like for someone else to touch them besides Jeff?" pleaded Liz.

"Yes, I guess so. Go ahead," I motioned.

I could tell Jenny was not comfortable with this situation and she was surprised at my reaction. But she didn't want to miss out, so she reluctantly decided to touch my boobs, too. So, at the same time Liz and Jenny had their hands on my boobs. I didn't feel myself getting warm down there. Their hands on my boobs felt like when I was getting a physical and similar to how the doctor pressed on my belly to see if it felt normal. While we are standing there, we all started giggling very loudly. It felt like a slumber party gone wild.

"Jump up and down. Let's see if they move!" said Liz.

I started jumping up and down to see them bounce and shake. This was great fun! "Look at these flashlights! Boom boom!" I started to get sexy with it and walked like a model in front of the girls.

"Take off your shorts," said Liz. "Do your panties match? You have to make sure they match when you see Jeff even if he doesn't take off your shorts."

"Duh, I know that," I said, acting like I was a professional at being a sex queen.

I took off my shorts and strutted around the room with my boobs out and panties on. I got on top of the bed and told Liz to turn on the music on my pink boombox that was next to my bed. Pat Benatar's *Hit Me with Your Best Shot* came on loudly. I started dancing and punching my arms and making sexy faces. I turned around sticking out my butt provocatively as I could at age thirteen. Liz and Jenny were going wild with laughter. They were turning away, but couldn't help but look, just like with all the images we saw in the magazines.

"Hit with me with your best shot," I sang loudly, and then put my hands inside the sides of my panties and started to pull them down so they could see my vagina. I got them down to my knees and Liz inched closer to get a better view.

"You have some hair there!" She was surprised.

It was just a light trail of blonde hair that had just started. Liz and Jenny were dancing and chanting,

"Take it all off Ashley!" I got the panties down to my knees and tossed the panties off into the air and I was completely naked. To my surprise, I started to get that warm feeling and tingly down there, so I continued to dance while Liz grabbed me a hat and tossed it on my head. Jenny grabbed a furry pink boa I had worn at a dance that was hanging off the bed canopy. I felt so good, a warm feeling in my vagina, and pure control of this situation. I kept dancing and the girls kept getting louder. My boobs were bouncing up and down while my butt was wiggling this way and that. Liz spanked me.

"Oh my gosh Ashley!" You have a heart shaped mole on your butt!! No joke!!"

At this point the girls were both rolling on the floor with laughter while I was in my glory. The more they fed me, the more I wanted. I was a shark who saw the path of blood in the murky water.

I wanted to search for more.

But it all came to a screeching halt, when my mom opened the door. She let out a loud gasp that scared the shit out of all of us. "Good heavens, what are you all doing?"

My mother had poise and prominence even in the most uncomfortable of situations. She walked over very calmly to the boombox, pressed stop, and spoke to us like she had just taken to the stage. The spotlight went on just over her. The air remained as quiet as a church until she broke the silence.

"Ashley, come down from the bed now and put your clothes on immediately. This is not at all as to what a young lady should be doing with her body for your friends to see."

I took off my hat and boa off, grabbed my clothes, and put them on fast trying to hold in my laughter as well as my sheer let down to be honest. I loved this attention I got. Of course my mom had to pop the most gorgeous balloon I had ever possessed. I didn't put the bra back on because I couldn't get it on quickly enough, so I just left it strewn on the bed laying limply and sad, just like me. Liz and Jenny were like statues and didn't say a word.

My mom broke the silence gnawing at our curiosity. "Girls. I know Ashley's body is growing and she is turning into a young woman. You will grow too in your own time. But to have my daughter on display for you like she is some kind of showpiece is not right. I'm disappointed you made her do something like this."

We all looked at each other, our eyes telling each other what to say.

Jenny spoke up right away because she never really wanted to do this. "Mrs Hayes?" said Jenny.

"Yes," said my mom in poised fashion.

"We just wanted to see Ashley's new bra so we can go ask to get one too. Then it turned into something else. We didn't mean for it to make Ashley feel bad, promise."

I looked at Liz and Jenny and grinned. Of course, for my mom everything came back to her dancing. You could give her any situation and she would bring it back to herself, guaranteed.

"Listen," she said astutely. "I was your age too, and Ashley inherited this beauty from me. I, like her, got my breasts when I was her at a very young age. I can remember this was the time the boys started looking at me differently at my dance recitals. I was one of the only girls whose breasts were sticking out of my leotards, even through the glitter." She droned on and on.

This was flat out embarrassing for her to be saying anything in front of my friends. It was bad enough that she saw me dancing naked in front of my friends. I wanted this to end.

"The other dancers wanted to see my breasts and were interested in how I got them and if any boys had touched me," she said looking at all three of us. "As dancers, we critique each other's bodies all the time because we spent many tight corners changing right in front of each other. But at no point did I let anyone touch me or tell me to do something I didn't want to do. Dancing was for recitals, practicing, and a little for fun in my own terms, but never to be on display so tackily as to what I just saw now." My mom stood there with her commanding presence and arms folded. Her silent stare could part the Red Sea.

"I'm sorry Mom," I said.

Liz and Jenny chimed in with some soft apologies as well, but I know they didn't mean it.

My mom picked up on this too, but she didn't have the energy to push it further. Instead, she walked past us in her recital of a walk.

"The door will stay open now girls when you are coming over. There is also no need to change in front of each other anymore now that you are becoming young ladies. Classy ladies don't do this unless you are at a dance recital. Do you understand?"

My mom walked out with even more poise than she walked in with like she had just finished a tragic dance piece. Once she was out of earshot, we all started laughing.

"All I know is you got the bod girl, and all the boys want to touch it. Now you know how it feels. Looks like you liked it until your mom came in and ruined it. So go have fun at four today with Jeff!" Liz grinned. And call us when you're back home so we know what happened," she said.

"Oh don't worry, I will," I said smiling with all the confidence of a Radio City Rockette kicking in a formation line at the Tony Awards.

When the girls left, my mom came back into my room.

"Ashley, I hope I was clear today with you. I know the girls are harmless here, but I have seen the way the boys have started to look at you. Don't let all of that go to your head. You are too young to let any boy touch you, do you understand?"

"Yes, I get it," I said. "I won't let them, don't worry," I lied.

This was her birds and the bees talk. I could give a fuck what she said to me. I just couldn't wait to see Jeff at four because I wanted him to like what he saw. Plus, I really wanted to get that warm feeling again.

Chris is still snoring but facing the other way. He will never get me to feel warm with him ever again.

Chapter 35

Tammy

> *"Seize the moments of happiness, love, and be loved! That is the only reality in the world. All else is folly."*
> - Leo Tolstoy

I awake after a long period of silence but I still feel like I never slept a wink. I really don't know how much longer I can go on here. This pain in my head is substantial like nothing I have ever felt before. I keep hearing voices. I want to run to them but I can't. I call back to the voices but no one can hear me. I have no other choice but to bend my mind towards good memories. I need something to hold on to. I slowly get up from the hammock. I need to walk. Every step hurts but I make my way over to a sunny patch of land where we used to have our swing set. There are only broken remnants now, but I strain really hard to see it in my mind. I want to go back to when we left Alex on family day. I remember the good feeling of being relieved to get a heavy weight off my chest.

On the way home from the trip Mom and I stopped off at a rest stop. We were eating our lunch at the picnic table under a lovely elm tree. We watched the kids playing on a swing set not far away. Their parents sat a little in the distance on a bench. The father was on his phone and never lifted his head the whole time, which I found troubling but not surprising. I've seen so many people who missed precious moments because their heads were buried in their phones. I wanted to go tell them to watch their children play, or better yet play with them.

All too soon that father will be at a rest stop wishing for the time by the swing again after dropping his daughter off to live her own life. On the other hand, the mother just sat and watched her child playing. At one point she got up to start the girl off on the swing. We listened to the happy shrieks of that feeling you get of your stomach dropping when you are on a swing.

Mom and I watched and reminisced about those carefree park days with our kids. Sometimes these moments felt like many moons ago. Other times it felt like five minutes went by when we were in this part of our life. Many of those moments could set anyone back to fire like a catapult down a black hole of tears and self-pity. To snap out of this trance I would smile and remember that these memories felt good, that's what mattered, not pining for time I couldn't get back.

Watching this girl reminded me of when I was a little girl and how I absolutely loved to swing on our swing set in the backyard. So many images go into the brain from day to day and all of those details get jumbled around or lost. But just watching this girl made me think about my own self many years ago and without fail, I could find that time in my brain where I had stored these joyous moments in my life and actually felt them.

My head was pounding before. Now I notice the pain has subsided, not sharp, but smooth with bliss.

When I was on a swing, I would feel weightless, carefree, and never more content. Dad had built this swing set for Dawn and me. We played on it all the time. I remember clearly swinging in my dress with my hair all done waiting for my grandparents to show up for birthday parties or events. I would swing and swing, higher and higher and just wait to see my grandparents' long black Buick kicking up gravel as it came down our long driveway. I loved that swing so much that Dad got tired of my complaints when the weather got too frigid.

He was such an attentive dad. To satisfy my happiness, he hung the swing down in the basement for me in the winter. It hung from the beams in between our laundry piles and his dusty workbench. This time was where I would enjoy my makeshift backyard on Friday nights after school, just swinging to my heart's desire. Mom would come in and out to do the laundry while I listened to sounds of the Johnny Carson Show blaring from the tv upstairs. I loved to hear my parents laughing from the couch. I can hear them now, faintly out of reach. These were the times I remembered with such fondness. I feel comfortable right here now even in this bare patch of land.

There was sun. It felt good on my body. I felt alive with wonder.

Mom sat quietly at the rest stop for a moment as I shared these stories with her. I loved her smile while I was telling them. "Oh, how you loved that swing, Tammy. There were many days I couldn't get you to come off and go to bed. I cursed Dad many times for putting that swing in the basement. But I couldn't stop him from loving you and your sister." She looked at me lovingly, tapped my knee, and then she looked back at the little girl. The smile that formed adorned her face like lights on a Christmas tree. She loved to touch me any chance she got. She would tap my shoulder, grab my hand, or squeeze my arm. I do the same thing with Alex. Instantly, I got that blissful feeling again like I had when I was a little girl on a swing.

Before Mom and I set off for home again, I turned around one more time to see that little girl. I was happy to see her father had put down the phone. He was now doing underdogs while the girl laughed and laughed in a high pitch giggle that the heavens could hear. It was music for my soul.

When we arrived back at Mom's house, she asked me to stay over, but I felt it was best that I went home. I had to learn how to walk into an empty house. She understood of course, but she always had my well-being first, even as an adult. I was somewhat getting used to being alone, but it still felt foreign to walk into an empty house at night especially. The noise of my keys felt so loud under the hush of a quiet night. I walked in and turned on the hallway light. I let the stillness settle in me for a little bit. My old self would head right for the refrigerator but I was trying to break a bad habit. I didn't want that competition of opening and closing that door competing with myself whether or not I should stuff my face to find relief.

I knew with a hundred percent certainty I would lose because I had an unhealthy relationship with food. This was getting better for me, so I didn't want to alter the new habits I was trying to attain. But I was jittery just waiting for what seemed like an hour of a world without noise.

I turned on the tv to create noise for me but I quickly turned it right back off because I was annoyed with channel surfing trying to find anyone chattering with meaning. These were people just spewing words out in the air that had no origin, no connection to anything. The words raced out the tv penetrating the air, which caused me to gasp trying to find my breath.

After I turned the tv off I picked up my book. I was reading the words while thinking about all the good times with Alex. I wondered if he was out with his friends. Would he find a girlfriend? I started counting the weeks to when he would be home before I figured out I had read an entire chapter without knowing what was going on.

I closed the book abruptly. The silence seeped into every pour of my being. And with that feeling, my gut-wrenching sobbing interrupted the silence, cutting the air right in half. I had been holding so much emotion inside. I was trying to be a hero, but there was no one to sing a victory song for me. It was time to let it all go. The empty nest was hollow. I had to let it naturally fall off the tree. The wind, the rain, and snow would change it throughout the seasons. Eventually it would fall down to the ground and decompose into the dirt. A new nest had to be rebuilt.

But I could not put a stop to this crying.

The only way out of this despondency was to shift my mindset. I had to physically talk out loud. I wanted to go for a walk but it was too late, so I walked and talked down my lonely hallways. Alex was able to understand the divorce, which ultimately was the best for all of us. As indifferent as I was to Bill, I was also glad to know he had made the journey to see Alex because I knew that meant a lot to him. When the salty liquid descended down the timeline of creases on my face, I let them fall off the edge. There was a pool of memories on the floor in front of me. I didn't want to slip, so I grabbed a towel to dry them up for good. I came to the conclusion that when the stars align you have to appreciate that gift. I was compelled to gear up for the next curve ball. Life was always around the corner while you were standing at the plate vacillating on whether to swing or not. Nightfall was descending over the warm patch of earth where the swing set once stood under the moonlight of my baptism.

I was a woman now, no longer a child carrying scars of the past.

I felt full not from my weight, but from an all-encompassing new found self.

She was a paradisiacal island.

CHAPTER 36

Ashley

> *"It is amazing how complete is the delusion that beauty is goodness."*
> *- Leo Tolstoy*

I can't even peacefully daydream because of Chris. As his snoring increases in volume, it raises my fuel level of animosity towards him to a high level. It's taking everything in me not to wake his ass up and show him that whore on his phone.

I cannot fall asleep while sleeping on a bed of dissolution.

I get up by flapping the covers off me to make some noise in an attempt to wake Chris. But no, he continues to snore flat notes on a staff measure. I get up and take another Xanax and wash it down with water. This is the only way I am going to be able to get some rest. I need to be ready for WW3 when this fuckhead wakes up. I lie back down. It will only take about fifteen minutes for the Xanax to kick in. It would be great if I could have an IV hooked up to me all the time. I could just press a pump when I needed to take the edge off. For now I gotta deal with my own thoughts.

I go back to daydreaming about my first sex experience with Jeff.

I made sure my body smelled good along with my hair, too. I put fresh panties on. I wore my new bra. I was ready to go find my womanhood. I lied to my mom when I left shortly before four and said I was biking to Liz's house for an early dinner. Mom fell for it and off I went. Some good things her talk did because she made me want to go out for more.

When I arrived at four at the park, Jeff was already there waiting for me with a big smile. I wondered if he put on fresh clothes. I wondered if he was as nervous as me.

"I'm surprised you showed up," he said.

"Why wouldn't I?" I said, my voice quivering a little.

"I guess I thought you would chicken out or bring your friends," he said so smoothly.

"Nope, just me," I said.

We parked our bikes together, then walked in the dry grass. It crunched under our feet from the lack of rain during the hot summer days. He led me to the bleachers. We crawled underneath where it was dark and a little musty. It was kind of creepy, but we needed to be out of sight. The light filtered in the perfect spot as we sat shielded and safe. It didn't take him long because he knew what he wanted. Before kissing me I could tell he wanted to say something. We sat looking at each other.

"Ashley, you are the prettiest girl in this town, you know that?"

I nodded a yes with an "Aha," in the sexiest voice I could at age thirteen.

He leaned in and kissed my lips very softly.

I closed my eyes because I didn't know what else to do. He closed his eyes too. I instantly started tingling. He kissed me a few times on the lips. Then after a few light touches of lips on lips, he parted mine with his tongue. It felt really strange at first to feel someone else's tongue in my mouth. All these years it was just for me. Then one day someone inserted their tongue in my mouth to invade a sacred area of my lifeline. I remember thinking that his breath smelled fresh, like he just brushed his teeth before meeting me. He swirled his tongue around and around with mine. Our tongues were dizzy with setting off distinct animalistic messages to all of our important parts.

We kept kissing for minutes on end before his hands started moving. I knew it was coming but it still startled me a little bit. I winced a little when he touched my waist inching closer up to my boobs. His fingers gliding off my nipple sent that warm feeling shooting down below. I could hardly contain myself. This was such a fabulous feeling. I instinctively moaned a little. He liked that because then he moaned a little too while keeping his tongue circling in my mouth. Then when our tongues were tired from working out, he pulled away slowly. He just smiled at me. My panties were soaking. I thought I peed in my shorts.

"Ashley, can you take off your shirt?"

I didn't say anything at all. I just looked him right in the eyes. I did not take my gaze off of his. I pulled off my shirt slowly. My bra was so pretty. It really was a shame to have it covered all of the time.

"Those are really big," he said and he started grinning nervously and kind of squirming.

"Do you want to touch them," I said.

"Yes," he said as his voice was trembling.

Maybe this was his first time, too. I really didn't know because it didn't matter. His hands were somewhat big, rough, but warm, and he squeezed my boobs gently.

"Can I take your bra off Ashley?"

I thought it was sweet that he kept asking.

"Yes," I said quietly, again not losing the stare I had with him. Amazingly he only fumbled for a little bit with the hook, but I had to help him until it came undone. Then my boobs were staring at him right in the face. I noticed my nipples immediately peaked again but this time it was not the cold air. He actually shrieked and I got nervous that he didn't like them. I think he realized it threw me off because I freaked out.

"Oh my gosh, do you think they are ugly?" I said and quickly covered them.

"No!" he said, interrupting me. They are perfect! I just can't get over how pretty you are."

He had both hands on my boobs. He was stroking them softly, then he came in to kiss me again. He kept feeling my boobs and then pinched my nipples softly. His kiss reached down off my lips, to my neck and then to my boobs. This is why the lady in the magazine looked so happy. This feeling was like nothing I had ever felt. Jeff's tongue on my nipple was silky, sending a wave of sensations throughout every inch of my body. I wanted to stop him because I wasn't sure if he should be doing this, but it felt so good that I couldn't get myself to make him halt. My vagina felt like a pool that had been filled too high overflowing around the rim. He then started to move his hand down my shorts and that's when I pulled out the reins. No one ever touched me there.

"Stop," I said gently.

"Why?" he asked. "I can feel that you are warm down there. Let me touch that too. It will feel even better than this," he stared at me like a puppy dog wanting a treat. "C'mon Ashley," he went on. "You're the prettiest girl on the block. Every guy would love to trade places with me now." He motioned for me to look down at him. He unzipped his jeans and out came his penis like the leaning tower of Pisa.

"Oh my gosh," I said, shocked.

I never went over with my friends about anything he had to offer. I thought this was all about me. I wasn't prepared to touch this alien thing in front of me. It was scary. It reminded me of a sword that would damage me.

"What happened down there?" I bellowed, feeling confused. This alien was interfering with my warm and tingly feeling. The whole affair stopped me in my tracks.

"This is what happens when I get turned on, " said Jeff. "And you are turning me on. Do you want to touch it?"

I couldn't do it. I just couldn't do it. It actually grossed me out.

The tingly feeling was gone like a tire that lost all its air. All of a sudden, I wanted out because I was a bit nervous about what I had gotten myself into. I had a different feeling here with Jeff than I had dancing on the bed with Jenny and Liz. I grabbed my bra and shirt and put it back on.

"What's wrong?" said Jeff. "You know you want it so why did you meet here then you tease!"

Suddenly, this sweet, green-eyed gentleman seemingly changed to a werewolf in a heartbeat. How could he be so gentle, then turn wicked in seconds?

"I just didn't want it to go this far, that's all," I said and started walking out.

"Well, you shouldn't have come then Ashley! You don't just show a guy your tits, let him lick you, and then decide to walk out," he said rather sternly.

"Oh yeah, watch me!" I said sternly right back.

I ran out of there, jumped on my bike quickly to get the hell out of there. I left him there alone with a boner. I could give two shits about what he was feeling. The only reason I went was for me, not what he wanted.

Of course, when I saw Liz and Jenny at the pool the next day, I told them everything while we were sitting with our feet submerged under water. They were giddy with excitement, yet floored when I told him about how far Jeff wanted it to go. They had all kinds of questions about his penis so we sat there talking about it to shrieks of laughter. "Ashley, you are like royalty. The boys are all staring at you, but not Jeff. He is checking out other girls. Apparently, you are old news to him already. Didn't take long."

"So, what," I said. "Who needs him? I can have my pick. All I have to do is show them my boobs and that's it. I get that warm feeling and I'm done. I don't need to touch their weird things."

We all started laughing.

I loved this new control I had.

I became the biggest tease, just like Jeff told me. While we were chatting, Mike came over and asked if I would meet him behind the pool where there are trees to shield the noise from the pool. Liz and Jenny looked with sly grins, "See you later," and they left.

Mike took my hand and off we went. Basically, the same thing ensued and then the unhappy ending for Mike left him aggravated too. It was almost like Jeff told him exactly what happened with him because it was the same scenario more or less, just a different guy. I guess news travels fast. Although this time I really felt like going further, something stopped me. I knew it was more about the control I had over this situation. I said to myself, who would know my tits would become more powerful of a weapon than a shotgun?

I started becoming addicted to my sexuality, so I turned it into a game with other boys. I really enjoyed the kissing and the teasing the most. I just didn't want to stop. One time I let a boy go a little further. He touched me on top of my panties. It felt strange at first, but then that warm feeling came to a toe tingling, juice flowing, outside body experience that I just kept wanting to come back to over and over again. I even figured out how to do this myself when a boy wasn't touching me. I needed that feeling like a strong drug that I craved. I had turned into a sexual creature seemingly overnight.

But pretty soon I figured out that these boys had started talking too much. They were getting aggravated about what was happening. I also noticed that Mike and Jeff had not been hanging out anymore. It looked like Jeff was hanging with everyone and Mike was left with no one. Liz and Jenny said some of the boys were coming up to them asking questions about me and so on. Before you know it, I was being called out as the neighborhood slut. None of this was good for my image.

I can remember clearly riding by the boys on our bikes one day when we heard them singing a song. When we got close, they started screaming to the melody of *Put Your Head on My Shoulder*, "Hey Ashley, Put your head on my boulder!"

They were all laughing so hard. I felt like they now were in control and it angered me. I was not going to be the passenger on the sex train. I was going to be the driver if it was the last thing I did. I was just fuming as we rode back to my house. I held the tears all the way home. Liz and Jenny just stood there, stunned at my tears. I rarely cry because not only is it too messy, but it also shows a strong weakness that others take advantage of.

"Why are you crying Ashley? You are the one that keeps getting these boys to lick your boobs. What do you expect?" Jenny said not so nicely.

"I even heard the older boys with my brother talking about it," said Liz. "Word travels fast, you know. "He even said you let a boy touch you on your panties."

This made me feel even worse. I thought for a moment that maybe this wasn't going the way I had wanted it to go. I did not want to look like I was the loser in this game.

"Well thanks Liz for backing me up and being a good friend. Thanks for telling your brother the truth!" I shouted. I went on through my tears, "Are you saying to them that I am a slut too?" I demanded.

"No, I didn't say that, Ashley. I am just saying that everyone knows. The truth is all of this is happening, Ashley. The boys aren't making anything up, that's all, so what could I say at that point?"

Jenny was listening quietly but then it was her turn to jump in. "I am not sure if you want to hear this either but Mike and Jeff have been going at it the most. They were good friends before you Ashley. But

Jeff found out that you and Mike were together the day after he was with you and that was it. He immediately got everyone on his side and they left Mike in the dirt. He's pretty much all alone now," Jenny said with a long face. "I feel sorry for him. It just doesn't seem right. I also heard that there is a fight being planned this Friday behind the baseball field at four o'clock."

"You bitch Jenny! You feel sorry for Mike? What about me? I'm your friend!"

"I know Ashley, but what are you doing with these guys? It's all so weird" Jenny said.

I didn't care for the way she turned on me, making it look like this was my fault.

I didn't care what Jenny thought anymore. She was just jealous because I was prettier than her. She didn't like that I had bigger boobs. No one liked her. I should have felt like a big whore here, but all of a sudden, I was thrilled that these guys were actually going to fight over me. This was all about my hot body, specifically my tits. With all my emotion leaving my body I felt superior here in this situation. I was the one holding all the cards. I loved feeling this way. My friends were just jealous.

"So, they are fighting over me?" I was intrigued.

"Yes, I guess so, are you happy now?" Jenny said.

"Yes, actually I am because now I am the one who is sitting pretty. We have to go see this on Friday," I said, like it was going to be the next blockbuster movie.

"Duh, of course we'll be there, it ought to be interesting," said Liz. "How about that, guys fighting over your jugs, who would know?" she said laughing.

Liz always sided with me no matter what the fight was about. I could count on her to stay with me, but Jenny was not finding any of this funny. She sat there with a bewildered look on her face. It was like she turned into a nun heading to the convent.

"What's your problem Jenny?" I said sarcastically.

"Since when are you friends with these stupid boys? Why would you be on their side? They are singing a song about putting your head on their boulders. You think that's okay?" Jenny lashed back at me.

"I never once touched these boys Jenny, not once! They sat there with their swords sticking out ready for a duel. Funny thing is that they were the ones touching me. I want nothing to do with their dicks, gross!"

She looked at me skeptically. "Well, how do I know you weren't putting your head on their boulders?" she snapped back not believing a word I said. Now she thought I was lying to her.

"I told you I didn't and even if I did, what does that have to do with us," I said.

"Well, I guess I don't want to hang out with a slut," Jenny said.

And that was it. That comment burned. I looked her dead in the eyes. I have known her all of my life. "You are just jealous Jenny because none of these guys would even look at you because you have the chest of a five-year-old. Grow up and maybe someone will fight over you," I snapped.

It got awkwardly quiet. She stared at me like a snake looking for its prey. Then she started to cry.

"You are a slut, Ashley, and a nasty person! I never want to see you again!" She stormed away crying, tail between her legs, and that was the last time I hung out with her.

I had Liz and that was all I cared about even after knowing Jenny that long. There was nothing left I could say. Another thing is she was not pretty at all, quite homely, I would add. This was bound to happen at some point. There was no way she would be able to hang with me or Liz. Later on she tried to mend the fences, but I couldn't forgive the name calling. She was just in my way from my own good time so I ignored every bone she threw until a dog buried it never to be found again. I needed to be with someone who agreed with me, idolized me and who was also pretty.

So, from then on, it was Liz and I. Even Liz didn't hang with Jenny anymore. Over time, I would wave to Jenny every so often since we lived next door, but that was it. Our moms kept trying to get us back together, but even they gave up after a while. I was interested more in the fight that was about to ensue than a friendship I no longer held interest in.

On Friday at four o'clock, Liz and I were front and center waiting for the boys to show up for the fight. When Jeff showed up, he had an entourage with him. As soon as he saw me, he gave me a wink and pushed up his sleeves. I was turned off by the wink because even if he won the fight, I wasn't going to show him my tits again, but I loved the thought that he was fighting for me. I was the princess that the prince wanted.

I felt special.

A few minutes later Mike showed up with one other boy, who looked older. He appeared to be giving him a pep talk like he was a coach in a boxing ring. Liz looked at me with her eyes wide, like she was chewing on popcorn during an exciting scene in a movie.

"Can you believe this is all for your tits?" Liz said.

We just sat there laughing. Within a few minutes, more people kept showing up one by one. It looked like a few moms had shown up as well sitting off in their cars. I couldn't believe any of them would condone this, but apparently things were brewing in our little town. I was the center of all of it. Within minutes, the boys were in the middle of semi-circle of kids chanting,

"Fight, fight, fight!" Mike and Jeff circled each other like lions circling their next meal. Jeff threw the first punch. I still remember the sound of his fist hitting Mike's nose. Immediately blood was spewing out of Mike's face. He retaliated back immediately with a hit to Jeff's jaw. Then they were rolling around on the ground like animals throwing punches into each other's sides. It got pretty ugly, but we sat there watching every minute of it, chanting the whole way. I kept thinking that this is all over me.

Liz kept grabbing my arm and not wanting to look. "I can't believe this all over you!" she kept saying.

"I know, how about it?" I said proudly.

It seemed like hours, but after a few minutes of the boys just pummeling each other, it appeared that Mike had made the final pin, blood spilling all over Jeff as he looked down upon him with one last kick in the side of his ribs. Jeff let out a bloody cough holding his side. Upon this bellow, out from the cars ran two moms coming to rescue their cubs. One mom picked up Jeff and the other picked up Mike. They were dragging their sons reluctantly to their cars, but not before Mike raised both hands high in the air like *Rocky*. The boys all started singing the Rocky theme and held him up like he was the heavyweight champion. I wondered if their moms knew they were fighting over my tits. I don't know how they would explain that one.

"Did these moms know about this?" said Liz.

"I don't know, but we better get out of here because I don't want to deal with the Mama Bears!"

So, we got on our bikes and got out of there quickly. When I jumped on my bike my whole body twitches hard making my body flop in bed. It wakes me up out of a tranquil state, along with Chris who rolls over putting his arms around me again. He's already had his way earlier, yet I still feel his sword in my back. How fitting.

Chapter 37

Tammy

> *"The beginning is always today."*
> *- Mary Shelley*

There's a chill in the air when the sun vanishes, especially in the fall. I can tell what's coming in the near distant future. The new season will be compelled to redesign the landscape for me. I want to start fresh.

I want this headache to go away.

The only way to release my pain is by mind-shifting again in this painting. I start the fire to sooth my rattling mind moving in all different directions. Maybe that's why my head is pounding. Once I get the fire going, I am at ease.

I remember when I let myself surrender to vast changes in front of me. I was no longer captive to obstacles in my way. After leaving Alex and coming home to my new empty place, my bed retained my rebirth. I was awakened with a revivification of the spirit. I got my morning coffee, ate a clean breakfast, and logged in my points on my Weight Watcher's app. I was resolute and unswerving this time to what I was eating. Because of this unwavering desire to make a change, I had lost thirty pounds. While I had a long way to go, this new weight loss left me with a sanguine complexion. I was defeating my demons and feeling victorious with my choices for the first time in a long time.

I walked to work on a glorious, unseasonably warm mid-fall day marveling at the last of the leaves departing with all their splendid colors. Breathing in the crisp autumn air made me feel lively. I was elated to actually feel better about breathing without it being too labored. My workday started pretty much the same every day. I started my crossing guard duty before the hustle bustle started. I liked to get there early so I could listen to the silence before the storm of cars that would roll in from all different directions. I knew everyone was trying to get from one place to the other, but sometimes it seemed like these cars were ants scurrying quickly to dive into their holes. I found myself questioning if these people were in the moment. It seemed like a mad rush most days. I purposefully walked very casually back and forth to slow everyone down when I crossed those white lines of peace. I wanted to create a safe gap that was hushed, yet peaceful. Everyone would benefit from a reset to their center for even just a fleeting moment.

Stop for a gap in time. Take it all in.

The judgmental people probably thought I walked slowly because of my weight, but that wasn't it at all. I marveled at the slow down, the stop and breathe method while collecting thoughts. But once my feet were off those white lines of peace, the push onward began in full force. Again the children crossed, the people walked. They went back to ants scurrying this way and that, feeling important on the way to where I didn't know. What made this intersection even busier and louder, was that my school was just down the street from the private school. So, there were many people dropping off kids at both places. The intersection reminded me of a beehive swarming with bees so active and strong until it was time to rest.

Crossing kids was truly my favorite time of day though because this is where I would connect with the kids who were walking, as well as chat with some of the parents. For many of them, I watched their metamorphosis from kindergartners to fifth graders and loved to see them grow. I knew everyone's life story because I took the time to listen.

After my crossing guard duty, I went right to the kindergarten classroom. This is where I spent my day tending to runny noses, wiping tears from missing their moms, enjoying recesses, playing games, and watching the excitement of kids learning how to read for the first time. I loved every minute of it. In a small way, I was able to relive being a mother of a young child every day. This job provided me with a tremendous inner sanctuary. The classroom was divine. The space was untouched by the grips of adulthood that were wavering outside the walls displayed with crayon scratched construction paper. What made it even better was I really enjoyed the people I was working with too. I didn't make a lot of money, but I was happy, and even received insurance. I had to feel broken to be whole again.

I was a part of something.

No longer was I the big lady just walking kids idly across the street. I walked with conviction now. When after school dismissal crossing duty ended in the late afternoon, I would set off for home to do my own homework for my education degree, as well as attend evening classes. I let my vigor lead the new path.

The fire pit glows a brassy incandescent orange in front of me. I embrace my surroundings knowing I can climb to the summit because I shed the shell of the old version of who I once was. I am entrenched in a cement casing heavy with chagrin for too long. Renascence is within reach for me. All I need to do is stay the course.

CHAPTER 38

Ashley

> *"The hottest love has the coldest end."*
> *- Socrates*

EVEN with Chris' sword in my back, I manage to fall dead asleep. I have no dreams that I can remember after my own daydreaming before I nodded off into the abyss of sleep. Everything is black out black from all the gin and extra Xanax I had taken to survive the slaughter of last night.

I wake up instantly and forget where I am for a moment. I don't know if I love Chris or hate him split fifty-fifty down the middle or up my ass. I open my eyes and stare at the ceiling trying to get my bearings on where I am. My body is soaked in sweat as I push the covers off me to let some of the heat escape. I have a headache that seems like someone was inside my brain poking needles into my scalp. I start to get the spins so I have to sit up and elevate my feet to make it go away. This always happens to me when I drink gin. I should have just stuck with wine as usual because my body has gotten so used to it. I can drink bottles of wine, somehow keep my buzz, manage my shit, and exercise to burn it off the next day without anyone knowing the wiser. I am a master of keeping my vices a secret, similar to the importance of guarding the vault of a bank. I know how to cover my tracks, dot my i's and cross my t's because I have been drinking by myself for years. Couple the alcohol with pharmaceutical pleasures and I have the perfect cocktail of distorting my reality. This is a great hidden secret, or at least I think it is.

But I don't know what I was thinking, drinking gin. It used to be a favorite of mine, but apparently it has caught up with me because I can't believe how shitty I feel being a seasoned drinker, or is it because my marriage has exploded like a bad stomach flu that hits you out of left field?

I don't feel the sword anymore. I look next to me and see an empty pillow. After daydreaming about everyone else but my husband, I remember Chris' muscular tree trunk arm covering me when I slithered into bed after being fucked through a car window.

"Holy shit, did that really happen?" I said out loud, scratching my head.

It seems too real to be a figment of my imagination or a daydream. Oh my God, what have I done? Our marriage had not been the best for a while and it was bound to bubble over at one point, but I hadn't imagined it would happen like this.

We just packed our problems away on the shelf, like a suitcase you don't use anymore, until one day you need it and find that it's not going to hold what you now have to pack.

I sit up in bed and I see a flash of Chris' pants and shirt strung carelessly over the hotel chair. He left his watch on the nightstand and his ring was left behind as well. It is a Saturday morning, so I know he isn't at work. I am sure he went to work out. But I notice his phone is gone.

I would love to see the look on his face when he opens his texts, but they will say "blocked" next to it. He will be able to see what I wrote back in return to the naughty "sexting." This image sends me into a quiet rage just thinking that I missed watching his glance of infidelity, trapped and no way out of this one.

While I lie there trying to put my brain waves together, I start to piece all the events from our first day of yesterday with Chris after a while of not seeing him. Upon waking this all feels like a nightmare, but this isn't a nightmare because I don't remember any dreams.

Everything is dark.

I have not even begun to think about how I will tell him about the conversation with that whore last night, not to mention the fuck romp I had in a car.

I start thinking about Surfer Boy again and to be honest, that sex was smoking hot, like something you would see in a movie. I feel moisture just rethinking it again. At this precise moment all feelings of guilt leaves me. I feel myself regretting not one second of my infidelity. I actually feel like violating Surfer Boy again, but I am sure this encounter would not be the same. There was too much energy last night. I'm not sure I can resurrect all that again on a dime. I decide to keep it in my conscience to have with me forever.

I am equally impressed at my idea to banter back and forth with Chris's mistress, but now I wonder what my next move will be. I have a pit in my stomach I cannot get rid of, but I have to figure out what to do next. What I figure is to get the fuck out and leave because there is no one here to get me out of this one. That's it, that is what I want to do. Chris will come back and find me gone. Then he will know why I left. I'm just not sure what he will do next. But he will have to be the one to come crawling back to me, begging me to stay and plead for my forgiveness.

He is the one that fucked someone first, not me.

I quickly go online and start looking for the first flight home. It will cost a pretty penny, but I find one and book myself on the flight, charge it to Chris's card, like everything else I do. I toss my adultery into my suitcase. It is easy to pack because I barely wore anything while being here for twenty-four hours. I gather an outfit and lay it out so when I get out of the shower, I can head out the door and immediately get out of this fucked up city. I have to get in the shower though to wash off my disgust, start over. I also have to hurry because I don't know when Chris left before I woke up. He could be running a fucking marathon in Central Park for all I know, but I have to move fast, and that is not easy with a hangover the size of Manhattan.

I am washing myself and moving fast when I hear the door open and shut.

"Fuck!" I say out loud in a harsh volume.

"Ash, are you ok?" I take in a deep breath of antipathy.

"I don't know if I'm okay," I say sarcastically.

The door of the bathroom opens and he lets in a burst of cold air.

"What?" Chris says. "I couldn't hear you."

"Why wouldn't I be okay?" I say back with even more sarcasm.

"Well, good morning to you too. I tried to get you up to go for a run with me this morning, but you were dead to the world from your drunken slumber. Don't you get sick of just laying around waiting for the booze to leave your pores? Then when you do get up your run around spending my money while I am working my ass off. Must be nice to live a life like that, sweets."

I let the water hit my face and body. The water no longer feels soft. There are ice chips shooting down on my skin.

Each particle stings. I turn the water off. Then there is silence. A rage of fire is rising up inside me with such fury that I am shocked the bathroom curtain doesn't rise up in flames.

"I'm just kidding Ash, lighten up. How about I come in, you wash the sweat off me, and we go at it again like last night? That was hot sex, just like our old college days. We have all weekend to do what we want."

I stand there dripping in disdain.

He has to know that I know about his mistress, I think. How can he not? Does he think I am just going to blow this off because he owns me in so many ways? He opens the curtain. I am on display feeling cold, naked, and twisted with sourness.

"Chris, I am getting out, and I'm leaving." I grab a towel, walk right past him, and start getting dressed. Just smelling him when I walk by makes me want to gag. He stinks of deceit and dishonesty. I think he knows exactly what is wrong and he wants to play stupid.

At this point, I know precisely that he knows nothing about me. He thinks I had become the rich, drunken housewife that doesn't have a clue what is going on. Maybe I choose to shove it under the covers for a while, but I sure am not going to let him know this. I am not going to stand here and play this game, but I don't know how to bring it up because I want him to say something first. This just blind-sides me really now that I stand there sober.

I have had my suspicions about his fidelity being gone all the time, but I had never thought he'd put it into motion. He was by no means a sex deprived man when he was at home, but when he was gone on these trips for a while, I did question how he got along without having sex. I gathered he took care of himself, but after a while, that would fizzle out like a sparkler on the fourth of July. We had our ups and downs, even though once we had kids our relationship changed. I could say Ava and Noah really fucked this up. I guess we both became quite distant, essentially just going through the motions of a marriage. I really felt myself moving away from him once he was gone so often in a world I was once in.

I think he felt the same thing.

As fit as I was, I felt my body changing, no longer the sex crazed serpent of my old days. My sexuality would ride in on waves. Sometimes the tide was high, but much of it was low due to his demanding ways. I had started losing my period, slipping into perimenopause, coupled with how I spent most of my time drunk. Therefore, I somehow missed all the signs, I guess. However, I always kept Chris satisfied because I felt like I had to, not because I wanted to all the time. Somehow, I didn't see how fucked up that was until this very moment.

Being made a fool is not the friendship I want to rekindle.

Chris comes around the corner of the bathroom looking all sweaty and rosy faced. I can tell he had been running. He is unphased at my flippant outburst.

"What are you talking about leaving for? You just got here. Quit acting childish, Ashley. I said I was joking about you not doing anything," he chuckled.

"It's not about that, Chris, and you know it. I'm not a fucking idiot," I say while dressing.

Silence remains in the air, similar to the smoke leaving a gun after the victim had been murdered, traces of fumes still leaves plumes in the air. The shell of the bullet has hit the floor with a loud clunk. We stand there not saying anything until he turns his head and breathes in deeply. I want him to fill the air with his lies.

Go ahead, I say in my head. Fill the room with your dirty lies.

"Ok, I'm at a loss, Ashley. Why are you acting so strange? Are you pissed because I went for a workout without you? I couldn't get you up, so I went on my own. I don't get hammered like you do and lie in fucking bed when there is a whole city to see. So, what's the big deal? Why do you have to create conflict all the time? We are in New York at a five-star hotel, can have sex all day if we wanted to, find marvelous restaurants, walk through Central Park, and hear a band or see a play. But you want to spend it miserable?" He stands and waits for me to say something. Anything.

I say nothing.

"I got two tickets from my boss tonight for front row seats on Broadway to try and be romantic. Now you are telling me you would rather pack your shit up and go home? Go home to what? For what? So, you can go play tennis with your friends all day? So you can talk about how hot the instructor is, then proceed to get fucked up afterwards on wine and talk about what shitty lives you think you lead while you drive home in BMW's and Mercedes to fucking castles?" He stops, trying to catch his breath.

I think he breathed easier running his miles today. I look at him with cynical eyes while he is on a superficial soapbox of a delusion. He finds his breath again.

"All this mind you, and you are picking up my kids, drunk! What a great idea. There. I said it out loud." He paced a little, then paused searching for his words. "You're an addict Ashley," he shouts. He waits for me to say something.

I said nothing.

"I am glad I grabbed the elephant out of the room already, and somehow you are mad at me? I keep kissing your ass and you turn this around with a poor me attitude? What a joke. You call this a marriage, Ashley? We keep coming back to the same fucking argument." His voice rose with each sentence. "I don't know how much longer I can go on like this. When I am gone from home, I don't have these issues. To be really truthful, I am happier when I am gone and that's not a good thing at all." He stops for a second and sits at the end of the bed holding his head in his hands like he just lost one of his best business deals.

I stare at him very crossly until it was my turn. "You done?" I say.

"No, I am fucking not, Ashley, no I am not." He goes on. This time his voice has hit a tone of a different octave I had not heard since we broke up back in college. He starts his finger-pointing like I was a little kid. This makes me even more uncomfortable. "Not one of your snobby friends has a job while your kids are in school all day. Oh wait, I am sure you will say you put in your mom-time, right? You had Naomi raise the kids as babies while you were out getting your feet and nails done, waxings, and massages to fill your empty time. You also treat Naomi like shit, by the way, and she can't be nicer. She is the exact opposite of you. You hate her because she's a good person. You are not. You are fucking not!"

"Are you done?" I interject loudly this time. "Are you fucking done?"

"No, don't fucking cut me off!" he screams.

This was a real bashing of me.

"You have cleaning ladies who do the laundry, get the groceries, and you get take-out food since you rarely cook anything on your own. Oh, and let's not forget the PTO time from school, right? You said that was a full-time job? But you managed to fuck that one up eventually because you talked shit about all the other moms instead of counting fucking box tops and serving cupcakes at the parties. Now you say you are working for charity, but you can't even do that right because your drinking gets in the way of you getting your shit done!"

He is out of breath again. He has to stop and stretch. I think he is burning more calories critiquing me than the fucking run he was on.

"The fucking balls to tell me you are going home," he says taking a break for a millisecond. "Who's paying for the ticket? Why don't I break out the fucking violin . . . poor Ashley isn't having a good time in New York so she has to go home." And he broke into a whiny voice singing.

He is not done. I let him go on his tangent because I am waiting to observe how he is going to get out the muck he is walking in.

"What the fuck Ashley? Are you going to have your Daddy come pick you up?" He sighs heavily. "I want to know why you started this shit with me. You at least owe me that right fucking now!"

I just sit and stare plainly right into his eyes. I am usually the yeller in our relationship but not this time. I can tell my reticence is fucking with his mind. I don't owe him a Goddamn thing. He will be owing me everything he has got.

"Well, are you going to answer me as to why you are leaving or just stand there shooting daggers at me?"

I sit there for another long moment and think of the balls of him trying to pin this all on me. My head is spinning with how could he not know that I had busted his affair? He is fucking with my mind too. This game is old.

I can feel myself brewing, like the hot coffee bubbling up at the top of the rim when the machine was done filling the cup. The cup was left there with steam until I pour some cream in to lessen the boiling point. When the coffee hits the right temperature, I come up for a breath, and then I poison the air we were breathing.

"Why don't you check your phone Chris and see if the kids texted you."

Now I start to get a little nervous and wonder in my head if he really did see the text stream. I think if he checks the phone now in front of me, he will see the kids hadn't texted, but he might see the other messages. Chris pulls out his phone from his running pants and glances at it. I watch it light up his face, like a spotlight under a hot seat.

"Yes, I do see a text from Ava. She asked if you got here and if we could send her a picture of us in Central Park," he says calmly with all of the authority of a father who loves his daughter. Chris comes over a little closer at me to show it to me, as if this was evidence he has caught me in something. I look away and take a deep breath. Somehow I hadn't seen that Ava texted Chris.

Chris takes a quick glance up at me rather skeptically. "Holy shit Ashley, please tell me you texted the kids that we were here, or were you too quick to get lit up with that fucking Gold's Gym bartender that you forgot about our kids? Quit playing these fucking games Ashley and tell me what the fuck is going on!"

Why did he bring up Surfer Boy again? Could he have been that intuitive without me knowing? He is making me nervous but I can't falter.

"Yes, asshole, of course I texted the kids. I did that as soon as I got here. Ava is just a daddy's girl, you know that. You think I am some kind of alcoholic who can't take care of my own kids? This is how you view me? Why don't you tell me how you really feel!" Unfortunately and reluctantly, tears start falling at this point. This is the last thing I want to do, but I can't help it.

I never cry. He broke me down. He made me feel like a fool.

I want to be the one who has it all together, but clearly, I do not because for a fleeting moment I am terrified my marriage is going to end, and then what am I going to do? I have settled into a lifestyle that is too hard to let go, yet too damaging to stay.

I make another attempt to fix this and get my way. "Is this how you really feel?" I regret this statement the second it rolls off my lips because now I look like a lost puppy.

He shouts back at me. "Well, if the shoe fits, Ashley!"

I hate that saying. It makes me think of fucking Cinderella. Did she really get a happy fucking ending?

"And if you're sitting here with a hangover, mascara running, and crying while I run through Central Park isn't a good enough example, believe me, I can find plenty more." He looks deeply into my eyes again and it makes me quiver. Those green eyes once held gleams of light, now they are diffused dark with hatred.

"You haven't been in this relationship for years, so why are you crying now, Ashley? I am not sure if you figured this out, but this trip was my last attempt to pull us a little closer, but I can see it has done the opposite. You failed my test. And now you have got the kids involved in your mess and that's not cool at all. Have you ever thought about them and their well-being, or is it always about you?"

I have to come back and defend myself. Now he is going to throw that card involving the kids?

"I didn't know I needed to prepare for a test when I came to see my husband or I would have studied!" I stomp over a little closer in a huff. I look at him with my livid sea blue eyes. The blue ocean was no longer calm. Waves came crashing in quickly. "Okay Chris, I know why Ava texts you but Noah doesn't! You are never home and they have forgotten what it's like to have a father. The only connection Ava has with you is worthless dialogue over a fucking phone. Noah is thrilled you are gone, but Ava spends most of her nights crying and comes in bed with me when you are not there!"

I think that will shut him up but it made things worse.

"I asked you a question on what the fuck your problem is. You won't tell me and now you want to throw the kids in as pawns for your stupid games?" he asks. "Okay Ashley," he counters. "I am sure you are there for the kids in between all of your activities. You know how many texts I get from Ava about how she is sitting home alone because you are still out? I have to answer to her that the strange noises she is hearing at night are nothing. I have to tell her not to worry that Mom will be home soon all while I am hundreds of miles away. And Noah, he doesn't even respond to my texts, and you? I can rarely reach you. So don't play these fucking games with me, Ashley. Does Ava come into bed with a passed out lifeless body next to her? She might as well stay in bed with her stuffed animals instead. They would provide more fucking warmth!"

Chris shakes his head and gets up and starts pacing. Again, he isn't finished. As I watch his face contort with anger it all becomes clear. He is throwing all of this back at me so he can make excuses for why he wants to be with someone else. This is a trap that he is setting down for me to walk into. I am walking over a landmine.

"We obviously have a lot of problems Ashley, but don't go blaming the kids for the way you lead your fucked up life. It's not their fault!" He sits down again on the bed after pacing the room. He runs his hands through his hair breathing deeply.

For one millisecond I think this fucker is right, but he is the one who cheated on me first. I want to clearly make this point as it will work in my favor should there be a divorce looming in our future. I need to find my backbone and go in for the kill, but he comes right back into the ring swinging. He is so good at arguing. I feel like I need a trainer to give me a pep talk, and splash water on my face.

"So, for fuck sake . . . are we going to get down to why you are leaving, Ashley? Because I should be the one walking out on you," he anounces.

"What the fuck?!" I scream on the top of my lungs. I physically and mentally lose it. I don't give one fuck who hears me. I am yelling so loudly that I start losing my voice. "Ok Mr. Perfect!! You want to know why I am leaving?? Look underneath Ava's text and see the text stream from the woman you are fucking! How about that? After you passed out after having sex with me last night, I noticed your phone would not stop buzzing. It seemed very strange to me the way it just wouldn't stop!"

Chris slowly gets off the bed to where I am standing and looks at his phone. He turns to me with a blank stare and wild eyes. "Did you look at my phone? How do you know the password?"

The nerve of him asking this question I think. "I have watched you before with your phone glued to your fucking face other than on me. I watched you enter your four-digit code because I was suspicious of who you were talking to. So what?" I say rudely. "That has nothing to do with what we are talking about now."

He shoots me a dirty look. He is going to try and use a privacy clause here? I am baffled.

"I beg to differ," he says, continuing to push me. "I don't look at your phone and check your texts. Maybe I should! But you shouldn't be doing that to me Ashley. What a breach of trust!"

My mouth is hanging open at this point. This is just another strategy he is playing in this game of chess. "Breach of trust you mother fucker! I grab the phone out of his hand and point to the sex texts. I scrolled up to the top. Start with this one you fucking liar!"

He scrolls up to the top and he starts scrolling down. I watch his face as he got lower and lower to the bottom of the thread. He moves towards the balcony, his back facing me as he drifts off into the noise of New York. I sit there quietly and wait. He is also quiet for what seemed like years. I decide to pop the bubble of air.

"I'll give you one thing. She's pretty hot. Got the blonde already, so had to get that conquest of a hot brunette, ha? How did it work out for you? God only knows how many others there are Chris. I want to go back home to get tested for STD's you mother fucker!" Now I started yelling and then before I know it, I lunge toward him. I am on top of his back pounding punches into his body with such force I can't stop myself. I am clawing and scratching because I physically want to hurt him.

"What in the fuck is wrong with you, you crazy fucking bitch!" Within seconds, Chris has me turned around and on the bed with his whole body over me. My hands are pinned back against my sides. I wonder what my dad would think if he saw Chris doing this to me right now. I am breathing heavily and crying. My head is pounding. He is staring at me with eyes I have never seen before. They are eyes of hate and disgust. I roll my tongue around my mouth and salivate, then spit right up into his face. He lets go of my arms, stands up, goes to the bathroom and grabs a towel.

"Real classy Ashley. Is this how your dad taught you to fend for yourself after fighting away all the men? Not here to save you now, is he?"

"Why do you keep bringing up my dad? He has nothing to do with this and you know it. You just keep diverting the attention from you. My dad would never do this to my mom, so don't even bring him into this. He's a real man. You're just a caricature of one!"

This hit below the belt for Chris. I can see him getting riled up again.

"Oh, and your parents are the Hallmark card of marriages, right?" He starts laughing sarcastically. "Give me a fucking break. You're a product of their fucked-up marriage. Just stop now because you're wasting words." He keeps going. I am wondering when this will ever end. I don't want to miss my flight.

"You know what, you whack job? If someone calls the police on us from another room, I could get a domestic battery charge and it could ruin everything I work for. Then where are you getting your money from? Have you thought of that? No, you didn't and that's why you think you can act this way. That's how unstable you are you fucking cunt." He says this word so calmly with matter of fact. It rolls off his tongue so easily.

It truly is the absolute worst thing a man can say to a woman and I have the pleasure of hearing it from my husband and the father of my children. A man can beat a woman down with insults of any kind, and she will be able to recover. But call a woman a cunt and it's game over. The word just rips me right in half and I am not sure which piece of me to pick up from the floor. I am astounded at how he managed to turn all of this around to make it look like it was my fault our marriage had crumbled.

"So, was it the ass? The tits? Does she suck you off, tell you nice things and make you feel good? How long have you been with her? Is she the only one? I am sure the kids will be thrilled to meet their new mom!" I keep pressing. No answers from him. Now he is the one that was quiet.

"Are you at least going to admit you are fucking someone else or are you going keep blaming me you fucking gutless dick? I really enjoyed texting her last night, Chris. We had some good dialogue. Didn't you see it?" This was it. I am really good at riling him up and I can see when he is getting ready to blow, and he blows.

"Yes, you know what Ash? She has an incredible body. In fact, I can't wait to fuck her every minute of the day. You know why? Because she is not a lifeless fucking corpse of a woman like you. Your body has always driven me crazy, Ashley, you know that. That's what landed you a ring on your finger and a good life, my dear, but you have pissed it all away. And over time your body no longer did it for me because there was nothing lying behind it. There was just anger, sadness, sourness, and flat-out lack of desire, not to mention scathing insecurity and it has made you so ugly to me. You think I don't know when I am fucking you that you're not in it? I have been getting my rocks off with you, a means to an end. You have become miserable to be around in the sack and anywhere else for that matter. When was the last time you and I actually had a good time? I don't even remember because you let this go Ashley, you! No one else. You have fucking everything, always have, yet you still can't find a place to be happy for you or anyone who is near you. You're like that iceberg the Titanic hit, secret, cold, and hidden way below the surface until an unsuspecting vessel comes along. You suck the joy and love right out of everyone. Helpless victims are sent plummeting down dying of hypothermia while you get on the safety boat. Well, not this time."

Holy shit he could write a fucking novel. I forgot how incredibly intelligent he is. To come up with these words spontaneously? I am being compared to the iceberg the Titanic hit. Wow. This is worse than him calling me a cunt. He is tearing everything out of me and the hole in my stomach widens into a vast sea of sadness. But I still am not going to admit that this is my fault. It isn't my fault.

He reads my mind. Somehow he can always read my mind. It fucks me up.

"But you don't see it at all. That's what makes it even worse. Or perhaps you do and you can't live with it or learn how to fix it, so you just became a drunk. You think I didn't notice? I tried many times to help you but you just pushed me away, drowning in your own sea of chaos, so I just gave up."

He turns his back again and goes to the balcony overlooking the scattered skyline.

"You were once a woman I loved with all my heart, and now a woman I love with nothing in my heart."

I sit motionless because this about took my breath away. These are some of the most hurtful words I have ever heard. I feel devastated. He turns and looks at me with tears in his eyes. I have never seen Chris cry one time in our life.

"It is time you go. Get the fuck away from me. I didn't know how long I was going to live this charade, but I am suddenly feeling better now that it's out there. I'm glad you are leaving. You are right about something for once, Ashley. Are you happy now? You leaving is the best idea you have had in a long time. I'm even happy to pay for your ticket out of my life," he says very forlornly.

As sad as this makes me, I still am not going to let him get out of this without a fight. I have to pull my shit together.

"How can you stand there and talk to me like this? You fuck another woman and I am the one to blame?"

"I guess you don't fucking get it, Ashley. I guess you just don't get it," he repeats.

I start screaming again because I am supposed to be the one on top.

"You're just going to let me go and sever the ties just like that? That's it? I have to go home and take care of all this and tell the kids, my family, my friends? What the fuck Chris? This is all your fault you fucker! I quit my job, gave up my life, had children for you and this is what I get in return? How dare you?"

I have all the rage of a tsunami wave crashing into a resort town, destroying everything in its path. I don't even think before I take a glass off the table and launch it at his head. It goes nowhere near him and hits the floor with shards flying everywhere. The noise cuts the air with a siege of anger as it splatters on the tile floor by the door of the room.

When Chris gets really mad, he grits his teeth and squints his eyes. "Ashley, enough already," he says firmly but with force. "You need to go."

It seems as if he is trying to talk me off the ledge.

"You are going to fuck up my job if the police get called. We are going to have to carry on with this another time and the time is not now when we are both this angry."

He walks back to the bed and sits down again heavy with his presence. I think I finally wore him down because he would have usually just walked away a lot earlier, but he is invested in ending this marriage. He is like the character in a cartoon who keeps getting beat on yet miraculously comes back for more. I can tell he is looking for more words but I think we used them all up.

"Why don't you get the bartender to drive you to the airport? I haven't seen that spark in your eye since I first laid eyes on you, Ashley. How do I know you two didn't fuck at some point and your casting fingers at me, ha?"

With everything in my being, I want to throw this in his face and make him feel like I did. I feel like I have been punched in the gut. "So be it. I'll pack my shit up and get out of your hair. Then you will have more time to fuck the ever so happy brunette. Give her some time and she will end up like me. You have that knack for people. I'm not a product of my parents. I'm a product of you!" I couldn't say anything anymore without yelling. I started packing the rest of my things.

He watches me closely as I furiously shoved things in my suitcase until he speaks again with such conviction.

"So, did you fuck that guy or what? I feel like there was a lot of time not accounted for. It also makes sense why you didn't respond to my texts when you were sitting in the bar flirting and drinking yourself into oblivion while waiting for me," he says with a smirk.

I don't recall seeing any texts from him or calls, but I was drunk.

"And somehow it is okay for you to have most of your days and nights unaccounted for Chris? God only knows how many women you have been fucking and for God only knows how long. Maybe that is part of why I am 'lifeless' as you say. Because now that I think about it, you have been distant for a while. This sure explains a lot. Maybe it was nice to be appreciated by someone who thought I was attractive for fuck's sake, so did you ever think of that Chris?"

I think I folded the same blouse twice. I zipper up the suitcase, grab my makeup bag, and my purse. I stand there in front of him gazing at him with full eye contact. There is no way I am going to tell him.

"So, does this mean you fucked him?" He breathes distinctly.

"No, go fuck yourself, Chris! I guess you will never know." I turn and head for the door.

Chris gets up after me and grabs my arm quite forcefully. "I don't think it is going to be wise to talk to me that way with an impending divorce coming your way, Ashley. You better be really careful in what you say. I also don't want you going home telling the kids and getting them involved making it look like I'm the bad guy. You won't tell me, but I know you fucked that guy, so the way I look at it we are on an even playing field here, Ashley. Safe trip home and you'll be hearing from my lawyer because I don't see anything left here but chaos and heartbreak."

All of a sudden, looking at Chris is like staring at a stranger.

I no longer know this man I once loved and I take his hand off my arm abruptly. "That is the very last time you will ever touch me! Are you prepared for the divorce you selfish dick? Because you will never find a woman who looks like me to cater to your whims and needs. You just won't. I hope you live out the rest of your days in misery you selfish fuck. I suggest you find a different place to move to when you do come back because I will be keeping that house!"

Now it was my turn. "And as for the kids, I'm not going to make up some shit for coming back early to tell them about what a great person you are. I will let them know you are a total asshole and found someone else to love. I am with them every day, not you. You're here pretending to be a good father because your daughter sends you texts. Big fucking deal! Your son thinks you're a cocksucker anyways, so he will be happy you aren't coming back." I am physically shaking at this point. I want him out of my way so I can get the fuck out of there. I wish I had made it out of there before he got back from his run.

"Way to be a great mother and drag our kids into our dirt, Ashley. You really need help, you know that? I guess you will tell the kids what you want, but I will also explain all of your skeletons too. They will know what a liar and selfish bitch you are, which I think they already do. I'll just confirm their suspicions. Fucking a bartender half your age," he says with a smirk and such smugness, not ever owning up to his own infidelity, but justifying it. "What were you trying to prove? That you are still just as narcissistic as you were when I met you many years ago?"

I don't know who is going to get the last word here because this has gone on way too long. I think it's the most I have talked to Chris in years. It is my final turn. "I think you are the one who needs to examine yourself, so you better look in the fucking mirror first." And with that, I walk out and slam the door on him.

I run down the hallway like the building is on fire. I am tempted to stop in the lobby to see if Surfer Boy is there. I want to tell him not to say anything to Chris and give him warning that he may come down to either talk to him or punch him in the face. But when I glance over at the bar, I don't see him.

There is another young guy, nowhere near as hot, and I breathe in a sigh of relief. I decide not to walk anywhere near that bar. My best course of action is to get out this time, so I ask the concierge to order me an Uber before I scurry out of the lobby and onto the sidewalk outside the hotel.

Chapter 39

Tammy

"Notice that autumn is more the season of the soul than of nature."
- Friedrich Nietzsche

THE fire glowing reminds me of the measures it takes to keep it burning, which are very similar to keeping up with the ever-changing seasons in the Midwest.

And in my mind.

My head is not hurting so much because I went backwards into the seasons to reminisce. I think about how my life was going in the best direction after yet another change of season. I think about days where it started off bright in the morning but the weather made sudden shifts in typical Chicago style. At some point during the school day, the wind would pick up, the temperature would plummet, and the light rain would start to mist within no time at all. Some days at work would entail completely different weather patterns in the morning compared to the afternoon. There was rarely consistency when seasons were about to change. I would walk out at the end of the day and it would feel as if the day changed to a different one altogether completely.

There are all different seasons of my life. It was how I prepared that counted.

Each day at work, I put on my safety vest, and always had an umbrella, poncho, and hat in my car. I called these my "trunk items." When I was new, I wasn't this prepared. I learned this the hard way from many years of being a crossing guard. Midwest comes with distinct changes, all leading one into the other.

The older I get, the more I see that these seasons are alive and innate within myself. I watch the fire burn. It is always mesmerizing. The heat warming the cool air in front of me smells so good. It smells like the season of November. I embrace the harshness on the way in more than the changing of the leaves in October.

In November, I knew what was coming. I also knew the harshness was not permanent. I enjoyed being well-informed about what would happen in a "brace for impact" style. It would get cold, stay cold, then leave quietly and mysteriously giving way to the spring. This gave me hope to roll through the seasons always everchanging.

Season change illuminated my way on this passage of time.

I stare at the fire again watching the flames flicker circular in motion. I can't help but hum along to Axl Rose singing his song, *Cold November Rain*. Sounds of his piano ring through me while a light rain falls on my aching head.

Having a job outdoors and living in Chicago could be a mixed bag of sorts, and not suited for the weak minded or porcelain doll figures. I enjoyed being a warrior as a midwestern lady because I had learned to take in all the seasons that nature had to offer. Sometimes I dreamed of living somewhere with a constant stream of warm sunshine, but they were just dreams. How would I prepare for the next season when there wasn't a next season?

The fire keeps moving, circling wildly with the wind. Dark smoke climbs up above the trees. I can smell my strength rooted from the fire pit of my life.

Chapter 40

Ashley

> *"It is not a lack of love, but a lack of friendship that makes unhappy marriages."*
> *- Friedrich Nietzsche*

As mad as I am at Chris, something inside me hopes he will come out of the hotel and get me. He will make this all right again. I am left here on the streets of New York City to deal with this by myself. Rapunzel was left at the top of the castle waiting for Prince Charming to save her.

He never comes down.

For the first time I have to figure shit out on my own and I don't know what to do. I feel like the last person standing after a nuclear war, lost and scared. I reach down into my purse to grab a Xanax because I need to take the edge off before I get on a plane heading back home. I swallow the pill dry. As I wait for the Uber to show up, a man, quite disheveled, comes up to me with a worn and rough face. He smells as if he hasn't showered in weeks. His hands look like cracked leather. His fingernails are filled with black dirt. He has missing teeth and cannot stand up straight. This is not an uncommon sight in New York, but this is not the time for me to have a conversation with anyone, especially a homeless man. I try to avoid any kind of contact and just pretend to ignore him, but he doesn't care. He must have spotted my anger and resentment thinking of me as vulnerable prey. Then he speaks with his breath too close.

"Hey young lady. Ya look like you could spare me some change to get something to eat. How about it?"

I try so hard not to look at him for fear of picking up a disease by osmosis. He is disgusting with his beard all twisted, pieces of food stuck in his whiskers. There is a thick layer of mold growing on his teeth. He was not a man.

"No, I don't have anything to give you." I turn away. You would think he would move on to someone else. But no, he keeps badgering me. What the fuck?

"I know someone like you has money. Come on now, can't you help me out lady?" I ignore him and look at my phone. I try to move to another place.

"Did you hear me lady?" he snaps back louder.

"Yes, I did hear you and I told you I don't have anything so leave me the fuck alone you junkie! And even if I did have money, I wouldn't give it to you to go buy cigarettes or drugs."

The people walking by give me a quick glance, but keep to themselves like robots moving to the next destination. Horns are beeping furiously in the noise of the littered streets. These people probably dealt with this nonsense on a daily basis. Tons of people in this city, and this fuck has to look for my sympathies just because I am a woman and look like I have money. He has no idea what I just went through.

"I don't have a job either, you know," I say. "So, figure out how to get yourself out of a jam from someone else besides me. Or here's a novel idea; get a job so you don't have to beg random strangers on the street. How pathetic. I have my own shit to deal with, not yours!"

The man utters something under his breath I cannot hear. He moves right on to another person. This lady proceeds to dig in her purse and gives this nutjob money. I shoot her a dirty look while shaking my head so she can see my disapproval. How can someone just hand a stranger money like that? I am quite certain he would just go buy drugs or cigarettes. What a complete waste of her own savings and a total sucker.

I just don't see how someone can end up on the street. There are plenty of jobs in this country. My Dad always said that if you help people like this, you just enable them to be moochers and the cycle moves on. But I can't worry about this anymore because I need to figure out my own life. I will never see that mess of a person ever again. I don't give a fuck. The Uber pulls up and I get in. I sigh heavily upon sitting in the seat. Oh fuck. I sound like my mother. She sighs all the time.

"Where to Miss?" the man says jovially.

I don't need to be around a happy fuck. "Get me to JFK Airport as soon as you can," I say.

The driver looks at me through the rear-view mirror. His eyes raised ready to start a pleasant conversation. "You've been here a long-time, lady? Looks like the big apple took a bite out of you," he says chuckling. My mind is thinking what is with these fucking men and their judgment calls? Can't they once try not to get into our pants? I shake my head.

"You know what," I say. "This city is a horrible place, ok? I don't want a bite of the apple because it's bruised and rotten. There is no need for anymore commentary, got it?" I am proud of myself that I can come up with a metaphor that quickly like Chris did. Too bad he is not here to knock him down a notch.

"Fair enough, JFK it is."

He doesn't say a word the rest of the time and neither do I. There is dead silence as I watch the skyline of New York pass by me like a dark and deep rainforest filled with the most hideous and dangerous kinds of creatures. I never want to see this fucking place again.

Fuck everybody, especially Chris.

What kind of husband lets his wife leave a big city all by herself?

Chapter 41

Tammy

> "I make so many beginnings there never will be an end."
> - Louisa May Alcott

THE fire continues to glow softly this evening. I hear familiar voices in the background of the cold room. My head feels soft and not so painful now.

I am filled with tranquility.

I lay my head back gently to try and view myself from the outside looking in.

I had lost fifty pounds. I was now at two-hundred and seventy-pounds but I honestly felt like I could run around the block. I felt lighter when I graced the white lines on the crosswalk. My skin started looking better. I was able to breathe a little easier. I was starting to move a little faster. I had been going out for walks every day, rain or shine. There is a bike path just behind my condo that I would head to before work. I would follow up again in the evening after work. I started off with short walks because I would get so winded because my top weight was three-hundred and twenty-five pounds. So moving around for me felt as if I was carrying loads of cement on my back. I couldn't fathom how I had become so complacent with myself. But I suppose that's what a parent's death and a bad marriage can do to someone. But I had no more time to make excuses. I had done this for years at the expense of no one else but myself. It took everyone leaving me to slap me into reality that if I didn't do something, I was going to continue to eat myself to my own death. I had already developed diabetes and a host of medical problems. My clock was ticking voraciously.

Enough was enough.

I was used to people's stares when I was on crossing duty. But when I first went out on the path to walk, I felt really nervous, not at all comfortable with how people were going to view me. When I came upon someone on the trail, I would receive a mixed bag of looks. Some people would snicker. Some people would smile. Some people would signal a thumbs up signifying they were happy I decided not to look like a Mack truck. Others would look at me with pity. I always hated that look. I am a person just like everyone else whether I'm three-hundred twenty-five pounds or one-hundred twenty.

I didn't need anyone's pity.

But after a while I just decided not to concern myself with what anybody else thought. I was doing this all for me. All for Alex. All for my mom and those who loved me. The person I really wanted validation from was Alex.

When he came home for his fall break, he was thrilled to see how I looked. I know I wasn't anywhere near my goal, but having fifty pounds off me was noticeable for Alex.

When I picked him up, he threw his bags into the trunk and jumped into the front seat. He leaned over for the best hug you can give in a car. "Hey Mom," he said so cheerily. "Wow, your face looks thinner! You're really doing it, ha?"

He had no idea how much those simple words made me feel because now for sure no matter what happened in the future, I was going to stay the course. "Thanks babe. I know I still have a long way to go, but I shed fifty pounds so far." I felt so good to utter these words. It really was a great start.

"Well, that's all-around impressive, Mom." he said. "So you're doing like you said with exercising and following the Weight Watcher's plan?"

"You got it kid! I even have a counselor once a week to go over my nutrition plan and exercise schedule. It really has been life changing, Alex. I'm not running marathons yet, but ya never know." I turned to see his face and he was laughing. I loved that he still laughed at my wisecracks. It was so good to see his face.

I meditate towards the fire now thinking of that face in my car on the way back to see our new condo that day. His smile imprinted in my memory is warmer than the fire in front of me. My head starts to hurt thinking about him because I so desperately want to see him again. I want to hear his laugh. I want to feel his hug. I am lost without him.

He truly is my light. I can hear his voice but it starts to fade.

I go back and relive that weekend to subdue the aching pain in my head. Alex loved my condo. He was happy I had an extra bedroom where he could lay down his head temporarily in a house of safety, and love. He wasn't in his old bedroom with the stars on the ceiling, but he would make it his own during this season change. He didn't need the stars on the ceiling anymore because they would always radiate from his childhood lighting any path he would take in the future.

The whole weekend went by so fast because while he stayed with me, he did spend a day with Bill, too. I hadn't talked to Bill since our divorce was final and left it that way. I figured Alex would connect if he wanted to. And he did. So one day he took my car and spent the day with Bill fishing. I was elated that Alex had this time with his father. It wasn't just about me. It took me some time to figure that out. We went to see Mom too and that was enjoyable. We talked about how good life was going now in a new direction. We had it all and it felt great.

I felt like Alex had just arrived when I was taking him back to the airport again. When I dropped him off this time, it stung, but nowhere near as penetrating as the first time. I marveled at what a few months could do for the soul. Before we got to the drop off at the airport, I looked over at him while he was telling me about all the things he had to do when he got back to school. I loved how excited he was to get back. This is what I wanted for him as hard as it was for me to see him leave. He would leave me over and over again until he wouldn't come back to his bedroom of comfort. I'd have to adapt to the seasons.

Nothing is permanent.

I looked at him when he was done talking.

He looked at me. "What?" he said. "Why are you staring at me? Kind of creepy." he laughed like a school boy.

"Oh nothing honey. You look like your father, that's all."

He grinned again. "I hope that's not a bad thing for you," he said, getting a little serious.

"Oh gosh no, Alex. Don't take it that way. I think it's a wonderful thing. I don't hate your father." I tapped his knee. To lighten the mood I started singing, "Here I go again, on my own!" laughing.

"Mom, you crack me up! I can't think of an eighties song without thinking of you."

"That's a good thing. kid. My parents would be proud," I said. We both started laughing.

When Alex is gone, that is what I miss the most. I miss laughing with him.

We got to the drop off. This time I was able to get out of the car somewhat easier than a few months before. I wanted to give him a proper hug before I saw him again at Thanksgiving break not that far away in time. I knew the older he got the breaks would be sparse, so

I had to take advantage of every moment with him right now. Days were always numbered.

There was no guarantee of tomorrow.

"Mom, stay with this weight loss program. You are so different in such a good way. I can see it in you . . . makes me happy." He smiled that infectious smile I adored.

"For sure Alex, honey!" Gosh I felt so good that he approved of my new life.

"Okay Mom, love you. Talk soon." There was no awkwardness. No nervous feelings at all. I loved this about the air we were breathing in this time.

"Love you to the moon, Alex. Safe travels."

He got out of the car and went on his way. When the door slammed it didn't sound like a crash as it did at the first drop off. Although we both changed, everything was the same. I was able to feel it.

The quietude yields serenity. The fire starts to dim. I can go lie down on the hammock now, dreaming of that weekend with Alex. I could dream about the next time I would see him. My head doesn't hurt. I think of that last embrace until I see him again.

Chapter 42

Ashley

> *"Fare thee well, and if for ever still for ever fare thee well."*
> *- Lord Byron*

THE Uber barely comes to a stop when the driver dumps me off at the airport. I get the vibe that he doesn't like my last comment. He drives me there fast and doesn't say another word. Fuck him. Maybe it will teach him a lesson to shut the fuck up and do the mindless job of getting people from one place to the next.

I get through the maze of security control at the airport, finally sifting through all the zombies. I don't want anyone to say a word to me. I want to go unnoticed for the first time in my life. Before I sit down, I check my phone to see if Chris texted me.

Nothing.

I am still in shock that he let me go like this, especially because it was him who had tossed our marriage into the fire and let it burn. I am feeling sick to my stomach and it takes everything in me not to puke right there in front of everyone. Fortunately, I am able to get into the Admiral's Lounge pretty quickly, go to the bathroom, freshen up and just sit before I board the plane.

The nerves and Xanax on a hangover stomach don't suit me well. I end up running back to the bathroom and start vomiting. I am an absolute train wreck, no denying this. I have to splash water on my face and swirl water around my mouth to get that acid taste out. I feel mildly better, but that pit in my stomach is still there. I have a feeling this day is going to fester in me a long while or maybe be with me forever.

When I reach for a paper towel to wipe my face off, I catch a glimpse of myself in the mirror. I have never looked uglier. I have dark circles under my eyes that lead to a trail of mascara running down my cheeks, along with hives on my neck. I hated Chris for making me look this way. This is precisely why I don't cry because no one looks pretty when they cry. In order to not look like a worn-out welcome mat, I brush my hair again, pull myself together and put a little more makeup on. I can't go into the lounge looking like this. It just doesn't fit my style, so I do my best to pull myself together.

I sit down quite heavily and sink into the chair like sinking into quicksand. It isn't five minutes that go by before a good-looking gentleman with tight dark jeans, a black shirt and sport jacket, complete with a stylish cowboy hat, sits down next to me.

"Anyone sitting here," he says with a deep voice.

I make the mistake of making eye contact. His eyes are striking, almost as much as Chris' eyes and it totally catches me off guard. Oh good God not another man with piercing eyes.

I kind of squirm in my seat and say, "No, not at the moment." I am hoping he isn't going to start flirting because I just don't feel like talking to anyone in the state I am in. I know my own makeup can't cover up the melancholy hue to my skin. All I want to do is check to see if Chris texted me back. I also want to text Naomi to let her know I will be home early. But I don't get a chance to check my phone or avoid him because he starts talking right away with the most charming of smiles of course to complete his whole look.

"So, you heading to Chicago as your final destination or do you live here in New York?"

I let some silence in here because I really don't want to get personal. I shrug my shoulders lazily. I swear to myself I am not going to get personal. I can't do it.

"Let me guess, you were here on business?"

I sigh a little while trying to look annoyed. I want to act like I am not very interested in his charm that could easily sweep me off my feet, yet again. I am in too much of a vulnerable state to let this happen again. Oh fuck, I catch myself not thinking with purpose. But I have to admit to myself that there may be purpose in this instant attraction along with an escape route.

As I sit there looking into his eyes under that sexy hat, my eyes make their way slowly down his body to his feet where his dark brown expensive cowboy boots are rooted to the ground. It has been less than twenty-four hours since I fucked a guy half my age in a car, but after that conquest, I know I could have more if I wanted. I don't need this temptation, but suddenly my stomach feels at ease at the fact that I can easily not spend my life wandering alone after Chris left me.

"Did you hear my questions?" he asks again, staring me up and down as well.

Thank God I had put my makeup on right before meeting him is what I was thinking.

"Yes, I heard you. The answer is no to most of your questions. I am heading to Chicago where I live, yes, but not for business. I am not from New York. Where are you from?" I feels it better to throw more questions at him.

"I was here on business, then a layover in Chicago before heading home to Houston," he says.

I smile rather flirtingly. I just don't have a clue how to turn it off. "Oh, that explains the hat and boots cowboy."

"Ha, that's right. You aren't used to seeing cowboy hats in New York or Chicago I suppose," he pauses a little with those dreamy eyes. His mouth curves up so cutely when he speaks, sporting a well-manicured beard. This instantly turns me on. He reminds me of one of those hot country singers who sings about a Silverado.

"What were you doing in New York if you weren't there on business and not from here? Family?"

I look at my watch to divert this game for a little bit because as quick as a wink my fear kicks in. I don't want to get involved in another tangled web. "Look, I am not in a good frame of mind here. I just need to focus on getting back home, ok?"

He turns and looks the other way almost like he is checking to see who is around. "Well, I don't mean to bother you and all. You just caught my eye because you looked preoccupied and all. I thought you might need someone to talk to you. You know, unwind a little bit, that's all. Can I get you a drink?"

I breathe in pretty heavily and he picks up on this. Asking me if I wanted a drink is like asking a kid if they wanted candy. Of course I want a drink. I always want a drink. "Well, I would love one to cure me from all the drinks I had last night."

He laughs out loud.

"Well, well, well. You know how to bite the dog that bit ya! You're my kind of gal. What will your poison be, my lady?"

Oh my gosh he calls me his lady. But this time I don't mind him calling me this. I also don't bother to correct him. This scene just falls onto me xoincidentally, so I have to go with it.

"I'll have a Pinot Grigio."

He gets up to get us drinks and I find myself in this mind game again with men. It is just so easy to play a game I enjoy, even in the shitty way I feel with my world ending rather abruptly. I pop another Xanax while he gets the drinks.

I'm not feeling completely tranquil yet because I think I puked it up earlier. I let the pill dissolve on my tongue until he comes back then I drink it down with the wine he gets for me. He of course settles in with bourbon on the rocks, a man's drink—so fitting for him. When he sits down, he puts his arm around my chair as if he has known me all his life. I'm not uncomfortable with this at all. I feel a calmness of being safe, which was odd because I've known this man for ten minutes.

"So, you were here on business in New York, then the final destination is Houston," I say. Again, I need to direct all the questions over to him instead of me.

"Yep. That's about it. I've been doing some business here. It's a boring ride back and forth with a layover, so it's nice to hang out with a pretty lady like you. Cheers," he says, and his eyes study my eyes like he is viewing artwork in an art gallery. He hits my glass lightly with a loving touch.

I imagine his kiss would be as delicate as these glasses clinking so softly. I drink the wine rather fast because I'm quickly falling into his presence, and just as quickly that gnawing feeling starts to come back again.

"Hey listen, thanks for the drink," I say, keeping his gaze. "But I have to check in with my kids and all, and just need to be myself now before we board the plane." I start to feel that I need to end this endeavor as quickly as it began because having sex now with another man is not going to help this situation, but I won't deny I am thinking about it.

He doesn't want to end our conversation. "What? We just started getting to know each other . . . kind of." And then he paused for a moment laughing and says, "I didn't even get your name." He looks disappointed.

I put the glass down on the table definitively so he can feel my resistance. "I don't think that's necessary Cowboy because this isn't going to be a rodeo. I just found out my husband is a giant asshole. I have to focus on getting home, that's all. So, if you don't mind, I can't go down the dusty trails into the sunset with you now. I have to get a hold of my nanny before we get on the flight." I am proud of myself again for coming up with some fancy words to fit the scene, but Chris hadn't heard it. I had lost my fancy words when I was arguing with him.

The Cowboy sits for a moment staring at me without any words. I know I could get lost in those deep brown eyes that match his hat. But that pit of a feeling in my stomach is saving my ass from more heartache and complication. I need to feel pain in order to save myself from more pain.

"You're a beautiful woman, whatever your name is. And that guy's an idiot for leaving you. That's all I'll say. When a lady says no, she means no. And I, my lady, am a southern gentleman and will honor your wishes."

He gets up willingly and straightens out his belt buckle that keeps his manhood at bay. He is tall and giant-like standing over me when he takes my hand and actually kisses it. I marvel thinking, is this guy for real? Why would I ask someone like this to leave?

He bends down towards me really close and says, "You let me know if you change your mind at any point and want to join me in Houston."

I let him keep hold of my hand for a moment. The warmth creeps over my cold hands like a fire burning on a winter evening. I don't want to let go.

"I appreciate the gesture and the company, but I need to be alone."

He winks, tips his hat and says, "As you wish my lady, as you wish." He walks away and sits down on the other side of the lounge.

I see him looking at me every time I look up. I am looking too. I finally have to tell myself to divert my attention so as to not meet his gaze. This is tough as hell.

I fumble around for my phone nervously, but before I find it, we are getting called to board the plane. I walk on the plane slowly and find my first-class seat somewhat in a trance from the wine and pill I took. I sit down with a slow thump. I close my eyes for a second.

When I open them again I see the cowboy has walked by to sit down in the row behind me. I can smell his aftershave from my seat. I close my eyes again. I see myself riding on his horse into the sunset.

I shake my head out of that fantasy and check my phone instead to see if I have had a text from Chris. I think he may be wondering if I got off okay. I put my code in waiting for my dot to light up that I had a message, but no dot. I can't believe he doesn't want to have the last word. I think over and over again, how can he not even care about me leaving? I know a stranger in the airport would fall head over heels for me. Yet my own husband hates me. This Cowboy would be concerned about my every move and would never leave me hanging and waiting. This fuels my misery even more. I open up a blank text to Chris and sit there for a moment. All the words I could use in the English language and I ponder about what I will write.

I can't think of anything fancy, so I start writing, "I am on my way home. Hope you're happy now you miserable asshole." That is the best I can come up with since I've used all my metaphors for the day already.

I open up a different text for Naomi. I tell her I am on the way home and will text when I land to see where she is at. I ask her to keep it quiet for the kids that I was coming home because I wanted to surprise them. Surprise them with infidelity I suppose, but any surprise sounds good right now. I wait there with my phone in my hand. I'm not going to put it away until the plane is getting ready to take off. I keep checking it incessantly like a gambler waiting for a match on the slot machines.

The first message back is from Naomi. "All good. See you soon and safe travels." There is no message from Chris. I turn the phone off, close my eyes and pass out for the entire flight.

We land quite abruptly into O'Hare Airport and it jolts me out of a lovely dream I had where I was riding on a horse in an open field for miles with the Cowboy. It throws me for a loop because I am quite certain I had an orgasm in my dreams because I feel warm all over, moist and so relaxed. I look around to see if anyone is looking at me because if I had an orgasm in my sleep as good as this one, I am quite certain I was not quiet. But no one is looking at me. When I stand up to get off, the Cowboy is standing too. I can feel his presence behind me because he is behind me in my dream. I have to turn around because it is killing me not to.

He shoots me a wink and tips his hat again. Then he leans over and gives me his card and says, "If you are ever in Houston, look me up, my lady. Welcome home to Chicago. I hope you get what you want and deserve here."

I smile back at him. I look at the card to see what his name is. The logo was the state of Texas.

"I hope I get what I deserve too, Colton Radley. And by the way, my name is Ashley Hayes."

He grins and says, "Lovely name for a lovely lady." He grabs hold of my hand. "I am guessing you don't have a card, but are you on Facebook or Instagram? I could look you up."

"Yes, I am . . . you can find me there waiting for you." My flirting is as natural as blinking. I blow him a kiss and I walk through the airport with him following close behind me. The sound of the roller bags is as heavy as my heart, as we all lug our safety nets behind us here and there. The whole time I am walking I want to drop everything, turn around and run into his arms, like some dopey

Hallmark movie, but this shit is real. No cameras and directors ready to shout "cut" when the scene doesn't look right. I have to go face my own scene, and none of it involves cowboys or romps in the hay.

My suitcase is loading me down. I need to repair the hole in my safety net myself this time. When I get down to the transportation area to call my car service, I turn around to see where my Cowboy is.

He is gone.

I am overwhelmed by my lonely stature. I stand there quietly for a moment, then turn on my phone. This is the last test to see if Chris texted me back. I open the phone. Up pops my screensaver of me and Chris on a beach in the Maldives. The water was so pristine that you could see the bottom for miles. Behind those miles of smiles, was a steep drop off of deep water.

There is silence from Chris.

I roll my bag to the outdoor platform where the cold, late fall wind hits me square across the face, like a slap from an angry friend.

No more Cowboy.

No more clear water.

No more Chris. I guess I never escaped from the castle tower and need someone to get me out of there, but who?

Chapter 43

Tammy

> *"The fall of dropping water wears away the stone."*
> *- Lucretius*

I wake up somewhat rested after a long night's swaying in this hammock. The morning appears later and later. I don't hear birds singing anymore. They must have all left when the wind called them my name. I wonder how long I am going to stay here. Can't I just jump out of the painting? I only hear silence in the cold room. I really want to see Alex. I am missing my mom. She has to be wondering where I am. I miss my walks, seeing the children, and my new life.

Interestingly enough, I don't long for food. I can't remember the last time I ate. I feel much lighter. I have to find a way out of here though because I've worn out my welcome. So, I've been trying hard to weave this plan in my mind to make the leap out of here. But I'm not so sure how to do this after the dream I had last night. And do I really want to leave?

I replay the dream in my head to remember the details. I woke up to the sounds of waves crashing along the beach. I was lost again, but in a place I didn't recognize. Sometimes I would have dreams replaying the time I was lost at the park as a child, but I always found my way back at the end. This time, I felt unsettled about the setting. The dream was bending my brain to comprehend what was happening to me. The dream was very vivid. So much so, that I thought I had left my home for good, perhaps on a vacation?

I was wading in the ocean. Someone was with me but I'm not sure who it was. I was in an area of waist-high water, but the waves were getting really large behind me. I was shocked at my buoyancy. I hadn't swum in a while for fear of my weight sinking me like a stone, so it felt good to be ensconced in water again. The water took over, seeped into every pore creating a wall of life around me. I turned around again to see those waves coming closer. In the distance, the waves started to appear higher, until the ripples of water started moving faster creating a wall that was way over my head. I needed to head back to shore. There was a high sand ridge in front of me that I needed to climb that led to a higher ground. I set out to move. I was moving faster than I used to, but this was a race of me against the water so I wasn't fast enough.

The water will always win.

Running through the water in slow motion wore me out. The water was so heavy against my body. The waves crashed on me and set me over the high ridge I was heading towards. I remember looking at the person next to me after the wave crashed and he said we were fine. I felt relief that I saw the land ahead of me within reaching distance. I started walking towards the sand, but all too quickly we were not fine. I slipped down backwards off the sand ridge, then back to little higher than waist deep water. The person next to me was now gone. Another giant wave rushed its assertiveness into my body with such great tenacity, that it kept pulling me back from the higher sand ridge area. I kept getting pulled out further and further feeling great panic. I kept seeing the shoreline move farther and farther away from me. I woke up once I got so far away that I could not see the shore anymore, just miles and miles of water.

There is nothing scarier to me than being surrounded by water and no sight of land anywhere. Who knows what is lurking underneath waiting to plunge me into an unknown, secret world. I am absolutely terrified when I wake up because I feel an overwhelming sense of impending doom.

My head starts to pound again. I hear beeps. I hear distant voices pleading with me about something. The voices sound distressed.

I need to get up again out of the hammock. A walk always help me feel better and that is just what I was going to do. That was just a dream. But did I have a dream while living in a dream? Is this about death? Perhaps I need to go back in my mind to remember the day my dad died, as painful as it was.

Walking quietly I move through the yard under the guiding care of the elm trees. I need guidance from my memories here at this glorious house.

CHAPTER 44

Ashley

> *"We can complain because rose bushes have thorns, or rejoice because thorn bushes have roses."*
> *- Abraham Lincoln*

WHEN I get home from New York, it seems like the whole town had left for their lake houses to pack up for the season. There are no kids on the street, no cars, and the house have not one light on as it is just starting to get dark over a dank November evening. The leaves are scattered on the lawn blowing gently over the grass, now just remnants of the seasons that passed. I wonder what is going to come of my life when the divorce comes knocking on the door, but I will deal with that later. I am sure this divorce will be uglier than November and its bareness.

When I walk in, the house smells nice and clean. Naomi knows what a neat freak I am, so there is not one thing out of place, but now it doesn't feel like my home anymore.

There is a note on the counter that reads, "Picking kids up for activities and heading out to eat. Come meet us there if your flight gets in on time. Text first before coming."

I text Naomi and she responds back that they would be at the Starline Café in our little downtown main street in a couple hours. I tell her I will meet her there. I could meet her before then, but I need some time to sit, unwind, and take another shower from the plane germs and duplicity. I think I will feel better upon showering, but there is no hiding this mess that is all coming to a head. I don't want to say a word to the kids, but then again, I don't know what I am going to say as to why I am home early without alarming them, especially Ava. But I know Noah could give two shits honestly. As long as he has his phone and his friends, he is fine.

I get myself a glass of wine, and then two, and before I know it the bottle is gone. I put the glass down, reach over and pull out the Cowboy's business card. I stare at the card for a while as my eyes start getting heavy like weights are being placed on top of them.

I fall sound asleep for what seemed like hours and wake up to the sound of my phone vibrating on the glass table next to me which causes me to jolt up suddenly. For a moment, I forget where I am. I think I was back in the hotel room with Chris.

My heart is pumping because I think for sure it is him, but it is Naomi and she sounds concerned. "Ashley? Where are you? We are here and I got worried that you were not here. Are you coming? We have been waiting here thirty minutes. I called you several times. Did you not hear the phone?" Her voice is escalating with more apprehension.

I think she is catching on to my drinking, but she would never say anything.

"Should I come get you?" she said skeptically.

I pause for a moment trying to remember where I was again. She is asking way too many stupid questions. I am getting confused because she just keeps firing off questions left and right.

"Naomi, no need to worry. I took a shower and fell asleep because I didn't get a whole lot of sleep with traveling and all. I'm okay. I am getting ready to head out right now."

"Ok," she says. "But we can just order here and bring it all home if you like. Does that sound good?" she continues in her German accent.

"No, it's okay Naomi. I said I'd be there shortly. Go ahead and order without me. I am not really that hungry." I don't want to eat and have to throw up in front of the kids.

"Ok," she says rather disappointedly. I feel her discernment through the phone. I pull myself together, grab my purse and head out the door to meet them.

When I walk into the cafe, I see Naomi sitting with Ava and Noah. All three of them are staring at their phones. I walk up to the table and not one of them looks up for a few minutes, oblivious to the world around them. My presence is not felt or known. I stand there acknowledging that exact same feeling. I for a moment think, are we all just oblivious to the demons in our lives?

"Hello?" I say sarcastically.

Ava looks up first. She seems bewildered, not enthusiastic that I am there. I know I am going to face a barrage of questions from her.

"Mom, what are you doing at home? I thought you were with Dad in New York? Is he with you?" She gets up from her seat and looks around to see if Chris is there as she talks right past me.

I want to tell her no that Chris was not here with me because he was too busy fucking a Barbie doll, but I hold in my angst. "Well, that's a lovely welcome home Ava, thanks."

"Oh, sorry Mom, it is just Dad texted me this morning and said he was hoping he would be home soon, so thought he would surprise me, that's all."

I guess his phone does work I think to myself. That fucker was going to use the kids to get out of his mess.

"Dad texted you, Ava?" I sigh. "When did he text you?"

"This morning. He said he was almost done with work and he would be home next week."

This whole conversation is taking place and Noah doesn't look up once.

Naomi nudges him and says, "Don't you want to say hi to your mother Noah?"

He takes his eyes off his phone reluctantly and stares up at me. Gosh his bright green eyes are the same as Chris's. He is a spitting image of his father. I have seen that stare before. Noah's looks are even more striking than Chris. He honestly could stop the oxygen flowing when walking into a room. He will break someone's heart one day I was sure of it, just like mine, which has had a bullet go through it. I have to double take because I can swear he is the younger version of Chris sitting right here with me.

"Oh, hey Mom. You're back early. Was Dad a crabby jerk like he is when he's home?"

Naomi looks shocked that Noah responds this way, but I'm not mad.

"Noah, do not talk about your father in that way. That's so disrespectful!" Naomi says.

Suddenly I feel Naomi has overstepped her bounds again the way she snaps at Noah. She doesn't know a thing about Chris, especially what I know. She is out of place here.

I make this known because she has struck a nerve in me, especially after my husband has been out fucking God knows who. He could have fucked Naomi for all I know, which is why she probably feels it so important to defend Chris. For the first time, I start looking at her a bit differently like she was under a microscope. She catches my skeptical glance. But this is a true classic tale of the husband fucking the hot Nanny, and Naomi is no slouch. I would not be a bit surprised if this had been happening.

I don't know what to believe anymore. "It's okay Naomi, and no need to reprimand my child for his comment. If you saw how Chris treated Noah lately you would understand why he said that, but you don't, so leave it be. When's the last time you saw Chris with Noah in the same room?"

Ava of course chimes in sensing the awkward air. "Mom, why are you so mad at Dad? What did he do?"

I am half out of it still and buzzed. I also do not need this third degree from my daughter because now this was just a big buzz kill. I could have stayed home and got some well needed sleep. I'm feeling like a flare being lit up by the truckers indicating a sign of distress on the side of the road. I don't answer Ava and I don't even look at her actually.

Ava isn't satisfied with my ignoring her because she's a bitch. "What's wrong with you Mom?" Ava says, while staring at her phone scrolling images of her teen friends scantily clad puffing out their lips for blowjobs, if they even knew what a blowjob was. If they did, they would not find themselves in this pose.

"Nothing is wrong Ava. When your dad gets home, he can explain everything to you about why I am home early, that's all. I'm done talking about it. I am home and he is not. It's that simple."

Noah looks up, rolls those piercing green eyes and goes right back to his phone. Naomi, not knowing what to say or do, apologizes for her outburst and gets up from the table because the pager has buzzed for the food. When she comes back with the food, the kids and her eat while I sit and watch in silence. Finally, the air is broken with some superficial conversation. We have no idea how to talk to each other.

"Did you bring us anything?" asks Ava half-heartedly.

Bring you anything? I say in my head. Is she fucking kidding? I had no time to collect my dignity, let alone stop and get some stupid keychain or t-shirt that she wouldn't appreciate anyways. I am losing my entire existence and this bitch is thinking about herself.

"No, I didn't bring you anything because I didn't have the time darling. Isn't my presence here enough?"

As the old and worn out saying goes, you can cut the tension at this table with a knife. I feel Naomi's stares going right through me as the kids eat with their heads down. I stare right back at her. I see her glance like she is trying to outsmart a cat. I hope she isn't going to fuck with me today of all days because she will fucking lose. How dare she think she can run this show better than me? Does she think she is capable of being a better mother, a better wife?

I want to say, "Oh, just wait honey."

One day she will see the illusions that are created in an alleged love affair, sober or straight, and it will catch up with her at some point. Then she won't be so quick to judge.

When the kids are done eating, Naomi brings all their things up to the garbage and throws them away without a word. I can tell she is still pissed off at my actions. I can tell she thinks I'm not a good mother. I don't fucking care. I sure as hell am not going to apologize.

She is the nanny.

When we get outside the kids want to go with Naomi in Chris's car. I guess they prefer the sleek gray BMW over my pearl white Audi complete with the mothering of Naomi. Naomi shoots me a look like she has conquered something because the kids want to go with her. Then she insists that I follow her home as if I don't know where I am going. I know this was her way of keeping control in an uncontrolled setting, similar to keeping a wild parakeet in a cage. I don't feel like hearing Ava chatter anyways so it is fine with me. I am too tired to fight her and fucked up, so I let her lead the way.

CHAPTER 45

Tammy

> *"No man stands taller than when he stoops to help a child."*
> *- Abraham Lincoln*

I take a walk over towards the front entrance of the house. It feels good to move around because it helps clear my mind from the depth of my dream. I can usually let dreams go, and don't really remember many of them, but I feel a strong desire to sort this one out for my own awakening. I walk to the tip of the horseshoe shaped driveway that leads to a nice front porch outside of the house. There are four steps up that lead up to the front door. The porch is wide and deep enough to fit a chair on either side of the doorway. There is a little table where Mom and Dad could rest a beverage to enjoy chatter under the stars.

Mom always stored these chairs in the basement for the winter months. They were left there to collect dust, yet also stay intact from the elements. So when she heaved them back up the stairs for some air, we all knew summer would be waiting to sit down and relax. The nice thing about this house is there were plenty of places to roam and find a quiet resting spot. We all spent a great deal of time around the firepit, or in the backyard. But Mom and Dad liked to sit on the front porch at night after dinner and just chat. This was their place. I can hear their voices talking and laughing, lamenting over their days. They shared so much great joy together. Dawn and I knew that was their spot, but as young kids, we would always want to join them. We would sit on the steps watching the lightning bugs showcasing their carnival lights in the black backdrop of the yard. Constant flickers of light would appear like a firework show without the noise. The male would light up in hopes to find the perfect mate. I was so happy that Dad's light attracted Mom. They never turned us away when we would ask to sit there and watch this spectacle with them. They were living proof of all that splendor in nature before us. I loved those days with all my heart.

I walk up the stairs but notice the chairs and little table are gone. I sit down on the steps like I did when I was a little girl. It feels good to be back, but like any space that was once loved and then abandoned, it feels completely different upon returning.

Nothing is the same in the sameness I once knew because everyone changed.

I breathe in the world around me thinking about my dream. I know someone was with me when I couldn't find my way back to shore. It had to have been my dad. I questioned if it was Alex. I definitely know it wasn't Bill. When I was flailing around trying to get back to shore, that is when he left me. If that was my dad in the dream, why did he leave me at the worst possible time?

This got me thinking about the events of the day that led up to the worst day of my life. It had started out just as usual. Dawn wasn't home because she had stayed near her college for the summer because she got a job there. I was still home living the summer life after high school before starting college. I had gone out with Bill that day. Dad went to work as usual, and Mom was home from work. She had a part-time job but was always home for dinner time. I was out and didn't make it home for dinner. Bill and I were out with friends, but I remember wanting to come home early because I was feeling oddly tired, along with a nauseous feeling.

I didn't know it then, but those symptoms were the hallmark symptoms of pregnancy. I remember pulling up into the driveway bummed that I missed dinner because Mom's meals were always delicious. Mom and Dad were sitting on the chairs on the front porch. They had a dessert Mom had made on their little table. They smiled when I pulled up, offered me dinner that was left on the counter, but I wasn't hungry. I didn't necessarily want to hang out and talk out in front because I didn't feel good.

When I was older, and Dawn was gone, my parents never pushed me to be with them, especially at my age, so they just let me go into the house without asking too many questions. I loved that about my parents. They knew when to give me space. They didn't mind that I didn't join them because they were in a conversation of endearment anyways.

Looking back now I can still see Dad sitting there on the porch that day. He was hanging on to Mom's every world dangling his feet off the porch of the home he built, the love he found. He was a man of riches for the soul, not the checkbook. He had found compatibility, trust and a natural affinity to my mom. I saw this on their faces most of the days of my life, even when Dad was gone. My mom never remarried and never will, because there is no one that would come close to the sagacious relationship they shared. I envied this about my parents, especially when I figured out that I was trapped in my own marriage not feeling a quarter of what they felt. My dad adored my mom. She adored him back. He loved what he built. And he loved that he found my mom in a sea of madness. She would always be the stable person in his life. Bill was never any of those things for me.

I stare at my parents on the porch. I see them but they don't see me. Then the chairs disappear along with them. All that is on the porch is an old spider web swaying in the corners.

I wish I would have gone back outside that evening after I went in passing them with a half-hearted hello and respectful smile. But I needed to lie on the couch and take care of a gnawing stomachache. I turned on the tv to take my mind off a strange feeling in my belly. I fell sound asleep to the monotonous sounds of nothing on the tv. I don't remember Mom or Dad waking me up asking me to go to my room. Sometimes I would fall asleep on the couch and one of them would always get me up and tell me to go upstairs to bed. But that night I did not get up from the couch.

Next thing I remember is that I was awakened at three o'clock in the morning with a startling phone ring coming from the kitchen. The phone was relentless. It kept ringing and ringing. It continued to get louder and louder screaming with intensity. I couldn't ignore it even though I wanted to. I wasn't moving quickly because I woke up disoriented, my heart beating fast. This ring had conviction so I had to pick it up. I made my way over to the kitchen fumbling through the darkness. It was a good thing my mom left the kitchen light on the stove every night or I would have fallen into the deep darkness. I grabbed the phone off the hook to end the fury of this ring, yet I paused fearing that the noise on the other end would be just as unsettling.

"Hello" I said, very confused and dazed with apprehension. There was some distance noise and some dead time of about a millisecond.

"Tammy, Tammy, are you there?" It was my mom.

"I'm here, yes Mom. Where are you?" I was confused as to why she was not home at this time.

"We are at the hospital. Dad had a heart attack."

Dead silence.

I won't forget those words. "Dad had a heart attack." There are just five words in the sentence that were single-handedly responsible for the next course of my life.

"What?" I said, even more confused. "Wait, What?" I must have been dreaming.

"Tammy, listen to me. I couldn't wake you before we left because there was no time. Your dad got up and said he didn't feel good. He said he felt weird. He was having a hard time breathing. I wanted to call an ambulance but he vehemently refused. I finally was able to convince him that I would take him to the hospital. I figured you went up to your bed like you always do and I'd wake you up when I knew more."

I guess she didn't see me on the couch, but this was not the time to correct her. I was trying to process this coming out of a deep sleep. I was still trying to figure out if it was a dream when I heard Mom again yelling. Her voice did not sound like the voice I knew.

"Tammy. Tammy! Answer me, are you there? I'm at the hospital now," she said with all the fear in her voice like someone was trailing her down a dark alley.

"Wait, I didn't hear you at all?" I said. My stomach was doing backflips now. "Is he going to be okay?"

Dead silence. Then a pause in time.

"Tammy, that doesn't matter right now and I don't know if he is going to be okay. That's why I'm calling. The doctors are with him now. I don't know anything yet, but I think you should get her as soon as you can. I need you to call your sister right now and then come to the hospital."

"It's three o'clock in the morning Mom, " I said, feeling scared to go out and venture out on my own at this time. My mom had a habit of over exaggerating everything. I was thinking this was one of those times.

"Tammy," she said sternly. "You need to do what I say and get to the hospital right now."

I knew then she wasn't exaggerating and needed to do what she said. The last thing she needed was no support. She was losing the support of her life.

"Tammy, can you hear me? You are not saying anything. Listen, I gotta go. I don't want to leave him and doctors are coming in now. Get going, please, right now," she said in a desperate plea,"

I didn't like anything about the pitch in her voice. "I'm calling Dawn and leaving."

"Okay, she mumbled, and then hung up abruptly.

I was finally awake. This was not a dream. It was a living nightmare.

I felt odd calling my sister and creating a phone ringing of fear for her too, but I had no choice. She was in a worse predicament than me. At least I was able to go to the hospital. She was hours away and now would be forced to sit in a dorm room the size of a closet and fear the worst. I wish mom had me call her later. I visualized her fright of a glaring phone ringing waking her up out of her beauty sleep.

I still feel guilty for the hours of pain I caused her to sit in a chamber of worrisome thoughts. But I had to get my shit together and left for the hospital. I remember running through the witching hour to get in my car. Remnants of days went flashing through my head when we would leave on a road trip vacation. Dad always arranged for the trip to depart at 3:00 am to get a jump start on the journey. And no one better have to go to the bathroom until at least noon! He was a man on a mission. Dawn and I would rise reluctantly, suitcases in tow with our pillows to go right back to sleep to the lull of the engine flying down a highway at lightning speed. It felt so promising and mysterious to set out into the night watching the landscape change when the sun would rise through the car windows. Dawn and I would sleep in great anticipation of where we would be when we woke up. And we always ended up somewhere glorious when we were with

Mom and Dad, except for their arguing moments over directions when they had to change interstates.

I chuckle trying to ease my mind a bit from the terror I was feeling thinking of their little spats. But leaving at this time with no vacation ahead formed a sense of foreboding, making my stomach turn even more circles. I knew where I was going to end up on this journey.

I had a bad feeling.

I sit here now as the evening light goes on over an empty porch. I can swear I just walked over to this porch in the morning. How did it get dark already? I have not thought about the details of this evening in years. I am amazed I can replay it all in my head and truly sense all that I felt. I need to stay on the path as difficult as it is to relive. Living it one time was bad enough.

When I got to the hospital, I met my mom in the lobby. She was still in her pajama top, but she had thrown on a pair of pants that didn't match. She wore a light jacket to cover her top because she didn't have time to put her bra on. Her hair was disheveled. Her eyes had dark circles on them. Her hands were shaking when she wrapped them around me in a tight embrace. How was this the same woman only hours earlier laughing with her best friend on the porch? She aged right in front of me.

As we passed through the lobby to get to the elevator, I noticed the hospital was eerily quiet. All the sick patients were being poked and prodded all night for their vitals while trying to sleep. Nurses tiptoed around. The staff talked quieter. The gift shop and cafeteria had prison bars over the doors indicating no one was going in there. When we got into the elevator Mom started talking. I liked it when she was quiet because then I didn't have to hear any bad news. But then she started talking while we were moving in slow motion up the elevator.

"So, they confirmed that Dad did have a heart attack. He's still alive."

Mom went on talking about what happened, what was wrong, tests being run, and emergency surgery. I know I missed ninety-five percent of what she was saying because all I heard was that he was alive. I immediately lost the power washing of adrenaline that was shooting through my body because I heard the word "alive." I breathed deeply and tried to focus on what she was saying. I had a blank stare because I figured out quickly that being alive didn't necessarily mean good by looking at the expression on my mom's face and hearing all the details of my dad's dire condition.

"Tammy. Wake up. Did you just hear anything I said?" She knocked me back into reality. I remember my mom being so put together in this chaos, but I was like a zombie, complete with motionless stares. I don't know how she was holding herself together. I felt like someone had ripped out my insides.

"Dad is going into emergency surgery to repair his heart very soon. I feel horrible that Dawn can't get here, but that's why I called you. I wanted to make sure you got here." She said something about blockages, blood clots, lack of air supply, and a stroke. It was like I had never heard these words before.

I never thought this strong man I loved would need any help from anyone. I didn't believe it because my dad was never sick a day in his life. I thought for sure he would get out of the bed, tell us it's all okay and he'd be fine. This was who my dad was. Nothing was going to tear him down. I firmly believed this. So, I felt my mom was jumping the gun here by calling me. She could have let me sleep. I'd have been none the wiser and then we didn't have to make Dawn worry needlessly. He would be home soon enough after doctors repaired his heart.

The elevator opened revealing the new road ahead. We found seats in this little family waiting room behind cold metal doors. No one else was there. The tv was off with *Reader's Digest* magazines strewn about the table. There was a lamp on the table illuminating a soft glow to balance the dimmed lighting. The lampshade was crooked. I wanted to go fix it but I had no energy to get up once I sat down. I imagined that people like me sat here not reading the books, but browsing through to distract the mind from horrible thoughts. No one else wanted to fix the crooked lampshade either. We sat uncomfortably waiting for someone to come get us.

It got calm finally and that's when Mom lost it. She put her head in her hands and started crying. This scene instantly made me cry. She was falling apart and I had to help but I didn't know how because she was always taking care of me.

I grabbed her trembling body and wrapped my arms around her. "It's okay Mom." I said. I had nothing else to say. I had heard people say this in bad times. But would it be ok? I didn't even believe myself when the words came out with no pulse riding through it.

"Thanks, Tammy. I'm sorry. I don't mean to cry, it is just I'm glad you're here, that's all." She picked her head up and sniffled.

I went over and grabbed a tissue from the box on the table. I'm sure there's a lot of crying that goes on in between these four walls of this dank waiting room. A candy striper's job would be to come find all the empty tissue boxes for the broken people who worried about someone they loved the most. Then the boxes would need to be replaced, making way for more broken hearts. It was a cyclical process.

"Did you call Dawn?" mom said. "I feel horrible because she is far away. I'm not sure if we can get anyone to drive her home. Or maybe you might have to do this Tammy, but we'll worry about that later."

I know it's selfish, but immediately I second guessed this decision. I would be forced to spend hours with my sister, who really had no use for me anymore in her life. What would we talk about? I could only reminisce or talk about the weather for so long. With the distance over the years, we just didn't have anything in common. She didn't bother to know what was going on in my life, and I felt the same about her. Maybe that would change down the road.

"Okay Mom, whatever." I didn't think I should say anything, but only agreed to what she wanted. I didn't want to make her life any more difficult than it was at the time.

When the nurse walked in, she wore scrubs and a heavy look. "Is this your daughter?" she said with no emotion.

"Yes, this is my daughter." Mom said.

"Come with me please. You will get to see him before he heads off for surgery. We are preparing for his vitals right now. He has his eyes closed because we have mildly sedated him, but it would be best to talk to him now. I assure you he can hear you." Her tone seemed warmer as she continued to talk.

I think she felt sorry for us. I felt sorry for her for delivering news like this so early in the morning. What the nurse didn't prepare me for was what I was about to see when I walked into the room. I saw my Dad lying helplessly in a hospital bed tied to machines beeping and breathing for him.

It took my breath away because he was my hero. Who was going to save him?

I wanted to rip all the cords out and attach them to myself so I could breathe better. I wanted them to sedate me and mom to strip the pain we were enduring. Dawn was lucky to be away at college. She always seemed to dodge dicey moments in life.

The doctors walked in similar to soldiers preparing for battle. One doctor was contemplative, while the other one kept an austere face while speaking. In all the medical jargon, all I heard was they were going to try their best. To me this meant yes, they would help save my hero, but there was an insertion of a disclaimer that this might not happen.

No guarantees in life.

We were told to give Dad our best wishes quickly because they were on a timeline. The longer he sat, the less chance he had to live. They motioned for me to go first, so I went over and stared at my Dad. He looked so helpless lying there. I grabbed his hand softly, told him I loved him, and that I needed him. He didn't squeeze my hand back. It was warm, but lifeless. His face stayed in the same position. I could see he had shaved before bed. He looked clean and out of pain. I told him he was my hero and he needed to come see me off to college. I told him Dawn loved him too and should be proud of how he raised us. I told him he survived Vietnam, he can do this.

I heard beeps. They pierced my ears with perturbation.

I have a vivid memory of remorse thinking I wished I had talked to him when I came home that day. I had buried these events in my subconscious until my dream about the ocean yanked it out of me with all the force of a tugboat pushing an ocean liner. Dad was the one standing with me in the water. He had to let go. But what about me now?

I kept all my tears inside at his bedside so as to not upset him. I gave him a kiss on the forehead to end my speech because I heard the doctor whisper that it was time to go. I remember feeling mad at the doctor because I had so much more to say. The nurse stepped in to lead me out so my mom could talk to my dad. As I was walking out I heard the doctors talking to my mom in serious voices. I waited out in the hallway for her with my ear attached to the door, which was slightly ajar. Then I saw her lean in next to Dad, grab his hand and lay her head down on him. She was sobbing like a baby. Her body looked decayed, like she could wither away right there with him. He was her best friend. They had fun together. I think that if she had the choice to go with him right then and there she would have jumped right in if Dawn and I didn't exist. My tears were being held in but the dam broke, and they poured out with potency. I couldn't believe this was all happening.

I hear beeps in my head now all of a sudden and my head hurts again. I grab my head and put in my hands for a self-massage. I heard these same beeps. They were high pitched in a rhythmic unison of music notes on a measure. I wonder if Dad heard this noise too. I look out into the cold room. I hear the beeps again with soft voices.

My mom walked out of the room and we watched Dad wheeled down the hallway in a parade-like fashion with lots of people surrounding him. He would never be the same again, and neither were we. Mom, Dawn and I would spend five agonizing days later watching him suffer. Then finally he took his last breath to the sound of beeps right in front of us. Then there were clicks on a metronome, right on beat until they weren't anymore.

Then no sound. No more beeps.

My head pounds the heaviest it has so far on this journey. I sit on the steps of the porch listening to silence, then the beeps.

Then soft voices.

CHAPTER 46

Ashley

> *"A false friend and a shadow attend only while the sun shines."*
> *- Benjamin Franklin*

WHEN I pull up on the driveway, I see the kids embracing Naomi and having what looks like a pleasant conversation with giggles and hugs, even Noah, which is mildly shocking to me. When we all go inside, the kids say goodbye to Naomi one more time. It seems like I am an intruder on their little vacation. They look disappointed that Naomi is leaving. They go right up to the rooms without one word or glance in my direction. I'm sure Ava is going to text Chris or go on her iPad for Facetime. I give up trying to form a relationship with her.

This noiseless house has turned gray and dismal and I can't do a damn thing about it. These kids are like strangers I walk by on the crowded street of a New York evening, unknowing and distant. There is mystery in the deep darkness that is unsettling, but no way to get fingers around the blackness of the night to create a sense of calmness.

Naomi is still there and reshuffling some things that are on the counter to look busy. Then she stands there awkwardly waiting for my payment, or my apology and not necessarily in that order. She isn't getting an apology, that's for sure. The payment I am able to do just to get her the fuck out of my hair. She stands there with daggers on her face like a little child because she is pissed that I raised my voice at her back at the restaurant.

She doesn't scare me one bit though. I think if I raised my voice at her again, she might wilt, or throw herself down on the floor in a fetal position claiming too much anxiety. Fuck her and the high horse she rode in on. This judgment of hers has been going on for a while and it has come to a head for me. I grab the envelope with money from the cabinet and turn to face her. Somehow I feel like I am going to pay her for fucking my husband. It feels like I am giving her call girl money from Chris.

"Here is your money, Naomi. It is payment up and through tomorrow evening as I thought you would be here the whole weekend. If you need to stay over, I would prefer you leave early as I have lots of things weighing on my mind and I need space."

"I think it is best that I leave, Ashley. That way you can have your space that you need," she says cynically.

She catches the pissed off look on my face and then stumbles in her language. I can tell she wanted to retract what she had just said.

"Um, a, um . . . It's just, like, that I have been with your family since the kids were babies. Is this how you want it to end Ashley?" She has tears in her eyes and then they just start flowing. It is so uncomfortable honestly. Clearly, she put more into this relationship she thought she had with me because I am not feeling the same way. I just want her to leave, that's all, no other bells and whistles were necessary.

"This is not the end, Naomi. I think you are being a bit dramatic." Does she want a fucking going away party complete with balloons and fan fair? I have my own issues to deal with and this problem with her is way low on the totem pole. I don't want to have to parent an employee, because that is what she is to me, an employee, but I have to say something, I guess.

I muster up my bullshit card from my business days. "C'mon now Naomi. There is no need to cry. Please don't embarrass yourself. You haven't been here every day because the kids are older. This was just like a visit, that's all, nothing else. The time has come to part and endings are inevitable. I am sure there will be times I will still need you. Looks like you had a nice goodbye tonight with the kids so that's what matters."

I stretch out my hand, smile a fake smile and extend my arm out with an envelope of cash. If she is able to take the money, then that's what it is about when it all comes down to brass tacks. She stands there for a few moments just waiting. I am able to see the wheels turning in her head, but I know she doesn't have the balls to tell me what she is thinking.

I am armed and ready for anything she is willing to throw at me though. A couple more moments go by as we stand face to face. She grabs the envelope weakly from my hands with tears in her eyes. My eyes are as dry as a creek in Death Valley. I just want her to leave. She grabs her own car keys, walks down the hall crying because I am able to see her shoulders shaking on the way out.

Even through the tears I question her sincerity because I view this as a business transaction. I imagine her texting her friends when she gets in the car telling them what a bitch I was to her or how I paid her for fucking my husband. They would give her all the pity she needed.

I go to the window, see her get into her Ford Fiesta and peel out of the driveway. I grab another bottle of wine, drink the whole thing scrolling through social media at all the lovely shining people all in love with life until I fall unsoundly asleep.

When I wake up on Sunday the skies were gray, the rain has been falling in a slow steady pace lightly tapping the roof. The kids are already up, quiet as usual just eating breakfast while watching

YouTube videos. I get a bowl of cereal and sit with them. I don't want to do this, but I have to figure out a way to tell them what is going on. This is not the time to sugar-coat a lot of shit.

"Listen," I say. "I need today to gather myself together. Your dad and I have not been getting along. That's all I am going to say, but I need to figure some things out." They both look up from their videos. I guess my statement gets their attention.

"Are you and Dad getting a divorce?" Noah said.

"A divorce?" Ava said, shocked.

"I don't know guys. Just relax Ava." I have to give her a hug and console her because she immediately starts crying. "You are overreacting Ava, now stop. I just told you I have to sit and think about what the next steps are to figure out our problems. Your dad is not who you think he is, that's all."

"I don't get it Mom," she says, still crying.

"You don't get it because I don't either, Ava. Don't make this harder on me than it already is. Just do your homework and play your games and relax today. Things will be better tomorrow. When I talk to Dad I will know more, then I can tell you more. So, stop crying because that is not going to help anyone. Does this make sense?"

"Yes," she says half vocally.

"Got it Mom," Noah says.

I think they are too shocked to talk about it or didn't want to tell me how they were feeling, but either way, they go upstairs for the moment. I need to be by myself anyway because I have no idea what to say to them and I don't want to say too much. I check my phone while finishing my breakfast.

This talk comes at a good time because I finally get a text from Chris. It reads, "I have lots of connections Ashley and I have been in contact with a lawyer. You will be served papers soon. In the meantime, I'll be home on Tuesday to go over all of this with you and the kids."

My stomach drops and I feel like it might come out and up my esophagus. He is seriously going to end this marriage. I throw the phone across the table and the cereal and milk splatter everywhere. I let it sit there for a while. I spend the rest of the day brooding over whether I should say anything back. I have several bottles of wine throughout the day, each bottle getting me closer to responding back.

By the third bottle, I grab the phone and started typing, "You want to pretend to be a father now Chris, when you have pretended to be a husband all these years? We have to wait for you like helpless turtles? I think you should tell the kids that you are a selfish, fucking machine and can't keep your dick in your pants. You cheat on me and I get punished? This is all about so you can keep your little whore, have your cake and eat it too. I want to watch it all blow up in your face, you shameless piece of shit of a man. I am going to take you for everything you have. I will be calling my own lawyer tomorrow!"

He is dead on the airwaves from there.

The kids eat Ramon noodles for dinner while watching their YouTube videos again. Ava wants to lie on the couch with me, but I send her upstairs. I tell her it is a school night and the best thing for her is proper sleep. She is not free from whining, but eventually she buys into it and goes to bed. I do not have the energy to take care of anyone at this point but myself, and besides, they are old enough to fend for themselves.

I lay on the coach and think about my strange encounter at the airport. I start thinking about the perfect timing of not only the Cowboy, but Surfer Boy too. I grabbed Colton's card and find his cell number. With more wine and a pill, I hit a courageous level and pull the trigger.

I send a text to Colton. "Hey, It's Ashley. Hope you made it to Houston all right. You were right, I should have come to Houston to check it out . . . never been there before. It all sucks here right now."

Within thirty seconds a text comes back almost as if it had been shot out of a cannon. "I was just thinking of you Miss Ashley Hayes. Sorry things are not good, but I can change that for you if you like. You would love Houston and I'd be happy to show it to you."

I have this guy in the bag, right away, but I am feeling like I could pass out because my eyes are droopy and my head is spinning. "I am going to bed, but will be in touch in the morning, promise." I attach a wink emoji with a heart.

Three seconds later, "Oh, c'mon. You can't reel me in like that and go to bed. At least tell me what you are wearing?"

Here we go . . . "I have a white shirt on, no bra and a pair of black panties."

A millisecond later. "Oh, that's hot Miss Ashley. I can feel the heat through the phone. Please text me tomorrow. Sweet dreams princess."

I drag myself upstairs, close and lock my door, and then plop into bed. I quickly delete this off the phone because now more than ever I need no paper trail during a divorce. I turn the phone off completely for the first time I think since I got it. I want to throw it right out the damn window but I know I can't because that device is a slot machine calling me back for one more pull.

"Fuck Chris," I said out loud while laying my head down on my pillow. He did me a favor because I take care of myself thinking of Colton and fell sound asleep.

I sleep as best as I have in years.

Chapter 47

Tammy

> "This is my letter to the world
> That never wrote to me."
> - Emily Dickinson

THE beeps are faint now and no longer hurting my head as much as they were. I wake up peacefully with a puddle of tears next to me. I cried myself asleep on the porch waiting for a new vision of what was going to happen to me. But I can't recall any new dreams. Turns out I was thankful for my lack of memory because tackling my dream from the ocean was taxing enough. I had finally confronted my fear of losing my father. Had I come to terms through a cathartic release? Maybe. Or am I just distracting myself from the fear of my own death?

The days after Dad died were the hardest I have ever had to endure. Mom was trying to hold it together for Dawn and me, but we knew once she was out of our sight she was in a lonely cave of sorrow. It pained us to see her this way. We did what we could to help make Mom's days bearable. But looming overhead we knew Mom would be really alone when we left. Dawn was working near her college over the summer so she was only home temporarily because of Dad's death and school would be starting for her too. I was also getting ready for college. Dawn and I had long talks about what to do, but we both decided Dad would want us to forge ahead with our plans. Mom is a strong lady and would survive, so she insisted we go back. She didn't want to even hear the idea of not going to college. Dawn left a week before me and got off with no hitch as usual, but not me. I had skipped my period prompting a test with a little pink symbol that would determine the fate of my life. I was a witness to death all while holding new life inside me. Life can be a strange juxtaposition at times. I remember when I told mom the news. She was just in shock, still barely breathing from Dad's death. I felt oddly similar to how fear riveted through my body the night I had to meet Mom at the hospital. Pregnancy was supposed to be a happy announcement. This felt like another kick in the gut instead.

I was in shock. We all were in shock.

And even though there was controversy on whether or not to keep the baby from Bill's family, my mom and I never thought twice about what we wanted to do. I know my mom was very disappointed that my college career had ended before it started, but she was instrumental in helping me move forward. I know Dad would have been disappointed in me too for not going to college, but if he saw Alex he would move on quickly. Alex was the best present I have ever been given. At first the disappointment of my college dreams derailing was overwhelming. I felt guilty for feeling awful about being pregnant, and still feel guilt sometimes for feeling this way because Alex was everything I could have asked for and more. After Dad died, the focus on Alex helped my mom and me heal day by day because we had each other. I do think we were meant to be on this passage in time together.

I step off the porch and try to think about what life would be like if Dad didn't die so early. I'll never know, but I can always dream. The best gift I could give to my dad was preserving his memory by keeping his spirit alive for Alex. I would tell Alex stories and show him pictures all of the time. While it was not the same, it helped. I did this for my mom and my dad.

I step down off the porch. I wish I could see them both, tell them that I love them one more time. Maybe I'll remain lost in this setting forever. Maybe I'll always remain in this beautiful painting because I just can't seem to break free. Do I need to?

I walk towards the front of the driveway and make my way down towards the busy street. I can hear cars rushing by. I think of death and it no longer scares me. I really feel like for all these years my fears of death were grounded in the unknown. I know now that I will not be alone when I go. I will be able to walk home with a delicate slip into another world beyond. This thought provides me with overwhelming relief.

I hear the beeps again. They are slightly louder than the cars going by and I feel tired again. I sit down on an old stump to rest. I hear soft voices coming from the cold room that suddenly lets out a slight movement of warm wind. I will follow my heart until it's time to go.

Chapter 48

Ashley

> *"Behind her smile is a hurting heart. Behind her laugh, she's falling apart."*
> *- Anonymous*

I wake up the next day to my door being almost pounded into the point of it breaking down. This noise wakes me up out of a deep slumber and scares the shit out of me. I had locked the door before going to bed and hadn't realized it was time to get up to take the kids to school because I passed out before setting the alarm.

Ava is screaming, "Mom!! Are you alive? Mom!!!"

Holy shit, this girl is so fricking dramatic. I stumble to open the door, and there she is standing in her school uniform crying again. "Oh Mom," she comes rushing in and gives me a big hug. She almost knocks me over because I stumble backwards losing my balance. She sobs and tries to catch her breath.

She hasn't hugged me in a long time. She has me worried.

"You never lock your door and I thought you were so upset about Dad that you just weren't going to get up, and then I was going to call the," she is cut off by Noah.

"I told you she was fine, Ava. Quit overreacting already. She got in a fight with Dad. That doesn't mean she would do something stupid, Ava. Stop being so dramatic"

She turns away and goes to the bathroom to wipe her face. Noah grins at me.

"Thanks Noah. I am fine. Just give me a minute and I'll be right down." On the way downstairs, I make my way to Ava in the bathroom. "Honey, I'll be fine ok. Haven't you ever gotten in a fight with your friends? I just needed time to myself, that's all."

Ava looks concerned still and I wish she isn't so intuitive sometimes. I don't know where it came from but a mother gene kicked in.

"You spent the whole day on the couch, Mom. When you weren't getting up this morning, I didn't know what to do, so I texted Dad and Naomi too."

My light switched from compassion to fury and my eyes are open with horror.

"You what?" I yell.

She jumps back a little at the tone and loudness of my voice. She is not expecting my reaction after I just tried my best to console her.

"Why did you do that Ava? Noah was right here with you. Why do you have to go running to Dad or Naomi with any little problem? They are not even here to help! I am fine and I am here. I am tired of you acting like a three -year-old, Ava. Now get your bag and let's get you to school. And don't tell any teachers or anyone else anything there, ok? We are taking care of our problems at home and I don't want anyone else hearing about it because it's no one else's business but ours!"

She stands there wide-eyed and stunned. Oh my, I hear my mother's tone all over this sentence and it makes me cringe but that was the problem with words. Once they are out in the open space, there is no taking them back. This was how my own mother handled our affairs. She always pretended everything was okay when it wasn't, and here I am doing the same thing. I have to say something to Ava because she is just standing there with pitiful eyes. Suddenly, I feel sorry for her because it is as if I am staring at myself as a child.

"Dad will be home tomorrow and we will all sit down and talk about things, okay?" I give her a hug and feel her pain for a short moment.

But at the same time, I can't have her sabotage any of what I have planned moving forward, so I have to console her and tell her everything will be okay, even though I know damn well none of this is even near being okay. But I have to take this stress out of the equation for myself and deal with the mess I am in without the kids fucking this up. It is much easier to lie to the kids and tell them everything is alright.

I am wondering how long it will take Chris to text me and bitch at me that I passed out. I know he will tell me I am not taking care of my kids. I fucking know it so I have to think clearly here.

We all get into the car, again silently, not talking too much until I decide to make small talk and make it appear that things are normal.

"Ava, what's on the plan today? Any practice after school or am I picking you up at the regular time? Noah, you as well?"

"I have chess club on Mondays, remember, no volleyball today."

I don't remember because I can't keep my shit straight. I lie through my teeth. "Oh yeah, I remember. What about you Ava?"

She looks at me almost like she is giving me a test. I think she wants me to say something instead. I wait.

"Regular time today, Mom. There was an email this morning that Mrs. Turner is sick, so no singing practice after school today. Didn't you see it?"

"Oh right, I saw it, but glad you reminded me." I lie again. "I'll be there later then."

It is one of those back-and-forth days for drop off and pick up. This is the routine-like story of my life, still not able to keep it in sync.

As we drive past the crossing guard we see every day, I take notice of her presence again and feel it necessary to speak out loud about my observations. "How does that woman do this job every day? And especially in this crappy weather most of the time? She does look a little less wide though, doesn't she? It's almost like someone pulled the air out of the balloon . . . just slowly."

The way she looks sparked a soap box speech for my kids that I would announce once in a while just to keep them in check. I do want them to be concerned about how they look in the world.

"You have to watch what you eat and exercise. No way you want to let yourself go like that. I don't get how she could be smiling day in and day out. She looks like any minute her heart could blow. She's a walking heart attack."

"Wow, kind of harsh Mom, don't you think?" I have Noah's attention. "You talk bad about that lady all the time and you don't even know her."

I find it interesting my Mr. know-it-all who barely talks, lifts his head off his screen and has something to say. I turn my head to look at his face and speak right to those green eyes that think they knew the world. He sounds like his father and I don't like that at all.

"No, I am not being harsh, I tell the truth. I think she is an example for both of you on what not to do with your life. The way she looks shows us what happens when you let yourself go and not push yourself to be better. She walks kids across the street back and forth every day and eats herself into an oblivion. What kind of job is that? What kind of life is that? She probably gets paid close to peanuts. How can you live on a crossing guard salary? Plus, you can't eat shit all day and expect to live past forty, that's all. She can put on that fake smile all she wants, but there is no way she is happy with her life." I can't believe this was getting their attention. They never speak but now they want to go against my opinions about the fat crossing guard? Really?

"How do you know her age?" asks Ava.

"I don't. But we have seen this woman every day for many years and every day I pass her I question what she does all day long. I wonder how she let herself get this way. I am going to work out when I leave and keep myself active and she just eats it seems."

Noah sighs as we pull into the school. "I don't know why you care Mom. See you later." He jumps out as quickly as he could.

I turn to Ava who is getting out slowly in a half daze. I can tell she is still thinking about her scare with me this morning and everything going on with Chris. Again, I feel sorry for her. "Ava, have a good day. I am fine, okay? I am going to meet my friends and play tennis today, okay? You go be with your friends too. She still looks confused.

"Why do you hate that lady so much mom? And why do you hate dad too?"

She looks sad so I have to reassure her. Ava is like an orchid. You have to treat her very lightly. You can't just throw water in the soil, you have to put ice cubes in the pot to let the water seep in slowly. I guess I need to be more understanding with her.

"I don't hate Dad, Ava. We just don't see eye to eye right now. As for the crossing guard, it's just not what I want for you, Ava. There is no way you could dance with a lot of weight like that, pitch well, or be able to sing clearly in your musicals, right? Keep moving, doll. You want to have a good figure, yes? I want more for you, that's all."

She says nothing back, but looks at me with sullen eyes and then says, "When will Dad be home?"

She just isn't hearing anything I am saying. She is focused on Chris.

"Did you get what I was saying about that lady more importantly? I told you Dad is coming home tomorrow and we can talk then." She turns and looks at me funny.

"I guess so Mom." She gets out of the car and says bye quietly.

She walks with her head down for a bit. I wait there until I see her move into a group of girls to line up with for class. I see her friends give her a hug when they see her. I can tell she is popular because the girls want to be around her. She always looks good and her hair is so pretty and pristine. She really is a trendsetter. She will forget everything I just said within a few minutes and find something else to fret about besides me.

Finally, I have time to myself again. I go home to change for my workout, then to tennis, and then to grab my clothes for lunch afterwards.

I'm not sure if I am going to share any of my drama, but my one good friend's husband is a divorce lawyer, so think I better get someone as soon as I can, so I feel like this is a good time to drop the bomb.

I am afraid to check my texts, but the first one I see is from Naomi. Her texts came this morning within a few minutes of each other, along with a missed phone call.

"I know we left off on kind of weird terms last night, but are you okay Ashley? Ava texted me and said your door was locked and she didn't know if you were alive. I panicked and called you to check in on you."

I don't respond.

Next text.

"All ok?"

I don't respond.

Next text.

"I know I shouldn't interfere, but I care about Ava and Noah. Hope all is well. I am going to take a drive over to see if all is okay." Then I have to text back.

"All good, Naomi. No need to drive over. I am fine and the kids are at school. It was just Ava overreacting again."

Within a minute, a thumbs up emoji shows up. Okay, check that one off the list. No text from Chris, thank God. At least not yet.

So, I head out and get my head clear while running on the treadmill. I have a great game of tennis afterwards and it feels good to be with my friends.

We decide just to hang in the club as usual afterwards for lunch. We always bring our own wine and set up a charcuterie board to hang and talk. I don't know why I feel nervous to tell everyone, but I do. I know I'm not going to be able to tell this story sober though, so I go to the bathroom and take a Xanax with a glass of wine.

I have to wait for the right timing in conversation to spill the beans. It isn't until after the second bottle of wine when I am feeling a little looser. Char has just finished telling a story about how she went to her lake house all weekend to console her cousin whose husband was cheating on her.

So, in the middle of the laughter and gossip, I say, "Well, you may have to counsel me too. I think I am going to need Ted's number too by the way."

They all stop rather suddenly.

"And what would you need for counseling or Ted's number for darling?" The smile leaves Char's face. "I thought you just got back from your romantic getaway to New York? You were so excited about this. What happened?"

"Well, let's put it this way. It didn't go the way I expected. To make it short and sweet, I started out having sex with Chris after hanging in the hotel bar all day waiting for him to get off work. I couldn't go to sleep afterwards, and while he was sleeping, I saw his phone lighting up with texts from the woman he is fucking."

It is like the air has been sucked out the room. They all sit there in horror. For a hot minute it seems like we are in the middle of filming for a fucked up reality show.

"Holy shit, Ashley! Are you serious?" says Lola.

"Serious as a fat woman having a heart attack, yes," I say.

"What did you do?" Lola asks.

"I did what any jealous woman would do when you realized cutting off his nuts was not a good option. I went and fucked the hotel lobby bartender out in the parking lot."

There is more jaw dropping silence. I think I sobered them all up at this point. Then there are shrieks of laughter and hands over their mouths, then more giggling.

"Wait, what the fuck?" says Lola. "Were you and Chris having issues? I know you would talk about a fight here and there, but you two always seem to have it all."

"Well, apparently we don't have it all," I say snottily.

Apparently, these women don't know me at all. I have been miserable for years. I should turn to acting because I must have hidden it well. These words spoken in my head resonate with me. These feelings made me realize we did have problems and I have chosen to hide them all. We sure had everyone fooled.

Suddenly, what happened with Chris and me doesn't even matter to them because they sit quietly for a moment staring at me like I was wearing the Scarlett Letter A. Then they quickly go right into *People Magazine* mode or fucking *Entertainment Tonight* news flashes. I go right there with them. There is no other choice because I'm not looking for a therapy session. I need a lawyer. Then they come back to me.

"Was he hot?" Char says.

"What do you think, c'mon. Do I look like the kind of woman who would fuck an ugly guy? Plus, he was way younger than me," I say.

They all start laughing again.

"Oh my gosh, tell us more!" It is like I was back at the high school cafeteria again telling a story for everyone else to live through my experiences, or fucking *Grease,* "Tell me more, tell me more . . ."

I humor them because I know they aren't getting any hot sex like what I had in that car with Surfer Boy. They are just watching the soft porn on the Hallmark Channel and wishing it was their lives, but they are just as miserable as me.

I have the balls to go out and make it real, not watch it on a screen. "Well, I basically ripped his clothes off and mine, sat on top of him in the driver's seat and rode him until I came and he did too. The car was rocking and the windows were steamed up like a glass door from a scathing hot shower. It was beyond sexy. And, the things he said to me were so hot. He was grabbing my ass and telling me I was so juicy and wet and he's never fucked a woman like me. He didn't want it to end and kept telling me to keep going. We were just clawing at each other and couldn't make it happen faster. I just think about it and gets me going." I want to shock them all. I think it works because they are all hanging on my every word.

"Oh my God this is unbelievable Ashley!" Char says.

"Wait. Does Chris know you fucked this bartender?" Lola says.

"Good God no! I told the bartender when our romp was over that I was like Cinderella and he'd never see me again because he was not my prince charming. He wanted to give me his number and for me to tell him my name but I said no."

"He didn't even know your name and you didn't know his?" Lola says, shocked.

"Wow, you had a total slut night Ashley, alright!"

They start giggling again.

"I left Chris the next day after we had a huge argument and I confronted him about texts and the whore he was with. He fucked another woman and flipped it all on me and that it was somehow my fault? Then to make matters worse, he let me leave New York by myself with a threat of a divorce that he is going to file."

They sit there, mouths open. I can tell they want to throw out their opinions. Then Char speaks up.

"But you fucked someone too, Ashley," she says.

There is the judgment.

"I know, but he fucked someone first. But wait, it gets better," I say.

"Wait, we need more wine!" says Char and they all started laughing and pouring more drinks.

I can feel my speech slurring a little and my head starts to feel fuzzy, but I have more to tell. "While I was waiting to get on the plane to come home, I was in the bathroom puking because I started feeling sick over everything that happened. I just couldn't believe Chris is going to divorce me. He's such a selfish prick." I say slurring again.

"Oh Ash, this sucks," says Char, interrupting.

We are all laughing here like schoolgirls.

"It's just that it sounds like a soap opera, but what are you going to do? Do the kids know?"

"They have an idea, but I kept it as simple as I could. I'll deal with them after I get this shit straightened out." I want a more dramatic effect. "So while I was waiting at the airport, I got this cowboy coming up to me, 'yada-yada', and he wanted me to fly to Houston with him."

"Holy shit Ash," says Lola. "I want to live your life. Was he hot too?"

I look at her and smirk again. "Hotter than the bartender, what do you think? And fuck Chris! I can fuck any guy I want. I don't need him!"

They start howling.

"Don't even tell me you fucked this guy too?? Did you 'yada-yada' the sex part of this story?" Lola says in suspense, mocking a favorite *Seinfeld* episode.

"No time for the sex just yet with the Cowboy, but I was texting him last night. There's just something about him, and Chris has turned this whole thing around on me, and fuck him. Just fuck him!"

I take another swig. The amount of alcohol is getting to me but I need this Chris bashing with my friends. I'm feeling like that weepy drunk lady you see in bars way past her bedtime. I surprise myself at this point with my sloppiness. My voice starts shaking and some other people sitting around us look at us in a scathing way. I don't know if it is the substances, but I start to feel so fucking angry all over again after telling this story out loud. I start shaking with tears flowing down my cheeks.

I hate to cry.

They all sit there speechless and not sure what to say when they see my tears. We had gone from high school girls talking about penis size to full on Alanis Morissette singing her *You Oughta Know* ballad for scorned women.

Char breaks the silence. "Oh Ash, you have every right to feel like you do." She grabs my hand.

"I will get you Ted's number right away and fuck him is right! He has no right to make you feel this way."

They all chime in and agree.

"Have another drink, Ashley. That will make you forget about that asshole," Lola says.

As we were carrying on, I notice my phone light up. "Oh shit, it's Colton!"

They all look confused.

"Who is Colton?" Char says.

"It's the Cowboy."

They all start giggling again like high school girls while the rest of the world is working.

"Did he send a dick pic? I hear that's what guys do nowadays."

I roll my eyes.

"Oh God I sure the hell hope not. You ladies have to go home and have sex, this is just fucked up."

I glance at the phone to see what Colton has to say to me. "Thinking about you today. Not that far from Chicago . . . just a thought. Can you get away?"

I will have to deal with this later because as we are sitting there the clock is getting closer to dismissal time for Ava, and I think I might want to stop so I can sober up a little before I have to pick her up. And then while Colton is texting, a text from Chris shows up right after and it is a serious buzz kill.

"Oh fuck, now it's Chris."

More shrieks again from the ladies. This sleepover party is getting to be too much for me. I don't really use this story for entertainment and that's what it has turned into. I am quickly regretting that I said anything, but the more wine I drink, the more I spill, but I find myself feeling very nervous again.

"What are you going to say to Chris? What does he want?" Lola chimes in.

"I don't know, but I'm going to have to go. I have to get Ava. I was late this morning and she was freaking out, so I don't want her to be a basket case again and text Chris that I am late. Can you send me Ted's number Char so I can have at least accomplished one thing today?"

"I am already on it," she says.

"Sounds like you will be on it too with the Cowboy!" says Lola and they all start giggling again.

"Are you okay to drive Ashley?" Lola says while sipping on her wine.

"I'm fine. Don't worry about me. I have to go. Thanks for your support as always," I say as snarkily as I could. I trip over my purse when I get up because I head for thr exit too quickly and feel the rush of alcohol upon standing up. This sends them into another tailspin of laughing.

How can they be my friends? My life is falling apart and they are concerned with the sexual details and make my problems a mockery. What the fuck? I turn around after tripping. "Maybe you all might want to go give your husbands a blow job before I come knocking on their door now that I am a free woman."

That shuts them up. I think they get the hint they have pissed me off.

Fuck them too.

They are no help for me.

CHAPTER 49

Tammy

> *"To die, to sleep; To sleep, perchance to dream."*
> *- William Shakespeare*

SITTING on this old stump is more comfortable than I thought it would be. I can still hear the beeps. I hear voices that fill every pore of my body. It seems as if this journey has brought me full circle back to the day I left to finish up for the day at work on a dismal November afternoon. I sit here thinking back.

When the door opened for the afternoon dismissal, the wind went right through me. But once I started crossing the kids, all the coldness went away like winter, who left a blue sky at night and made its exit slowly over time, leaving an entrance to the spring.

There were cars whizzing by as the sound of the tires on the wet street sent a sizzling effect with streams of water spraying up off the tires, even at slow speeds. Over the last few years, I noticed an increased lack of awareness in these cars drifting by me as I would see the same people every day. It seemed much of the time lately, I would just shake my head at the drivers who wouldn't slow down until the very last minute. I would use my whistle to get their attention, but no one seemed to care.

People were in a hurry to get nowhere.

They were either too busy eating, adjusting their make-up in the car, or worse, texting or staring at their phones instead of the road, basically doing everything else but driving. Over time, I became well aware that if we didn't have crossing guards, so many parents would not be tucking their children to bed at night all due to sheer ignorance and careless behavior. They would be bringing flowers and pinwheels to graveyards instead. I stood on this corner thinking about what was more important than taking care of a moving vehicle with precious cargo inside? Everyone was just going home to someone or someplace where the person or people, or animals at the other end would be grateful they walked through the door. It felt like so many people have become focused on their own little nucleus and no one else. It really was a shame at how we have evolved into such selfish humans, yet I tried to shake it off. I just try to take life at a slower pace in the hopes that others would follow.

As I walked a small group of children across, I chuckled to myself as they went spraying by and yelling, "We are like ducks, Mrs. Tammy!" They started to waddle. I laughed and joked with the kids all of the time.

"Oh, hello my little ducklings. Let me lead you across the pond." They laughed again and waited for me like they always do, very careful never running, just waiting for my lead.

Oh how I loved the innocence of children.

I was thinking about moving even slower after thinking about all the selfishness with the rain that was forming puddles at my feet. Everyone needs to slow down into a safe gap and rest, take pause, and appreciate how small we are in a vast world of beauty.

I took a deep, cleansing breath.

As the children passed, I said, "Thank you my little ducklings for always following the rules. You may go home now and dry off." They always smiled back.

"Quack, quack, Mrs. Tammy." Shrieks of laughter followed them mixed in with the noise of wet streets and cars. I waited there for a bit on the other side while cars blew past me spraying up water as they flew by. I wondered if they even bothered to notice I was there. I was always on the lookout for cars, but more importantly I needed to watch for children and people coming back and forth across the white lines.

I was getting ready to cross again to the other side when I noticed children quickly approaching the intersection waiting to be crossed. I could see their umbrellas pointing like soldiers on the horizon. I used my whistle to motion for them to stay put and wait for me. They did as they were told and waited patiently for me. When I was getting ready to cross the street, I saw a white car that seemed to be approaching the intersection rather quickly. I always made sure to ease out onto the white lines so drivers know they need to check behind and around them to start slowing down for the crossing. But this car looked like it was going rather fast and the streets were wet, which made me feel apprehensive and not at all sure what this person was doing. I got worried.

Was this car going to stop?

I moved out just a little to make my presence known, with my large body and bright yellow reflective gear. How could someone not notice me? I had lost even more weight, but I was still a large flashing construction sign blinking for a safe passage and a warning to slow down. I got out far enough out onto the white lines but this car was coming in so fast that I had little time to react. Also, because of my size I couldn't get out of the way in time causing me to endure the crashing impact of doom. I felt an enormous wave of solid steel overcome my body that lifted me straight up onto the hood of the car. The upward force on impact flipped my large body like a cork. What happened next was a split second of blurriness and jarring chaos of upside-down scenes. The last thing I heard were brakes screeching, a pungent smell of burnt rubber, terrible shrieks, and primal cries from children. The hard hit of my head went into thick glass, and then everything went black.

I get up from the stump and walk to the street, but I turn around. The cars are too loud with no sense of direction. There is nothing for me outside of the area that is appeasing. The beeps are at a lower pitch and my headache is very slight. I hear a voice calling me.

I need to take steps down the driveway back to the house before it fades away again.

Chapter 50

Ashley

> *"The darkness that surrounds us cannot hurt us. It is the darkness in your own heart you should fear."*
> *- Bernardus Silvertris*

I'm prepared for the weather when I hustle to my car. The temperature has dropped and it starts raining from the lovely fall morning, that quickly. And of course, I should have stopped drinking earlier because I am now running late as usual. Gosh, I miss California and question just why I came back here for midwestern life again. I am miserable with this weather.

When I run outside through the rain to my car I know I am in trouble. "Shit!" I see the clock. I can't get anywhere on time. Thank God I don't have a job. I have to gun it over to the school so Ava doesn't think I am dying again. I am more than a bit buzzed, so I grab a piece of gum out of the glove box and check my phone again. I see that Chris has texted a few times, along with Colton as well.

I start off driving to the school. When I come to a red light, I open the text from Chris. "So, you still drink yourself to oblivion and can't get our kids to school on time? What the fuck are you doing locking your bedroom door, Ashley? None of this good. You scared the shit out of Ava and that's not right. She called me crying. I think Naomi needs to come there and take over. You need help. I don't think my kids are safe with you."

I don't see that the light has turned green in front of me because I am reading this text and people behind me start beeping. "Fuck off!" I yell at strangers through thick glass.

I am driving but all the things going by my window are like a dream. I look up at one point and can't remember how I got to the spot where I am. It's like my car is on autopilot.

The phone buzzes in the cup holder and it's Chris again. "Furthermore, I think you fucked that bartender and you have the nerve to question me. I went and talked to him after you left and he gave me every indication that he was hot for you and that something happened. You want to talk?"

"Damn it!" I hit the steering wheel with my fist. I knew he would find Surfer Boy. I had hoped he wouldn't squeal. Or is Chris just saying he talked to him and is trying to trap me.

I decide not to say a word about Surfer Boy and ignore this inquiry. How dare Chris think I can't take care of my own children? And God damn Ava and her texting Chris. She is going to fuck this up for all of us and she doesn't even know it.

I hit the steering wheel with my fist again. No more walking on eggshells. Ava needs to know the truth so she gets it in her head that she needs to keep her damn mouth shut. If I am going to get a divorce, I am going to make sure I get out of it what I am entitled to, and that is a substantial amount of money.

At the next light I grab my phone again and text Chris. "How dare you tell me how to raise my kids you fuck when you are never home. Fuck you! You can keep trying to make it look like I fucked someone, but we both know it was you, not me. Why would I fuck a twenty-something bartender with you there? You have no proof of anything, so let it go."

I hear beeping from behind me again. Fuck them and their impatience. It's just a stop light that we are at momentarily in our lives. This text is important. I take off slowly on purpose to piss off the drivers behind me.

From the light on my phone I see that Colton is also texting. I have to open it. I don't want to wait to see this one. He intrigues me. "Too much time has passed. Did you think about coming to Houston? I know we'd have a hell of a time."

I breathe in. Chris texts back.

"All I care about is my kids, that simple. You are a fucking mess of a person."

My head is screaming inside of me with horrible thoughts of Chris. This motherfucker, really? Now all of a sudden, he gives a fuck about his kids? He is just going to use them as pawns in his own twisted game.

I feel so driven to text Colton that I can't wait. As I come to a light, I look down at my phone in my lap and reply back. "Coming to Houston would be the best thing for me. I know you would treat me much better than my husband ever could, that's for sure."

Not even within a second of taking off from the light, Colton texts. "Are you going to answer? You know you swept me off my feet. Can't stop thinking about you."

"What? I just answered him, what is he talking about me answering?" I say aloud.

The phone buzzes again from Chris. "Who the fuck do you know in Houston, Ashley? He can treat you better than me, ha? This must be the bartender you are talking to . . . hmmm."

"Oh, my fucking God," my heart drops and I drive off the road and then swerve back on. I look at the texts again. My car skids off the road again and I swerve out of the gravel quickly. I had sent my response to Colton to Chris instead! Adrenaline rushes at me at such speed I feel like I am flying down a tunnel at a hundred miles per hour. I cannot believe I fucking did that. I am losing it. Holy shit.

"Fuck!" I scream out loud. I hit the steering wheel so hard that my hand starts bleeding.

The mist has picked up and there is a deluge of rain on the windshield that clouds my view. I'm not paying attention and I throw my phone down in anger. When I look up, I am moving into the school zone faster than I realize because it's too late to swerve. I don't see the crossing guard walk into the intersection and as fast as a bullet powering out of a gun, I hit her dead on the target.

I slam on the brakes, which sends the tires screeching over wet pavement. The force of her large body brings my car to a complete halt. Within a split second of impact and deafening silence, I see her body fly up onto the hood with a thunderous flop. I hear her head hit the windshield with a thud and then the cracking of glass with blood splatter. The thud is so loud it makes my whole body shutter as the airbags come out with a bang simultaneously.

I get knocked back into reality. I feel like my heart is going to bang out of my chest. I can't see over the airbag, but I think she fell back down to the ground near the side and towards the front of the car because I don't see where she landed.

It is like I hit an elephant. When I look up after my shock and daze, I grab my head and my chest and lean my head back in sheer panic mode. My heart does not stop beating fast and my whole body hurts from the brick wall that came out of my steering wheel. I am trying to get my heart to slow down but I can't do it on my own. I went to reach for another Xanax to block this hysteria, but I can't reach my purse over the airbag. I start sweating like I'd been in a sauna and my body is shaking like I have a fever.

What happens next seems like a dream. I need air and need to get out, but I am afraid to stand up. I roll down the window a little and cold air blows in with rain drops soaking the side of my face. The drops are a welcome reprieve to cool me off from the heat that is rising inside my body from deep below. I look out at the corner of the sidewalk and I see kids.

They are screaming and crying because they must have seen the whole thing. Oh fuck I hope I didn't hit a kid too. I manage to take my seatbelt off, and I stay still for a minute, stunned. Good thing I sit farther back from the steering wheel because the airbags didn't hit my face, but they are obtrusive and the smell of nylon soaks into my lungs.

I feel a bizarre taste in my mouth. My whole body feels like I have just endured a marathon, but without the spectators ringing cowbells at the finish line. I move the seat back away from the air bag to spread out a bit to maintain my composure. I put my head down towards my knees in a prayer-like position even though I have never knelt in a church one day in my entire life.

I want at that moment to melt into the seat and slither down into a deep hole and disappear. Maybe I can just pull away and play stupid, act like this never happened. But I just keep hearing that sound of hitting this woman and it is like a wicked awful pummel I can't get out of my head and it grounds me right in that spot. I am fucked up from the wine and Xanax, but I try to remain calm even though my head feels like it is in an alternative universe. I put the car in reverse to get away, but then I shift right back into park, right where my head is at as well. I look straight ahead feeling the intensity in the air I am breathing.

My phone buzzes jolting me into reality. I feel trapped and I need to get out of the car. I grab the phone and put it into my pocket. I step around the side of the car hiding behind the door so no one can see me. That's when I notice the large crossing guard lying on the ground. Her stop sign is bent in half and her body is lying limply on its side. She is not even moving. Blood is streaming out of the side of her head and from her mouth. Her leg is bent in an awkward position behind her shattered in a few spots. Parents are shielding their kids from looking and going near the crosswalk. I hide making sure they can't see me. I sit there hiding listening to the bedlam because I can't bring myself to go near the body. This is not my fault and now I am going to be blamed for a stupid fat woman not being able to get off the street in time for a car coming. I don't understand how she didn't see me. I sit here like a soldier in a bunker, just anticipating, and waiting for the worst.

A few minutes later, I hear the loud speaker come on from the school with a panicked principal talking in what seemed like another language. I think she is telling all the kids to come to the playground and no one should go towards the crosswalk because an ambulance is on its way for an accident.

She drones on but all I hear is the blah, blah, blah blah blah like a Charlie Brown Peanuts skit. A few kids are also screaming, "Miss Tammy! Oh my God Miss Tammy is not moving!"

I breathe in deeply. I hover there, frozen. "Tammy," I think. This is not what I pictured her name to be. I thought it may have been Martha or Vera or something blah like that, yet Tammy wasn't all that exotic or pretty either.

I can't move. I just stand there like a statue. I am so grossed out by the crossing guard's body lying there. I don't want to be a part of this commotion, so I slowly move back to the car and slide quietly into the front seat. I think I could leave and no one would know. I wait for the right time. From the inside of the car, I see a group of women that formed a circle around the crossing guard down on their knees. The strong rain has dissipated now to a cold and gray mist, but the women don't have umbrellas and they also don't seem to mind getting wet. One woman grabs the crossing guard's hand and smooths her hair off her face. The women, who look like moms, are probably telling Tammy that she is going to be okay. In the distance, I hear the sirens edging their way closer and closer to the scene. Everyone is so focused on the crossing guard that they aren't looking out for me and what I have done. I have my foot on the brake and the car in drive. Would they know I left? My phone starts buzzing like my heartbeat pumping blood to every part of my body. I put the car in park. I reach in my pocket and open it up.

The text streams are filled with expletives and question marks. "Are you there?" and then dead on the airwaves.

"Of course, you have nothing to say," was the last one I saw from Chris.

Then the phone is ringing and it is Ava.

"Of fuck, I forgot about Ava." I have to answer. As soon as I pick up, I hear the anxiety in her voice, the paranoia. This time she has every reason to sound panicked.

"Mom, where are you? You're late and everyone got picked up so they had me call to see if you were on your way. Are you coming?" she pleads. The sirens are getting louder and I can barely hear her.

"Ava, don't get nervous, but there's been an accident. I am okay, tell Mrs. Lane that I've been in an accident and you are going to call our nanny to come get you. Naomi is listed as an emergency contact, so if there's any trouble, tell them to call me back. Listen to me now. Call Naomi and ask her if she can drive you home, then text me back to let me know what's going on."

Of course, Ava can't take my advice as an answer so she keeps going on and on. As I talk to her, I lock the door and start the car up again to see if I can just pull away and use the fact that I had to pick my daughter up from school as an excuse, but a man comes running up to me with an umbrella and he starts knocking on the window. Ava fucked this up again!

"Fuck!" I scream out loud. I don't think I am going to get out of this now. This man looks frantic and he sees I'm in distress. He waits there fidgeting and pacing back and forth. I give him a look indicating I'm on the phone.

"Honey, I have to go, but I'll call as soon as I can, promise. Text Noah too."

"Are you okay Mom?" Then I hear her start crying.

"Ava, don't make this worse for me, now stop crying right now. I'm on the phone talking with you so I have to be fine, right?"

"Okay Mom, I'll call Naomi."

"Okay," and I hang up. The man starts knocking again to get my attention. I put the car in drive and start to move the car to get away from him. Then he starts banging harder on my window and it startles me. I think he is going to crack the glass because he is banging so hard and with such desperation.

I put the car back in park because he scares me.

"Don't move!" I hear him say and his voice was escalating loud enough to where I am able to hear him clearly through my closed window. "I already took a picture of you, your car and your license. You won't get far!"

It's game over. "Fuck!"

I have to roll the window down at this point, but I don't want him to get too close for fear of smelling the booze on me, so I avoid his gaze and space when I open the window with just a small crack.

"Is this your car?" he says, sounding stressed.

I don't look at him, but I mumble quietly because I have no volume in my voice.

"Yes."

My phone keeps buzzing like my lonely heartbeat. I pick it up to see who it is. I don't know this man and I don't feel I owe him an explanation.

"Hey, are you here lady? Forget your fucking phone already. Do you realize you hit the crossing guard? I saw the whole thing happen in horror. Were you not aware that you were driving?"

I sit still and quiet and don't move because I don't know what to say. I look at my phone again to see if it's Ava.

He steps in closer to see if I'm going to answer him. "Really, with this phone?" He moves in a little closer and smells the air. "You seem fucked up to me, you know that? Our crossing guard is laying on the street dying and you're more concerned with your fucking phone?" He starts raising his voice now. "This is probably why you fucking hit her!"

A woman comes running over and steps in. "Luke, this isn't helping now, ok?"

He breathes in starkly and looks the other way. She looks at me and asks if I'm okay. I shake my head no. I have no words. My heart is still beating very fast, like I have never felt before. I finally find my Xanax but these people at my car door get in the way of me taking it. My skin is clammy and cold now in contrast to the heat I had felt a few minutes before. I feel like I can't keep up with my breathing. I have a dry mouth like I hadn't had a drink in days. I sit there frozen like a stranger in my own body.

I need an ambulance, too, for my defective existence.

"Look, stay here please," she says. "We've called 911 and they are on the way. They'll straighten this all out."

The sirens are looming in the distance and my phone keeps buzzing and vibrating through my whole body.

"This lady is drunk!" the man shouts again. "She's glued to her phone and drunk!"

The woman steps in again, this time holding him back to try and calm him down. I worry he's going to jump into my car, but there's nothing I can do or say to change this horrible situation.

My stomach has grown a pit the size of an apple and I feel that at any moment it was all going to come up. I vomit more than I cry in life.

"We're going to have to let the police take care of this," she says.

He paces back and forth. "I don't want her taking off. I don't trust this lady. She's a piece of shit, look at her. Drunk in the middle of the day, not aware she's driving and hits someone and traumatizes all the children. Are you happy with yourself lady? What the fuck!"

The woman motions for me to roll down the window. Reluctantly I do and she reaches through the window and put her hand on my shoulder. I feel like I am stuck in quicksand ready to go down.

"Just wait here, ok?" she says.

I look up at this angelic woman and as clear as day I see her soul. I wish I had her compassion. I want her to stay with me, tell me all is going to be okay. Her eyes look sullen as a mother who had just lost her child. When she looks at me again with those same brown eyes with accents of orange, the colors send a wave of nurture through my body that bestows upon me an inner peace in this madness that I can't clearly define. It almost feels like seeing her eyes places me in the eye of the hurricane, calm and still while terror hovers close in proximity all around me. My phone is buzzing again, and then it starts ringing. I look at her and then look at my phone.

"Do you want to pick that up?" says the woman longingly.

"It's my daughter. I have to," I say on the verge of tears.

"Of course," she says.

"I'll stand outside the door. But can you do me a favor?"

I look up blankly and nod.

"Can you please give me your keys?"

I think for a minute. No way I can get out of this now with everyone seeing what happened. Like a teenager being punished from the car, I have to surrender and give her the keys. It is a weak moment for me.

"Mom, are you ok? Are you ok?" Ava says louder.

The ambulance, two fire trucks, and three police cars arrive and the noise is deafening. I feel like they're signaling to the world that there is an evil human in their midst. The rain falls mixing with the bright hues of blue and red flashing lights. I take a peek out the window and see my reflection, the red lighting up the craze in my eyes.

"Mom, are you there? Answer me!"

I take a deep breath in because I'm exhausted and she's exhausting me even more.

"Ava, I'm here. Did you get a hold of Naomi?" I honestly felt like I haven't slept in days. I just want to go home to my own bed. And to think I was fucking a hot guy in a car almost less than twenty-four hours ago in New York City and now this.

How life can change in an instant.

"Yes, I did and she's with me now," says Ava. "Naomi said she can see there are flashing lights down the street by Lincoln. Is that where you are at? We can come over there."

Oh fuck, I say to myself. This is not what I need at all. Damn this kid. Why can't she just go home with Naomi for fuck's sake. "Ava! I am fine, I told you. Put Naomi on the phone now!"

"I am just making sure you are okay and . . . "

I cut her off. "I said put Naomi on the phone now!"

Naomi got on. "Ava is freaking out here, so I had her call you to let you know I've got her and can get Noah later on."

"Okay, Naomi. I'm okay, it's just a little fender bender. All good, I just have to fill out a police report. I'll call you when I'm on the way home. Sound good?"

"Yes, Ashley. That sounds good."

I can tell she is not satisfied with my explanation again like last night, but I don't give a fuck. I hang up and motion back to the angel of a lady, but she is gone. I want to fall into her eyes again while I wait for her to tell me what to do next. But then I spot her by the police officers who are getting out of their cars. She comes running back over to my car.

"Just stay here. I'll have the police come talk to you." She disappears like a warm blanket being taken off a child sleeping in a peaceful slumber. I am left there to watch the November rain fall on the windshield, smearing the blood from the glass where the crossing guard's head cemented an imprint.

I watch from the car as the parents and children all circle around the crossing guard. There are sobs and caresses, well wishes and parents hugging each other, and their kids. "We love you, Miss Tammy. We love you," they chant.

As I look at her lying there on the street, I just can't understand how she got that big. Maybe I put her out of her misery. How does one person eat that much to be almost three hundred pounds and be okay with that situation? I am embarrassed for her that it takes more than three men to hoist her body onto the stretcher. I think they are going to need a crane at one point because even these big, strong men struggle to get her up into the ambulance. I'd rather die than suffer that humiliation.

The door to the ambulance shut with a loud slam as a group of medics frantically tend to her injuries. The sirens go on again, while the crowd parted like the Red Sea. The ambulance makes its way through piercing the ears of everyone close by. I see some people do the sign of the cross as the ambulance speeds off as if that's the magic remedy for making this all go away. They should do the sign of the cross for me. I am the one left here suffering alone.

My phone buzzes again. It was Colton. "What happened to my lady? Are you looking for a plane ticket? Don't leave me high and dry now . . ."

I start biting my nails and peeling off my nail polish. I do this when I'm nervous, and I don't recall a time when I have been this nervous in my whole life. The police are writing notes down in their notepads from the people standing where the ambulance was. I see that guy that was yelling at me pointing towards my car and swearing. The lady with the welcoming eyes and friendly face is standing beside him. Her head is down now not looking in my direction because she's busy consoling the kids around her. I then notice several police officers starting to walk towards my car and it makes my heart thump with fear as they are approaching. I watch the rain tap lightly on the windshield to avoid their attention. The water slides down in tiny bubbles on the glass. My phone buzzes. It's Chris.

"What the fuck now, Ash? Ava just texted me and said you were in an accident? I called Naomi and she said it was a fender bender, but I'm guessing a DUI. Possibly on the way to the airport to go to Houston, right?"

Boy, he has perfect timing. I text him back with angry fingers hitting each key on my phone.

"Go fuck yourself." This is a welcome diversion at this point.

The police appear like Godzilla walking over the buildings and crushing everything in their path. I wish I had the keys because I would take off at this point. What was I thinking about handing over my keys to a stranger? She had put me in some sort of weird trance.

I start to shiver when I hear a buzz again. It's Colton. "Earth to Ashley, what's going on? You're off the airwaves darling, don't do this."

I sigh and watch the police coming over. I have no idea what I'm going to say to them. My heart starts beating a thousand times a minute and I am sweating again like I just finished a dance routine. My phone rings and it almost makes me jump out of the car.

I answer it. "Ashley, it's me Colton. Why are you not answering my texts?"

I speak but I can barely get a breath out. My voice is cracking, "I got in an accident. It's so fucked up. This woman came out of nowhere and I didn't see her and I hit her and now the police are coming to talk to me. It was just an accident."

I'm talking so fast I can't get it out fast enough.

"Oh, shit Ashley, are you ok?" he says sympathetically. His voice sounds like my father.

"No, my neck hurts and my muscles are starting to feel achy. My ribs hurt from the airbag coming out and it's a fucking mess. I don't know what to do. Oh shit, here they come!" I cry.

He chimes in. "Ashley, what can I do for you? I want to help you. You are just having a bad way lately," he says.

"Hang on Colton. The police are at my window."

Two officers are knocking on my window with billy clubs. They motion for me to roll down the window.

The officer starts talking. "You need to hang up the phone. We'll let you have your own phone call after some questions. We need to see your driver's license and proof of insurance first.

"Colton, I have to go now. I'll call you soon. I may need your help. Will you help me?" I am begging him like I used to with my dad when asking for money.

The cop sighs. He looks irritated with me. "Mam, I asked you to hang up the phone and get your license and insurance card. I'm not sure if you know this, but you have seriously injured the crossing guard. Now hang up the phone!"

Like a true prince charming Colton hangs on. "Call me back Ashley. Of course, I'll help you sweetheart."

I look at the cop as calmly as I can.

"That was my daughter." I lie. "I had to make sure she got home safely since I'm here and was on my way to pick her up from school."

"Where does she go to school?" the officer inquires.

"Right down the street at St. Anne's."

"So, do you drive this way daily? Would that be a safe assumption if you were going to pick up your daughter?" he says seriously.

"Yes," I say while handing him my license and insurance card.

He takes my cards.

"Stay here, I'll be back." The other officer stands next to my car with his hand on his gun. I see another officer on the passenger side checking the dents and the crack in the windshield. Another officer appears at the back of the car. Then I notice the only female cop. I am surrounded. Cops are coming out of the woodwork. I feel like the doors of the car are coming in on me. I see no way out of this one. I wish I hopped on that plane with Colton, then I wouldn't be here. I wish Chris hadn't fucked anyone else.

I thought that problem was serious.

"What the fuck was going to happen to me?" I start crying and I loathe crying. Maybe they'll feel sorry for me if they see me crying. I sit there for what seems like hours waiting to get into the gates of hell. The officer comes back to my car and knocks on the window again.

"Step out of the car," he says with a commanding voice.

I'm afraid when I get out that my legs will buckle due to the stress I'm undergoing now. I'm sweaty and still fucked up and I'm trying so hard to hide it. I step down and stumble a little. There's a small crowd of people holding umbrellas in the light rain. I can feel them all staring at me with their judgment looming heavier than the gray clouds above.

"You smell like you've been drinking. Where were you before you arrived here?" He looks at me with dubious eyes. I can tell he doesn't like me or believe anything I say.

"I was playing tennis and went to lunch with my girlfriends, that's it." He breathes in and lets out a huffed breath.

"And did you have anything to drink at lunch?" I look right at him, serious as I could. "Yes, I had one glass of wine, that's all." I lie again.

I had at least three to four bottles of wine, no doubt about it because I'd lost count. I wouldn't have drunk so much if Chris was just able to keep his dick in his pants, that fucking prick. The cop looks at me and stares. The other officers come walking over like a pack of hyenas ominously laughing while surrounding their prey trying to intimidate me. Their tactics were working.

"Smells pretty strong like alcohol and again, not sure if you are aware, but you just hit someone. You could've possibly killed her. Do you understand the seriousness of this situation? There are witnesses telling us you never got out of the car to check on who you hit. Is this true? The man over there says he stopped you from fleeing the scene."

Damn! That guy was way too involved. He fucked this all up for me I could have left.

My phone starts ringing. It is Chris. Good fucking God. He was the last person I want to ask, but maybe he can help me rather than Colton.

"Can I answer this please? It's my husband. Maybe he can help me out of this," I plead and against my will, I start to cry.

The other officer grabs the phone out of my hand and swipes the red arrow. "No one is going to help you out of this," he says defiantly while raising his voice. "You'll have to talk to him later. Right now, we need your full attention, do you understand?!"

"I told you I had one drink, that's it. The crossing guard came out of nowhere, I swear. She didn't even see me and she was getting ready to cross the kids. I thought she had them staying where they were at. She was not clear as to what she was doing and she is the one who caused this accident, I swear. She just jumped out right in front of me and I had no time to stop! She was the one who should have waited for me to pass. I don't know what she was thinking and now somehow it's my fault?" I start slurring through my words because I really don't even remember the events leading up to hitting her. I start to sob like a three-year-old.

"I'm not sure if you are aware, but the moment a foot goes on the white lines, Illinois law says the car needs to stop. Witnesses say you didn't attempt to stop because you were not watching the road. Another witness behind you said your car swerved several times on the shoulder before hitting this woman. The crossing guard didn't have to wait for you, just like no one has to get you out of this. The laws apply to you too, honey, and you may want to brush up on those laws before you accuse someone who is seriously injured because of your actions!"

The other male officer with the dark hair and serious face inserts himself. "Furthermore, I think you had too much to drink and we have reason to believe you're under the influence. We're going to ask you to blow and take the sobriety tests."

I hear my phone ringing in the officer's hands.

"You can't do this!!" I shout becoming unglued. "You can't just make me do things without my lawyer. I hear my phone ringing. That's my husband and he knows some very powerful lawyers. My dad is a lawyer too. You are fucking with the wrong people. This was an accident! She crossed the street too early and didn't see me! I am not going to tell you anything until I talk to my lawyer. I know my fucking rights!" I scream and my voice is shaking in primal defense mode.

"You need to calm down, ma'am and watch how you're speaking to me."

The other officer gets closer while the other officers stalk around my car.

I see the serious one put his hand on his cuffs moving closer to me. His voice is low and he is losing patience. "Apparently you don't know your rights. We have every right to search your car and ask you to blow. We have probable cause as to what caused this accident and you don't seem very stable right now. You also smell like booze. You also have been slurring your words and acting irrational. Furthermore, if you drive in Illinois you agree to give a breathalyzer test when asked. This is the law." He is very stern and unwavering on letting me say a word. "You do NOT have the right to ask for a lawyer before you take the test, but you can refuse the test. If you refuse the test, your license will be suspended. Now step out of the car or we're going to have more trouble."

I get out grudgingly.

I stumble again and the officer has to catch me.

"I haven't eaten all day so I'm a little dizzy," I say, trying to act sober. The rain is starting to increase a little and I'm getting soaked. The cool water rolls down my back as he makes me touch my hands to my nose, walk a straight line, and recite the alphabet. Fortunately, being a dancer helps in the balance department, but the breathalyzer doesn't work in my favor at all. And then he mumbles out a lot of words. "So, a DUI that results in an injury or death is called an Intoxication Assault and a third-degree felony. I have reason to believe that alcohol is not the only culprit here. I feel a blood test is needed too, and we have witnesses that say they saw you were on a phone while driving, and driving over the speed limit in a school zone. Not one of these things are good, and you very well may have killed someone as a result. We are taking you to the station and you are under arrest."

He starts reading the Miranda Rights and I don't even listen. I am insulted for being treated like a common hoodlum criminal. They will be sorry about this when my family bails me out. I hear my phone ringing in the distance and wonder who it was. I am thinking of who I will call. I think of my dad. He'll be able to help. I'll get out of this somehow and he'll be the one to help me, not Colton, not Chris. There is no way I'm going to jail. I think of my mom's reaction and the thought of that makes me more fearful than going to prison. Maybe if she hadn't been such a cunt I'd be living a different life. Not a life where my husband fucks everyone else but me while I stand in handcuffs.

I stop talking and let the rain fall down on me without resistance. It makes me ache, yet all my senses are awakened and strangely enough I feel very much alive.

I was uninvited here, to everything in my life.

The handcuffs are blending in with the blood on my wrist from hitting the steering wheel.

The handcuffs are tight. I have had them on for a long time.

They are never coming off.

I feel as if I have invaded something sacred, something whole. It takes everything in me not to run, but I know I wouldn't get far and that would give them one more strike against me.

The officer is done giving me my rights, and the handcuffs feel like ice cubes. The cold dull ache went down to the bone and the steel is tight pinching my delicate wrists while the rain follows its relentless pattern.

I retort. "You don't know if I killed that woman because you only talked to a few witnesses! You haven't talked to her at all and asked her why it was okay to just walk into an intersection without looking. What kind of crossing guard doesn't look to see if cars are coming? This was not my fault. You've got this all wrong. You'll find out, and you'll all look like assholes."

They start moving me towards their car. My feet are barely leaving the ground. They must weigh a hundred pounds, for each step feels like I am pulling them out of cement. I get a good look at the female officer finally. She hasn't said a word the whole time, but I can see her disenchanted eyes through a veil of darkness. I am able to feel her judgment similar to lips touching a lemon. Right before I am ushered in the police car, I asked for my phone again. "I can hear my phone ringing. I want my phone. I want to call my dad."

They all stop and the female officer chuckles acerbically, shaking her head.

The serious officer says, "You'll have to wait until we get to the station to make a phone call. Think you can survive the ride without your phone sweetheart?"

There it is again, "Sweetheart." That word goes right through me. I don't have a sweet heart. My beating heart had turned slowly harder each day, chiseled by the artist, one piece at a time.

Those pieces of the once beating machine ended to the way a dead battery just fizzles out and no way to replace it, like this finality in front of me. I was an unsolicited intruder to the womb and paid for it every day my feet touched the ground and my heart pounded beats.

The female officer is staring at me when I am getting into the car. She gives me the whole up and down glance-over with a disdainful look on her face. I can tell she wants to say something to me because I have been the receiver of this look many times in my life, mostly from other women. She is certainly not the first.

They're all just jealous.

With all the confidence of a five-star general, she says, "You think an orange jumpsuit will match your style, Barbie?"

She grabs my head to lower it and shoves me in the car with a forceful push. My whole body is trembling with anger.

The door slams on me and I can hear them all laughing through the glass window as the handcuffs behind my back are uncomfortable and unyielding. I am unsettled and unhinged and sit here in my own shame, degraded and belittled like a trapped animal. The hyenas devoured me on sight.

At least the crossing guard doesn't have to endure my misery. She will somehow come out of this as the hero I just know. I can see it now. The community will come together with signs and balloons and flowers. They might even hold an annual 5K for Miss Tammy annually to repeat my misfortune of being somewhere at the wrong place and time.

This woman walked kids across the street and she's a hero. If I had been catapulted over the hood of a car and died, would anyone care? Would someone brush the hair off my face and touch my cheek so gently and tell me everything will be all right?

When I settle into the backseat it feels like a trench. I look out the window and stare into an unknown world. The rain stops and, the red and blue flashes circle above my head in dizzy blurs. The male and female cop open their doors and get in the front seat. They don't even look at me. I see the backs of their heads creating heat that encompasses the car swiftly. I wish they would give me my phone. I can hear it buzzing calling my name. I look out the window again. An eclipse comes over the sky like a dank and caliginous cloud that creates a vast depth of darkness for me to fall into the shadows, never to return from the abyss.

Chapter 51

Tammy

> *"The best portion of a good man's life: his little nameless unremembered acts of kindness and love."*
> *- William Wordsworth*

AND everything is black until it isn't again. Small waves of light come into the foreground, like an old television getting ready to warm up and then slowly it comes into view. I find myself walking back down the horseshoe shaped driveway.

When Mom sold the house after Dad died we had endured another death. Losing this house was similar to a surgeon removing my heart from my chest. To be back here again fills me with an overwhelming presence of heartfelt joy. I keep walking closer to the backyard towards the fire pit. My feet feel so light. I notice that when I look down, I am able to see my shoes.

It sounds disgusting but because of my steady weight gain over the years, I could barely see my feet when I looked down because my gut was so large. This time where my feet are planted, I feel weightless like a child, almost like I am walking on airy, soft feathers.

I can't tell if I am a child or not because it just seems like I am ageless. I also don't know where to go first because my senses are fully awakened.

I want to capture all of these moments at the same time. The landscape of this painting is keeping me grounded and the leaves on the trees are taking on their crisp form before they fall to the ground in splendid colors. I reach the clearing with the sound of the brush crunching under my feet.

I remember well a little sidewalk that I start walking on that bends around the house and onto the patio towards the fire pit. I follow it slowly, almost like it is my first time there. As I draw nearer, I see the smoke coming off the top of the dark stones once placed there.

I can smell the crisp air, hear the crackling of a fire and the ashes burning on a cool fall evening. When I get closer, I see the back of my dad's flannel and a stick at his side for stoking. The sight of my dad makes me jump into a full gallop to see him.

I have wanted so badly to see my dad, hear his voice and stories, and give him a hug. Finally!

But the beeping continues softly and stops me like I had stepped in wet cement. I stand there bewildered and disappointed like when a good dream is interrupted abruptly. I feel something warm on my hand, like another hand pulling me back. I can't hear anything but the beeps, but that warmth feels good, like a cozy blanket on a cold winter night.

I feel a strong calling to follow the warm hand first before running to Dad because I hear a noise that sounds like someone is pulling up the road. This time, I see Mom, Alex, and Dawn driving down the long driveway. They pull up to where I am standing kicking up a cloud of dust from the gravel they are gliding over.

My head feels clear, the beeps stop and I feel myself free of pain. They are steeped in laughter about something and I hear this musical sparkle very clearly from a distance. The music is enchanting and I gravitate to it innately. I step up out of the wet cement and run towards them wanting to be part of this infectious joy. They open the door, and I slip in light as a feather. It is beyond thrilling to see them all together, so happy. I cry sobs of relief. They have finally found me. They are still laughing. I don't know what is so funny, but I start laughing with them. Mom and Dawn take off their seatbelts and turn around to look at me in the backseat. Alex is right at my side. They are all smiling at me longingly without words.

I look at them too for a long time, not wanting to see them leave.

They each grab my hands and pull me towards them. I hold on tightly and try not to let go. I am pulling so hard, but I feel that force again of not being able to keep their grip and I lose it.

The car door opens and I feel an overwhelming presence that I have to leave even though I desperately want to stay with them forever. My head throbs again and the beeps start chiming slowly as they increase in frequency pretty quickly.

I vehemently try to ignore the sounds, and then I hear footsteps on a cold tiled floor. Each step that hits the floor hurts my head. I am floating again in a different direction without my own doing and need to find my place in time. I feel tears that go from cold to warm and caress my face on the way down my cheeks.

Dawn grabs my hand and squeezes it. This warm touch fills my whole body and reminds me of how we would run through the trails together hand in hand holding on to our innocence. "I've always loved you even though we are far away," she says.

I kiss her cheek that we share. I can feel our tears connecting our soul in the conscious stream of sisterhood.

My hands are warm and I feel a gentle kiss on my forehead that is so soothing, like how I remembered my mom putting a cold washcloth on my forehead to break a high fever. She would run her hand across my head and tell me everything would be all right. I hear her say these same words like when I was a child.

A wave of light air crosses my face and I feel a tranquil voice in my ear. "Love you my dear precious daughter. Hang on darling, hang on to me always."

That voice transcends unconditional love into every cell in my body.

She catches my tears that are slipping into her palms. I feel my mouth move into a smile and sweet feelings of nurturing overcome my being and encompass my soul. I feel my mother's warm hand in mine while she guides me towards the lightning bugs that are flickering with soft lights around the fire pit. I sit on her lap, innocent as a child, up and away from harm. I lay my head on her shoulder watching the soft glow of yellow lights in the summer sky. I feel her arms around me placed so serenely.

Only a mother can provide this kind of warmth and love on my forlorn attempt to be present and awake. I have never felt so loved and at peace. I will never be alone in the darkness on my way home.

In my other ear I hear a deeper voice filled with tremendous sorrow. "Mom, Mom please, you can't leave us, don't go yet, please! I need you more than ever, don't go." His voice trails off into sobs that make me feel like I could explode into a million star-shaped pieces that weigh so heavy on my chest it hurt.

He places one of the plastic stars from his childhood room in my hand. The star glows in my warm palm all the way to my heart.

I feel Alex with all of the weight of me because he is my always and my forever. I can sense his body in mine just as we started years ago. I want to tell him I love him, that I need him, that he is the only true love in my life, but all I can do is try and stop the beeping because I have no speech to give, just remnants of my broken body. He knows I love him with all my being. I feel his tears fall on my face, merging with my own delicately moving creek of tears behind my childhood home.

I held Alex in my arms as a baby and embraced the young man that had emerged before me. I fiercely want to hold on to him, but he is water moving in the creek peacefully over rocks, bubbling, tranquil, constant and flowing. I have no right to stop it.

The years were too short.

I feel with all my being that I am running out of time under a night filled with gleaming stars that will soon fade away. Even though I have the plastic North Star to guide me, I am torn between where I should go. Yet I know there will always be light where there is love.

So, I realize I have to run to Dad and jump back into the painting.

I feel the squeeze of both of my hands and a temperate feeling all over my body fills me with as much peace that anyone could ask for. The pain I held in my body was overwhelming and as difficult as it is to leave, I know it is time to let my feet glide over the stars and let it all go.

I am the last leaf clinging onto the tree on a raw November evening. I have to make my way down the bark landing ever so lightly to become mulch for the Earth's soil.

I am walking home and have company to guide me on my next journey. The pain in my head subsides in slow motion while the beeps slowly fade into space and time. I sense warm bodies on top of mine filling me with overwhelming gratitude for life.

A vision of the fire pit releases a red hue and a spark, and the smoke clears, leaving a quiet hush, similar to the freeing moments of a safe gap. And there is Dad. He never left my side.

He has been waiting for me this whole time.

About the Author

LISA STUKEL was an elementary classroom teacher and reading specialist for the last twenty-four years. She recently shifted her career path to working for the National College of Education department at a university in Chicago. Besides teaching, one of her many passions includes writing. She has written a few short articles published in *Chicago Parent*, and an article about the birth of her sons was published in *Twins Magazine*.

The Safe Gap is her latest work, which is her first adult novel that has been a work in progress while raising her family and attending to her educational career.

Lisa is an Illinois native, who spent her final year teaching in a private school in Miami Beach last year but is now back residing in Chicago for her new career path. She lives with her husband Tom, and their sons, Dante and Ezra, left the nest last year for college.

Made in the USA
Monee, IL
29 November 2023

47773024R00277